BEAT to a PULP

ROUND TWO

Edited by
David Cranmer and Matthew P. Mayo

Foreword by
Sophie Littlefield

Cover art by
James O'Barr

Cover design by
John Bergin

ISBN: 978-0-9833775-1-1

BEAT to a PULP
PO Box 173
Freeville, New York 13068

CONTENTS

FOREWORD

"I'd rather write an entire novel than a short story," a well-known crime author told me not long ago. "I just don't have it in me."

I beg to differ. I think that inside each of us—especially those who dwell in the darker reaches of humanity, at least inside our heads—are the seeds of a thousand stories. These dramas turn on the thinnest edges of coins tossed by fate. A chance meeting, an offhand snub, an unlucky break, a dashed hope, a spurned love, one more pull on a flask. A last straw in a relationship that has ground along for years, accumulating hurt and rotting from within. A weapon too handy for anyone's good.

A misunderstanding.

A grudge.

An unholy longing.

You and I—for if you are reading this, I claim you in my club, this loose association of people who find each other by the words—we see things differently. We wait to pick up our child at the dentist and the man chatting up the receptionist takes a new shadow. In his pocket—why not?—is an old photo, an address on a page torn from a paperback, a tooth rimmed with blood, a lucky penny stamped 1962, a string of pearls.

It happens at the ball game, the grocery store, the subway, church, an anniversary dinner, the hospital waiting room. It happens when we're trying to pass ourselves off as just another classroom mom, middle manager, neighborhood Joe, lector, cashier. It's inevitable, unquenchable. Long-standing friends and partners accept us this way. Or not, and our pasts are often littered with their parting shots. New acquaintances find us in-triguing or off-putting or fascinating or scary—*other*, at any rate. It's hard to dim this particular flame, even when we put on our best game face.

We find each other, we storytellers, and these days we gravitate to places like this. BEAT to a PULP takes its place with other story homes, virtual and print, where dark fiction thrives.

Not very long ago I was an unpublished author. In my desk drawer is a folder—a very fat, ragged folder stuffed with dozens of pieces of paper—holding rejections dating back a decade and beyond. Many more are on my hard drive. Most are terse; some are kind, several are not. No matter, I could not stop writing stories.

It was the online noir and hardboiled short fiction community that first made room for me at the table. Between 2008 and 2009, editors at *Thuglit*, *Pulp Pusher*, *Yellow Mama*, *Out of the Gutter*, and others accepted stories from me, encouraging and guiding me to improve them. Then they published them. No milestone in my career will ever top those early publications for pure joy. I was proud, honored, and more determined than ever to write my heart out. As I got to know others in this community—authors and editors and readers—I felt like I'd finally found a place where I belonged.

I wonder if they will ever know what an impact they had on me: Craig McDonald and Todd Robinson and MysteryDawg and Neil Smith and Patti Abbott and Kieran Shea and Chris Holm and Patrick Shawn Bagley, the first to read my words and suggest that maybe I had something there, that it wouldn't be the worst idea in the world to keep going.

I don't remember the first time I encountered David Cranmer. He, like so many in our community, was simply there, a supporter of our craft who walked the walk and made sure the short story stayed alive long after its Golden Age had waned. BEAT to a PULP was a place to go for the good stuff, the hard stuff; Bill Crider identified its spirit as "pulpy vigor" with a modern sensibility and I think that says it well. But I especially appreciated David's editorial expansiveness—a willingness to blur the lines, to turn expectations upside down even when it seemed there were no more corners of the genre to explore. Raw, campy, melancholy, cerebral, experimental, explosive, subtle, retro, futuristic—David has a remarkably broad vision. All voices welcome here, as long as they speak to the human experience— the palette is as much every man's as Everyman's.

Sample, in this new volume, a cross section of the stories by newcomers and experienced hands alike, and you'll be impressed as much by the broad swath they cut as by the stunning quality of the work. Hilary Davidson's prose burns so clean you barely notice until it's too late in "A Special Kind of Hell." Glenn Gray spins dream-circles of fraught possibility in "The Little Boy Inside." Dave Zeltserman twines pity with loathing and makes it look effortless in "King." And then there's Vin Packer, born Marijane Meaker, who rose to pulp bestsellerdom in the '50s and '60s. Her story, "Far From Home," compresses such a wealth of emotions into a compact and elegant form, it's sure to inspire readers to search out her backlist.

My hat's off to David and Matthew, not only for their brave and skilled editing but for their devotion to pulp in all its forms. I hope you'll join me in celebrating both this collection and the work published regularly at www.beattoapulp.com. With admiration and gratitude,

Sophie Littlefield
California, 2012

In fond remembrance of Howard Hopkins, whose passion for the Pulps was surpassed only by his kindness.

THE SPACE KILLERS
Bill Pronzini

The door to Rnfibl's Outpost Grattl Shop opened and two Terrans came inside. They sat at the counter.

"What'll you have?" sPfzl asked them.

"I don't know," one of the Terrans said. "What kind of grattl do you want, Big Ernie?"

"I don't know," Big Ernie said. "I don't know what kind of grattl I want."

It was dark outside. There were no street lights. That was because there were no streets. The robot labor crews hadn't got around to building them yet.

The two Terrans at the counter read the menu scanner. Down at the other end, Nikkk watched them. He was drinking a Lyran yerfulmus latte. It was early in the evening so he was still sober.

"I'll have the Rigelian wild rrfim *au jus* with a side order of grrib," the first Terran said.

"We don't have any Rigelian wild rrfim," sPfzl said.

"What the hell do you put it on the scanner for?"

"It isn't on the scanner."

"So you think it isn't on the scanner?"

"Well, it wasn't on the scanner this afternoon."

"Oh, fleek the scanner," Big Ernie said. "What kind of grattl have you got?"

"I can give you Beta Hydran, Low Brmian, Sigma Draconan—"

"Give me Titanian yatz, medium rare, with fragm sauce and candied summitan."

"We don't have any Titanian yatz," sPfzl said.

"Everything we want you don't have, eh? That the way you work it?"

"I can give you Beta Hydran, Low Brmian—"

"I'll take Low Brmian," the Terran called Big Ernie said. He wore a dark green loose-fitting oxy suit with a bulge under the right arm of his tunic. One of his ears looked like a *bas relief* of the surface of Mars.

"Give me Sigma Draconan," the other Terran said. He was nine inches shorter than Big Ernie, seventy-three pounds lighter, and had a long red beard and a bronze Gork ring dangling from one nostril. The bulge under his tunic was on the left side. The two Terrans didn't look like twins at all.

"This is some crappy little hunk of rock," Big Ernie said. "What do they call it?"

"Outpost Fourteen."

"Ever hear of it?" Big Ernie asked his friend.

"No," the friend said.

"Must be out in the middle of the asteroid belt."

"It is," sPfzl said.

"You think we don't know that?" the friend said. "How could we be here if we didn't know that?"

"So what do you do here nights?" Big Ernie asked sPfzl.

"They eat and drink," the other Terran said. "They all come here and eat the grattl and drink the fleeking yerfulmus."

"That's right," sPfzl said.

"So you think that's right?" Big Ernie asked.

"Sure."

"You're a shiny freeb, aren't you?"

"Sure."

"Well, you're not," Big Ernie said. "Is he, Bruno?"

"He's as stupid as an Acheiportyx zirp," Bruno said. He turned to Nikkk. "What's your name?"

"Nikkk. With three k's."

"What kind of name is Nikkk with three k's?"

"It's a Terran name with a Martian spelling."

"Another shiny freeb," Big Ernie said. "Ain't he a shiny freeb, Bruno?"

"This crappy little outpost is full of shiny freebs," Bruno said.

sPfzl put two platters, one of Low Brmian zullf, the other of Sigma Draconan hado xthan, on the counter. He didn't set down any side dishes. Low Brmian zullf and Sigma Draconan hado xthan didn't come with side dishes.

"Which is yours?" he asked Big Ernie.

"Don't you remember?"

"The Low Brmian."

"Some shiny freeb," Big Ernie said. He leaned forward and took the dish of Low Brmian zullf. Both Terrans began eating.

"What are *you* looking at?" Bruno asked sPfzl.

"I was looking at your beard," sPfzl said. "It's longer on the left side than on the right."

"So you think my beard's longer on the left side than on the right. You hear that, Big Ernie? The shiny freeb here thinks my beard's longer on the left side than on the right."

"It is," Big Ernie said, and went on eating his Low Brmian zullf.

"This is lousy hado xthan," Bruno said.

"I know it," sPfzl said.

"What the hell do you serve it for?"

"On account of Rnfibl can make it cheap," sPfzl said.

"Oh, so Rnfibl can make it cheap. He's another shiny freeb."

"What's the shiny freeb's name down at the end of the counter?" Big Ernie asked Bruno.

"He says it's Nikkk with three Ks."

"Hey, Nikkk with three Ks," Big Ernie said. "You go around on the other side of the counter with your friend here."

"Why?" Nikkk asked.

"Because I told you to."

"You better go around," Bruno said.

Nikkk went on around the counter.

"Who's out in the kitchen?" Big Ernie asked sPfzl.

"Nobody," sPfzl said.

"Where's the Melnusian?"

"What Melnusian is that?"

"The Melnusian that cooks."

"There isn't any Melnusian that cooks."

"Every grattl shop on crappy little outposts like this has a Melnusian that cooks."

"We don't," sPfzl said. "We had a Rhyx dishwasher for a while, but he quit to take a mining job on Altair IV."

"Just a shiny freeb," Big Ernie said.

Bruno got off his stool and went around behind the counter and looked into the kitchen. "Nobody there," he said.

"Say," sPfzl said, "what would you have done to the Melnusian if we'd had one?"

"Zirp stupid, all right," Big Ernie said. "What would we do to a Melnusian?"

sPfzl looked at the wall. If there had been a clock there, it would have said a quarter past six. But there wasn't any clock on the wall. The only thing on the wall was a dried spot of Lyran yerfulmus.

"Well," Bruno said, "why don't you shiny freebs say something?"

"What's it all about?" Nikkk asked.

"You hear that, Big Ernie? Nikkk with three Ks wants to know what it's all about."

"Why don't you tell him?"

"What do you think it's all about?" Bruno asked Nikkk.

"I don't know," Nikkk said.

"What do you think?"

"I don't like to think too much. It hurts my head."

"You hear that, Big Ernie? The shiny freeb says he don't like to think too much because it hurts his head."

"You don't have to repeat every fleeking thing," Big Ernie said. "I'm right here and I got ears."

"Talk to me, Nikkk with three Ks," Bruno said. "What do you think's going to happen?"

Nikkk did not answer.

"I'll tell you," Bruno said. "We're going to skrank a Terran spacer. Do you know a Terran spacer named Otto Andersson?"

sPfzl and Nikkk looked at each other. "Yes," sPfzl said.

"He comes here for grattl whenever his ship vectors in, don't he?"

"Sometimes he does."

"He's due in tonight, ain't he?"

"I suppose he is."

"We know all that, shiny freeb," Bruno said. "You think we don't know all that?"

"What are you going to skrank Otto Andersson for? What did he ever do to you?"

"He never had a chance to do anything to us. He never even seen us."

"And he's only going to see us once," Big Ernie said.

"How come you're going to skrank him then?" Nikkk asked.

"We're skranking him for a friend of ours. He's paying us ten thousand credits for the job."

"Ten thousand credits?"

"That's right."

"You know how we're going to do it?" Bruno asked sPfzl.

"No," sPfzl said.

"Well, I'll tell you. We're going to do it with the lasers we got hidden under our tunics. What do you think of that, shiny freeb?"

"Oh, skrut," Nikkk said, and he took the Orgellian blaster out from under his tunic. He shot the Terran named Big Ernie through the head, and then he shot the Terran named Bruno through his off-center red beard. Then he put the blaster back under his tunic and went around and sat down at the counter again.

"Bring me another yerfulmus," he said to sPfzl.

sPfzl was looking down at Bruno and Big Ernie lying dead on the floor. After a while he made another Lyran yerfulmus latte and took it to Nikkk.

"That was some nice shooting you did there," sPfzl said. "But you took quite a chance, didn't you?"

"Well, all that talk about skranking Otto Andersson for ten thousand credits made me mad."

"I know what you mean," sPfzl said. "It made me mad, too. You know, I can't help wondering what he did."

"Who?"

"Otto Andersson."

"Got fleeked up with some corrupt politician in the Federation. That's what they have contracts put out on them for nowadays."

"He must have got fleeked up with more than one corrupt politician," sPfzl said. "He must have got fleeked up with a whole bunch of them."

"I guess he must have."

"It's a hell of a thing."

"It sure is," Nikkk said. "I'm going to get out of this business pretty soon."

"Yes," sPfzl said. "That's a good idea."

"I can't stand to think about those two Terrans getting ten thousand credits for skranking Otto Andersson. It's too damned awful. All we're getting to skrank Otto Andersson is five thousand credits."

"Well," sPfzl said, "you better not think about it." †

FAR FROM HOME
Vin Packer

Around here they still talk about the fire at Far From Home. That small landmark cottage on the point of the bay, burned to the ground. Fishermen going for clams waded ashore and watched helplessly. My father was gone by then. Everybody said he'd set the fire. He used to work at Far From Home. He used to open his big mouth mornings he was getting coffee at Springs Store, nearby. He'd laugh about his bosses and call them names. I can hear him now.

"Ah, it's spring and the pansies are back," my father said. He was checking our phone messages. "What do they want me to do now? Put a tub of posies out by their mailbox?"

I never said anything when Dad made fun of Paul and Robert. It made my life a lot easier than if I'd ever let on to him that I didn't think they were bad guys at all. The few times I'd been to Far From Home they didn't seem any different from other New Yorkers who came to spend the summer in our town.

I remember once I called them a couple and Dad blew.

"Don't call them that! Your mother and I were a *couple!* They're fakes! They're phonies!"

After Dad erased the messages, he said, "This job at Far From Home has your name on it, Sonny Boy. They want their house opened."

"Why does it have *my* name on it?"

"You're the neatnik. I'm not as good at dusting as you are, either."

I let him get away with a lot. If I didn't, he'd see an opening and go in after me. He'd call me Girl instead of Gil. He'd make fun of my idea to be a chef one day. He'd go for the throat, as only Dad and his buddies could when they thought they saw a weakness in someone.

My dad called himself a contractor, but he was really a carpenter, a plumber, a yard man—he did what work came his way. He was more than an unskilled laborer but not much more. None of the men he hung out with ever went to college and like Dad, some of them never finished high school.

You can imagine how they resented the rich gay fellows who have summer homes here. Double it where my father was concerned. He was afraid his own son had tendencies.

Before my mother died he'd tell her I was beginning to look as pretty as her when they first started dating. I did have her blue eyes, and there were a few summers my blond hair was long. I liked to bake and I *was* a self-proclaimed neatnik. That was all Dad needed to get on my back when he was tired and depressed. Then he'd call me "Girlie" and he'd see if he could make me mad.

I felt so sorry for him, the way he missed Mom, and sorry for me the way I missed her, too. I let him say things Mom would have left the room over.

❖

Now I have to confess something even Dad didn't know. It happened the summer before the fire. I'd worked as a waiter/bus boy for a big party Paul and Robert gave at Far From Home.

I was just fourteen. They were paying me fifteen dollars an hour to pass trays of food, keep the floors clean, and clear tables of empty glasses and dishes. I wore a white jacket and black pants, a white shirt and a black bow tie.

I'd pop shrimp into my mouth before I passed a tray around. I tasted the baked clams, the raw oysters, and I had a hamburger and a hot dog fresh from the grill a cook tended in the back yard. There was that thin salmon, caviar, all the rich cheeses, then tiny pastries you could pick up in your hand. Or you could have big slices of chocolate cake, or key lime pie you could eat with a fork, sitting down somewhere to enjoy the string quartet playing on the terrace.

I was looking good and feeling good, just as though I was at parties like that one all the time. There were piles of throwaway cameras on trays in case anyone felt like having a photographic record of the evening. There were sterling silver key chains for souvenirs with round silver discs that said Far and Away.

Right in the middle of things I saw this wad of money held together by a gold dollar-sign clip on the floor of the hall closet.

I picked it up, took it into bathroom, and counted 10 one hundred dollar bills. One thousand smackeroos.

I put it in my pocket. I'd give it to Paul or Robert before the evening was over, I decided.

But it also occurred to me that no one could have seen me. And who walks around with a thousand dollars in his pocket at a party? Somebody who'd probably never miss it.

I wasn't a bad kid. For one thing Mom had been too sick for me to give her more to worry about. I studied, took odd jobs afternoons and summers to make spending money and buy my own clothes.

Money was always a problem. Dad and I talked about it all the time. How much we had for this, what we couldn't have, and what there was so far in my college fund.

Dad said, "You're going to college if I have to rob a bank."

"Things aren't that desperate," I said.

"Don't kid yourself, Gil."

The house Paul and Robert lived in was really a cottage. It was two hundred years old and it had been "fixed" by men like Dad time and again. One year during a hurricane, the bay rose and water came into the first floor. Dad said they spent a fortune repairing it, that they could have built a new house for what it cost. But it was one of those historic places. The original owner wouldn't sell it until he found buyers he trusted to keep it the way it was.

It only had two baths and three bedrooms. It faced the bay, no near neighbors, but beautiful gardens on both sides, mostly Robert's handiwork. My father used to say that you could tell which one took the garbage out in that house: it was Pauline, as he liked to call Paul. Roberta, Dad said, was the one with his nose in the daffodils and his hands in the salad bowl.

❖

"Don't leave yet, Gil," Robert said that first night I worked there.

I waited until the last guest was out the door. I was sitting on the terrace, looking at the moon's reflection in the water, wishing we didn't live in such a crappy house, dad leaving his clothes where he took them off, never washing a dish, never giving a damn how anything looked.

"You had a rough winter, didn't you, Gil?" Robert said from behind me.

Then Paul said, "We liked your mom a lot, Gil. We're so sorry."

"Yeah. She liked you guys, too." Mom had helped out at Far From Home nights they had dinner parties, but the three of them had had a kind of friendship, too. She'd given them cuttings from plants and they'd brought by lilac bushes or dwarf evergreens. Once, Paul gave her some goldfish complete with a fancy bowl. Our cat ate them that very evening, but we never let Paul and Robert know.

They had sent a couple dozen white roses to the funeral home and later they wrote Dad and me saying how much they'd cared for her. Enclosed was a photograph of Mom stretched out on a chaise in their yard, with their black toy poodle in her arms.

I could feel the money clip in my pants pocket. I was thinking of all the stuff I could buy with it. I'd never be able to put it in the college fund because Dad would want to know where I got it. But I could use it for special occasions, special treats.

I couldn't believe that Robert was smiling so sweetly yet asking me, "Do you want to return the gold clip you found, Gil?"

I was about to deny it but Paul said, "We were going to pay the help with that tonight. Then I saw *you* pick it up."

I could feel how hot my face and ears were. I took the clip out of my pocket and handed it to Robert.

I mumbled, "I meant to give it to you, then I forgot."

"Bull!" said Paul.

"What?" I was surprised at the sharp tone of voice.

"I said bull! You were going to walk off with it!"

"Don't be harsh, Paul," said Robert.

"When he stops lying and starts apologizing, I'll stop being harsh, not before!"

I heard myself let out this big sigh and say, "Paul's right. I was going to keep the money. I'm very sorry."

"Apology accepted," said Paul.

"Thanks," I said. "I guess I'll never be asked to work for you again."

"Sure you will," Robert said. "It's over and forgotten."

Paul drove me home.

He didn't say anything until the car stopped. Then he said, "Want to hear my rules for a good life?"

"Okay."

"Keep your body clean and your head clear and earn your own money."

I gave him a guilty smile and said thanks.

They weren't out from the city, yet that afternoon I rode my bike over to open their house.

Enchanted Waters had already opened the little round pool in back. It was an unusually hot day for May, and I'd decided I'd take a swim later.

They had the kind of house that was a maid's dream. You had to look hard for any dust. I mostly opened and cleaned windows, and I mopped the kitchen floor. The funny thing was I liked to clean. I was good at it. I was fussy about my own things, too: my clothes, my room. I liked to try and create one little perfect area in our jungle house where I could be peaceful and forget what was in the other rooms.

When I had finished my housework at Far From Home, I shed my jeans and T-shirt and took a swim. Then I flopped down in the rope hammock and enjoyed an eyes-shut daydream of owning this place, of having a gorgeous wife and well behaved, great looking kids who were off at the beach.

"Well! Well! Well! Our little Girlie is having herself a sun-bath."

"And you've had a few beers, hmmm, Dad?"

"You walk around in your underwear here?"

"I went for a swim."

"Where are Pauline and Roberta?"

"We're right behind you, Mike." And there they were suddenly, and there was my father red-faced but with that defended posture, hands on hips, jaw stuck out, speechless for once. Furious, again—that pointless, humongous fury smoking away inside him ever since Mom died. I wasn't afraid of him, but I knew not to count on him anymore.

"Hello, Gil," Paul said, and Robert asked me "Is the water warm?"

"He's coming home with me now!" said Dad.

"Water's fine," I said.

"Get your clothes on, Girlie!" Dad said.

I said, "I'm coming."

"I don't want him swimming here!" Dad said, shaking his fist at them.

Paul said, "Whatever."

"Hey, Dad," I said, "Dad, for Pete's sake."

"What is *whatever* supposed to mean?" Dad demanded.

"It means whatever you say, that's fine," Paul said.

"You bet it is!" Dad said. "He's my son!"

"Cool it, Dad," I said. "I'm coming."

"He only *works* for you," Dad said, "and you remember that!"

"Not to worry, Mike," said Robert.

Then Dad said, "Wipe that smirk off of your face!" and went for Robert, knocking him down.

Blood was running from a corner of Robert's mouth.

"You get out!" Paul shouted. "Get out now!"

"C'mon, Dad," I said. "C'mon, it's time to go."

Dad wasn't all bad, believe me. The next day he felt terrible about punching Robert. He told me I should go over there and give them his apologies, but before I could do it, he said no, he'd go himself.

He called them up to be sure they'd be there, and he drove off after bragging that he was an honorable man and an honorable man always owned up to his mistakes.

"Let that be a lesson to you," he said.

"Let it be a lesson to *you*," I said. "Don't lose your cool."

The thing was Dad stopped off for a few beers to work up the courage an honorable man needed. When he got over there, Paul and Robert were gone.

"Hey, Gilly boy?" he shouted at me over the phone. "I'm alone here at Far From Home. I've got an idea!"

"What, Dad? You've had a few beers again, haven't you?" I could always tell by his voice when he'd been drinking.

"Before I got here I stopped off to do some thinking. You're right about not losing my cool, son. We need the work."

"And they've been darn nice to us, Dad."

"You're right," he admitted after a short pause. "Your mother liked them ... so I'm going to do them a favor over here and you could help me."

"What are you going to do?"

"I'm going to paint that little kitchen of theirs without charge. I've got that can of white enamel in my truck and I just had it rotated yesterday."

"Dad, they may have their own ideas about it."

"Naw, no, they spoke before about painting that little room. Paint's peeling in there. I'll give them a makeover."

"All right," I said. "I'll come by just so you don't mess it up!"

No surprise, Dad was sleeping in the rope hammock when I got there. He'd only finished one wall.

❖

"What was destroyed was priceless," said Paul. "We saved for years and years to buy the Pollack painting. We couldn't afford to insure it."

"Our family photographs, our books, oh, everything," Robert said.

"Everything. And this house … this house."

"Where is your father now?" the policeman asked me.

"He took off. The fire was raging and he just got into his pickup and went for help."

"Why did he set the fire?"

"He *didn't*," I said. "Why don't you listen to the truth?"

"Gil," Paul said, "don't protect him."

"*I* set the fire!"

They still wouldn't hear that.

Robert said, "Mike claimed he was coming here to tell us something. He sounded furious!"

"That's just his way," I said. "He knew he was wrong! He was going to apologize."

"Let's go downtown," said the policeman. "Let's get all the facts straight."

❖

All the while I painted the kitchen that afternoon, I thought of how Dad ruined things, of what a ruin he was himself since Mom had died, of how I didn't think I could stand living any longer with damn Dad, out there snoring in the hammock!

I was mad! You bet I was mad!

But I worked on the ceiling, even while I was cursing my father. I was careful, too, neatnik that I am, I'd covered everything around me so paint wouldn't get on it.

I put newspapers down to keep the stove and the icebox clean.

I was about to do the last wall when I went out in the yard to shake my father and tell him he had to wake up and help! This makeover was his idea, not mine!

The thing was, I'd never thought about that old gas stove. We had an electric stove, and so did everyone I knew.

While I was out yelling at Dad, the pilot light on the stove must have worked through the newspapers.

"I'm not going to paint anymore until you get up!" I told Dad.

"Who said you had to paint?" He had one eye open.

"You called me for help, remember?"

"I changed my mind." He turned over in the hammock, his back to me.

The fire must have been running along the walls just as I sat down in the beach chair and said, "Have it your way, Dad."

I don't know if he heard me.

But soon we both heard the whoooosh and then the roar of the fire as it hit the propane gas tanks.

I can't stand to drive down Bay Street and see the lick of land where Far From Home used to be.

Robert and Paul are long gone from this town now, but in my mind's eye, I still see their shocked, sad faces as we stood out on the lawn that sunny afternoon, the smell of burnt wood in the air, what was left of the house black and smoking.

Everyone, including them, still believes my father set that fire somehow, even though I figured out how it started, and later an inspector from the fire department confirmed it.

There are certain truths no one wants to hear. No one can believe truths that are hard to accept, either.

For example, who would ever believe that the real reason Far From Home burned down was that my father was trying to do a makeover for Robert and Paul? †

KING

Dave Zeltserman

The children jeered Mary Crowley when she tottered past them. Their voices, though, were cautious and their smirks hid an uneasiness, as if they weren't quite sure whether to ridicule her or be afraid of her.

Mary paid them no mind as she continued on, her ankles swollen thick by rheumatism, her lips frozen in an awkward half-smile, her eyes dull and glazed. A patchwork of white scars could be made out under her grayish complexion and it gave her large broad face the appearance of being a wax mold that had been scratched repeatedly by razor blades.

None of the children knew her name. No one in the neighborhood knew it any longer. To them she was the crazy pigeon lady. She herself sometimes forgot the name her parents had given her. It had been ages since anyone had called her by her name; her poppa being the last person to do so, and he had died almost twenty years ago.

Mary cautiously approached the bench that had been her destination. For a moment her body seemed to shrink inward, and timidly she glanced left, then right and over both shoulders as she searched past the children for the white-haired man—the Evil Wizard as she thought of him. That she didn't see him caused a tear of joy to worm its way down her waxen cheek. She carefully lowered herself onto the bench, her lips still pulled into an idiotic half-smile.

Her thick fingers worked the coat buttons as she unbuttoned her large ratty cloth coat that she had had for over forty years and took out from it a bag of bread crumbs that she'd brought. After carefully scattering a few of the crumbs by her feet, she waited. First one pigeon arrived, then another, and within minutes a dozen of them were pecking at the crumbs. She looked around once more and, satisfied that the Evil Wizard wasn't in sight, spread a pile of the crumbs on her lap. Before too long the pigeons were jumping on her and her smile changed, becoming something warm. A light also began to shimmer in her eyes. More pigeons came and soon they were all over her; on her shoulders, her head, pulling at her scraggly gray hair, prancing up and down her swollen thighs. The largest of the pigeons sat in her cupped palms. A great black and white bird with a tuft of gray feathers that ran down the middle of its head. The sight of this bird made her eyes glisten with tears.

"King," she cooed, her voice faltering and unpracticed. "How is my darling, Kingie?"

In response, the pigeon snatched at one of the bread crumbs, its beak ripping the skin of the old woman's palm. One of the children yelled out that the crazy pigeon lady was going to start French kissing the bird. Others laughed and started singing that Crazy Lady and King were sitting in a tree, K-I-S-S-I-N-G. Mary didn't notice. At that moment her universe consisted only of herself and her king.

"Oh, Kingie is hungry, huh? You glad to see your Princess Mary?"

One of the other pigeons tried to jump into her palms and King turned and pecked angrily at it sending the bird back onto Mary's lap.

"Bad Kingie. Don't be jealous," Mary reprimanded, her face blushing. "You know you're my favorite."

A whirl of motion sent the birds in flight. Mary sat frozen, petrified in fear, as a wooden cane swung wildly over her head. The Evil Wizard had come. For a moment she was lost in a chaotic cloud of gray feathers. When it had risen, he stood in front of her, the Evil Wizard, his staff in hand.

"What's the matter?" he bellowed, his eyes shining furiously, his withered face bright red. "You too stupid to understand what you're doing?"

Mary tried to look away from him, but she couldn't move. A sob escaped from her. He lifted his cane and jabbed it at her, stopping the tip only inches from her face.

"Try and get it through your thick skull that those damn birds are nothin' but filthy, lice-infested vermin!"

He clamped his mouth shut and stood staring at Mary, his face growing redder as rage burned like fire in his small black eyes.

"Because of you these damn birds keep coming here dirtying everything up," he finally forced out, his voice strained with emotion. "How many times do I have to tell you to quit feeding them!"

He stopped and waited for an answer that wasn't coming. Mary Crowley had disappeared inside herself. Her lips were again pulled up in a frozen idiotic half-smile, her eyes blind, her low sob had changed to a dull moan. The white-haired man stared furiously at her until he lost the last remnants of his patience. His face twisting into something horribly ugly, he grabbed the bag of bread crumbs from her.

"You're not going to feed them again. You understand? Just because you're too stupid to know better I'm not going to let you filthy up this neighborhood!"

He once again shook his cane at her face.

"Just keep sitting there grinning like an idiot!" He lowered his cane and looked away from her. "It's filthy what you do. Letting them crawl all over you like that. I've never seen anything so disgusting, and it doesn't matter that you don't know any better."

He turned and walked away.

The children played until dark, and it was a long time after they were gone before Mary Crowley could move. Slowly, rigidly, she looked around, then hobbled to her feet. Even then she was still too petrified with fear to feel the cold wind biting into her arthritic joints.

She headed home taking slow, shuffling steps. Her thoughts were filled with worry about her birds. It was so cold and she didn't know if they had gotten enough to eat. And King? What would he think of her, letting the Evil Wizard chase after her birds with his wicked staff?

She was so afraid of the Evil Wizard. And he was wrong. Everything he said about her pigeons was a lie. They weren't dirty, and they weren't the ones ridiculing her, or yelling at her, or swinging wicked staffs at her face. If it was anyone who dirtied up the neighborhood it was the Evil Wizard and his terrible yelling.

She wanted more than anything to tell him to leave her alone, but she had trouble finding the words to speak when he was around, and whatever words she found she knew he would ridicule. The thought of his ugly red face and bulging eyes made her shiver. Then she blanked her mind of any thoughts.

Mary's father always greeted her the same way after work. With a big grin on his face he'd ask how his princess was and Mary would always giggle and run off. Then after dinner, he would read her stories and play tic tac toe with her, and most of the time he'd let her win.

A few days before he died he called her over and spoke in a tone she'd never heard before. "Mary, my darling," he said, "I am so afraid for you."

At first she couldn't figure out when he meant, but after the days following his death turned into months she understood. There was nothing left for her but loneliness. She would sit alone all day and wait and nothing would happen. Sometimes she would get up and look out the window and then sit back down, waiting for everything and nothing. There was no longer anyone coming home to call her his princess. There was no poppa to smile at her or to eat dinner with her. And there was no one anymore to protect her from the loneliness.

Her poppa had saved enough money to buy an annuity so she could stay in their three-room apartment and have groceries delivered weekly, but as much as he had hoped otherwise, he failed to save enough so she could be taken care of professionally. So there she was.

For years she was terrified of leaving her apartment, but eventually something became even more terrifying. The loneliness.

The first few times she ventured outside her apartment she only made it a few hundred feet before her heart would start racing so that she would have to head back. But she pushed herself, and after several months she made it all way to the park. That was when she first saw the pigeons. There were only a few of them and they looked hungry. The next time she brought bread, and the pigeons were there as if they'd been waiting for her. She tore a piece of bread to small bits and tossed it to them and watched as they pounced on it. That was when she saw her escape from the loneliness.

Every time she'd go back to the park there would be more birds waiting. Then one day King showed up and she knew he was special. That he would be her king and she his princess. And she was happy, almost as happy as with her poppa.

Then the Evil Wizard with his wicked staff started to show up. He would shout at her and make her cringe. She tried to pretend he wasn't there, but that only made his shouting more horrible with spittle flying from his grotesque bloodless lips. He would spy on her so he could chase away her pigeons with his staff and try to hurt them.

It seemed so cruelly unfair.

❖

Mary hid in her apartment for the next three days. Every time she would think of her birds she would start to put on her coat, but then the image of the Evil Wizard's awful face would stop her. It would make her put away her coat. After three days of doing this the thought of her birds being hungry and missing her was too much for her. Especially King. She put on her coat and headed to the park, afraid to even move her head and let her eyes wander for fear of spotting him. When she reached the park, she cautiously lowered herself onto the bench, her lips frozen in a half-smile. And she prayed that the Evil Wizard wouldn't find her.

At first she couldn't move as she sat there. Minutes passed before she was able to reach for her bag of bread crumbs. As she was spreading the crumbs along the ground, the Evil Wizard came out of nowhere to stand in front of her. The sight of him made her suck in her breath.

"I told you I'd be watching for you," he said as he leaned on his staff.

Mary couldn't breathe. Her body became every bit as rigid as her half-smile. The Evil Wizard stood over her, his eyes shining cruelly as he smiled at her. After a while he sat down next to her. All Mary could do was let out a sharp gasping sound. Like a small animal caught hopelessly in the teeth of a steel trap.

"I do love the park," he told her after a while. "So calm and peaceful. I come here every day now." He waited for her to respond, but she was lost in an ocean of terror. He sighed and placed both hands on his cane so he could lean forward.

"You were going to feed them again, weren't you?" he asked. The wounded animal noises only came out faster from her then. He listened to the noises and shook his head. "I guess you're not capable of understanding me. I'm tired of this. You won't be feeding them again."

Mary Crowley got to her feet. Somehow she managed to escape him, and as she fled for home, the wounded animal noises came out in a sharp, frantic beat. By the time she reached her apartment, she was sobbing uncontrollably, her mouth still frozen in her half-smile.

A thought penetrated her mind. The Evil Wizard would think she was too scared to go back there, at least for a long time.

Which meant if she went back now he wouldn't be looking for her. And that meant she'd be able to take care of her birds. And King. How glad he'd be to see her.

It was still light when she returned back to the park. She sat down on her bench and took out her bread crumbs. The park was mostly empty. Only her and two other men she'd never seen before. They wore blue uniforms and moved around by the bushes as they picked up and put gray things into a barrel. Mary decided not to let them worry her, and she spread the bread crumbs by her feet and sat back and waited. Her birds will be so happy to see her. They will be so hungry and grateful. And King will be with her again soon. She couldn't wait to have him sitting in her hands. She couldn't wait to tell him how she fooled the Evil Wizard.

The men finished what they were doing by the bushes. As they carried the barrel by her one of them spotted the bread crumbs.

"You waiting to feed the birds?" he asked.

Mary pretended she didn't hear him. Pretended he wasn't there. The man shrugged. "Sorry, lady, but they ain't coming," he said.

Mary squirmed and tried to look past him.

"They'll be here," she croaked uneasily.

"No ma'am, I don't think so. They already came tonight. They're in this barrel now."

Mary giggled at the thought of that. "No they ain't," she said. "They wouldn't hide from me."

The man looked at his partner and then back at Mary. "Someone poisoned them dead," he said.

His partner reached into the barrel and took out a dead pigeon. As Mary stared at it, comprehension slowly worked into her eyes and she let out a low cry before covering her face with her hands. Tears streamed through her thick swollen fingers. The man holding the dead bird dropped it back into the barrel and both men carried the barrel away.

When Mary took her hands away from her face her mouth was twisted into a crazy parody of a smile. Moving unsteadily, she headed to the bushes.

"Kingie," she cried. "Please, Kingies, not you."

Something moved then in the tall grass behind the bushes. Mary dropped to her hands and knees and crawled toward it.

It was King! Mary rubbed her eyes, but there was no mistaking King's black and white coloring and the gray streak on top of his head. And he was moving.

As Mary crawled closer, she saw he wasn't really moving. Or rather, something was making him move. A rat was tearing at King's body.

"No!" Mary screamed. "No! No! No!" The rat stopped to look at her and then continued with its mauling of the dead bird.

Frantically, Mary flung a handful of bread crumbs at the rat. The rat only sniffed indifferently at them. Mary searched through her coat pockets and found a partially eaten peanut and chocolate bar. She tossed that. The rat looked at it curiously, its nose twitching, and then left King's body for it. Mary scooped up the dead pigeon and held it tight to her chest.

"Poor Kingie," she whispered through her tears. "Poor, poor King."

She had her eyes squeezed tight and gently rocked the dead bird back and forth. When she opened her eyes, she saw the rat standing on its hind legs chewing on a piece of the candy bar, grasping it between its front paws. As Mary watched her eyes widened.

She buried King in the park and then headed home. Her legs ached from the cold and her body was near exhaustion, but she no longer feared the Evil Wizard. She no longer walked with blinders on and instead let her gaze wander.

When she had passed a house near the corner of the park she saw him. He was behind a front window, his grim face searching into the darkness. She stopped to meet his stare. Then her eyes glazed over and she looked through him.

❖

For the next month Mary Crowley went to the park every night at eight o'clock. Every night she would pass the Evil Wizard's home, and he would stare at her from his front window, but other than that, he didn't bother her. No one did. At that hour the park was hers.

One night she did see the Evil Wizard. He had ventured out and was walking along the periphery of the park. When he got within thirty yards of her he stopped and shook his head in disbelief. Then, with his wicked staff in hand, he came toward her. Mary giggled at the sight of him. When he got within ten feet of her he stopped dead in his tracks. His jaw dropped open and his awful face grew whiter than his hair.

The gray things on her weren't pigeons, but rats. Dozens of rats. Jumping wildly on her. Running along her body, their claws cutting her exposed flesh as they scampered about feeding on the peanut butter she brought.

She met the Evil Wizard's stare and smiled. Then she ignored him. There was nothing he could do. Even if he poisoned them, there would always be more. There have always been more. Mary knew he wouldn't even try. He was too terrified to try. As far as she was concerned he no longer existed.

A large rat, the largest of them, jumped on her shoulder. He was all black except for a triangle of gray on his head. Her eyes melted seeing him.

"King!" she gushed. "How's my Kingie!"

More rats joined the bench. Before long she was covered with them, and they moved over her as if they were a living grayish quilt. Nothing of her was visible any longer, but her voice could still be heard. A strangely contented voice. The voice of a princess who found her king. †

MISSED FLIGHT
Steve Weddle

She had one of those doctor's office names: Tori or Lori. And dark, wet, curly hair tied up with a pink hair clip to match her yellow shirt and purple scarf.

"I'm sorry, sir. This can't be your name."

All I had to do before I left was close up some loose ends. Simple. Which is why the old man picked me. Simple. "So you found the boy and then what?" I asked Georgie Martin.

"I took him back to his mom and dad, like I was told to do."

Georgie was sitting across from me in a booth at Harry's restaurant in Pittsburg, Kansas. It was a straight-shot diner: booths down the left, tables in the middle, counter on the right. I took the last bite of my burger. Some coffee. "You didn't notice any marks on the boy? Cuts? Burns?"

Georgie was looking past me, to the big windows in the front, trying to keep his mind off things. "I dunno, Oscar. I just figured whatever had happened to the boy, you know, he'd gotten beaten up or something."

"And you handed him off?"

"That's what the old man told me to do. I swear. Find the boy. Bring him back to his parents. It took me three goddamned weeks, man. It wasn't easy."

"Sorry it was so difficult." I drank the last of my coffee, looked at the grounds in the bottom of the cup. Tried to take a breath so I wouldn't kill him right there. "I'm sure if the boy was still alive he'd feel bad for you." I set the cup down on the table as carefully as I could, trying not to rattle anything.

Georgie flapped his mouth like he was letting air out of a balloon. "C'mon man, it ain't like that. I'm just saying I *didn't* know. Wasn't any way for me to know. I just did what I was told."

"The kid was twelve, Georgie. Didn't you even talk to him?"

He wiped some ketchup off of his mouth with the inside of his wrist. "Kid didn't talk. Just cried. All the way from Cassoday to Wichita."

"You tried?"

"Tried, hell." Georgie was shifting around now, pulling at his collar. "He wouldn't talk. Just cried."

"You ever think why he might be crying?" The space behind my head was throbbing and I was trying to take another deep breath. Keep this all calm.

"Somebody had kidnapped him. Molested him. Whatever. If they'd have just gone to the cops." Georgie looked around the restaurant, maybe looking for support from people he didn't know. Maybe looking for a way out.

"You know they couldn't do that," I said, holding my empty coffee cup out for the waitress, a pleasant enough teenager without any apparent piercings or ink.

"I know the old man said that," he said. "Hell, even people like us can get help from the cops sometimes."

The waitress stopped moving when she heard the "people like us" and "cops."

"We're fine here," I said to her without looking. She reached down to take away my plate. I grabbed her wrist and moved it away from the table. "I'll let you know when we need you."

She left in short, skidding steps to the back of the place. I leaned forward. "Keep your voice down. This has to end here."

"Sorry," he said. "I'm just, it's just." He stopped for a second, took a deep breath. "I feel responsible."

"For turning the kid back over to his parents so they could continue to molest him? Yeah. I can see how you might."

Georgie rubbed his eyes.

I leaned back into the bench. He wasn't a bad guy. We'd worked together before. He'd always done right before. He'd just made a mistake this time. That's what he'd tell you.

"I didn't know that. How could I know that?"

I leaned over the table and said in a harsh whisper, "You were *with* the kid. Did you even think to ask him why he was crying?"

"He wouldn't say nothing. Not one thing." His jaw was shaking. Caffeine. Fear. Realization.

"Okay."

" 'Okay?' That all you got? I take the kid back and he hangs himself because of that and all you got is 'Okay'?"

"Yeah."

"Geez, Oscar. I thought you were here to help me clean this thing up. I thought you were on my side. Isn't that what you do? Isn't that why the old man sent you?"

"That's right." I looked into my coffee cup, swirled it around like I was looking at tea leaves. Nothing. "So you didn't discuss this with anyone? No cops? No reporters? Not your barber?"

Georgie ran his fingers over his stubbled head. He smiled. "No, man. I do what I'm told. Me, you, the old man. That's it."

"And the parents?"

George screwed up his face. "Who?"

"The kid's parents. The congressman and his wife. You talked to them when you dropped off their son."

The life fell out of his face. He stared at me. "Oh, yeah. Geez. How are we gonna handle them? Think they'll talk?"

I signaled for the waitress to bring the check. "We'll have to think of something. They know who you are?" She put the check on the table next to ours and went away.

"No, man. I just dropped the kid off and said we'd be in touch. They grabbed the kid and carried him into the house. I never got out of the car."

I frowned at Georgie's word choice. "You said 'we'??" The question hung there for a second.

"Yeah. I didn't say who, though."

I nodded.

I took the check and Georgie made a show of searching his pockets for money.

"I got this, Georgie."

He dropped his shoulders and breathed out of his nose. "Thanks, man. I'll get the next one."

"It's Okay. Don't worry about it."

"No, really. I'm good for it. Next meal is on me."

I threw an extra twenty on the table. "Fine." I stood. "Where'd you park?"

He scooted out from behind the booth and took a step toward the back. "I'm out behind the place. Where are you?"

"I'm out front. Lemme pull my car around back and we'll come up with something."

"Okay."

He walked toward the back door and I went out the front.

When I got out the door, I turned and headed behind the building, checking my pockets, feeling the weight.

Georgie was standing beside his car, smoking a cigar when I came around the corner. He jerked up. "Geez, man. You scared me." He looked past me. "Where's your car?"

He looked surprised and a little air came out of his mouth when I caught him in the temple with the brass knuckles. He dropped between his Taurus and a pickup, so I was able to snap his neck without too much trouble. I pulled his wallet out of his back pocket, taking the credit cards and a couple hundred bucks in cash. Looks like the next meal was on him.

"Your name is on here twice, sir." Tori picked up the sheet of paper from the airport counter and held it in front of her face, as if things would be clearer in the horizontal, as if confusion would fall off of the page with gravity.

The flight was boarding. I didn't have much of a chance.

❖

I was supposed to just get a hotel, catch a flight in the morning, and be in Chicago by noon. That's not what I did. The boy's name was Blake Goodwin. He was twelve, the same age my son had been when his mother took him. That was ten years ago.

I dumped Georgie off at a speed zone in the road called Frontenac. All I knew about the place was that a hundred years before the town had lost forty-something miners in a collapse. I was hoping they wouldn't notice one more corpse.

I stopped near Fredonia, gassed up the Buick and made a phone call to find out where the congressman lived. Picked up a lighter from a counter display, some cigarette butts from the ground, and put them in a bag. I was at the congressman's house in time for dinner. The neighborhood was gated, but the entrance was automated. I parked at a dentist's office across the street and watched the SUVs roll up, wait for the machine to register and the gate to swing open, then pull through. I drove around for a few minutes to find the closest gas station. I parked at a fast-food place and grabbed something they thought was a milkshake.

After another half hour at the gas station, I found a Lexus with the right tag. Got it started while he was inside buying breath mints. He'd parked away from the only camera, on the edge of the lot. Lucky for me the driver didn't want any scratches on his car. I'd try to take good care of his baby.

I pulled up to the gate, slowed, then went on through after the gate opened. A couple of turns toward the water, then down Tall Timbers Lane, in a little section that didn't have a tree older than ten years. I took the photo of Blake Goodwin from my pocket. A newspaper story about his disappearance. Grieving congressman and wife, begging for the safe return of their only son. Yeah, safe until he returned.

He had the same haircut Sean had when he went away. I'd kept up the best I could, being so many states away. Sent money that was returned. They didn't need any dirty money, she'd scrawled back. They didn't need a lot of things. Money. Toys. Visits.

Me.

The wooden fence behind the house was high, but the gate was open. I dropped a couple of the cigarette butts there and went in back. Through the ten-foot windows, I saw the wife making drinks at the bar. The congressman was laid out in a leather recliner staring at some wall-sized TV, watching a colorized version of *Casablanca*. I felt bad I could only kill them once.

The scene where Ilsa pulls the gun on Rick was starting when I walked through screen door and shot the wife in the shoulder. They were screaming "Oh, my God" and "Jesus Christ" like they were at some fundamentalist snake-kissing service.

"The safe," I said to the husband as I was walking over to the wife.

"Safe? What safe? We don't have a safe."

I shot the TV, which I was going to do at some point anyway.

More screaming. I picked the wife up and put the barrel of the pistol into her mouth. She stopped moving.

"The safe."

She looked past me to her husband. In the reflection of some big, sun-framed mirror in the kitchen I could see him reaching for the phone.

"Tell 911 to bring a bucket for your wife's face."

I had to keep her alive so he had a reason to open the safe. And he had to open the safe for this to look right. I'd kill them both either way, but I hated to see a good plan wasted.

He moved away from the phone toward me. "Office," he stammered. "In the office."

I picked the wife up by her good shoulder and we all walked into the office in the next room. Behind the big desk were pictures of the son they'd spent years molesting. Little league. Class photos. Family shots. He went to the bookshelf, pulled off some books he'd probably bought by the foot, then opened to the wall safe. "I don't know what you're looking for," he said, putting envelopes from the safe onto the table.

"No," I said, splattering the back of his head across the wall. "You wouldn't."

The wife fell down to the floor face-first screaming. I looked at the bookshelves. Bloody chunks clumping along the spines of unread books, sliding down pictures of their son. Violence won't bring back the dead. I'd been told that before. No. It won't. I pulled the wife's head up, her back bending like a yoga pose. "You had a son. You had everything."

"I don't know what you're talking about." She was about to hyperventilate. Short words, clipped, full of snot and tears. Like a beaten child. "Why are you doing this? What do you want?"

I want my son back, I thought. *I want what you destroyed.*

"My husband," she said, shaking through the tears, "is a very powerful man."

"Was."

"Please. God." She was having trouble breathing. A cracking sound at the back of her throat. Bile. Fear. "You don't have do this," she said, twisting her head, looking around the room, looking for some way out, searching for help that wasn't there. "Please. We are very powerful," she said. "Powerful people. Please. God."

Begging. I thought of their son. Maybe he had begged them to stop before he ran away. Took off. Their own son. I looked at the pictures on the shelf. The same haircut my son had at that age. The blond bowl cut with the part on the side. The last time I'd seen him. And then the family photos. At the congressman's office. In front of the big politician's desk. Yes. Look at the power. Look at what I can control. Look at what people can take away and destroy.

"When you get to Hell, say hello to my ex-wife." I took a step back and put a bullet through her head. I pulled the slug from the floor and the other from the bookshelf, took the envelopes from the desk.

I knocked over some stuff on my way out. Grabbed the other slugs I'd left. Went to the back fence, dropped the lighter and the other butts out of the bag. Fingerprints from all the cheap folks at the gas station who used the lighter. Cigarette butts from a few people. Let the cops spend their time on all their tests. I like to keep the geeks employed.

I took the Lexus to the burger place and swapped it for my car. Tossed the slugs down a grate as I pulled around. Found the interstate and headed for the airport. I stopped at a lousy diner for some eggs and bacon, left the pistol in the bathroom garbage. Didn't matter if anyone found it. No numbers. No prints. Probably the cleanest thing in the bathroom.

I parked in long-term, dropped the gloves I'd been wearing into a trash can, and took a trolley to the terminal. At the ticket counter, I reached into the wrong pocket and pulled out the newspaper clipping about the boy's death.

"Sir?"

I put it back in my pocket and found the fax from the funeral home.

The woman looked at it. "I'm sorry, sir. This can't be your name."

She looked at me, then back at the fax.

The flight was about to board. If I missed this one, the next one to Chicago was in a few hours. Being the holidays, most of the flights were booked solid. I could still make the service with the later flight, but I wanted to keep moving.

She looked at me and raised her eyebrows. "Your name. Twice."

I took the paper from her, pointed to the last part of the name the funeral home had typed in for the deceased.

"Junior," I said. Of course, he'd gone by Sean. "Sean Martello. Junior." I took a breath. "I'm senior."

"Oh, sir. I'm so sorry. Yes, we can find room for you. But you just missed this one. The next flight is scheduled to leave in three hours."

I looked at her. I hadn't seen my son in ten years. What's another few hours? They'd be putting him in a suit. Arranging flowers. Whatever it is they do. I wouldn't be any help. Never had been.

She typed, handed me the ticket and the fax. I looked at the ticket. "Bereavement Fare." I folded the sheet of paper and put it in the pocket with the newspaper story.

"You can wait in the lounge if you'd like," she said. "I'm sorry for your loss, sir. And I'm sorry you missed your flight."

Yeah. I'd missed a lot of stuff. †

PURRZ, BABY
Vicki Hendricks

When Mary Lou came to the door in a red velvet robe, exactly like mine—except for the smaller size—I knew it was no coincidence. What I'd been suspecting for months was clear. How smart of Jack to save time on Christmas shopping by making one stop at the department store, a robe for his wife and one for his lover! I saw the competition in her eyes as she boldly sized me up, thinking she could snatch him away from me on sheer intelligence, never mind looks. She was only wondering how long it would take. I saw his eyes flick down the front of her robe, which was loosely tied, although there wasn't much to see in there. She must have worn the robe to taunt me, secretly, not figuring that I had one just like it. Of course, mine didn't have embroidered initials. That ML stuck in my mind.

It was early morning and we were dropping Purrzie off before we flew out to visit my mother. Jack had suggested that ML, as a cat lover whose elderly pet had just passed away, would take good care of our little sweetheart. After seeing the robe, I wouldn't have entrusted my beloved Purrzie to her, but we barely had time to get to the airport, and Purrz seemed comfortable sniffing around her living room, which was the most important consideration, after all.

I had to wonder what Jack's motivation could be in taking me to this lair. Did he want to get caught? More likely he thought I was too stupid to have a clue. His underestimating my intelligence had been an issue for years, mainly because I didn't read continuously like he did or appreciate the arts. I was proud of my down-to-earth personality, but he just got snootier as the years went by. He'd been spending a lot of time away from home lately, but I wouldn't have figured on a lover if I hadn't seen that robe and the calculating look on ML's face.

Maybe ML had suggested the idea of watching Purrzie, so she could check me out. Of course, Jack wouldn't have thought she'd wear the robe. On the way to the airport I mentioned the identical style, and he shrugged as if he was barely listening. His acting was decent when he was desperate.

I forced myself to put all my feelings aside while we were at Mother's. After the trip when we picked Purrzie up, I looked around her place. She had her Ph.D. diploma on the wall, and tons of books, Shakespeare plays and novels and poetry I was supposed to read in high school but never had time because I had to work. She had a lot of female poetry writers that I never heard of, Marilyn Hacker, Elizabeth Bishop, Adrienne Rich, many more. I glanced into the kitchen. Only a toaster on the counter. She was no doubt a feminist who couldn't cook. Women's poetry was her specialty. While ML and Jack were discussing "school business," I scribbled down a few of the poets' names, thinking I might catch up.

Back at home, I'd kept my suspicions to myself for a couple of weeks, when I heard Jack having a quiet phone call. "Who was it, honey?" I asked him.

"Somebody from school about a meeting. Nothing."

I let it go, but my guard was up. I heard him again, with that same tone, two days later. Then one morning he was on the phone before I even got out to the kitchen. I punched *69 on the extension, and checked ML's number on information. I was no fool.

Jack was slathering cream cheese on a bagel when I confronted him.

"Why were you talking to Mary Lou so early?" I asked him.

"What?" He looked up from the newspaper like he was dazed.

"I just did *69 on the phone."

"Huh?"

"Star-six-nine. It gives you the number of the last caller."

"Oh. Why'd you do that?"

"I wanted to know who called so early. So answer my question."

"Mary Lou is having trouble with her department head. I was just giving her advice."

"Oh, really?"

"Yes, Georgia. What's your problem?"

Of course, I shouldn't have tipped. He was too fast to get caught like that. However, he wasn't aware that I could hear the change in his voice, the soft tone like he used to use on me, and I kept that to myself.

By afternoon I started to feel bitter. I tried to concentrate on reading email, but it was tough. I slopped a shot of Wild Turkey into my chamomile tea and took a long gulp. Son of a bitch. For fifteen years, I'd cooked, waited on him, and took care of the home, so he could keep his nose buried in print. Now he's sniffing up another woman. In the fall when ML took the job teaching English literature, he mentioned that they had known each other in college. I should have been more alert. I remembered her name from years before. She was a fantasy that never came true. Now was his chance.

I heard Purrzie's toenails trickling down the wood hall floor and called his name. He always came when I called him, unlike Jack. He stopped at the doorway of the office and yawned. This cat was a beauty, streamlined and muscular, a lovable, perfectly marked tabby, and smart as all get out.

"Oh, did I wake my sweetie? Com'ere, sweetie."

He came to me and I petted his back and gave him smooches on the head. He was warm all over, probably just got up from his window ledge. "Oh, precious sweetheart. How's my sweetie?"

He took a leap and settled on my lap. He loved me more than anything else in the world, including food. You couldn't say that about any dog, or dog's best friend.

I started down the spam awaiting my attention, deleting the hundred or so about Viagra, penis enlargement, and the latest assortment of sleazy sexual promotions. "Masturbate to dilated teen rectum movies," "Mature lesbians rubbing their vulvas," "See me playing with my rectum." Christ. Rectums? I couldn't really understand the attraction. Nobody would have believed this five years ago, or twenty years ago, when Jack tried to woo ML.

It was bad luck that she'd turned up now, when adultery seemed minor compared to the popular sexual perversions. ML wasn't gorgeous but different from me. Neither of us was a spring chicken at forty-five. I was stocky and muscular with a round face and dark hair, while she was a tall blonde, thin, and sleepy eyed, with narrow shoulders and dangling arms that seemed to lack solid bone or muscle, the feminine kind of woman Jack always looked at. ML had a slight edge that gave the impression she was only interested in what life could do for her, and the world could go fuck itself otherwise. I might've enjoyed her attitude if she wasn't enjoying Jack.

I closed out of the email window and started typing up a list of Jack's new behaviors and the times and dates of the calls when he'd walk into another room to talk. I realized that lately, he'd mentioned going on a diet. Damn, that made sense. Bony ML wouldn't like sweaty flab interfering with her breathing, and Jack was smart enough to figure he'd better get rid of some before the newness of the sex wore off. Of course, he hadn't yet managed to cut his food intake. I could probably end their relationship if I just kept cooking his favorites, but it wasn't a sure bet and could take a while.

Had he started getting haircuts more often? Tweezing the hairs from his nose and ears? I wasn't sure, but in general he was a little more attractive these days. It didn't look good for him.

I made a note to keep track of the crossword puzzles. It occurred to me that I hadn't seen Jack with his pencil poised over the newspaper in weeks—so romantic for the two of them, fact master and wordsmith, the perfect couple.

I had counted the condoms, the stash in his nightstand. I was sure he'd bought a full dozen in the month when I'd forgotten to take my pills, and his sex drive hadn't been that strong. Now there were only three left. He was thrifty enough to finish up the open box rather than buy a separate supply for ML. I hadn't had the sense to check the quantity before I confronted him about the phone calls. Since then the three hadn't been touched.

I went back and continued to delete spam. It was comforting to know that if I ever needed sex, *of any kind*, I could find it easily. I'd put dinner in the oven earlier, lasagna, rich with cheese and tomato and béchamel sauce and it began to send its aroma my way. I'd also gotten in a couple bottles of good Chianti. Italian food was Jack's favorite. I planned to start over that night, convincing him that my suspicions were gone so he'd be off guard. I wanted to catch him for pure shock value and to show him how smart I was, in spite of what he thought. Then maybe we could restart our marriage on more equal ground, him being in the hole he dug with his guilt.

I used to think Jack was cute and funny when he got into a rant, but now I realized that most of the joy he got from our marriage was by emphasizing my stupidity, and more than that, he enjoyed the company of somebody on his own level. I began to resent his intellectual monologues and use of words I didn't know. He was a professor of history, with his endless stories and details about wars and slavery. On a weekly basis, I listened to repeated critiques of Dee Brown's bad writing and poor research in *Creek Mary's Blood*. ML was, no doubt, impressed that Jack knew the facts better than the guys who wrote the books.

I hadn't attended college, but my life never lacked for it, until now. I had my restaurant and made a much better living than Jack did teaching, but I knew deep down that he was only concerned with facts, how many he knew and how many I didn't. He'd always thrown me crumbs about how our differences made us so good together, but being smarter than me was what puffed him up, besides eating the great food I cooked. I think those were the reasons he was keeping me around, since he'd found ML again.

I tried to pay the phone bill online, but I was so upset I kept misspelling my password. I pictured her and Jack together in the library at school, fondling each other under the table, her reciting poetry or him explaining how the Indians ate six pounds of meat a day in winter, because they had no vegetables—Indians as thin as her, he'd say, and poke her in her flat stomach. It would be his dream to have a woman who enjoyed listening to all his factual crap. I poured the empty teacup full of Wild Turkey, chugged it. I wondered if they snickered together about all the things they figured I couldn't understand.

Purrzie stretched and jumped off my lap. I followed him into the kitchen to heat his rotisserie chicken. I shredded it into tiny bits so he wouldn't gobble big pieces and choke. He wasn't piggish by nature, but I wanted to make his life safer and more enjoyable in any way I could.

I looked into the oven. The lasagna was beautiful but couldn't compete with ML. Besides being an intellectual who shared Jack's tedious book interests, she was the lost love of his life, and now he had a chance to regain his self-esteem. Years before she surfaced, he'd told me they'd once smoked dope and had sex. Now he probably didn't remember telling me, or more likely never realized I would put together the name with the information after so long.

I'd made the salad and was just sliding the bread into the oven when the keys rattled in the door. I reminded myself to keep a lid on conversation about ML.

Jack came in and gave me a big hug and kiss, and I sniffed his mustache and neck for any unfamiliar scents. I wasn't sure. He started to sniff too, maybe at the Wild Turkey, another thing he was always on my case about.

"Lasagna, your favorite," I said. "Garlic bread on the way."

"Yum. I don't deserve you, Georgia."

"Why not?"

He kissed me quick and headed into the bathroom, his mind already elsewhere.

The Wild Turkey had a kick. I realized I'd better calm down. I wanted to ask him if Mary Lou could cook, although I knew it didn't matter to him anyway. It's one of those things you list when you're judging your pros and cons, but it doesn't weigh a feather against that hot rod of wild passion. I'd been riding the hot rod less and less.

I was pulling the pan of lasagna out of the oven when the phone rang. Jack was still in the bathroom. I shoved the pan on the counter and answered it.

"Is this Mrs. Lewis?"

"There is no Mrs. Lewis," I said. Telemarketers. Shit.

"Oh, sorry."

I'd been pretty harsh and I could hear apology in her tone. Maybe she thought Mrs. Lewis was dead, or else that I wanted to be Mrs. Lewis and couldn't get Jack to marry me. The truth was I'd never changed my name to his. Whatever she thought, she hung up fast—something to remember for future use.

Jack yelled from the bedroom. "Who was that, sweetie?"

"Telemarketing."

"What were they selling?"

"I don't know. They asked for Mrs. Lewis and I said there wasn't one."

"Oh?"

"Yeah. She hung up."

"Good job." Jack came strolling out in his jeans and ivy-league shirt, looking his casual academic self, his face a little too happy for a weekday. It could have been because I was pouring the wine, and the lasagna was browned perfectly and bubbling in the center of the table, but I started to think. We'd had a telemarketing call a week earlier, and about an hour later he went to the gym and didn't come home until near midnight, after supposedly meeting friends and having a few beers. I fell for it at the time, but now I realized the call could be a trick, in case I answered the phone, or a signal that ML was waiting for him.

I remembered something else too. Jack had been keeping his cell phone turned off while we were together. That way he could get back to her at his leisure. Fucking asshole. He thought he had it made because I was such a dope.

I set the garlic bread on the table, sliced out a chunk of lasagna and put it on Jack's plate. It was oozing cheese and red sauce and he licked his lips. He was so good at this. Getting ready to chow down and enjoy his dinner, then take off for some poetry and wild sex, leaving me with the mess.

He held out his wine glass and toasted me for the nice dinner. It started to gnaw at me, the way he was so cool. I used to admire that in a man, but now I saw the down side. They never flinch, no matter what you do. Teflon personalities. Nothing sticks—until the Teflon gets scratched.

I got involved in my plate as he started up a lecture about slaves. Topics were always swimming around in Jack's head. I nodded and chewed.

"I was reading the other day about cat-hauling."

"Cat-hauling?" The word *cat* caught my attention. "A service to take Purrzie to the vet?"

"No, the slave owners did it before the Civil War as a form of punishment, to make examples of the tough, hard-to-coerce slaves. It's in Charles Ball's slave narrative.

"Were the cats all right?"

"I guess. You might not want to hear about this during dinner."

"As long as the cats were fine."

"The idea was to tie a man down on his stomach, naked, with his arms and legs staked out, drop a big tomcat on his back, and pull it by its tail. The cat clawed and ripped into the skin and muscle, trying for a foothold to get away."

"Ooh, I can imagine."

"They would do this until the slave was unconscious from the shock. Of course, there were no antibiotics so the infection was often deadly.

I cringed. "Brutal." I looked over at Purrzie on the window-sill, who was licking his asshole peacefully. "God, that's horrible."

"Certainly was. Imagine getting ripped to shreds then left to get infected and die."

"Besides that, the cats were probably scared to death." There was probably something wrong with me that I couldn't feel as much sympathy for a man as I could for a cat, but nothing could be done about it. I took a big slug of my wine to get past the vision of an agonizing cat, screaming as he was being yanked by the tail, not having done anything wrong, not knowing why he was being punished. I shivered. "I didn't know cats were kept as pets back then."

"I don't think they cared for them like we do." He looked at Purrzie still licking himself and shook his head. "Not like His Majesty. Cats were kept to kill mice."

I ignored his cut at Purrzie, but it registered in my brain. He started up about some Civil War battle tactics, where the Union army made tunnels like mice, but there was no further mention of cats so I lost interest. When he stopped talking, I smiled. Now I was just waiting to see how long he'd hang around.

"There's ice cream for dessert."

"No, thanks. I'm stuffed. I'm going to head over to the gym after I digest this great dinner."

It was an hour and a half between the time of the telemarketing call and when he left the house. I figured he didn't want to jump up from the table immediately and risk trouble. I thought of telling him I was going along to the gym, but I hadn't worked out in two years and I knew he'd be suspicious. I didn't want to follow and risk getting caught. I was biding my time to figure out a better plan.

He came home late again that night and said the guys wanted to make racket ball and drinks a weekly thing. He had showered, so there wasn't any evidence to sniff. These were guys I hadn't met, so I couldn't call to check anything out. I didn't bother objecting. The jig would soon be up.

The next morning he made love to me, pay back for the lasagna, no doubt, so he wouldn't feel guilty. I started to think maybe I was making too big a deal out of all this, and I could win him back.

"I was thinking we could take a long weekend and go to Cancun or somewhere to get away from the cold," I said.

"I don't know. I have to keep up with my syllabus."

"Oh, take a day or two! The students will be happy. My treat." I knew ML, being a teacher, couldn't compete when it came to money.

"We practically just got back from Christmas. How can you take more time off from the restaurant?"

"I trust my new manager completely." I studied his face to see if the word *trust* made him flinch, but it didn't.

"I'll think about it. It's true we have Mary Lou to take care of Purrzie now. She still hasn't gotten another cat." He smiled. His whole demeanor brightened up at the thought of ML watching Purrzie. So why didn't the cunt get a new cat? I bet she couldn't wait to have Purrzie to herself again.

He was off to school early. Said he had papers to grade and had forgotten to bring them home. I bet they were meeting for coffee. My stomach started to burn as his car backed down the drive. So that was it. Purrzie was his ace in the hole—working better than what he had in the hole during his younger years. He knew I'd never let Purrz go, but ML didn't. ML knew a one-of-a-kind cat when she saw it, and Jack was a fringe benefit.

I couldn't take it any longer. I wasn't a wimp who could live like that, waiting and hoping. I took another day off at the restaurant so I had time to work out my scheme. I sat down at the computer and looked at my email. All crap. Not a single note from a friend or relative. Nobody I could talk to.

I deleted more rectal spam as I formulated the details to catch Jack and ML. I closed my AOL and used Jack's password to open his account. Sure enough, there was email from mljonson45. What luck! It had to be Mary Lou, and she was on AOL too.

The mail wasn't anything interesting, just a fast note: *Don't worry. I have a great idea. Will talk to you at school.*

It didn't sound like good news for me. I deleted it. I'd heard about setting up false accounts where the address was one letter off from the real address. If I used a capital *I* instead of a small *L*, and pretended to write from Mary Lou, Jack would never know the difference, and I would receive his reply. I went back to my account and added a new screen name, mIjonson45. With the AOL font, only the computer could tell what letter that line stood for. I was damn smart.

I decided to keep the note to Jack plain and mysterious, since I didn't know their little love names, or what fancy expressions an English professor might use.

Come to my place at 8 P.M. tonight. I have a secret surprise for you.

I thought about the word *secret*. Was it too much? *Surprise* sounded too ordinary. I wanted him to build up anticipation so when I answered her door, his balls would shrivel into prunes.

I also wanted to be sure ML was home that night or I wouldn't have any way of getting inside. It was complicated. Jack's email address was historybuff1860@aol, which I changed to historybutt1860@aol, and sent the message to ML: *Busy with grading today. I can come to your place tonight at 7:00. Let me know if it's okay.*

The address change was little risky, but it was too cute to resist. If ML thought it was a hoax, she might still be home anyway. At worst, I was wasting my time and would have to try something else.

I knew Jack would check his email a few times from school. I sometimes left him messages there instead of calling. I was a little worried that he might say something to ML, but she was in a different building, and if they thought they had secret plans for later, they'd be unlikely to look for each other. Worst case, he would mention the email and they would figure it was some kind of mistake. It might give them the creeps, but they couldn't trace it to me.

I took the gun from my panty drawer and tucked it into my big purse. My brother had given me the Glock when Jack and I moved to the big city. Jack didn't know I had it. He'd never have let me keep it. My gun in his face would show him I was serious, and teach him a good lesson. He would see how smart I was and never try anything again. I found a roll of duct tape to use on ML. I loved it. A dope like me teaching two professors a lesson.

ML's reply came back to historybutt within the hour: *Okay. I'll be home tonight. See you!*

She was already excited, the tart. I checked the other screen name at noon and still nothing. I needed to know whether my plan had worked, so I could beat Jack to her place, surprise ML, and get her out of the way. Finally, at three o'clock Jack's reply was there. It was also brief: *Why so mysterious? See you there.*

I had defrosted homemade minestrone soup and bread from the restaurant for dinner. I wasn't in the mood to cook. Jack came home acting normal, as he was so skilled at doing, and we ate and he talked some facts about the Seminoles' turbans and jewelry. I couldn't really pay much attention. I thought I heard the name Mary Lou, and almost questioned him, but then I realized it was my imagination playing tricks. My mind kept racing over my plan and my feet were in a nervous jitter under the table.

Jack ate two full bowls of soup and I thought he'd never get done. When he finished, I said I had to help out at the restaurant for the evening. Actually, since I hadn't been there for two days, there was plenty I should have been doing. I slugged down some Wild Turkey in a corner of the kitchen, and then put Purrz in his carrier. Jack knew Purrzie always sat on my lap while I did bookwork.

It was 6:45 when I left. I'd be a little late to ML's but she wouldn't expect Jack exactly at seven. He seemed relieved to see me go, so I knew he was planning to keep his date at eight o'clock.

It was dark when I arrived. I walked to the porch, set the cat carrier down, pulled out the gun, and rang the bell. Footsteps started up immediately and ML opened the door. She gasped. Her face was priceless.

I had the gun pointed at her skimpy chest. "Keep quiet and move back into the house."

She was good at taking orders. I kept the door open with my foot as I picked up Purrz and stepped inside. I set him on the couch and closed the door behind me.

"We're going to play a little trick on Jack," I said.

She started to disagree, but I poked at her small tit with the Glock and directed her to sit on a chair. She didn't put up a fuss, not that I gave her much chance. I pulled a piece of tape off the roll and slapped it over her mouth. She knew it was her own damn fault for starting up with Jack. I made her tape her own legs and one wrist to a wooden chair so I could continue to hold the gun. I put the gun down, wrapped the last wrist and tightened up the rest, then scooted her into the bedroom and moved Purrzie into the kitchen.

It wasn't long until I heard a car pull up. I got into position behind the door, expecting that Jack had a key, but he rang the bell—as formal as ever. I opened the door. He started sputtering something when he saw my face behind the Glock, but I barked my order, "Not a sound. Get in here or die," and he moved fast. I kept the gun on him and told him to march into the bedroom. He acted like he didn't know where to move, but I mentioned that the gun was loaded, and he backed up till he nearly fell over ML's chair. He looked at her all taped.

"Why are you doing this, Georgia?" he asked in a controlled scream.

"You know damned well why!" I yelled back.

"No, I don't. What kind of stupidity is this? Put that gun down. You don't know how to use it."

He couldn't resist bringing up my "stupidity" and that set my head on fire. Any regard for him or my own good burned up with those hateful words. At this point I would have expected him to be begging my forgiveness, so I would put the gun down. I couldn't believe he would continue to insult me and play out the lie this far. I was going to get a confession, one way or another.

I pointed the gun toward his chest. "Sit."

He sat on the bed and I tossed him the roll of tape I'd been wearing on my wrist. ML's bed was perfect for the job, kind of old-fashioned like I expected a poetry reader to have. "Lay down and tape your ankles to the bed posts," I said. I glanced back at ML wondering if the word should have been *lie*, knowing she would catch that kind of error, but she just looked terrified. Jack gave me a look like he was humoring me, but he started unreeling the tape. It was a double bed, so his legs reached okay, but he was slow at taping and the result didn't look too secure. I wouldn't dare let go of the gun to help, so I pointed it at ML's head.

"Hurry up, and tape it right, or your girlfriend's gonna git it." I was starting to enjoy my role.

"Girlfriend? What?" He looked at ML, blank for a second. "She's gay!"

ML started to squeal behind the tape, like she wanted to tear him to pieces for calling her a lesbian.

I had to laugh. "Good try. Keep it up, asshole. What are you doing here then?"

"I told you I was stopping by."

I could see him searching his head for another lie. His mouth moved, but despite his intelligence, nothing came out of it. Finally, he took a breath. "Look, we can clear this up. Put the gun down so we can talk. This is ridiculous."

"Oh, Mr. Information can't come up with a lie fast enough!" I pointed the gun back at him. "Tape your wrist to the top post."

He followed orders clumsily, and the time he took enraged me more. He was muttering that he didn't deserve any of this and that I was insane, but I ignored him as usual.

"This is nothing compared to what they do on the Internet," I told him. I had him tear off a long piece of tape so I could hold the gun and finish the last wrist. Finally I set the gun down, slapped a piece of tape over his mouth, double taped the wrists, and then went back over the ankles.

Now that he was taped up solid, I realized I had wanted him face down, but there was no way I was about to start over. Face up might work even better to get a confession. However, it was impossible to get his shirt off like that.

I went into the kitchen to look for scissors and also found a bottle of Cuervo Gold. Two quick shots and I felt adequate to the job. Jack went white as the bedspread when he saw scissors in my hand. The shirt was an ugly striped golf shirt, so I enjoyed cutting straight up the front, watching his chin quiver. I pushed both halves back over his arms to expose his chest. I opened his zipper and slid his pants partially down his thighs and took my time snipping off the Fruit of the Looms. Mostly I wanted to freak him out, not hurt him too much. He wouldn't have the nerve to press charges once his lies were exposed. I looked at ML to see how she liked the look of lover boy's balls right now, but she had her eyes closed tight. She might have thought I was about to cut those balls right off.

I heard yowling from the kitchen and went to get Purrzie. I felt terrible I'd left him in that carrier so long. I took a second to pour myself another shot. When I stepped back into the bedroom with Purrzie, Jack's eyes popped. He knew what I had planned— we were going to do a little cat-hauling. "See, I remember everything you tell me," I said. "This form of torture comes from so and so's slave narrative."

I slugged from the bottle of tequila that I found I'd carried with me and lifted Purrzie from the carrier. Jack was squirming, a frown on his face, and I knew he was itching to name the slave I couldn't remember. No doubt, he thought I was drunk too, and I'd taped him wrong side up in my usual dumb-ass way. "We'll be working on your chest, so you can watch," I told him, to set the record straight.

As mad as I was, I couldn't imagine grabbing Purrzie by his tail, so I held him under his armpits. "Now we'll see if you have something to confess." I pulled Purrz down Jack's chest noticing the evenly spaced stripes that immediately began to bleed. Jack moaned. Purrz was squirming and sure enough trying to get a grip with all four paws, just like the history book said. I held him a little lower to extend the rows of scratches and realized he'd got a foothold into one of Jack's balls. It was an accident. The son of a bitch moaned real loud. Purrzie was yowling even louder in my face, but even as I pulled the claws one by one from Jack's right ball, not a single word of confession came from those lips. I closed my eyes and gritted my teeth in frustration. "I'm listening—whenever you want to start!" I yelled.

Purrzie dug the claws of his left front paw into Jack's dick before I could lift him to threaten again, and it took some time to detach each hooked claw without further injury. I didn't want to ruin Jack for life. I had just pulled out the last claw when Purrz broke loose, scrambled up Jack's chest, and leapt to the floor. I watched him dash into the kitchen to hide.

Jack was still quiet, the damn fool. I looked back. "Shit!" The tape was covering Jack's mouth and he couldn't say a word.

He looked to be passed out, so I ripped off the tape and gave him a few slaps. His mouth fell open and some minestrone fell out.

I gave him a few more slaps. "Wake up, Jack," I said. "Now it's time for your fucking confession." I decided to play it like I'd planned it this way, rather than have him think I'd been too stupid to take off the tape.

In a minute, I realized he wasn't going to wake up. I didn't figure he'd lost that much blood, but he must have choked on those words I wanted to hear. That minestrone had backed up and clogged his windpipe and nose. My cooking had killed him. I felt a black mood come over me.

ML was conscious. I ripped off her tape and stuck the gun in her face to think, but I knew I had to kill her to get away with this.

She started to cry. "Okay," she said. "I'm sorry. I confess everything. Please don't kill me!"

Her confession was meaningless by now. I was in big trouble, and my gun hand fell down by my side. The deed was done. The victory was shallow.

I left her taped there, sobbing, and coaxed Purrzie out from under the kitchen table. Cat-hauling was better in the telling than in the doing. The facts hadn't given a clear picture. I realized I would miss Jack when the shock wore off, even his stories. I put Purrzie in his carrier and drove home.

The food is lousy in prison and the restroom facilities are primitive, but I've had plenty of time to catch up on my reading. I even found some of ML's women poets in the prison library. Come to find out, they're all lesbians. Thinking back to the look ML gave me, I'm sure she was sizing me up in a different way from what I thought. It's possible I imagined all the evidence.

However, one thing is sure. ML came out on top. She wrote to me that she adopted Purrzie from the animal shelter—at least he has a good home. Despite my mistakes, I feel like the smartest person here at the prison. Being smart just isn't the daily thrill I expected. †

THE LITTLE BOY INSIDE
Glenn Gray

At first, Greg thought he might be choking. After all, he did have
acid reflux and maybe his esophagus was inflamed and irritated.
He lost his breath for a moment and then it felt as if he would
vomit, a little gagging, and then he coughed up the little boy right
onto his desk.

The boy was naked and he was tiny, no bigger than a pen cap.

The boy was alive, somewhat lethargic, but alive; and covered in mucous.

Greg was shocked and thought that maybe the couple of beers
he downed might have had something to do with the whole thing.
Was he that buzzed? Greg jolted up from his desk, scared and
vaguely appalled, not knowing quite how to react.

His first impulse was to get some tissues and clean him up but
he didn't want to leave him alone. What if the little guy disappeared or woke and ran away? He didn't want that.

Greg scanned his study, grabbed one of his medical journals
from the stack on the floor, the firm glossy blue one, the
American Journal of Neuroradiology, and carefully tapped and
slid the little boy onto the cover.

He practically tip-toed to the bathroom, one hand holding the
journal, the other cupping the edge so the boy didn't slip and fall
off. He rested the journal on the counter and studied the boy
closely in the brighter light, noticing the sandy hair with the bowl
cut, matted down in splotches from the phlegm.

The boy was on his side now, in the fetal position, looking cozy and comfortable.

Greg ripped some toilet tissue from the roll on the wall and patted the boy gently, drying him off, and the boy seemed to enjoy it, bending his knees closer and hugging himself tighter.

Greg draped the boy's body with a few sheets of dry tissue and the boy fell asleep.

❖

Greg rummaged around in his garage until he finally found it, the cardboard box that his recently purchased computer came in. He hadn't thrown it away yet, just in case something went wrong with the computer and he had to return it.

But now it would serve a different purpose.

He tore off the top portion and flattened out the bottom.

Greg got one of his old T-shirts and a couple of old socks and arranged them along the bottom of the box.

He gently slid the sleeping boy onto the fuzzy sock, covered him with some pieces of another soft shirt he had ripped up.

The boy rustled but didn't wake.

The boy looked relaxed and snug.

Greg crumpled up a chocolate chip cookie and let the crumbs fall next to the boy. From his kitchen garbage, he fished a cap from a two-liter bottle of diet soda, rinsed it and filled it with milk, plopped it in the box.

Greg stared down at the boy in his new box-home, fascinated, and thought that he absolutely without a doubt must be losing his mind.

❖

Greg didn't know what to do.

He brought the box to his study, placed it on his desk next to the computer. He poured himself a Jameson and sat there staring down into the box.

The boy slept soundly.

He got up, paced the house, and then sat back down.

He thought about going to the ER. But then thought again. What the heck would he do? Walk in with the box, set it down and say, *I just threw this up? Look?*

Besides he couldn't see going to his own hospital, the one where he worked. He could just hear the staff now: "Dr. Baxter in Radiology has lost his mind. Walked in with a mini boy in a box, said he threw it up. Guess he's had too much radiation exposure."

No way.

And out here in the sticks there wasn't another ER for a hundred miles. Greg figured that's what he gets for taking the job nobody wanted in Upstate New York, middle of nowhere.

Greg thought maybe he should get a CT scan in the morning. What if there were other boys living in his abdomen. A whole swim team? A fraternity? Christ. But surprisingly Greg felt fine now; he didn't even have the slightest hint of bloating or epigastric pain he had usually experienced every day for the past several months.

He felt totally normal.

❖

Greg admitted to himself that he would need some help, someone to talk to, and he knew who he had to call.

Cindy.

Greg had basically just met Cindy.

He thought he was falling in love with her. No, he definitely had fallen in love with her.

But he didn't want her to think he was a freak.

Could he really call her now and tell her he just threw up a mini boy and could she please come over. Could he? They had been dating for only two months.

And he had just broken up with her the day before last.

Screw it.

Greg grabbed the phone, held his finger above the number pad for a long moment, then punched her number.

"Cindy?"

"Greg?"

"I know it's late, but I need to talk to you."

"You're kidding, right?"

"No. No I'm not. I need to see you."

"Hellloo? Greg? You said you didn't want to see me any-more. Getting too serious, remember?"

"I'm sorry, Cindy. Really, I am. It's just, well, something's happened."

"Yeah so?"

"I'd like to talk."

"I wanted to talk, you didn't. Now you want to talk."

"I know. I need to talk now."

"I was trying to get close. You ran."

"Not really."

"Now you call, late Friday night, say you want to talk."

"Well, I need to show you something."

"You tore my heart out, Greg."

"I didn't mean it."

"And I'm not doing it again."

"But I have this thing …"

Click.

Greg stood for a moment in the middle of his study with the phone to his ear, sighed.

The old clock on the wall ticked and ticked.

He finally clicked the phone off and placed it on his desk, next to the box.

He looked into the box.

Greg startled.

The little boy was lying on his back, eyes wide open, a swath of material pulled to his chin like a blanket.

Greg reflexively backed off, as if he were not supposed to be looking, caught peeping. He then slowly peeked back over the edge.

The boy met his gaze and tilted his head.

Greg stared. He leaned closer. He could hear his own breath whistling through his nostrils.

The clock.

"Who," Greg finally said, coming out like a whisper, "… who are you?"

The little boy looked puzzled, scrunched up his face.

The boy's voice was a distant soft squeak. "I don't know."

The little boy's eyes shut and he nodded off to sleep.

Greg watched the sleeping boy for an hour.

He had another Jameson and two beers and then brought the box into his bedroom, put it on the floor next to his bed.

Greg changed into flannel pajamas and climbed into bed.

He intermittently woke up to check on the boy.

In the middle of the night Greg was roused by a funny noise. He flicked on the lamp, leaned over to look in the box. The little boy was hunched over on his stomach, sobbing.

"Hey, little boy," Greg said, leaning on an elbow. "You okay?"

The boy turned to his side, looked up at Greg. He took a few breaths, wiped his face. "I feel scared."

"What's that? You're scared?" Greg lowered his ear, reached into the box. "It's okay, little guy. It's gonna be okay. Here."

Greg splayed his fingers, creating a welcoming flat surface. The boy hesitated, then crawled on hands and knees onto Greg's fleshy palm.

"There you go." Greg lifted him out of the box, brought him close to his face. "Everything's gonna be just fine, little boy."

The boy twisted, pushed, then stood, a scrap of cloth twisted about his waist. He smoothed his face with both hands. "Thank you."

Greg lay back in bed against two pillows, turned his wrist and let the boy roll onto his chest. "You're safe here."

The boy curled into a flannel fold.

A moment later, they both fell asleep, Greg's chest rising and falling like rolling waves, his heart rhythmically thudding beneath the boy.

❖

Greg woke at dawn, still on his back, and the little boy was still curled up on his chest.

Greg cupped the boy in his hand and gently maneuvered his little body onto the bed next to him, in a fluffy roll of covers. Greg watched him sleep.

Greg thought about going over to the hospital. It was Saturday after all and things would be quiet in Radiology. He thought again about getting a CT scan, just to check things. He knew Mike was the tech working today so there wouldn't be many questions.

He also thought that maybe he would bring the little boy, put him on the table next to him. Secretly, of course. And then he thought about the radiation dose and if it would be okay, given the boy was so small. He figured, gosh, we scan little premie babies when we have to and if it's just once that should be harmless.

He had to see what this boy was made of.

Greg showered, got dressed and had breakfast. He kept checking on the boy, who continued to sleep comfortably in the bed.

He figured he'd phone Cindy again, see if things were different now, given it was morning and she had time to think.

There was no answer, just the machine, which he hung up on.

He then remembered that Cindy sometimes worked on Saturday. She was a physical therapist at the hospital and often times she would spend Saturday mornings working with some difficult patients.

When Greg entered the bedroom, he abruptly stopped in the doorway. The little boy was running and jumping on the bed. Sliding down some of the bunched up covers, rolling around.

Greg went to the bed and kneeled at its side.

The boy stopped and smiled at Greg. The boy was breathing heavily.

Greg said, "Hi."

"I'm jumping."

"I see."

"I feel better now."

"You want to go on a trip?"

"With you?"

"Of course."

"Where?"

"To my work."

"Okay."

Greg put on his navy blazer and slipped the boy into the breast pocket.

"Ready?"

The boy pulled up on the edge of the pocket, peeked his head out.

"Yes," he said. "This is fun."

"I'm having some abdominal pain," Greg told Mike the tech. "I just want to get a quick non-contrast abdomen and pelvis. Check things out."

Mike smiled, made a goofy face. "You're the doctor, Doc."

Mike helped Greg onto the CT gantry, positioned him. Greg didn't say anything, but he had the little boy in his hand and he was going to place him on the table at the right time.

"Okay, Doc," Mike said. "I'll do a scout view and you know the drill."

"Right."

Mike went into the CT control room, watched from behind the glass as the CT whirred into action. Greg's right hand was opposite the control room. He let the boy out onto the table. On the way over, he had instructed the boy as to what would happen. The boy got on his back along side Greg's abdomen.

After the scan, Greg cupped the boy in his hand, met Mike in the control room.

Mike was looking at the images on the screen. "That good, Doc?"

"Yes, yes. Fine," Greg said. "Just save it to CD and then delete the case from the system. This is off the record, okay?"

"You're the doc, Doc." Mike grinned.

Greg changed back to his shirt and blazer, got the CD from Mike.

He went to the reading room and punched in the extension to physical therapy.

"Cindy?"

"Greg?"

"I'm here in the hospital. Just did a CT."

"You okay?"

"Fine. Had some abdominal pain," Greg lied. "Can we talk?"

"I have a lot of patients."

"I really need to talk to you. Seriously."

"I thought we had something, Greg. This isn't easy for me."

"I know, I know," Greg said. There was a long silence. "Cindy?"

"Yeah."

"Um. I love you."

Another even longer silence.

"Now you love me?"

"I always did."

"Christ, Greg," Cindy said. "You're like a child."

"What'd you say?"

"You're like a child. A typical man."

Greg's head was spinning. He looked into his pocket. The little boy was looking upward, smiling.

"Greg? You still there?"

"Oh. Yes. Yes, yes."

"You were telling me you wanted to show me something."

"Um. No. I wanted to talk to you."

"Last night. You said you wanted to show me something."

"I did. Well, I wanted to show you my love."

"You've lost your mind."

"I'm lost without you."

Greg could hear Cindy inhale, breathe out heavily. "So you wanna swing by PT?"

Greg stood at the door to the physical therapy department, watching Cindy work with a stroke patient on a mat. The gaunt, skeleton of a man was hemiparetic, his right arm and leg paralyzed, spasm twisting his limbs inward. Cindy was gently stretching his arm, doing some range-of-motion exercise.

Greg realized then how much he loved Cindy. She was loving and caring. She understood things. It was the first time in his life he could remember feeling this way. There was a sense of calm, a warmth that infiltrated his gut whenever he studied her.

Greg decided that he wanted to marry her.

Cindy looked over and smiled at Greg.

She gave the man an elastic band, had him start an exercise on his own.

She walked over.

She stopped in front of Greg, held his gaze.

Greg said, "Hi."

"Hi."

Greg moved in close and hugged Cindy, pulled her toward him. Cindy was stiff at first and then softened.

"You know," Greg said. "There is something I want to show you."

Cindy made a face. "Oh?"

"Really. But you have to come over. Now is not the time or the place."

"Is this a joke?"

"No. We need to talk anyway. I've been doing a lot of thinking. I made a big mistake."

"Really."

"Yeah, really."

"How so."

"I don't want to lose you. You, you make me whole. I love you, Cindy."

"Hmm." Cindy narrowed her eyes, smiled. "I guess we can talk."

❖

As Greg exited the hospital through the sliding glass doors he realized that probably for the first time in his life he felt happy. Not just a pleasant transient happiness but the deep kind of solid genuine happiness that is filled with hope and great possibilities.

The air outside was crisp and he cherished the feel of it across his face. The sunlight glinted off a mountain in the distance and he felt as if he could climb that mountain, dash up the green slope and reach its peak, breathless.

He hurried to his Lexus and climbed in, careful not to squish the little boy in his pocket.

As he pulled off the lot onto the road, he thumbed open the pocket of his coat, "You okay old chap?"

"Yes," the boy said. "I feel happy too."

"Well good thing," Greg said and slapped the steering wheel, sounding silly. "Cause we going on a special mission, my boy."

❖

Two hours later Greg pulled into his garage, twisted the key from the ignition and exhaled. He was giddy. "Can't believe I just did that," Greg said in a sing-song way.

The boy was in the cup holder on the center console. "I'm glad you did."

Greg reached in his coat pocket, pulled out a small box, flipped it open.

"So am I," Greg said. He pulled the two-carat flawless princess-cut diamond ring from the velvet and held it up. A kaleidoscope of light shimmered before their eyes. "It's a beaut."

"It makes me happy," the boy said.

❖

Greg couldn't contain himself. He was so excited.

He called Cindy and arranged to meet. She would come over in a few hours. He thought about waiting, maybe going on a special trip like Paris or something and pop the question there. But he decided he couldn't wait. That he would do it tonight and then show her the boy.

Things were good.

He and the boy had some lunch; a sandwich and apple for Greg and a tiny chunk of apple for the boy, followed by a tiny pinch of turkey breast and more chocolate chip cookie crumbs.

Greg and the boy played a bit on the living room rug and then Greg put a little water in a bowl for the boy to bathe.

After, the boy settled down for a nap.

Greg cleaned the house and then remembered the CD.

He went to his study, slid the CD into the computer and waited for it to load.

The phone buzzed.

"Greg?"

"Yes?"

"Hi Greg, it's Frank."

"Frank. Everything okay? Weird to hear from you on a Saturday."

"Everything's fine with me, Greg. It's you I'm concerned about."

"How so?"

"I heard you were in the hospital today."

"Well, yes. Had some abdominal pain. Just wanted to get a CT."

"Turn out okay?"

"Yes. Yes, fine. Probably gastritis."

"Good. I came in to do some paperwork. I occasionally do that. We have an inspection coming up as well. Wanted to get a jump. One of the transporters saw you. I spoke with Mike and he was real reluctant to talk. Don't blame him. I pressured him."

"There's nothing to hide, Frank."

"Well. Some of the other docs, even some techs, they say you're not yourself."

"I'm fine. Just the gastritis."

"Even Mike. Said you were acting weird. Like you were hiding something, fidgety."

"I have a lot going on. A little stressed."

"That's what I'm saying, Greg. As your Chairman, but also as a friend, I think it would be helpful if you took a week or two. Relax a bit. We'll be fine. I've got coverage, no problem."

A long silence.

"Greg?"

"Um. Okay. Sure. I'll take the week. Thanks, Frank."

"Good. I'll give you a call."

Greg set the phone in its cradle.

He went to the bedroom, saw the boy sleeping soundly on the bed.

He went to the kitchen and poured a Jameson and noticed the clock.

Cindy was due to arrive in twenty minutes.

Greg couldn't get the conversation with Frank off his mind. He took a quick shower and shaved. He put on fresh clothes.

Who was talking about him? Frank made it sound as if everyone thought Greg was acting strangely. A subtle paranoia started to take hold and Greg pushed it aside. Told himself that he would relax, forget about that and focus on Cindy.

Just a few hours ago he was on top of the world. He tried to tap back into that zone. He thought about Cindy, watching her at work, and the warmth rose up in him again. The happiness was breaking through.

He went to the bedroom and saw the boy, awake now, sitting on the bed. Greg explained what had happened.

The boy said, "You'll be fine."

"You're right. I'm just dandy. And I'm gonna ask Cindy to marry me. Tonight. I'll just put you in your little box-mansion here and later, I'll introduce you."

"I love you," the boy said.

"What?" Greg was taken aback. He picked the boy up and brought him close to his face. "Well, I love you too."

Greg placed him in the box.

There was a knock on the door.

Greg padded across the living room floor, could see the outline of Cindy through the stained glass. Greg could feel the ring in his pant pocket, pinching his thigh.

Greg pulled the heavy wood door. There she was.

The warmth rose up in Greg, flooding his muscles.

Cindy tilted her head, smiled through the glass of the storm door.

Greg leaned and pushed open the door.

Cindy twisted in and went right into his arms in the foyer.

Greg shuffled back, intertwining his body with Cindy's. They said nothing.

Greg pulled Cindy's torso close, his nose at the nape of her neck, inhaling deeply, feeling like some kind of addict, her scent the drug.

After a long moment, they came apart, eyes connecting.

Cindy said, almost as if she would cry, "It's so good to be here, Greg."

"I really missed you," Greg said. "Really, really missed you."

"We've gotten real close real fast."

"I know."

"Does that scare you?"

"Not any more."

"We can do this."

"I know," Greg said. "Come inside."

Greg took her by the hand into the kitchen.

"You want a drink?"

"What did you want to show me?"

"Not yet," Greg said. "Well, two things now. Wine?"

"Two things? A little white would be nice. Anything bad?"

"No, no, no." Greg reached into the fridge, pulled the cork from a half-filled bottle of Pinot, poured. He cracked a beer for himself. "Come out to the porch."

He led her out onto a wood deck behind the house, which had a wonderful view of the mountains. They sat on a cushioned loveseat, sipped their drinks.

They sat for a couple of minutes, cuddling. There was a strong scent of evergreen from the line of trees bordering his property. The sun was low, the sky reddish brown.

Greg couldn't take it any more. He felt as if he would explode.

In one motion, he reached in his pocket and twisted onto his knees in front of Cindy.

She looked surprised. Greg brought up the box, clicked the top open, held it up.

He waited a beat for Cindy to comprehend. He met her eyes.

"Cindy?" Greg inhaled, cleared his throat. "Will you marry me?"

Cindy's face stretched, eyebrows arched, eyelids lifted, teeth. She was holding her breath, then let it out.

"Oh my God, yes. Yes, yes." Cindy gushed, and then a shriek. "YES!"

They embraced and kissed and Cindy stood up, hopped around a bit, hugged some more.

When they settled down, Greg finally said, "Now for the second thing."

"It's in here." Greg had Cindy's hand, guiding her into the bedroom. The box was on the bed.

"It's in that box?"

"Yup. Come here."

Greg and Cindy peered into the box simultaneously.

Cindy gasped.

Greg's mood flipped from jocular confidence to one of utter seriousness. "Hold on."

Cindy had her hand over her mouth. She stepped back.

Greg reached in and picked up the boy.

The boy had somehow solidified. He looked like a little sculpture, perfectly chiseled as if from a master artisan. He was a dull gray, but perfectly formed.

"Greg?" Cindy said. "What's that?"

Greg had to think quickly. Cindy was clearly terrified and he had just asked this woman to marry him. And she had said yes. He had to think of something.

"Ah. Just a joke is all." Greg floundered. "Yeah. You said I was like a child. Just a joke. Thought it would be funny."

It was half-hearted. Cindy backed up a few more steps. Greg placed the boy back in the box, took Cindy by the hand back to the porch.

"Are you okay, Greg?"

"I'm fine. Sorry about that. Thought it would be funny."

Cindy was definitely having her reservations. She was uneasy. She started to screw the ring off her finger.

"What are you doing?"

"I need a day to think, Greg." She set the ring on the glass-topped wicker table with a clink, next to her wine glass.

"Cindy, please."

"I'm sorry, Greg. It's all been so fast. Something tells me to sleep on it. I don't know what's happening here. With that little statue. Why did you have that thing in a box? Like you made a home for it?"

"I was just kidding. Please. Believe me."

"You know." Cindy seemed to loosen a bit. "I do love you, Greg. I really do."

"I love you too. So, so much"

"Think I better go." Cindy looked around, her hands fidgeting. "Why don't we meet tomorrow?"

Greg figured maybe it was the best thing. He was thrown off and she was uncomfortable. He needed to play it cool.

"Yeah. Okay," Greg said. "I'll call you in the morning."

❖

After Cindy left, Greg went back to the box. The boy was still there, immovable.

He remembered the CD in the computer. The CT scan.

He scrambled to the study.

Clicked the mouse.

The scan was on the screen as he had left it, when Frank called.

He scrolled through the images and there he was.

The little boy.

He was right along side his abdomen on the CT table, right where he put him. He zoomed the images.

He was astounded.

If the boy was stone or clay or whatever he would have appeared as a dense block, similar to some calcification. Like bone.

But no.

The lungs were aerated. The soft tissues were the same density as his own. The flesh was real. The bones were dense and the organs were proper organ density. Liver, spleen, pancreas and gallbladder. Stool in the colon. Fluid density in the bladder.

Greg rushed back to the box.

The boy hadn't moved.

Greg spoke to him. Called him.

Nothing.

Greg cried.

He poured a Jameson and sat with the boy on the desk in front of him for two hours.

Greg waited for something to happen.

Nothing happened.

He spoke to him until he was talked out.

Finally, Greg took the boy to the bathroom. He thought maybe some water might somehow bring him back. Rehydration? Yeah, that's it. He opened the faucet and ran warm water.

With the boy in the palm of his hand, he tested the boy's foot first. He let the water trickle, then course over the foot and lower leg.

The foot started to dissolve.

It began washing away like a sugar cube dissolving in a cup of tea.

Greg jerked his hand back.

Bewildered, Greg pinched some of the granules with his other hand, rolled them around between his fingertips, and then they were gone.

Greg started to sob softly, tears plopping into the sink. He ran more water over the boy's thighs after the feet were gone, and then the abdomen, all dissolving into nothingness. Then the chest and finally he was left with the little boy's head wobbling on his palm.

The boy's eyes were closed and he was smiling. He appeared content.

Greg sighed, said, "See ya, little guy," and let the warm water course over his face, running in little rivulets around the curves of his cheeks, nose, eyes.

After a minute, Greg's hand was empty and the water flowed through the creases in his palm, trickled between his fingers and around his wrist.

Greg stood and examined his own face in the mirror. He thought he looked different, aged somehow.

He shut off the faucet.

Greg grinned weakly, slowly dried his hands on a small cotton towel. His movements were slow, robot-like.

He shuffled back to the study, pushed the button on the front of the computer, retrieved the CD. He turned it over in his hand as if looking for some hidden code or message. It was just any old CD. Finally, he folded it and folded it until it cracked and then cracked again. He dropped it in the trash and sighed.

Greg lumbered to his bedroom, drained. He set the box on the floor. He undressed and lay flat on his back. He stared at the ceiling, the shadow from the lamp casting a wide, undulating arc.

He knew the little boy was okay.

Wherever he was.

He thought about Cindy and smiled, the warmth permeating, beginning to caress his entire body.

He would call her first thing.

Greg flicked off the light. †

AN OPEN DOOR
Chris F. Holm

"... *leave* ..."

When Simon heard the voice, his mouth went dry, his palms went slick with sweat, and his heart pounded like a drum line in his chest. It wasn't so much what the voice had said that spooked him, or the menace its throaty whisper conveyed. What spooked him was that it was so clear, it sounded as though it'd spoken directly into the digital recorder in his hand—and yet he hadn't heard the voice at all until he played it back. Add to that the fact there wasn't another living soul for miles around—the old Amalgamated Paper mill had been left to rot damn near seventy years ago, and Simon himself had been forced to scale one fence and shimmy through another to even get inside—and that voice seemed downright otherworldly.

The thought sent gooseflesh spreading down Simon's arms, and slapped a dopey smile upon his face. After all, that's why Simon was here.

His obsession had begun innocently enough: a day home sick from work, a ghost-hunting marathon on cable. Simon marveled at these regular dudes—no training, no bullshit claims of psychic powers—wandering through decrepit mansions and mental hospitals and communing with the dead. Sure, skeptics might scoff, but as far as Simon was concerned, the evidence they obtained was astonishing: strange mists and orbs on their night-vision cameras, spikes in the electromagnetic field surrounding them that caused their hairs to stand on end and signaled ghosts were near—and who could ignore the chilling electronic voice phenomena they recorded?

Those EVPs were what really blew his mind and stoked the fires of his imagination. The idea that spirits' whispers were just out of reach of human hearing, but that electronic equipment like the recorder in his hand was sensitive enough to pick them up— and that by alternately recording and playing back, one could literally converse with the other side? It beat the hell out of the fifty hours a week he spent entering data in a drab, gray cubicle on the fifteenth floor of a drab, gray building on a drab, gray Boston block—all so he could afford a bunch of useless crap that never seemed to bring him any joy.

So he poked around. Did his research. Bought himself a night-vision camcorder, an EMF detector, and a digital recorder. Put pins in maps, identified potential hot spots within a day's drive of his and Maggie's Brookline condo. Hot spots like the abandoned Amalgamated Paper mill in central Maine, where, in 1948, a young boy named Timothy Driscoll was murdered, stuffed into a steel drum, and dropped into the river by four boys he'd thought had been his friends. Driscoll sat undiscovered for the better part of sixty years, during which time all four friends met unseemly ends. If it hadn't been for a freak flood a couple of years back, his body never would've been discovered. It seemed to Simon all that violence, betrayal, and unfinished business *had* to leave some kind of imprint. That old mill was his best bet to capture evidence of a world beyond his own.

Maggie, of course, thought he was nuts. No matter how many episodes he made her sit through—no matter how much evidence of the supernatural he dug up online—she just shrugged it off, like the good Catholic that she was. "Nothing but fakes and charlatans," she once told him. "Not a bit of truth to any of it."

"How can you say that? The voices they've recorded have to come from *somewhere*."

"Oh, for God's sake, Si—it's a TV show, not a research expedition. If they're talking to anyone at all, chances are it's their producer playing Casper so they'll look good for the cameras."

"But what if you're wrong? What if they truly are communing with the other side? I mean, they bring regular folks in all the time. Folks with connections to the places they're investigating. Folks who often don't even *believe* in ghosts until they experience them firsthand. If they were faking, don't you think somebody would've outed them by now?"

"*Communing with the other side?*" she'd scoffed. "Do you even hear yourself right now?" But when she saw the hurt on Simon's face, she'd changed her tack, replacing sarcasm with a sort of gentle condescension. If his credulity with regard to this ridiculous obsession could not be shaken, she'd have to discourage him from pursuing it on its own merits. "Okay," she said. "Let's say they *are* communing with the other side. Who's to say that's a good thing? An open door's an invitation, as my Gran always used to say—and it seems to me some doors should remain unopened. God only knows who—or *what*—they might really be making contact with."

"They're just ghosts," Simon replied. "All they want is to be put to rest."

That's Si, she thought. *Trusting to a fault. Only he could have faith in the decency of cable TV hucksters and imaginary bogeymen.* "How can you know that from a shadow or a couple whispered words?" she asked.

Simon, of course, was not an idiot; he knew what she was doing. Humoring him just enough to steer his interests elsewhere. Thing was, he was pretty sure beneath her smug superiority and half-assed indulgence of his interest lay deep-seated fear and superstition—but on the rare occasion he tried to press the issue, Maggie bristled, so he thought it best to leave it be. Just as she thought it best to leave his newfound hobby be, figuring if she couldn't dissuade him from it, a couple nights spent wandering around old buildings and recording fat lots of nothing surely would.

But as he stood in the old mill, that ghostly syllable echoing in his mind, Simon thought, *If I can just make contact—have an actual conversation with someone long-dead—I can prove to Maggie once and for all that ghosts walk among us, and that they're to be helped, not feared.*

"Timothy?" Simon called, his digital recorder running in his hand. "Timothy Driscoll? Don't be afraid—I'm here to help. I invite you to come forth and speak to me!" His voice echoed through the dark expanse of the time-ravaged mill. He'd brought a flashlight to navigate by, but once he'd positioned himself roughly where he figured the boy'd bought it, he'd turned it off, leaving the greenish glow of the viewfinder on his night-vision camcorder the only illumination in the room. Ghosts, he figured, preferred the pressing, choking dark.

As the echoes died down to nothing, Simon strained to hear any sign of a reply. On TV, sometimes the guys would capture footsteps, or rhythmic banging. But there was nothing, only the sound of his own labored breathing.

After a few moments spent standing in the dark, he clicked off his recorder and rewound. "Timothy?" he heard himself say, tinny and static-filled as the tiny speaker in the recording device strained to replay at maximum volume. "Timothy Driscoll?"

After the echoes of his words died down, there was a good ten seconds of silence. He was about to kill the playback when he heard it—faint, but unmistakable.

"... you ... shouldn't ... be ... here ..."

A chill passed over him—through him, perhaps—and a cold sweat sprung up on his face and neck. He aimed his camera at the EMF detector clipped to his belt, and tasted the bitter tang of adrenaline as he realized the needle, which had sat at zero all evening, was now pinned as high as it would go.

Something was with him in the darkness.

His Adam's apple bobbed as he swallowed hard, trying to muster the spit for a response. He was shaking with fear and excitement. But he forced himself to hold his ground. Once more, he hit record.

"Why, Timothy? Why shouldn't I be here?"

Rewind. Playback. His own voice, a crackly artificial shout. And afterward, the distorted whisper of a disembodied reply.

"... *danger* ..."

The word chilled him. Somewhere in the distance, a chain rattled—like, Simon thought, the chain Timothy and his friends had played on, swinging from it, on the day he met his awful fate. He felt animal panic rise inside him, and he swung the camera around, peering at his viewfinder to find the source of the rattling. But he saw nothing.

Click. Record. "Danger? Danger of what?"

He paused a while, then rewound and played back. His own voice sounded shrill, afraid. The voice that replied seemed all the stronger by comparison.

"... *pain ... suffering ... DEATH.*"

The last syllable was a ghostly shout, straining the speaker till it crackled as Simon's own voice had done. How he'd failed to hear it with his own ears was beyond him. And there was something else as well, just behind those ghostly words: a keening, high-pitched scream. *Like a child's,* he thought. *Like Timothy's.*

Had he just heard the anguished cry of Timothy as he died?

The thought—and the violence implied in the specter's words—shook Simon to his core. His knees felt like jelly; his stomach seemed full of angry, crawling things. It was everything he could do to hold his ground. But he told himself the spirit he was communing with was that of a child—one that, in its own frightened and confused way, might be asking for his help. What he was hearing was an echo—the ghost-child relating its emotions in some sort of post-mortem attempt at closure.

"Are you telling me that's what you felt here? Does talking about it help to bring you peace?"

"... *no* ..."

"What, then? Are you *threatening* me? Do you want to harm me in some way?" Whatever he was talking to, it couldn't, he told himself. It had no form, no strength—no dominion in the world of the living. All it could do was talk.

"*... leave ... now ... Simon ...*" crackled the recorder.

At the sound of his own name, something broke inside him. Now he held his ground not out of bravery, but out of fear. He simply couldn't seem to get his legs to move.

"Or what?" Simon shouted—his voice breaking, tinged with hysteria.

But this time, the playback was garbled by a burst of static. All Simon caught was something "*needs.*"

He repeated his question. Again, the same response.

"I don't understand!" he called. "*Needs* what? What *needs*?"

But when he played the recording back, there was nothing. Five *minutes* of nothing. Somehow, playing back that much silence seemed to amplify it until standing there in that dank, still place that smelled of rust and rot and stagnant water was almost too much to bear.

No. Not *still*. Not quite, at least.

At first, the movement was scarcely more than a shifting in the darkness along the far wall. But as Simon aimed his camera at it, trying to decide if his mind was playing tricks on him, it coalesced into a sketchily defined figure—like some kind of living shadow. Simon couldn't tell if it was tall or short, male or female, heavyset or thin—it simply *was*.

He looked up from his viewfinder, but without night vision, the figure was impossible to make out. He glanced back down, and there it was.

For a moment, it seemed to stand there, though *stand* may be too strong a word for something with no discernable legs.

And then, without its outline suggesting even a hint of human movement, it advanced toward him—covering fifty yards of junk-strewn, half-collapsed floor in no time flat.

Simon couldn't move. Couldn't speak. He clenched shut his eyes and threw his arms up to protect himself. His recorder and his camera clattered useless to the ground.

Cold breath kissed his forearms, the apples of his cheeks. Warmth spread down his right leg as Simon pissed himself. And in a rasping voice as audible as any living one, and as black as darkest night, the thing before him whispered "*Maggie*."

That one word was like a starting pistol. It broke Simon's paralysis, and set him hurtling through the darkness. Twice he tripped and was sent sprawling, but he just as quickly found his feet. To rust and mildew was added the fresh copper scent of blood, the result of a nail that pierced his side when he went down. But the patter of blood dripping freely from the wound was drowned out by his gunshot footfalls and his hoarse, wheezing, panicked breaths.

Simon had no patience to retrace his steps and instead leapt out an empty window frame, spilling out of the ink-black mill and into the relative comfort of the watery moonlight, cold and faint as it filtered through the canopy of trees. Inasmuch as he thought anything at all, he was dully grateful the panes of glass were decades gone—for he would have likely leapt through the window either way. Lungs on the verge of bursting, Simon ran for the car, scaling the first fence in seconds, and tearing fabric and skin both as he dove through the makeshift aperture in the other.

He'd thumbed the ignition of his Accord before he'd even shut the door, and sprayed gravel as he fishtailed and lurched away. Though he'd lost signal somewhere around Augusta, Simon tried to dial home anyway—but predictably, no luck. And when, an hour later, he finally did get a signal, his worry only deepened, because there was no answer—the phone just rang and rang.

Why wasn't the machine picking up? And where the hell was Maggie?

Next he tried her cell. Straight to voicemail. Again—the same result. Finally, he threw his cell phone into the back seat in disgust and drove, white-knuckled, the three hours home.

Though he kept the needle at eighty the whole way, and worried for Maggie still, the drive calmed Simon some. He told himself these sorts of encounters weren't abnormal—that spirits were known to taunt, to frighten, to antagonize. He told himself there was no reason to believe anything at all was wrong. Maybe Maggie was on the phone with her mother when he called—she never answers call-waiting when she's talking to her mom. Or perhaps the answering machine was on the fritz.

Problem was, he didn't quite believe it.

Low-slung clouds blanketed the city by the time Simon reached Brookline, reflecting back the amber streetlights. And, as he approached home, they reflected flashing blue as well.

When he turned onto his street, he saw them: four police cruisers, at odd angles in the street, effectively closing it to traffic. A boxy fire and rescue vehicle idled half on and off the curb, lights off. Folks in everything from bathrobes to business suits jostled for a look behind yellow tape that fluttered in the chill night breeze. A uniformed policeman held a hand palm-up to stop him, and Simon automatically complied, throwing the car into park and climbing out, the driver's-side door left open behind him. The cop stepped in front of him, said something Simon didn't process about staying clear of the scene, but Simon just shrugged him off. He staggered like a zombie through the crowd, breaking the police tape as he approached his open condo door.

Simon and Maggie's unit was the first floor of a modest Victorian home with a large bay window and a small patch of grass out front. The grass, Simon noted, had been trampled, and every light in the place looked to be on. Through the bay window, he saw uniformed policemen and the oddly out-of-scale hulk of fully decked-out firemen milling about his living room—or what was left of it. Every bit of furniture in the place looked to be upturned, every breakable broken. The flat-screen had been yanked from the wall, leaving nothing but frayed wires. And on every surface, from the gauzy off-white curtains to the eggshell wainscot to the period wallpaper, blood. Not great gouts of it, mind, but tiny spatters. *Enough tiny spatters to fill a person?* Simon wondered. But then he reached the front door, and saw the great lake of crimson on the floor—his Maggie lying in the middle—and he didn't wonder any more.

Simon doubled over, vomiting. Rough hands dragged him back outside. The vague impressions of a coarse blanket draped around his shoulders, of time passing, of a cup of coffee held untouched in both his hands. And questions. So many questions.

Like where he'd been. What he'd been doing. Like did anybody have a grudge against him or Maggie. Like did he know why the door had been unlocked.

"Wait—what?"

"The door," said the detective, a gruff, tired-looking man, his face nearly as gray and lifeless as his trench coat, "it was unlocked."

"Maggie *never* left the door unlocked—not since that string of home invasions over on Boylston a few months back. She always at least set the chain," Simon said, almost to himself. Unbidden, the sound of chain links rattling in the darkness of the mill seemed to echo in his mind. Chain links, and a horrid high-pitched scream. Like a child's. Or like a woman's. "An unlocked door's an invitation."

"Yeah, but an invitation to *what*?" replied the cop. "Wasn't nothing stolen."

That was the question, Simon thought. The one he'd never be able to let go. Because much as he thought about that night in the years that followed, there was one thing he could never square. One question with two possible answers, both horrible. But one offered him a certain hollow absolution, and the other nothing but blame.

Had that voice in the darkness been a warning—or a threat?

†

THE SHADOW LINE
Charles Ardai

You can never know too much about the shadow line and the people who walk it.

—Raymond Chandler

They don't have woodpeckers in Mexico, they have Ivory-bills, but you wouldn't know the difference by listening to one take its feelings of inferiority out on the wall beside your head. I opened my eyes to find that the sun hadn't quite come up yet. It was inching its way toward the top of the Cerro de las Abejas with no more enthusiasm than a schoolteacher on the first day of class. There were still traces of last night's rain on the window glass, and near the top two fat droplets hung, trying to decide which would start the long, slow crawl to the bottom first. It was a race neither one of them could win.

I tossed aside the blanket and climbed back into the pants I'd left hanging over the arm of the chair. It was made of wicker and shellac, and aside from the bed it was the only furniture in the room. You paid extra in Tijuana if you wanted two chairs, and there weren't enough pesos in the city to get you a table.

My wallet was still in my pocket where I'd left it, and when I opened it to check I saw the proper number of folded dollar bills on one side and the miniature Photostat of my license on the other. My gun was in its holster, and a quick inventory revealed a bullet in each chamber. You might attribute this lack of overnight larceny to the honesty of the good, hard-working citizens of Tijuana, but you would be wrong. I didn't know what to attribute it to, other than the bad weather. Second-story men don't like to work in the rain.

I made my way down to the lobby, resisting entreaties from the elevator boy to let him show me around town. "You can't abandon your post," I told him. "It would cost you your job."

"Some job," he said with a sneer, looking from corner to corner as though in search of a place to spit. "Anyway, they let me take breaks, señor."

"Save them up," I said. "Give yourself the afternoon off."

Out front, the street was already busy. A young girl took hold of my sleeve before I'd set both feet on the pavement. "Come, mister," she said in a soft voice, "you come see my papa's zebra. You can take picture. Two pesos."

I shook her hand off my arm. "No camera," I said.

"One peso," she said and looked up at me hopelessly. Her eyes were no larger than bicycle wheels, and you couldn't count more than a dozen ribs through the faded fabric of her shirt. My hand ducked into my pocket of its own accord. It found a peso coin I hadn't even known was there.

She took it and latched onto my sleeve again. "Zebra?" she said, nodding.

I'd seen Tijuana zebras before. Every American who ventures south is offered the opportunity. They're the result of an enterprising program of cross-breeding between a donkey and a bucket of paint. "Thanks," I said, freeing my sleeve again. "Try someone else."

She came forward a third time—you don't survive on the streets of Mexico by taking no for an answer. But this time my jacket swung open and the holster must have been roughly at her eye level because she stopped dead and looked up at me with an expression that told me all I needed to know about her lifetime experience of men with guns. She backed off a step, then turned and ran full-tilt down the street, vanishing around the first corner she came to.

I did the same, only at a more measured pace and in the opposite direction. The neighborhood cantinas weren't open yet and wouldn't be until the heat of the day made their services indispensable, but one peddler with a pushcart and a giant metal urn was doing a brisk trade in sweet rolls and mugs of steaming, bitter coffee. I slipped the photograph out of my inside jacket pocket and showed it to him between swallows.

"One moment, señor," he said, holding up an index finger to indicate how many moments he meant. He tipped the urn forward and worked the spigot to refill the mug of a workingman in paint-smeared khaki pants.

" 'chas gracias," the man said. He had the build of a wrestler or a stevedore, but the same soft voice as the little girl. I wondered if this was papa, he of the zebra farm.

"All right, señor," the peddler said, turning back to face me, and he pushed his glasses higher on his nose. "Let us see this photograph." He looked at it, tilted it slightly from side to side. "No, señor. I don't think I have ever seen this man."

"You're sure?" I said, and handed him a dollar.

"Quite sure," he said after a moment. He handed the photograph back to me. He kept the dollar. "I would remember."

This was true. For all the violence you could witness on the streets of Tijuana, it wasn't every day you saw a man with scars along both sides of his throat, and when you did it was more likely to be a tough, down-at-heels pachuco than a man like the one in the photograph, with his refined features and faintly arched eyebrows. "He goes by Mendoza," I said. "Francisco Mendoza."

The peddler shook his head. "I do not know him, señor."

You get lucky sometimes. The first person you show a photograph to says, "Yes, of course, that's Mr. Smith. He comes by every Tuesday at four. Look, there he is now!" When it happens, you raise a silent hymn to St. Teresa of Avila, patron saint of headaches, for sparing you one. But it rarely works out that way. People haven't seen Mr. Smith, or pretend they haven't; they don't speak English, or pretend they don't. You ask and you ask, and you get nothing for your trouble other than raised eyebrows, apologetic expressions, and doors shut in your face. And St. Teresa does her worst. She's a diligent worker, that St. Teresa. By noon she'd given me one of her Grade A specials.

Fortunately, by noon the cantinas were open, and I sat at the bar in the largest of them, wearing a track with my thumb in the condensation on the side of a beer glass. The photograph of Señor Mendoza lay beside the glass, and when I saw the bartender looking at it, I rotated it to face him.

"You know this man?" I said.

The bartender took my glass, refilled it, and set it down again. He looked me in the eye and didn't answer my question.

"When did you see him last?" I said.

"I didn't say I know him," the bartender said.

"You also didn't say you're not Anita Ekberg, but I'll trust the evidence of my eyes."

"What do you want from him?"

"An old friend of his asked me to give him something," I said. The bartender's eyes narrowed. "Not what you're thinking. Just a letter."

"Let me see," he said.

I reached inside my jacket and pulled out enough of Roman's envelope that he could see the corner with the return address written on it in pen. *Hank Roman, Desert Springs Resort, Reno, N.V.* Roman had given it to me at the same time he'd given me the photo, which he claimed was the only one in existence. It may well have been. The one time Señor Mendoza had come to visit my office I hadn't reached for my Leica.

The bartender seemed still to be mulling it over.

"Sometime before the tide goes out," I said.

He shrugged, then pulled out a rag and began using it to polish a section of the bar that looked no duller than any other. "He has been here a few times."

"How many?"

That got me another shrug. "Five, six."

"What has he ordered when he's been here?"

"Whiskey," the bartender said.

"Straight?" I asked.

He shook his head. "With lemon juice."

A whiskey sour. It was as good an identification as finding a fingerprint. But the bartender had another.

"His hair doesn't look like that anymore," he said, aiming a thumb at the photograph. "It's all gray now. That must be an old picture."

"Not so very old," I said. I thought of the one time I'd seen him with the dye in his hair. Together with the surgery it hadn't been a bad disguise. I guess he felt enough time had passed, that he didn't need to pretend to be a Mexican anymore. The news reports of Rudolph Hopper's death might have had something to do with it. I assumed they'd made the papers even down here where Hopper hadn't owned them all.

"So," I said, "do you know where I might find him?"

"Last I knew, he was living over on Del Volcán," the bartender said, "near the park. I had to ... help him home once."

I nodded, remembering our first encounter. And our second. "Yes, that sounds like Señor Mendoza."

The bartender looked honestly puzzled. "Señor Men ...?"

"Well, what name did he give you?"

"Moran," the bartender said. He stopped polishing, slung the rag back under his belt. "One thing I can tell you, the man is no Mendoza. He is like you—a gringo."

I left a couple of bills beside my glass. I got up. "He's a gringo, all right," I said. "He's nothing like me."

The avenue was near enough to the water to appeal to American travelers but far enough away that you were spared the racket of boat engines and of hawkers shouting for attention. You still got the smell of salt and from time to time the wind would slap you across the cheeks like a rival inviting you to a duel. The park the bartender had mentioned was a long narrow stretch of green starting at the edge of the beach and ending at the edge of the highway four blocks east. A winding footpath led between the dusty trunks of tamarisk and jacaranda, and in the center a beach umbrella the size of a sideshow tent spread its shade over a half-dozen wooden chairs. In one, a man was dozing with a cat at his feet and a woven straw hat pulled low over his eyes. The cat kept craning its neck as people walked past, clearly wishing someone would bring it indoors. I knew how it felt.

The bartender hadn't given me an address and it wouldn't have helped any if he had, since none of the houses had numbers. What he'd given me was a description of the building at whose door he'd deposited Mr. Moran the night Mr. Moran had had too many whiskey sours to manage to stagger home unaided. I found it without any difficulty, the only three-story house on a block otherwise devoted to one-story buildings and fenced-in empty lots. In the States, there would have been a panel showing the tenants' names together with a buzzer for each, to activate the house phone. And in the States you would have needed it, because the front door would have been closed and locked. Here it was helpfully propped open with a broken cinderblock.

"He was on the first floor," the bartender had told me. "On the left. I saw the light go on." The light was off now, or maybe it just didn't show in the daytime. Heavy curtains were drawn in the windows. When I went inside and knocked, no one came to the door.

I took a close look at the lock. It was a Rabson, a respectable American make, which probably made this the best-protected apartment on the entire block, if not in the entire municipality. The door itself was made of wood and looked as though it would withstand one or two swift kicks, but probably not three. I didn't do it. I knocked again.

This time, footsteps sounded on the other side. They started out quiet and then got louder before stopping directly on the opposite side of the door. I pictured him standing there— Francisco Mendoza, Peter Moran, Leslie Madison, and who knows how many other names he'd tried on over the years. Quite a crowd for a one-room apartment in Tijuana off the Avenida Del Volcán.

"Leslie—" I began. But I heard another sound before I got any further. It was the sound of the hammer of a revolver being pulled back.

I dropped to my belly on the hallway carpet as the wood of the door exploded outward in a shower of splinters. The noise that went with it rang in my head like a gong. Somewhere under my jacket I could feel my holster and in it my gun, but I couldn't seem to untangle the weapon from the fabric surrounding it. Nice way to go, Fletcher: shot to death in a hallway in a Mexican rooming house because you couldn't get your gun out when you needed it.

I rolled onto my side, freeing my right arm, and yanked my jacket open; a thread snapped and my jacket button went spinning out of sight. Out of the corner of one eye I saw a pair of brown leather wingtips swiftly approaching and I looked up in time to see a PPK leveled at my face. I didn't look any farther. There was no point. There was a gun; there was a trigger; a finger was on the trigger, tightening. I wanted to say something, something that would stop him, but talking wasn't the way you stopped bullets, whatever they might tell you in the halls of diplomacy. Not when you have a gun in your hand, too, and only seconds to live.

I swung my arm up, past the other gun, past the hand holding it, to a broad chest clad in a silk shirt and necktie. A broader chest than Leslie's. A man might get fat living in Mexico, but he couldn't give himself broader shoulders or a bigger chest, not this much of one. I kept raising my gaze even as I jammed the muzzle of my weapon against the unfamiliar torso. Above was an unfamiliar face. "You're not—" we both began, only he said it in Spanish.

We were both right: he wasn't Leslie Madison and neither was I. But this revelation didn't seem to stop him for more than a moment, any more than the fact that I'd been knocking at the door rather than using my own key had. He'd been assigned a job, to shoot the man who came to that door, and by god he was going to do it. His finger, briefly stilled, began tightening on the trigger once more.

But when the gunshot came, it wasn't from his gun, nor from mine. The gunshot came from the pistol wielded by the man standing behind my broad-chested assailant, outlined in the open front door; a man wearing denim trousers and a linen workshirt and a woven straw hat, with an overheated cat lolling in the crook of one arm. The bullet tore through the other gunman's chest, spraying blood against the wallpaper. His hand slackened and his gun tumbled to the floor. I leaned out of the way as the body fell forward and collapsed beside me.

The cat leaped out of the man's arm and scurried into a corner as far from the action as possible. Once again I knew how it felt.

The man swept the hat off his head with the hand still holding the smoking gun. Under it I saw the silver hair, the scars.

"Well," Leslie said. "Hello there, Fletcher."

We dragged the dead man into his room, left him on the floor beneath the curtained windows. A quick search of his pockets revealed nothing in the way of identification. No wallet, no tags on his clothing, not even a library card. Torpedos south of the border didn't used to be so careful, but lately they've been learning from their cousins up north. When you go out on a job, you leave anything with your name on it at home. If the job ends well, you can pick it all up later, and if it goes as badly as this one had, well, what difference does it make?

We didn't hear any sirens on the breeze, and this being Tijuana I knew we might never. There weren't enough police to come running every time a gun went off. On the other hand, someone had sent this man to go wait in Leslie's apartment, and whoever it was might have stayed within earshot or scheduled a time to come back.

"Come," I said.

"You've got …." He made a gesture with his hand. "Blood on you."

I looked in the mirror over the washbasin standing in one corner and used a hand towel to wipe off the worst of it. The stains on my shirt and jacket were beyond repair.

I dropped the towel and took his arm. "We can't stay here."

"No, I suppose not," he said. He looked around on the floor. "Now, where do you suppose Cordelia has gotten to?"

"Outside," I said. "Because she's smarter than we are."

He followed me reluctantly. When we got to the hallway, the cat was nowhere in sight.

"Do you think she'll come back?" Leslie asked, and it dawned on me that he probably wasn't entirely sober. Either that or he wasn't entirely sane.

"I'm sure she will," I said. With one hand between his shoulder blades I steered him to the street. I flagged down a passing taxicab and shoved Leslie into the back seat. "Go," I told the driver.

"Where to, señor?"

Where to. I gave him the name of my hotel and off he drove.

Leslie was shaking his head. "Cordelia," he said.

I didn't know what to say. "You named your cat after your dead wife," I said finally.

"You may not understand this, Fletcher," Leslie said, "but I miss her."

I let it pass. "Here," I said, and I took out the envelope I'd been carrying around. Some of the dead man's blood had gotten on it, but you could still read the address. "Hank Roman asked me to give you this."

"That why you're here, Fletcher?"

"Yes," I said.

"I thought maybe you wanted to see me," Leslie said.

"No you didn't," I said.

"No, I didn't." He ran a thumb under the envelope's flap and pulled out the single sheet of paper it contained. He read through it in silence, then folded it, replaced it in the envelope, and handed it back to me. "You'll never believe this, Fletcher, but Hank thinks someone is trying to kill me."

"Does he say who?"

Leslie shook his head. "Just urges me to be careful. To 'lay low,' as he puts it. Lay low, Fletcher. Grammar be damned."

Hank Roman was an ex-Commando who had served with Leslie in the war. Leslie had saved his life—it was how he'd gotten the scars on one side of his neck. The ones on the other side were the work of an ingenious plastic surgeon who couldn't erase the first half but could give him a matching set.

"How much did he pay you to find me?" Leslie said.

"Nothing," I said.

"Then why'd you do it?"

"I owed him," I said.

"And now you owe me," Leslie said.

"For what?"

"Saving your life back there," Leslie said.

"I'd have survived," I said.

"One of you would have," he said.

We were both silent for a while. Up front, the driver whistled reedily through his teeth.

"What do you want?" I asked.

He looked me over, bloodstains and all. "Now that's one hell of a question, Fletcher. It is one hell of a question." He turned to stare out the window of the taxicab. It hadn't been washed anytime recently. "You remember all those stories from the Arabian Nights, about genies and lamps and wishes? Did you ever daydream about having one?"

"No."

"I did, Fletcher. I used to make up lists. Of what I would ask for if I had three wishes. Do you use one up wishing for wealth beyond measure? No, you can do better than that."

Spoken like a man who'd had wealth beyond measure— twice. And lost it both times.

"For happiness?" Leslie shook his head. "Too soft, too ... inchoate."

When I didn't say anything he put a hand on my leg.

"You know what I decided, Fletcher?"

"No," I said.

"Would you like to know?"

"Not very badly."

"I decided what I would ask for if I ever found a lamp with a genie inside of it was for the genie to stay with me always. As a friend, you see. I thought, what a wonderful friend to play with a genie would be."

"How old were you?"

He took his hand off my leg. "Nine. Ten. I was a lonely child, Fletcher."

"And now?"

"Oh, you get used to it. Being alone."

The driver pulled the cab to a halt at the front door of the hotel. I half expected to see the little girl from the morning, but she was nowhere in sight. It was probably just as well, as the bloodstains would have confirmed the impression she'd formed of me earlier.

We rode the elevator upstairs. The boy I'd ridden with on the way down must have been on one of his breaks because the operator now was an old hunchback who kept one hand on the lever and his eyes aimed at the wall. He'd seen plenty of bloodstains in his day, and plenty of pairs of men riding up to hotel rooms together, and he'd learned it was best to look the other way.

While I opened my valise and took out a new shirt, Leslie sat in the chair, one leg slung over its arm. I stripped off the ruined shirt, balled it up, and considered whether the undershirt had to go, too. I decided it did.

From the chair, Leslie said, "I used to think you might be my friend, Fletcher. My own genie. Sit with me, drink with me, talk with me. Protect me from the cops. Take me home when I couldn't make it on my own."

"It was nice while it lasted."

"I didn't mean for it to end," he said.

"You made it end," I said. "You ended it."

"You know I couldn't tell you I was still alive—"

"That's not what ended it." I remembered Maureen Carson's last words. She'd written a nice note, then gone and swallowed three dozen sleeping pills. "You know what ended it."

"What. Tell me."

I stood before him, a bloodstained shirt crumpled in each hand. He looked up at me. I watched his leg swing back and forth. "For a long while there, Leslie, I thought you might be my friend too. I learned better."

"I never meant to deceive you, Fletcher. I never wanted to."

"You just did it."

"That's right," Leslie said. "I did what I had to, to survive. But I didn't want to."

"Poor Leslie," I said. "Poor, poor Leslie."

He sprang out of the chair. "Poor Fletcher! Did I ask you to go on a crusade for me? Did I ask you to do any of it? I asked you to have a drink to remember me by, that's all. None of the rest of it. That was all your doing."

He was right, of course. And that was the worst part of it. No one had asked me to clear his name. No one had asked me to dig up all the dirt I'd dug. I'd just gotten myself a spade and started digging.

I threw the shirts on the floor, faced away while I unbuckled my belt. The blood would come off the belt—it was leather—but the pants had to go. It was a good thing I'd brought a second pair with me.

I heard his voice behind me, nearer by than I'd expected. "I'm sorry, Paul," he whispered. "I really am." His fingertips alit on my shoulder like a bird testing a branch to see if it would bear its weight.

I turned. He had his own shirt half unbuttoned, though there wasn't a bit of blood on it. His skin had gotten naturally darker from months in the southern sun, and the sharp lines of his scars stood out in pale relief. I traced one of them with my thumb, from below his ear where it began to the hollow of his throat. This was the one the Nazis had given him. The one he'd gotten for saving Hank Roman's life. I could feel it against my fingertip like the edge of a page in a book, a page you're coming to and about to turn.

"Who wants to kill you, Leslie?" I said. "You know who it is, don't you."

He nodded hesitantly. "I think so."

"You'll tell me," I said. "You'll tell me everything. No lies, no omissions. Everything."

He nodded again.

I moved my hand to the back of his head, felt the weight of his skull against my palm. He was not a small man, but his head felt small in my grip. Small but warm.

"Your cat's not coming back," I said. I said it brutally. He shook his head slightly and I saw his eyes glistening.

"I'm not coming back either," I said. "I'll find the men who are trying to kill you, I'll deal with them, and then I'll leave, and you'll never see me again."

I could see he believed it as much as I did. I shook his head roughly. "Never," I said. "Just this once and never again."

He tilted his head back and his eyes slid shut and he found me with his hands. "My genie," he whispered. †

RANSOM AND RED FINGERS
Garnett Elliott

Turquoise water poured in through the scuppers. The newly captured British ship was sinking.

Lorenzo splashed across the deck, rapier drawn. He nearly tripped over the corpse of a uniformed officer. An eight-inch splinter jutted from the lace ruff covering the man's throat. More wooden shrapnel, torn from the ship by cannonball impact, dotted his face and arms like a grotesque pincushion.

Lorenzo was about to step around when the 'corpse' let out a moan.

The man's eyelids snapped open. "B-bastard," he said, reaching inside his vest. Out came a silver-inlayed pistol.

Lorenzo threw himself to the deck just as the gun boomed. Lead scorched a furrow along his buff coat sleeve. Prone, he whipped the rapier sideways and thrust at the officer's neck. Toledo steel buried itself in the lace alongside the splinter. Hot blood splashed his wrist, as the Englishman thrashed out his last.

"Careless," came a voice from behind. A dark-skinned hand descended and helped Lorenzo to his feet. "All this time and you still assume a wounded man's a dead man."

Michaud snatched back up the wicker cage he'd been carrying. Inside, a listless chicken squawked. Over one lean shoulder he'd draped a burlap sack, and that hand also gripped a naked straight-razor. Blood dripped from the blade to join the saltwater eddying past their boots.

"That's our haul?" Lorenzo asked, nodding at the chicken.

"*My* haul, at least. Plus our shares, when the tallying is done."

"There won't be anything to tally. Look."

Lorenzo nodded to larboard, where the rigging from their ship, the *Whore's Promise*, loomed. The pirate two-master had rammed the larger British ship during the boarding, staving in her hull below the waterline. But the *Whore* had been damaged, too. Caribbean blue was sweeping through a ragged hole in her prow.

Michaud grunted. "Both bloody ships sinking. No way they'll be able to patch that."

"The most valuable loot right now would be a boat. And I bet this old man-o-war's got a couple."

They paused long enough for Lorenzo to pry the officer's pistol from his stiffening fingers. Several of their fellow crewmen rolled barrels past, whistling cheerfully. Others wrestled boxes and bales up from the flooding holds.

"Half those bastards don't realize the situation," Lorenzo said, "they're so intent on looting."

Michaud shook his head. "They'll be floating on those barrels before long."

Lashed to the gunwales along the quarterdeck they found a small boat. The Haitian cut the stay-lines loose with swipes of his razor, while Lorenzo worked the block-and-tackle to lower them toward the water. An old tarpaulin covered a man-sized bundle at the boat's stern. As Lorenzo heaved, the tarpaulin rippled with movement.

Reflex made him grab for his rapier. The rowboat dropped eight feet and smacked the water, almost throwing Michaud overboard. Lorenzo steadied himself and flicked the tarpaulin aside with his blade.

A woman in several layers of silk petticoats stared up at him.

Michaud slapped Lorenzo's shoulder. "Introductions will have to wait. We're taking on water."

Lorenzo saw the drink welling along the boat's keel. Some lax sailor had neglected his caulking. "You want me to bail or row?"

"Bail." Michaud unshipped the oars. "I'll keep an eye on the Lady, here."

❖

Not too far away rose a sandbar's white crescent. Michaud angled past it, making for the small island where the *Whore's Promise* had lain in wait.

Lorenzo bailed with nothing more than his cupped hands. He could've sworn their stowaway was quietly laughing at him, whenever he turned his back.

She had a narrow face tapering to a pointed chin. Her eyes were too close together. Lank brown hair swept past a pale forehead. And yet, somehow, she was the most attractive woman Lorenzo had ever seen. He kept stealing glances at her as he worked.

Michaud's strokes brought them into a palm-lined cove. They beached the little boat and dragged it behind the concealment of a hibiscus bush.

"I don't understand," the woman said. "Are you with those pirates back there or not?"

Michaud leaned against a palm's trunk. "We are."

"But we're gentlemen, too," Lorenzo added.

"Why did you hide your boat, then? And why did you row off like that, without waiting for your crewmates?"

"Well …" Lorenzo began.

"It's every man for himself, when a ship's sinking," Michaud said. "And my partner and I, we've never been too comfortable with the command structure aboard the *Wh—*, I mean, the *Promise*."

He didn't add that they were new arrivals to the crew. And, as usual, not well-liked on account of their respective nationalities.

The woman squared her shoulders. "I'm Mary Hurst, Lady in Waiting to the Baroness Montcalm, who was aboard the *Weathersby*. The ship you just plundered."

Lorenzo fought the urge to seize her hand and kiss it. "Lorenzo de Silva."

"Michaud d'Arcy."

Mary's too-close eyes narrowed. "I remember a story about a Spaniard and a Haitian who overtook a slaver's vessel. Made pirates out of the human cargo. Quite a terror to French shipping, for awhile."

"Never heard of 'em," Lorenzo said.

Crouched under a hibiscus, they watched several of the *Whore's* and the *Weathersby's* longboats row past. The craft rode low in the water, overloaded with pirates and stolen cargo. Lorenzo kept his eyes sharp for the Baroness Montcalm, but couldn't spot her. The boats slipped away toward the far end of the cove.

"What now?" Mary asked.

Lorenzo's stomach rumbled. He looked at the forlorn chicken, then at Michaud. The Haitian shook his head. "No fires. And I'm not eating that raw."

"What's in the burlap sack?"

"Coffee beans. Not even roasted."

Mary cleared her throat. "Now that the food situation has been addressed, what, may I ask, are your larger plans?"

Michaud rose and brushed sand from his breeches. He thumped the side of the rowboat. "The closest inhabited island is St. Kitts, and I doubt this old tub would make it. Also, we've got no water. Captain Dray will be sending out hunting parties soon, and that'll make it difficult to stay hidden. I think we need to rejoin the crew."

"Not much choice," agreed Lorenzo.

"But what about me?" Mary said. "What's to stop three score bloody pirates from, from—"

Lorenzo shook his head. "Our captain is a former Puritan. He'll flog the first man so much as touches a woman without her permission, high-born or not."

Michaud added: "They'll want to ransom you, Miss. You're worth much more unharmed."

"I suppose that's a comfort."

"Though we'll have to watch old Red Fingers," Lorenzo said.

"*Red Fingers?*"

"He means Gonsalves, the First Mate," Michaud said. "Something of a lecher. Not to worry, though, as you're under my protection."

"*Our* protection," Lorenzo corrected, tucking the officer's pistol through his belt. He wished to God he had some powder to charge the thing.

❖

Hot sea-breezes knifed the jungle foliage. Michaud led the way, after arguing with Lorenzo who would have the privilege. He made a point of pushing aside branches and other obstacles so Mary could pass in comfort. Lorenzo, taking up the rear, contented himself by imagining what the Lady looked like under all that silk.

She had to hoist her skirts at one point to step over a rotten log. Lorenzo caught a glimpse of white ankle, and looked up to see Michaud staring as well. The Haitian winked.

A little further and they heard the rhythmic thud of axes biting wood.

Michaud sniffed the air. "Smoke ahead. Dray's already got fires going and—"

A sheaf of nearby ferns rustled. Lorenzo started to draw his rapier, but slid the blade back when he saw MacReady's lanky form blunder out onto the trail. The *Whore's* bosun had a bandaged shoulder. His eyes brushed past Michaud and Lorenzo to fix on Mary Hurst.

"Stragglers, eh?" he said. "And you've found a woman of quality, too."

Lorenzo stepped in front of Mary. "She's Lady in Waiting to the Baroness."

"Is she now? Well, her lordship will be happy to hear that."

"The Baroness is alive?" Mary asked.

"Very much so. And in her cups, too. We're not all animals, Miss." MacReady cocked a hand to his hip and leaned over Michaud. "You two have some explaining to do. Gonsalves had you figured as deserters."

"We brought a chicken," Lorenzo said, pointing at the wicker cage.

"Well, that'll smooth everything, won't it?"

MacReady led them down the trail and into a clearing set back some thirty yards from the beach. Men were cutting palm fronds and assembling lean-to's, while others dragged felled trunks to a wooden mound taking shape along the shore. A one-handed pirate approached and snatched the wicker cage from Michaud. He withdrew the squawking chicken, thrust it under his left arm, and snapped its neck. Not far away, two cooks roasted a freshly dressed pig over a traditional *boucan* grill of green saplings. The crackling fat brought water to Lorenzo's mouth.

"Three more for supper," MacReady announced, addressing the sole pirate who wasn't hustling from one chore to another. He sat on an unopened cask with his arms crossed; a short, thick man wearing a scarlet cloak and a gentleman's wig of curled black locks. Silver beads weighted the ends of his mustachios. He glowered at Lorenzo and Michaud.

"My favorite pair. And where were you two, when the hard work of loading the boats was being done?"

"We don't answer to you, Gonsalves," Michaud said. "Where's Captain Dray?"

"Met with an accident, I'm afraid. Shot during the boarding. I'm captain now."

MacReady's face clouded. Several pirates laboring close by muttered, but no one said anything directly to Gonsalves. The Portuguese shifted off the cask. He slapped his hand against the double-brace of pistols stretched across his chest. "Anyone with the piss to claim otherwise?" He looked around. "I thought not. So captain I stay."

"Captain of what?" Lorenzo said. "We're marooned."

Gonsalves smiled and jerked a thumb over his shoulder. Behind him, a blonde woman in elaborate pearl brocade lolled on the sand. She had her head tilted back and swigged wine straight from a bottle. "We won't be stranded here long," he said. "Not with the Baroness as hostage. She was sent over to marry the limey governor of Barbados. We can ransom her for enough coin to get off this rock *and* buy a new ship, with drinking money left over."

"Those logs," Lorenzo said, looking at the pile of tree trunks. "A signal fire?"

"*Verdade*. Ships pass this island almost every day. The next galleon will surely send out a boat, and we can relay our terms to the governor."

Lorenzo hadn't realized Mary Hurst was hiding behind him. She craned her head out to glance at the Baroness. Recognition flashed between the two women, and for a moment the pearl-bedecked blonde looked sober. Mary's mouth curled.

"So *that's* why you two holed up," Gonsalves said, grinning. "Found yourselves a handmaiden and decided you wouldn't share."

"We haven't touched her," Lorenzo said.

"She's with the Baroness," Michaud added.

"That true, Miss? This lusty Black-a-Moor's not ravished you? The Spaniard, either?"

"They have not," Mary said.

Gonsalves smirked. "Always figured 'em for buggery."

Several of the surrounding pirates laughed. But not all, Lorenzo noticed. MacReady remained stone-faced.

"No man calls me a bugger and keeps his hamstrings taut," Michaud said, his razor flashing to his hand.

Gonsalves took a step back and bumped into the cask. His fingers touched the butt of a pistol. "What's this? You'd dare draw on your new captain? Bosun, restrain these two. Ketch, O'Shaughnessy—lend a hand with that wild Haitian."

Lorenzo's head jerked back as MacReady seized him in a choke-hold. Two burly pirates grabbed Michaud by the wrist and ankle before he could spring, sending him flopping to the sand. The straight-razor spun away.

"Steady now," MacReady whispered. "Don't get yourself killed."

Michaud wriggled like a snake, but one pirate pinioned his arms while the other rapped his skull with the hilt of a heavy cutlass. The Haitian slumped. Lorenzo started forward, then checked himself when MacReady's hairy forearm pressed against his throat.

"We'll handle this proper," Gonsalves said. "Pirate's trial, to commence now. The charges are desertion and insubordination. As we're already marooned, I sentence the Spaniard to fifty lashes from the Cat O' Nine and a hundred for the Black. Further, total forfeiture of all shares—"

"A hundred lashes will kill him," Lorenzo managed to croak.

"That as may be."

Murmurs from all around. The sounds of work had ceased; only the cook-fires still crackled. Lorenzo figured the whole camp was watching them now.

MacReady spoke up. "No disrespect, captain, but aren't we supposed to put such matters to a vote?"

"Aye, a vote," someone else said.

More murmuring. Gonsalves' eyes raked the crowd. His newly-won authority was being tested.

Lorenzo gestured to MacReady, who loosened his grip enough for him to speak. "If this is a proper trial, I would like to place a counter-charge. Namely, that you, Red Fingers, murdered Captain Dray to gain position. Likely you shot him in the back during the boarding."

Gonsalves' cheeks glowed as if rubbed with rope. "What? You're accusing *me*, now? Bosun, shut that man up or I'll find someone else to do it. As for the rest of you—"

But the rest of the crew grumbled. Lorenzo could feel the suspicion rippling through them. He pressed his attack: "I say you're a murderer, Gonsalves. And a coward."

"A coward, am I? You son of a Castilian whore."

"Goat-pleasuring Portagee."

The captain drew a pistol and cocked the hammer back. "Say that again."

"I will, if you'll give me satisfaction."

There was a harsh sound as roughly sixty men sucked in their breath and held it.

Gonsalves smiled. "You've got yourself a duel. Pistols at ten paces."

"Swords," Lorenzo said.

MacReady released him. "We'll flip a guilder for it," he said, reaching into his pouch. "If it's the Lady, then swords. The lion means pistols." He tossed a silver coin into the air, then backed away so others could approach and verify.

" 'Tis swords," said Kearny, the one-handed cook.

Gonsalves huffed. "Back then, you bastards, and give us room to fight." He removed his cloak and shrugged the gun belts off his shoulders. For a moment he seemed to consider tossing the cape away, but then wound it loose about his left forearm.

"Mayhap you should've chosen pistols," MacReady whispered to Lorenzo. "Old Red Fingers was a champion fencer in the court of Lisbon."

Lorenzo massaged his throat. "I've had some practice myself."

Two pirates dragged Michaud's unconscious form away. Lorenzo saw Mary Hurst give him a concerned look before she was jostled into the surrounding circle of grinning, gap-toothed spectators. Odds were already being argued in loud voices. Wagers taken. Lorenzo wondered if goading the experienced Portuguese was such a good idea.

Well, as his mother would say: *Este arroz ya se coció*.

That rice has been cooked.

He drew his rapier and tried a few swipes to loosen his wrist. The *Whore's* quartermaster handed Gonsalves a naked saber, which he raised in brief salute to his opponent. Lorenzo did likewise. Their swords lowered, the tips meeting together with a *clank*. Lorenzo took a deep breath.

But before he could exhale, Gonsalves' left hand snapped the cloak into his eyes.

Blinded, Lorenzo threw himself backward and heard steel whistle past. He opened one tearing eye in time to parry the follow-up stroke. Gonsalves pressed, his saber weaving lightning-arcs in the tropical sun.

Had Lorenzo not befriended a certain Italian, Signiore Marozzo, years before, the next few seconds would've been his last. The aging fencing instructor had taught him the value of deft footwork. He used it now, giving ground before Gonsalves' assault. Back, back he went, until his heel bumped against something behind him.

He fell.

A rustle of skirts. Mary Hurst threw herself over his prone body. "Hold," she cried.

Lorenzo looked up to see Gonsalves drawing his saber back, readying for the *coup de grâce*. "Move, woman," he said, "or I'll skewer you both."

"But he doesn't have a cloak. It's not fair. And his blade, it still has dried blood on it." She crouched over the rapier, rubbing it with a handkerchief.

"Out of the way." Gonsalves kicked her aside.

Lorenzo rolled, sprang to his feet. Instead of retreating, he feinted and thrust in *messo tempo*. The rapier scored a bloody gouge along Gonsalves' cheek. Roaring, the Portuguese tried to counter, but Lorenzo smacked the saber away with a neat riposte and nicked him once, twice, in the wrist.

They circled each other. Gonsalves' steps became sluggish, as if tired. A haze came into his eyes. "Damn you, Spaniard," he said, his voice slurring, "stop all that prancing about and let me stick you."

"Are you drunk, man?"

"Head's clear as glass." Gonsalves stopped moving and peered at him in surprise. "Why's there two of you all of a sudden?"

He lowered his saber.

Lorenzo thrust so hard a shock traveled up his arm as the rapier entered Gonsalves' chest. Three feet of bloodied steel exploded out his back. The pirate captain made a slow, shuddering turn before he fell.

❖

Chaos followed. Hoots. Shouting. Cheers. The clink of money changing hands. People surged forward to slap Lorenzo's back. Others cursed and spat.

Dazed, he watched as the two pirates who had hauled Michaud away knelt to pick up Gonsalves' slack body. The black wig slid off his head and struck the sand.

"Excellent swordsmanship," said Mary Hurst.

She'd pushed her way through the crowd, and without hesitation, embraced him. The smell of her hair filled his nostrils. He swayed, his heart still thundering from the fight. "I believe I had some help."

"Perhaps."

"What did you do to my sword?"

She lifted her skirts over her left thigh, revealing a small bottle strapped there. A Death's Head had been stamped into the glass. "I bought an unction from a mountebank, so mortal that but dip a knife in it …"

"What's a Lady in Waiting doing with poison?"

"A fair question. The answer: I'm not said Lady. The blonde sot is. We switched places when it looked like the *Weathersby* would be taken."

"But that means—"

"I'm the Baroness Montcalm." She dipped her head in a courtly bow. "As for the poison, I brought it along in case I don't like my new husband, the governor of Barbados. He's old and fat, and I'm told he has a horrible temper."

Lorenzo stepped back, uncomfortable about touching a royal.

"Oh no you don't," the Baroness said, seizing his hand. "You're staying close until you get me out of this mess."

"I will. I promise."

"Good. Now let's see how your friend's doing. He should be coming around by now."

They walked away from the cluster of pirates. MacReady was arguing in a hoarse voice why he should be appointed the next captain.

"You and Michaud weren't being truthful before," the Baroness said, "about not having your own ship and a crew of freed slaves."

"No, we weren't."

"Then what happened? How'd you end up with this sorry lot?"

Lorenzo sighed. "A long story. It starts in Port Royale, with an angry Vodou *houngan*, an apothecary's shop, and an earthquake ...." †

PILLOW TALK
Jodi MacArthur

Henrietta wrapped her arms about her pillow. "I'm still awake, Charlie. I can never sleep anymore." Charlie's body spooned hers. His arm wrapped around her waist, hand pressed against the silky hollow of her stomach. "Charlie, are you listening?"

Silence.

"Sleep. That's all you do anymore. It's not fair. It's never been fair." Henrietta felt sweat drip down her neck, the base of her spine. She scrunched back the sheets and adjusted her pillow. The mattress was a full size. It was her bed. He had his own room, but he never wanted to sleep there. "Afraid of the dark aren't you, Charlie? What did you do before you moved in with me, huh? Sleep with dolls?"

Charlie hadn't been afraid of the dark until he met her. He had told her this once, after she blindfolded, cuffed him to the bed, and inked a black heart into his skin, right above his own heart.

Henrietta pouted. "You liked our romps through the sheets." She could almost hear his voice now, *Jesus, Reta, when romps turn into stilettos and needles it becomes .... It's just that I ... I feel afraid.*

"It becomes what, Charlie? You never finished your sentence. Afraid of what? Me? Little ol' me?" Henrietta laughed. She watched the alarm clock tick to 11:59 P.M. "Get off me will you? I'm burnin' up here."

Henrietta sat up. He remained on his side. His hand slipped down between her thighs. "You always hit right on the money, didn't you, Charlie?" She rolled him to his back. His head thunked on the headboard. "Ohhh, ouch ...." She bit her lip and sat on her knees in the darkness. A thread of city light found its way through the long crack between the curtains. It highlighted his skin, giving him a pale, ghostly look. She swept her hand across his cool brow. He didn't move.

"Out like a light. Damn." She snatched the box of cigarettes and lighter off the night stand, then sat Indian style on the sheets, her knee pressing into Charlie's ribs.

She lit up, breathed in deep, and let out the smoke. "You asked me why I did it. I know you couldn't speak at the time. But your eyes spoke to me, the way they always do. I mean, yeah, you told me you wanted to sleep with me. Keep your arm around me, so you knew where I was." She brought the cigarette to her lips. "Did you really think I was going to stick you in the middle of the night?" Henrietta laughed and shook her head. Curls of smoke drifted up into the darkness, disappearing into the glare of city light.

"You know, my kid brother Tony, he caught me doing ... *things* once. It was none of his fuckin' business. I was out behind the shed, by myself, but he had to be nosy. The kid was always rattin' me out. Anyway, he promised me he wasn't going to tell. And thinkin' about it now, he really meant it. I was a teenager then. And believe you me—" Henrietta flicked her ashes on the carpet. She took another puff. "Teenage girls don't trust their brothers with secrets. That night, I snuck into his room and put a pillow over his head."

Henrietta leaned back against the headboard. The cool wood felt good against her hot body. She rolled her head to look at Charlie. "No one ever knew. They thought he'd rolled over and suffocated himself." She drew the cigarette between her lips and took one last puff.

"So when you caught me with the old man last week. Well, it was sort of the same deal. I could see in your eyes you were too scared to call the police. But I know you would have. You would have ratted me out. Shit, Charlie. You selfish son of a bitch.

Why'd you have to go snooping in places where you don't belong? I am happy with who I am."

She smooshed her cigarette into the ashtray. "I need to get some sleep. We both know it doesn't happen when you're in here with me." She leaned over and straddled him, his body cold between her thighs. She stroked his black heart, then felt the gentle curves of his face. Charlie would never be afraid again. And he would never tell what he'd seen her do. She had lovingly sewed his eyes and mouth shut.

Henrietta stood, grabbed the bottom of the sheet and gently placed it over his face, his body. Then she rolled him. He flopped off the bed onto a flat cardboard box. She grabbed the edge of the box and dragged it into the walk in closet.

She stood and pressed her hands to her back. Her silky nightgown clung to the sweaty wetness between her breasts. "Things haven't been the same since you died. The bed is just too cramped with your deadweight in it. So, I'm not sure when I'm going to pull you out again."

She turned to go. Stopped. Looked back. Dark clothes hung like beasts from poles. "Life is more scary than death, Charlie. You should thank me."

Henrietta shut the closet door, then walked to the window, brushed aside the curtains, and opened it. Streetlight trickled in, highlighting an intricate tattoo on the inside of her wrist. She stroked the name. *Tony*. No one could fill that darkness inside her, that void.

A flutter of movement below drew her eyes to the sidewalk. She saw a cigarette light, and recognized the figure that held it. He worked at the 7-Eleven across the street.

"You afraid of the dark, big boy?" she whispered. †

SKYLER HOBBS AND THE COTTINGLEY FAIRIES

Evan Lewis

I was parked in front of the TV, scarfing down a pizza and checking out the Channel 2 news. My friend and landlord, Mr. Skyler Hobbs, lounged in his armchair with a pipe and a book, doing his best to ignore me.

The newslady had just finished a heartwarming report on a baby that had disappeared and been quickly found, and started on a piece about a carnival opening, when Hobbs bolted from his chair, his pipe and book tumbling to the floor.

"What did she say about fairies?"

I stared at him. I'd been concentrating on my pizza, and heard only that the traveling show had just opened for a short run at Portland's Waterfront Park.

"Turn it up!" he roared. "Quickly, Watson!"

"Wilder," I mumbled. "Jason Wilder."

Mr. Skyler Hobbs, you see, believes he's the reincarnation of Sherlock Holmes, and that I—because my initials happen to be JHW—was sent by Fate to be his Doctor Watson.

He's nuts, of course, but it's a benign madness, and I could stand it. Up to a point.

Grabbing the remote, I cranked up the volume, but too late, as the newslady was already cracking wise with the weatherman.

Hobbs looked stricken, even frightened. "I must know what she said!"

I rolled my eyes. He was in one of those moods, so I snagged my laptop from under the pizza box and punched up the KATU

Channel 2 website. And there it was: Fairy Act Shines at New Carnival.

I motioned him to the couch. "Read it for yourself."

And he did, while I skimmed the highlights.

The Cottingley Fairies, the reporter said, were so impressive he'd been transported to a magical realm, and recommended the show for kids of all ages. When asked how the illusion was created, the carnival manager had insisted, with a broad wink, that the reporter would have to ask the fairies. The fairy act was making its world premier right here in Oregon, and the first public performance would be this evening at 7 P.M.

Hobbs twitched as if he'd swallowed a mouthful of bees. He raced to the closet, pulling out his violin case. "Quick! That performance begins in less than twenty minutes. We must be in attendance. And please, Doctor, do not fail to bring your revolver."

"*Computer* doctor," I said. "Remember? And who packs heat to a fairy show? I'll bring my brass knuckles instead."

❖

We arrived at Waterfront Park in record time. Hobbs insisted I park the Cruiser in a truck loading zone, and promised to pay any and all tickets, towing and impound fees.

On the drive, he'd steadfastly refused to explain his peculiar behavior. Of course, his behavior was always somewhat peculiar—that's to be expected from a guy convinced he's the second coming of Sherlock Holmes—but this was strange even for him.

Along with his violin, he carried a cast-iron box about the size of a kid's lunchbox. Forced to theorize, I'd come up with only one possible explanation. After the show, he intended to take up a position on the midway and entertain passersby with his violin, hoping they'd toss coins in the box.

The problem, of course, was that his violin playing was so wretched that folks would be more likely to take money out of the box than put it in.

People stared at us as we crossed Front Avenue, and with good reason. Hobbs, in one of his wilder flights of fancy, had decreed we must wear our clothes inside-out. For me, in sweat pants and T-shirt, this was barely noticeable. But Hobbs' tweed suit had wide, ragged hems, his pockets flared out like tiny flags, and his deerstalker cap looked even more ridiculous worn upside-down.

At the carnival gate, Hobbs requested and was denied a student discount, but received directions to the tent housing the fairy show. Then on we went, running the gamut of hucksters offering myriad ways to win stuffed and inflated animals.

"Hobbs," I said, "if you don't tell me what's up, I'm going to stop and play Whack-A-Mole."

"How much," he said, "do you know about the life of Sir Arthur Conan Doyle?"

"Just what everyone knows. He wrote the Sherlock Holmes stories."

"No," Hobbs said with a grimace, "he did not. But he did write an ill-advised tome entitled *The Coming of the Fairies*."

"So," I said, "you're scared of fairies because your crea—, because old Sir Arthur was."

"No. That was precisely the problem. He was *not* afraid of them."

The tent dead ahead bore a huge banner emblazoned with the words "See ... Hear ... Experience ... The Incredible Cottingley Fairies!" Adorning the sign were sketches of four lissome maids in diaphanous gowns. Three had wings like butterflies, while the fourth, wing-free but no less fetching, danced about playing a long black flute.

The tent entrance was jammed with bodies.

Hobbs wasted no time on courtesy. "Emergency!" he said. "Coming through!" And jabbed his violin case into the ribs of anyone in his path.

Within seconds, the crowd was behind us, and we pushed through a curtain into a dimly lit theater. All the chairs were occupied, and we were lucky to find standing room at the rear.

Hobbs thrust the iron box into my hands. "Your job, Doctor, is to open this box and hold it, being prepared to slam it shut and turn the key when I give the order. If you fail to follow my instructions to the letter, we are lost."

I stared at him. "Lost?"

"As in dead. Deceased."

"Oh."

He extracted the violin and bow from his case. "I can only hope they fail to recognize me, lest they flee before we can contain them."

"Contain them?"

"Of course. In the box."

"And why would they recognize you?"

"We met once before," he said. "Ninety years ago."

Before I could comment on the absurdity of that statement, a spotlight stabbed through the darkness, and into the spot stepped a wizened little man in an ill-fitting tuxedo.

"Ladies and germs, I advise you all to hold onto your socks, because you are about to witness the most astounding event of your lives. I am proud to present, for the first time on any stage, the amazing Cottingley Fairies!"

As the crowed whooped it up, an eerie music filled the tent. I strained my eyes for some sign of the fairies. They had to be fake. I knew that. But contrary to all common sense, I held my breath and my heart started doing the polka.

At last a light flickered at one corner of the stage. Another winked from the opposite side. Then two more toward the center. Suddenly, popping like flashbulbs, all four flickers erupted into light, and I was momentarily blinded. But as my vision returned, I could only gape in amazement. Three lovely ladies, each about five inches tall, flitted about on butterfly wings, while the fourth perched on a white pedestal, a tiny flute in her hands.

The wingless fairy put the instrument to her lips and began to play. The tune was indescribably lovely, and when the three flying fairies broke into song, the music flooded into every dark corner of my soul. Their words were unlike any language I had ever heard, but the message was clear. They sang of peace, contentment, and everlasting love.

I knew the fairies had to be fake, probably the product of hidden projectors, but they seemed so lifelike—and so endearing—it was hard to hold a doubting thought in my head.

Curious how Hobbs was taking this, I glanced sideways and got a shock. Far from being mesmerized, he was tucking the butt of his violin beneath his chin. And as I watched in horror, he scraped the bow across the strings, producing a sound halfway between a strangled cat and stuck pig.

The effect on the fairies was sudden and brutal. The flute player dropped her instrument, collapsing in a faint, while the airborne beauties faltered in flight, their wings beating in fits and starts. From all four came a mournful wail, loud even above the screech of Hobbs' violin.

"Come, Watson." Hobbs said. "Bring the box!" Then he was off, racing up the aisle toward the helpless fairies.

Still under the fairies' spell, I deemed him contemptible, even evil, but as he stepped on stage I shook my head, reminding myself he was my friend, and relying on me to do my part. Maybe, as I'd long suspected, he was truly insane, but on the off chance he wasn't, I could not afford to fail him. Clutching the open box, I bulled down the aisle after him.

The winged fairies had lost their battle to remain in the air and lay cringing on the stage.

"Into the box," Hobbs shouted. "Quickly, or I will destroy you!"

I'd been so focused on Hobbs and his victims that I'd paid no attention to the audience. I paid for that oversight as a foot hooked my ankle and sent me sprawling. Jarred from my grip, the box clanged across the stage and came to rest upside down.

All around me, people were jeering and booing.

I saw Hobbs' eyes widen in alarm, then lost sight of him as the angry audience surged up to engulf him in a flurry of fists and feet. The cry of his violin died with a loud crunch, and bits of shattered wood skittered in all directions. Still on the floor, it was all I could do to protect my face and privates from the kicks of the maddened crowd.

Above the chaos came the sound of singing, and at last the mob began to melt away. The singing, I realized, was coming from the fairies.

Two of them, their wings once again in service, hovered a scant foot above my head. Though they smiled as they sang, the smiles were malignant, and their eyes, previously bright as tiny suns, were black as pitch.

And they sang a different tune. This one was dark and dreary, with all the joy of a funeral dirge. Try as I might, I could barely keep my eyes open.

And then I couldn't.

❖

I hurt. Everywhere. And when I finally got my eyes open, there was nothing to see. Wherever I was, it was black as my mood. And to make matters worse, I discovered I was bound hand and foot.

I said, "Damn you, Hobbs."

"I very much fear," said the voice of my friend, "that the fairies have already done that."

"Where are we?"

"As near as I can determine, we are on the floor of a travel trailer manufactured by the Airstream company sometime in the mid-1960s."

"How could you possibly know that?"

"Really, Doctor. Have you not read my monograph on the history of criminal behavior involving the use of mobile homes?"

"Sorry I asked. How do we get out of here?"

Hobbs was silent a moment. "As near as I can tell, we don't."

I felt a chill. I had never heard such defeat in his voice. "Well then, since your little fairy hunt is going to get me killed, how about telling me why?"

"I had assumed," Hobbs said, "that as a human being of average intelligence, you were familiar with the story of the Cottingley Fairies."

"If my hands were free, I'd be punching your nose right now."

"My apologies," Hobbs said. "At one time, the Cottingley Fairies were as famous as ...." He groped for an analogy.

"The Andrews Sisters?" I said. "The Dixie Chicks? The girls of *Glee*?"

"I am not familiar with those individuals," Hobbs said, "but I believe you take my meaning. I shall endeavor to explain."

And he did.

The whole mess started back in 1917, when two young girls in the Yorkshire, England village of Cottingley photographed each other in the company of fairies. The pictures caused quite a sensation, and many people, including such famous folk as Arthur Conan Doyle, pointed to them as proof that fairies were real.

One of the many skeptics was Conan Doyle's friend, Sherlock Holmes. When Doyle wrote a book singing the fairies' praises, Holmes was determined to prove him wrong. Instead, Holmes discovered the little creatures were not only real, but far more dangerous than anyone had dreamed. Luckily, by delving into arcane legends, Holmes also discovered their weakness. The fairies were extremely sensitive to music, and found certain high notes to be intolerable—even deadly, particularly when performed on a violin. He also learned they were weakened by close contact with iron, and had an aversion to humans wearing their clothing inside out.

Holmes was still contemplating plans to deal with the fairies when, in the spring of 1920, Conan Doyle's friend Harry Houdini brought his remarkable escape artist act to England. Houdini, like Doyle, believed in the supernatural, and eagerly accepted an invitation to visit Doyle's home and meet the fairies.

This was Holmes' opportunity. Meeting with Houdini prior to the visit, Holmes convinced him of the danger, and the two conspired to put the fairies out of business.

Once the audience with the fairies was underway, Holmes burst in unannounced, sawing on his deadly violin, and forced the little monsters into an iron box of Houdini's design. Despite Doyle's outrage, Houdini promised to sink the box to the bottom of the sea, where it would never be found.

The only downside was that the fairies had not gone quietly. They put a curse on Holmes, proclaiming that the public would forget he had truly existed, remembering him only as a fictional character created by their friend Conan Doyle.

"So there you have it, Doctor. The fairies were gone, while I—that is, Holmes—was relegated to the world of fiction. But somehow, Houdini's box must been found and opened. Sensing that their old enemy had been reborn, the fairies came here to Portland seeking revenge. They know I am the one thing standing between them and the subjugation of the human race."

"Assuming I swallow any of this," I said, "there's one point you've yet to explain. Just what is it about these little babes that makes them so dangerous? They seem perfectly harmless to me."

"Don't you know what fairies do, Doctor?"

"Sure. They dance and sing and make people happy."

"Too true. But they also kidnap human babies and replace them with changelings."

"Why would they do that?"

"To wreak havoc upon the world, of course."

"Oh," I said. "Of course. And what sort of havoc do they wreak?"

Hobbs sniffed. "Have you ever perused a list of individuals born between the years 1917 and 1919?"

"You're kidding, right?"

"Not in the least. I suggest you check those lists at the earliest opportunity. You will find the exercise quite instructive."

I was stewing over that when I recalled the iPhone stuffed into the inside-out pocket of my sweat pants.

As my hands were bound in front of me, I was able to confirm the phone was still there, and soon managed to dig it out.

My thought had been to get online and see who was born during the years mentioned. But I now saw another option. "Now that I have my phone," I said. "I can call the cops."

Hobbs snorted. "And tell them what? That we're being held captive by fairies?"

I knew I could think up a better story than that. But in the meantime, I couldn't resist Googling "famous babies of 1917." As I scanned the list, my eyes nearly fell from my head. I quickly brought up the next two years.

I sat quiet for a time, stunned.

"Well?" Hobbs said.

"Do you mean to tell me all those people were changelings?"

"Of course not. But many of them certainly were."

"I don't believe it. Some of them did great things."

"As is quite natural. Changelings thrive upon attention, leading them to excel in their fields. But you may be certain that whatever good works they accomplished were more than offset by the evil behind the scenes."

"But Good Lord, Hobbs! JFK is on one of those lists. So is Indira Gandhi, Billy Graham, and Betty Ford."

"True," Hobbs said. "But so are George Wallace, Spiro Agnew, and Howard Cosell. And, I shudder to say, Phyllis Diller."

Other names jumped off the lists. Philip Jose Farmer. Nat King Cole. Arthur C. Clarke. Mickey Spillane. Zsa Zsa Gabor.

"I don't believe it!" I insisted.

"No? What about Jeane Dixon? Desi Arnaz? Bobby Riggs?"

"But Hobbs! Raymond Burr?"

His silence was damning.

I hung my head. "Now that the fairies are back," I said, "will this start happening again?"

"Almost certainly."

The names still haunted me. Ann Landers. Joey Bishop. Jacqueline Susann.

"Then we have to stop them."

"That was my intent. But events did not proceed as I had hoped."

How far into the depths of depression I might have gone I do not know, because at that moment a door creaked open. A bright spark of light hovered in the doorway, and a musical voice said:

"Wake up, gentlemen. Your presence is required."

The tent theater was deserted except for ourselves, the fairies, and two short, pot-bellied creatures with green skin, forked tails, and horns. The green guys freed our feet, prodded us with pitchforks, and forced us into chairs facing the stage.

"Changelings, I presume."

Hobbs nodded.

He addressed the fairies. "Why are we still alive?"

The wingless fairy, who appeared to be in charge, said, "You may rest assured, Mr. Hobbs-Holmes, that you will not suffer that state much longer. We wish to offer you one final performance."

"Then let us get on with it."

Shooting Hobbs a sour look, the head fairy called one of the changelings to her and whispered in his ear. The little monster turned and scampered off toward the rear of the tent.

Hobbs nodded toward the side of the stage. "The iron box is still here. If only I had my violin."

I had a sudden thought. "Uh, Hobbs. Remember that video I put on YouTube? The one you didn't like?"

"Of me performing Paganini's *Moto Perpetuo* on the violin? I do indeed, and you swore upon your honor to remove it."

I squirmed a little. "Yeah." The video had gone viral, accumulating half a million hits in a week, and I couldn't bear to take it down. "But as it happens," I said, "I forgot."

Hobbs began to scowl, then thought better of it. "You mean—?"

I nodded.

"Then by all means, hurry."

I did, fumbling for my iPhone, but hampered by the necessity of hiding it from the fairies.

The changeling who'd been sent away was now returning, a bundled pink blanket in his arms.

The head fairy said, "Please be patient, gentlemen. The performance will begin shortly."

I was now online, but typing with bound hands was a chore.

The head fairy leapt into the air, allowing the changeling to place the bundle on the white pedestal, then floated down on top of it.

Hobbs whispered, "Watson!"

"Wilder." YouTube was finally coming up. "Almost there."

The winged fairies hovered above the bundle, tugging back the folds of the blanket to reveal the pinched face of an infant.

At the same moment, the changeling who had delivered the child began to shrink, and the air about him grew hazy. His green skin faded to gray, then brightened to pink. As in no more time than it takes to tell it, he had become the spitting image of the baby on the pedestal.

Hobbs swore under his breath.

I typed *geek with violin* into the search field.

The second changeling yanked the blanket deftly from beneath the real baby and wrapped it around the imposter. Then, with an evil grin, he lifted the bundle and scampered from the tent.

The head fairy said, "Have you gentlemen every wondered what happens to the babies?"

Her sisters hovered inches above the infant. The four fairies looked at us with huge smiles, smiles that grew even larger as their lips peeled back and their mouths opened impossibly wide, revealing rows of fangs.

Hobbs said, "You don't mean—! You can't possibly mean that—"

"Oh, but we do!" the boss fairy said. "We mean exactly that."

The video was finally loading.

All four fairies dipped their chomping teeth toward the baby.

Hobbs roared, "Stop!"

The fairies looked up, just to mock him, but it gave me the time I needed.

I hit the "play" button.

From the phone's tiny speaker came the mind-piercing strains of Hobbs' violin. The fairies' eyes grew wide. Their little bodies twitched. I jump from the chair and ran toward them, music blaring.

Hobbs bolted for the far side of the stage, scooped up the box and rushed back toward the fairies.

I said, "You know the drill, you little bitches. Into the box!"

The fairies were weakening fast. Two of the flyers collapsed on the baby's legs.

"Inside, you demons." Hobbs grasped one by wings and dropped her into the box.

Two others rolled in after her.

The leader was on her knees. "I curse you again, Skyler Hobbs! The world shall never know that you truly ex—"

I'd had enough of that. I flicked her into the box and Hobbs slammed the lid before she could finish the word.

"Were we quick enough?" I asked. "Did we stop the curse?"

Hobbs turned the key in the lock. And for the first time all day, I saw him smile. "Time will tell, Doctor. Time will tell."

The cops had way more questions than we wanted to answer. Hobbs told them only that we'd heard a baby crying, and felt it our duty to climb the fence and assure the child's safety. The cops put their hardest questions to the carnival manager.

"What will happen," I asked Hobbs, "when the cops try to return that baby, and the parents already have one?"

Hobbs shook his head. "Thankfully, that task falls to them rather than us. The important thing is that we stopped those monsters in time to prevent more substitutions. Another generation of changelings could be the ruination of humankind."

We were still congratulating ourselves when a uniformed cop approached, a manila folder in his hand.

"That creepy manager dude denies everything. But we did find something strange in his file cabinet."

Hobbs accepted the folder with trembling hands. The tab was labeled "Cottingley Fairies."

With great trepidation, Hobbs opened the folder. And gasped.

I swore.

The file was thick, and held nothing but magazine covers. The covers had been ripped from magazines like *People, Us Weekly, In Touch, OK!*, and various supermarket tabloids. All featured smiling celebrities and their babies, and some went back several years. We saw Tom Cruise and Katie Holmes. Pitt, Jolie, and their twins. Elizabeth Hasselbeck. Even Anna Nicole Smith.

The cop eyed us curiously. "What do you think it means?"

Hobbs and I exchanged a worried look. We both shrugged.

"Time will tell," we said in unison. "Time will tell." †

THE KING OF MARDI GRAS
Anthony Neil Smith

Obie's cellmate was an older man, lifer, who led Bible studies and attended creative writing classes. Obie was new, just convicted a week ago. He knew the old man asked for rough new fish like Obie so he could get his hooks in early, keep the boy from a life of gangs, rape, senseless violence. Lead him to Jesus, self-expression, and rehabilitation, whatever that was.

Old man had killed three women in the seventies—his wife, her lover, and his mother-in-law who knew about it.

Obie wasn't that bad. Just pummeled his prom date nearly to paralysis when she wouldn't give it up after. Changed her mind. Obie hadn't.

He shouldn't have done that. He knew that. He'd really liked that girl. Now she wore a back brace. He wished he could take it back, not drink as much beer, maybe not spend all that money on a casino hotel room. Everyone else was doing it, so why not? Still, he wrote letters to the girl, asking her to forgive him. He never got a response.

The old man kept telling him to pray about it. Told him forgiveness was like a magic trick, because it happened when you weren't looking for it.

The hell was he talking about?

This day, out in the yard, Minnesota's November chill in the air, Obie was sitting with the old man at a table while the old man read a book. Tourist's guide to New Orleans. Been flipping through it for a week.

He took a deep breath, looked at Obie, and said, "I visited Louisiana today."

Obie shook his head. "Bullshit."

"In my mind. I did. I was there sure as I'm sitting here talking to you now."

So Obie grabbed the guide book, tore out a bunch of pages, and tried to make the old man eat them. Kept shoving them in farther and farther until the guards came and beat Obie till he blacked out.

❖

Once he was in solitary, Obie found he still had a couple of pages of that New Orleans book balled in his fist. Like the guards couldn't unclench it or something and left it alone. Just a couple of pages, but good ones. Lights and beads and floats. Bourbon Street. Parades. Krewe of Zulu. Bacchus. Hermes. Grand balls. Debauchery.

Once out, he went to the library, found the same book he'd tried to make the old man eat. Same copy, those same pages torn out. He fit them back in and smoothed them out and started to read about the history of Mardi Gras. It gave him an idea.

Obie told his new cellmate, a bitch he called Kreacher, like the elf in Harry Potter, to round up the heads of all the gangs in the prison. He wanted a meeting in the common area. And if Kreacher got beaten or killed along the way, Obie would find someone else and then someone else again and again until his message got through.

Luckily, the convicts only broke one of Kreacher's arms and knocked out one tooth while raping him. But he got them all there—Aryans, Blacks, Indians, Hmong, Christians. They sat in plastic chairs around a plastic table and stared at Obie as he made his entrance, most certainly all thinking of ways to kill this idiot. They knew he'd been the old man's roomie, and sent the old man to infirmary for a long time, but he wasn't an Aryan and he wasn't a Christian and therefore he was a problem.

But he descended the stairs with a string of beads around his neck made from paper balls—using the Louisiana book again—and melted bits of plastic he'd picked up around the joint and shaped by burning them above toilet paper fires. His fingertips were scarred and blackened but it had been worth it. He made a mask from the back cover of the book. Wearing it along with his beads with Kreacher behind him, arm in a sling while his other pantomimed a trumpet, Kreacher kazooing that old New Orleans standard with his lips—*Br br br BRRRRR/Br br br BRRRRR/Br br br BRR BRR BRR BRR BRRRRR ...*

The gang leaders were too annoyed to laugh, but it was funny. They knew it was funny. They also knew the first one to laugh would get punctured in the showers.

Kreacher stopped when Obie slapped his bad arm, turned to the convicts, and proclaimed, "Gentlemen, we're going to have fucking Mardi Gras!"

They all said, "Fucking Mardi Gras?"

"Yeah, and I'm the King of Mardi Gras."

The head of the Hmongs—called himself T.C.—cursed and said, "The fuck you know about Mardi Gras?"

The head of the Blacks—Federal Keith—grinned. "You know, I've got family from down there. I remember seeing parades when I was little. Zulus throwing coconuts and shit. That shit was *sweet*, man. Tight."

"And that's what we're going to do. Mardi Gras. Everybody's Krewe throws me a parade."

"Why we doin' this for you?"

"Cause I'm the King of Mardi Gras."

Shrugs and nods around the table.

"So you guys build some floats, makes some beads, and figure out how the hell we're going to get coconuts. I'm going to sit in a throne and watch it all pass by. And you've got three days."

The head of the Christians—Pastor Kill—raised his hand. "But it's December. Mardi Gras isn't until the Tuesday before Lent. That's three months from now."

The others booed him and punched him and sent him out of the common area back to his cell with a bloody lip.

Obie raised his arms like a real king. It shut them all up. "Okay, then you have your work cut out for you. Three days."

He made a grand exit with Kreacher right behind pretending to play sax this time. The head of the Indians—Rabid Wolf— threw a shoe at his head.

❖

But they all got right on it. Really dug the whole she-bang. Each gang rounded up all the bitches and fish they could get, plus some called in favors for bitches owed to other convicts for cigarettes or Internet time or five extra minutes in the shower alone. The guards should've confiscated all the materials—cardboard and construction paper and cell-made dyes and the slowly growing wads of wet newspaper taking on a coconut shape as they grew (don't ask what they used for glue)— but they were intrigued. What the hell was all this? It was better than having to watch the assholes makes shivs all day, or try to hide their gang rapes with strategically hung sheets. This Mardi Gras stuff was colorful, brightened up the industrial beige and steel. Purple and green and gold beads decorated the bars. Crowns made of magazine covers, cardboard, or in the case of Obie's majestic fucking crown that invoked the Kings of France, aluminum foil.

Obie luxuriated in his cell, Kreacher acting as his envoy to the rest of the cellblock while convicts came and went, seeking approval of their Krewe names, float ideas, themes, costumes, etc. Obie would approve, disapprove, or have one of the two bruisers, one each on loan from the Indians and the Blacks, throw the offender out roughly.

That happened less and less the closer "Fat Tuesday" (actually December 4th, a Friday) approached. The costumes were looking good. The Indians were actually dressing like Mardi Gras Indians, which in New Orleans was actually African-Americans dressing like Indians, but okay. They made ornate feathers out of chicken bones they'd saved from evening mess, gluing giant strings of dyed lint to them (don't ask what they used for glue). The blacks decided against the Zulu theme, against Obie's suggestions. After all, the Zulus were one of the greatest Mardi Gras krewes of all time. They're the ones who threw the coconuts. But no, the Blacks decided on a Viking theme. Plunder and pillage from the great white north. Sure, why not? The Christians abstained, so Obie commanded that they be mercilessly taunted until "Lent." The Aryans were thinking of a Klan theme, but Obie vetoed it. "This isn't the time nor place for hate. Have some fun." While the Aryans argued that hate *was* fun, Obie kept his resolve until finally threatening to throw the bums out of the parade. The Aryans relented and chose "Carnival Under the Sea" instead.

The bar were covered in dyed paper streamers. Men made kazoos and other instruments from toilet paper tubes, bits of plastic, letters from home, and drinking straws. Buzzing jazz riffs all over the cell block, day and night. Convicts on the balcony would shout at the bitches in the common area, a promise of beads if they would "show their tits!" Plastic cups full of prison hooch were passed around, the guards looking the other way until after the big parade.

Obie wondered if he could keep it going even longer. Mardi Gras all year, and him the king. What a way to do your time, he thought.

❖

On the day of days, with weather outside was chilly, but the convicts lined up for the parade looked warm as the crowds on Bourbon Street had looked in the guide book. Yelling, shouting, taking off their shirts and whipping them around above their heads. A goddamned celebration!

Obie sat on his throne. Right beneath the basketball hoop, made of three plastic chairs tied together and padded with bed pillows. Lush. His cape was dyed purple, and it had made by layering six clean sheets, sewn together with thread made from towels. His scepter, thirteen toilet paper rolls linked together, covered with tin foil and Scotch tape.

And then it began. As all parades began, this one had a marching band. Nine homemade kazoos in harmony playing a New Orleans party classic, "Don't Mess Wit' My Toot-toot," which, as interpreted by this band, also sounded like a plea for mercy. Kreacher led them, but was pelted by plastic cups full of prison hooch so mercilessly that he fell to the ground and was stomped over by the rest of the band.

After dragging him aside, the first float traveled down the route, eight bitches on their hands and knees carrying it slowly, a cardboard castle, the type you might find in an aquarium, surrounded by large white guys in Swastika tattoos wearing fishlike masks, throwing beads and shivs and even candy to the crowd. How'd they get the candy? Obie had no idea, but when the float stopped by his throne to allow him a bounty of the "throws", he enjoyed the hell out of some Starburst and Skittles.

Next came the Blacks, a Viking ship. Impressive. Even made the bitches underneath wear blue like the ocean. They'd gotten hold of some glitter, so they glued it all over plastic cups (don't ask, etc.) so that the glitter spelled out their name—The Krewe of Fuck You—and threw those into the crowd.

All very cool, sure. But Obie was pissed. Mightily pissed. Murderously so. Because riding at the back of the Viking ship, in a crown bigger than Obie's, sat Federal Keith, waving to the crowd like *he* was the King of Mardi Gras.

Obie ordered the ship to stop. A few bitches fell off their knees, wobbling the ship until it rested at a slope.

He shouted, "There is only one King here, Keith!"

Big smile. "You didn't read the book close enough. Each Krewe gets a king."

"Maybe so, but they're not real Kings. More like servants to the real King. And the real King is me!"

"Seems to me that everyone here should have a say in who their King is." Keith turned to the crowd. "Am I right, convicts?"

A big roar. Obie's chest tightened. He looked around. Must've missed it the first time—The Aryans had them a King, too. Carrying a trident. Behind the Viking Ship came the Indians' buffalo float, the Buffalo carrying the Indian king Rabid Wolf in an exotic headdress.

All three Kings descended from their floats and stepped up to Obie's throne. Obie stared down at them from his footstool made of old phonebooks.

Keith said, "That throne rightfully belongs to all of us. Not you."

"You want it, you'd better be ready to fight for it." He pulled his scepter apart at the middle, revealing a nasty sharpened twist of several stiff wires. About a foot long.

Keith beamed. "I was hoping you'd say that."

He pulled out a long, slim blade of hard plastic. Rabid Wolf hefted his ax, the metal obviously from his toilet lid. The Hmong float hadn't even made it through the doors yet, but here came T.C., ready with a broken baseball bat. The Aryan king wore makeshift brass knuckles—duct tape—but with glass and screws sticking out rather than brass.

Obie felt the guards getting nervous. Not just about the ensuing violence, but about their jobs. They had let this build. They should've known better. One said to Obie, "Uh, come on, wouldn't you just like to finish the parade and maybe have a dance off or something for the King's throne?"

Obie glared. "What did you say?"

The guard backed off. "I'll be inside if you need me. Just shout."

Federal Keith looked at his allies, all of them cracking their necks and flexing their muscles. "Let's do this."

Obie was about to land the first blow when he heard someone shout, "SINNERS!"

They all looked around, the word echoing back and forth between the high walls around the yard.

"SIIIIIIINNNNNNNEEEEEEERRRRRRSSSSSS!"

The crowd parted near the door, and the Old Man, Obie's first cellmate, stumbled thorough. His hair was wild, on end. He had bags beneath his eyes. Hands held hihg in the air, palms out, like a prophet of old. And he still wore his infirmary gown, which added to the wonder of him. Barefoot, in a clean white gown, cuts and blood around his mouth where Obie had forced the pages into his mouth.

One by one, the convicts began to fall to their knees before him. A wave of them, sweeping across the yard as he stumbled around the floats toward the kings. The Kings dropped their weapons, stunned. As he arrived at their circle, they all knelt before him as well.

At first he stopped, looked at each of them. Then he bent down and picked up a handful of dirt. He walked past Obie and sat on the throne, then licked the index finger of his free hand, stuck it into the dirt he held, and lifted the dirty finger to his forehead, where he drew a dirty cross.

He said, "All of you line up for Lent and think about what you've done."

And they all did, the four kings going first. That was the problem with Mardi Gras—it always ended with Lent. Always whooping it up just to have to give something up the next day. Not even the next day now.

Obie took his cross, told the old man he was going to give up raping or beating or some shit like that. But that was a lie. He really knew that he was never going to give up anything anymore. He had been the goddamned King of Mardi Gras, and that was as good as it would ever get. *

THE LAKE BOTTOM BONES
a "Joe Hannibal" story
Wayne D. Dundee

Sheriff Gene Knaack held the palm of one hand to the back of his neck and rubbed it from side to side as he stared down at the muddy depression in the ground. After a long moment he lifted his gaze and fixed it on Dusty and me.

"You sure this is the right spot?"

"Yeah, Gene," I growled. "I'm pretty sure I'd be careful about remembering the right spot."

"But there's nothing there."

"I can see that."

"But it *was* there," Dusty insisted with the urgent certainty that only a twelve-year-old boy can muster. "It was a human skeleton, just like we told you—and it was right there under those old steps."

The three of us were standing on what had for many years— until the continuing unbroken string of drought seasons—been the bottom of Lake McConaughy in west central Nebraska. Moreover, we were standing in the middle of what had once been the original town of Lemoyne. When the North Platte River was dammed to create the lake back in the 1950s, the town was moved north to higher ground where, in its reincarnated state, it continues to flourish as a nice quiet little community overlooking the very spot on the lake from whence it sprang. All that was left of the original community—exposed recently for the first time in decades by the receding lake water—were rows of tree stumps, bottles and twisted scraps of hardware debris, a barely discernable grid pattern where the streets once ran, and a handful of ragged building foundations. Some of the latter surrounded faintly sunken areas that had at one time been basements. A few, like the one we were standing in front of, had the remains of concrete steps, now tilted precariously and badly eroded.

Under furrowed brows the sheriff swept his gaze in a slow hundred-eighty degree arc. To the south of where we stood a narrow band of the North Platte still flowed, feeding to a spot a couple hundred yards east where it began to fan out again and swell to fill the remaining three-quarters of Lake Mac. To the west and between the shorelines—well, what had once *been* shorelines—there was nothing but sandy, muddy flat ground, a handful of puddles, and various types of weeds that seemed to be growing with a kind of wild urgency to fill the void left by the departed water.

Knaack rubbed the back of his neck some more. "Maybe dogs or some kind of wild animal might have dragged it off."

"It would have to've been the neatest damn pack of wild animals I ever saw or heard of," I responded. "It was a whole skeleton, Gene. Intact. Judging from the size of the skull and the bones I examined, a full-grown adult. Now every shred of it is gone. No dogs did that."

"The rain last night could have been enough to wipe out tracks," he said. "Or maybe the rain is what flushed out the skeleton and washed it away."

"That rain last night was barely a measurable amount."

"It was enough to cause you to hold off calling me until this morning."

"Yeah, and now I'm sorry I waited."

Like too many of the storms we'd been getting for the past summers, the one last night had blown in all black and rumbling and ugly-looking only to roll past and break apart after depositing a mere spatter of moisture. When Dusty, after discovering the skeleton during his late afternoon explorations of the formerly submerged old town had excitedly dragged me back to look at it, the storm appeared on the brink of busting wide open. Plus I was late getting started on my evening patrol rounds. So I'd convinced the boy—and myself, too—that it would be okay to wait until this morning and then bring the sheriff out to view the discovery under brighter, drier conditions. A few more hours, I figured, weren't going to make any difference to what was left of that poor devil stuffed in the swampy void under those old steps.

My name is Joe Hannibal. I guess I should explain that I am a licensed private investigator, although I don't work the investigative side of things much these days. I did, though, back in Illinois, for over two dozen years. When I relocated to Nebraska I'd applied for a license out here more or less from habit. But instead of hanging out a PI shingle like before I had instead started a private security patrol operation, called Lake Mac Security, providing a little extra protection and peace of mind for paying residents and businesses scattered around the perimeter of the popular lake where regular police patrols tend to be somewhat sporadic. It's a set-up that's working out pretty well. Dusty, by the way, is the son of Abby Bridger, a pretty divorceé who runs a general store and lodge at No Name Bay on the north shore. I rent a cabin from her and somewhere along the way we struck sparks that resulted in a romantic relationship between the two of us.

"So what does that leave as far as what could've happened to the missing bones?" the sheriff asked irritably, still pawing at the back of his neck. "Pranksters? Somebody's sick damn idea of a joke?"

"I'm not sure what to think." I ran a knuckle along the ridge of my jaw. Maybe this rubbing thing was contagious. "It could have been a prank I suppose. But that skeleton sure looked authentic, all brown and weathered, covered with mold and muck—exactly like you'd expect for remains that had been at the bottom of the lake since the town went under."

Knaack focused on Dusty. "You tell anybody else besides Hannibal here what you found, boy?"

"No way. I rode my bike back to No Name Bay as fast as I could and went straight to find Joe. I haven't talked about it to anybody but him."

The sheriff asked a few more questions, then eventually sent Dusty and me on our way. Before doing so he outlined some of the steps he would take to try and get to the bottom of this puzzle, including a thorough sweep of the area by his deputies, some dirt and mud sampling from around the old steps, and a check of records as far back as 1950 for missing persons or unsolved disappearances.

"That much activity is bound to draw attention, so word's going to leak out soon enough about what you found here," he summed up. "But if you two would keep mum about this for as long as you can, I'd appreciate it. I don't want to alarm people unnecessarily and I don't want to tip anybody off in case we actually turn up some kind of lead that might solve an old crime."

Even though I understood trying to hold in that kind of exciting news would cause Dusty—or any twelve-year-old kid, for that matter—to practically explode, I promised on behalf of both of us to keep a lid on things as best we could.

The rest of that day and the next went by uneventfully, as far as anything else out of the ordinary taking place. The sheriff and his men continued to search for some clue to the missing skeleton, but as far as we heard they weren't turning up anything significant.

It was the middle of July so there were plenty of other things going on around No Name Bay and the lake in general. Even though drought-depleted on the western end, where the old town had resurfaced, the rest of Lake McConaughy still had a great deal of water available for fishing, boating, swimming, and camping along its remaining miles of white sand shoreline. Shaped sort of like an elongated teardrop, the lake is widest and deepest at its eastern end, where it butts up against Kingsley Dam. No Name Bay is a few miles west of the dam and if the drought continued another summer the receding water might cause it to be redubbed No Bay Bay, but for the time being it still had boat ramp access and therefore was attracting its fair share of height-of-the-season visitors. Abby was doing a hopping business at her store and the other cabins of the lodge were filled to capacity every night. I, frankly, could have done without all the hubbub around me but since the summer months are what allows businesses like Abby's to survive, I could hardly begrudge them the flow of paying customers.

The second evening after Dusty and I showed Sheriff Knaack where the skeleton *had* been, I'd just headed out on patrol rounds when I received a call on my cell phone. It was Jean, one of the young women Abby hires to help work the store counter. "Mr. Hannibal," she said, "some young punks have shown up here and they're hassling Abby and Dusty pretty bad. I think you'd better get over here."

I was less than two miles away. I burned a quick U and held the gas pedal stomped to the floor all the way back to No Name.

I came barreling down the gravel road that leads from the highway to the marina and pulled up next to the store. Abby and Dusty were standing before the building, confronting a group of young people—three guys and three girls. All looked to be in their early twenties, sun-burned, scantily clad, and giving off an unmistakable air of pampered youth.

I piled out of my vehicle and walked over to them. Abby had taken up a somewhat protective position slightly in front Dusty. I moved up beside her. "What's the problem here?" I wanted to know.

"Whatever it is, it's none of your business, Pops," said one of the young guys, marking himself as the apparent leader of the bunch. He was tall, fair-haired, probably handsome by most standards, except for the well-practiced sneer on his kisser.

"Thank you," I said, "but I'll be the judge of what is and isn't my business."

"Might be poor judgment on your part, Pops."

"I don't know how, but they seem to know all about the skeleton, Joe," Abby spoke up. She was the one other person Dusty and I had confided in about his discovery. "I caught them giving Dusty a hard time about it. They're making ridiculous accusations that he stole it or hid it or something."

"How *do* you know about the skeleton?" I asked the sneerer.

"Right back to none of your damn business," he replied.

Another of the young men stepped forward, this one quite a husky specimen. Crewcut hair and gym muscles—a jock of some kind, maybe a would-be tough guy. "Wait a minute, Danny. Don't you see?" He made a flourishing gesture to indicate the blue light on my dashboard and the magnetic stick-on Lake Mac Security emblem on the door of my vehicle. "This must be a genuine descendant of Matt Dillon or Barney Fife or one of them other legendary lawman-types. Patrolling the Wild West to keep it safe for school marms and wide-eyed little kids and Mom's apple pie, by golly. That's why even a tiny little disturbance like this one *is* his business."

The two of them snickered nastily and pretty soon the others all joined in.

"All right. You've had your fun, had your little laugh," I said. "Before this turns into a *real* disturbance, why don't you just move along. Go on back to wherever you came from."

The husky guy's expression suddenly went cold and hard. "To hell with you, old man. We don't come and go on your say-so." He jabbed a finger, pointing at Dusty. "*That* little brat has got something of ours and we ain't going nowhere until we get it back. If I have to I'll grab him by his scrawny little neck and squeeze until he damn well tells us where it is."

"I don't have your stupid skeleton. I don't *know* where it went," Dusty insisted.

"That does it, you lying little—"

The husky guy made a move toward Dusty. I got in front of him. Body-checked him, levered one arm briefly to turn his upper body, then shoved. He went staggering.

As soon as he caught his balance he whirled back around to face me again, enraged. "Nobody lays their hands on me like that!"

"Let it drop or I'll do worse," I tried to warn him.

But of course he wouldn't listen. He charged straight at me. I sidestepped the reach of his bearlike arms and hammered a right hook to his ribs. This abruptly stopped his forward momentum and knocked him a jerky half-step to his left. I followed up, leaning in with a hard jab that landed just ahead of the hinge of his jaw. His shoulders sagged and he dropped to his knees.

I can't be sure where things would have gone from there. The way the others sort of shrank back and looked stunned by the apparent ease with which this old he-goat had handled their enforcer indicated none of the rest of them were ready to try and get aggressive. But if the husky guy had the endurance and heart to rise up and come back for more, he might have been able to give me a harder time of it. I've been in enough skirmishes to know a trick or two, but these days my dented old gas tank runs empty a lot quicker than it used to. It turned out to be a moot point, however, when a Keith County cruiser suddenly appeared, rolling down from the highway in a cloud of dust and gravel. Apparently I wasn't the only one Jean had seen fit to call.

The deputy who got out was young and ramrod-straight. All business. He was one of Sheriff Knaack's newer men and I didn't know him as well as I did some of the others on the force. But he did everything by the book and did it right. When he started hearing the answers to the questions he asked it didn't take him long to realize that, in view of the two-day search that had been taking place in regard to the missing skeleton, the sheriff himself would want to be in on the rest of this.

The police interrogation lasted until after dark. When it was done, the following had been determined:

The six young people were college students from the Denver area. They were vacationing for a week on Lake McConaughy, staying at the north shore getaway cottage owned by the parents of Danny, their pseudo-leader.

One of the girls in the group had an older brother who, on a whim, had purchased an authentic-looking movie prop skeleton off of eBay. Said skeleton had since been making the rounds of friends and family, often used as a party prop or Halloween gimmick or the means to play a prank on some un-suspecting soul. This time around the prank had been planned for the residents and law enforcement officers of Keith County. Having heard about the remnants of Old Lemoyne being exposed by the lake drought, the band of merrymakers had decided it would be a big hoot to bring the skeleton along, plant it somewhere in the ruins where it was sure to be found, and then sit back and watch the fun as a "bunch of hick cops and local yokels" scrambled to try and figure out the origin of the mysterious bones. Danny and his playmates had been secretly watching when Dusty and I took Sheriff Knaack out to the spot where Dusty had made his predictable discovery, their delight growing as the team of deputies got called in to scour the surrounding area and take their dirt samples and so forth. But delight turned to eventual dismay and confusion when no actual bones were brought to light and when, after taking their samples, the deputies simply left and nothing more seemed to be happening. Dismay and confusion built to frustration that finally manifested itself when the college brats spotted Dusty again outside the No Name Bay general store and accosted him there, blaming him for somehow spiriting away the skeleton and ruining the big entertaining hoax they had cooked up.

For the time being, things were put to rest by filing a handful of misdemeanor charges against the pranksters and shooing them off with their tails tucked between their legs. But that still left the nagging question of what *had* happened to the skeleton that once occupied—no matter how briefly—the muck under those old steps?

After the brat pack and his deputies had all taken leave, Gene Knaack hung around for a while longer, sipping coffee and talking with Abby and me on the front porch of her store. Not having all of the answers was clearly gnawing at him and I didn't mind playing the role of sounding board if it helped him try to come to grips. I'd called in one of the part-timers I sometimes use to take over my evening patrol, so there was no place else I had to be. And it was a nice enough night for lingering out of doors with the lake waves softly lapping nearby.

"Do you suppose," the sheriff was saying, "we could have *two* hoaxes going on here? First the college kids trying to play us, and then somebody else trying to play *them*?"

I replied, "It's possible, I guess. But where's the payoff in causing the first hoax to backfire?"

"Maybe we just had it," Abby suggested. "Getting the college kids to tip their hand about what they were trying to pull and then getting in trouble over it—maybe that was the payoff for somebody."

"But who? Those kids aren't from around here—who would even know them well enough to know about the skeleton in order to be in a position to get a kick out of seeing them squirm and get caught like they did?"

"Maybe it's somebody from *within* the group, playing a trick on all the others. What about that?" Abby said.

"Questions and possibilities," Knaack muttered. "But no answers ... and no damn skeleton."

We kicked it around another half hour or so without arriving at any kind of conclusion. When the air coming in off the lake started to turn chill we called it a night. We had no way of knowing that the answers, which seemed so elusive in the moment, would be revealed through a totally unexpected sequence of events less than twenty-four hours away.

❖

I had begun my patrol rounds the next evening and had just reached the town of Lemoyne—the new and current version, that is—as twilight was starting to settle. I only had a handful of accounts in the little community and had never had a hint of trouble at any of them so I'll admit my mind was not intently focused on matters of high security as I prepared to make my sweep. I couldn't help glancing off to the south whenever a view of the lake presented itself and each time I caught a glimpse I felt a pang of sadness at seeing mighty Lake Mac so diminished. On top of that, the mystery of the skeleton that had vanished from down there amidst the ruins of the old town also continued to tug naggingly at my thoughts.

I made the turn on Overlook Drive, heading for Dennamore's Bait Ship, when a very distraught-looking young woman came galloping out from between the houses and shrubbery on the right side of the street. She was in her middle to late twenties, wearing blue jeans and an untucked sleeveless blouse. She had medium-length brown hair and a face that was pretty in an unpretentious, suburban mom kind of way. But there was nothing pretty about the anguished expression pinching it right at the moment.

I braked. She came scooting around the front end of my vehicle and up to the driver's side window that I had rolled down.

"Have you seen an elderly lady anywhere out here?" the woman asked breathlessly. "She may have looked … well, lost. Or confused. She's my grandmother—quite short, pure white hair, wearing an old-fashioned house dress and probably an apron."

I shook my head. "Sorry. I just pulled in off the highway."

The woman's brows knitted tighter still. She turned her head and looked one way up the street, and then down the other. She appeared as if she wanted to break into flight but couldn't decide which way to go.

"Is she in trouble—or at risk in some way?" I asked.

The woman nodded, still looking up the street. "Yes, I'm afraid she may be at risk … from herself. Her mind wanders sometimes, you see. More and more often lately … she loses sense of time and place … and what her limitations are."

"Is she likely to have gone far?"

"It's possible. She's rather frail, but when her mind wanders she seems to forget that. More than once she's done things she shouldn't physically be capable of."

"I'll help you look, if you like," I offered. "We can cover ground more quickly in my car, and I've even got a spotlight if we need it. It's going to be dark pretty quick."

Her restless eyes cut to me, peering in through the open window, really looking at me for the first time. I don't wear much in the way of a uniform when on patrol—only a long-billed ball cap with the Lake Mac Security logo in front. Plus the stick-on emblems on the vehicle doors and the blue dashboard light. These credentials, combined with what I like to think of as a mug with a certain amount of character, were what the young woman seemed to be weighing as far as whether or not to take me up on my offer.

"All right," she decided, snapping a quick nod. Around the front end of my vehicle she scooted again, then piled in beside me.

As we rolled forward, she talked nervously. "I was gone barely half an hour. I went to that little store up the road to get some ice cream—Grandma loves a dish of ice cream before she goes to bed at night, and I realized we had run out. She was napping on the couch when I left. When I got back she was gone."

"Has she done that before? Wandered off unexpectedly?"

"She's gotten to where she tries to sometimes. Last winter we had to put special locks on the doors, way up high where she couldn't reach them, so she wouldn't roam out in the middle of the night after my husband and I were asleep and end up freezing to death or something. That seemed to be working ... until the other night, anyway."

We drew abreast of a middle-aged couple dressed in matching jogging suits, out for a brisk evening walk. The brown-haired woman seemed to know them. She rolled down her window and asked them if they had seen her grandmother. They said no, shaking their heads in unison. Then they flashed brief, concerned, somewhat pitying smiles and assured the granddaughter they would let her know immediately if they did run across the old woman.

We rolled on.

"What happened the other night?" I asked. "Your grandmother got out past the locks somehow?"

The young woman rolled her eyes and made a dramatic gesture with her hands. "She *climbed* OUT *her freakin' bedroom window* .... Can you believe it? Like a college frat boy or something. And that was the night that sudden late storm blew through. Right out into the heart of it she went. My husband works nights at the truck stop in Big Springs, gets home after midnight. When he pulled up he spotted her huddled in the bushes beside the driveway. Soaked, muddy, disoriented ... God knows how long she might have cowered there or how bad off she would have been if he hadn't come along when he did."

Something fluttered through the short hairs across the back of my neck.

We'd gone past the bait shop by that point and were coming up on a grassy area to the right where a handful of young boys were shagging fly balls in the rapidly dimming light. To the left a twisty, unpaved narrow lane meandered down toward where the lake should have been. Somewhere down there an unseen dog was yapping persistently at something.

The brown-haired woman called out to the boys, asking if any had seen her grandmother. They stopped their play long enough to give negative head shakes in response.

The woman sank back in her seat, her level of anxiety obviously on the rise.

"How about trying down there?" I said, jerking a thumb in the direction of the dirt lane. "Would she have been drawn toward the lake for any reason?"

"It's hard to say ... who knows?"

The yapping dog was still going at it strong. "Well something down there has sure got that dog excited," I said. "Come on, let's have a look."

I nosed my vehicle off Overlook Drive and down the lane, flipping on the headlights as I made the turn. Underbrush and stands of trees crowded the lane close on either side, hurrying the murkiness of dusk. The scent of damp earth and pools of stagnant water wafted up from the empty lake bed that lay just ahead of us. The lane was rutted and rough, forcing me to proceed slowly.

We emerged from the fringe of trees onto a flat of weed-studded sand and mud. I braked and cut the engine. We could hear the dog barking more clearly now but still couldn't see the animal. Its barks seemed to be coming from a line of high, sharp, brush-covered embankments running back in a line more or less parallel to Overlook Drive.

I tugged a long-handled, high intensity flashlight from the door pocket and stepped out. "I think we need to see what's got that mutt so worked up," I said.

The brown-haired woman climbed out on her side and sailed around next to me. "My God," she said. "You don't think my grandmother may have tried to come down that embankment and ...."

That's exactly what I was thinking ... or fearing, I guess would be a more accurate way of putting it. No matter how clichéd it might be—Lassie barking to draw attention because Timmy has fallen down the well and all that—it's what came to mind and there was no getting around it. But of course I didn't want to say that to the already-distraught granddaughter. So, instead, I made no reply at all. Just snapped on the flashlight and started walking toward the sound of the barking.

When we finally came in sight of the mutt we saw that it was some kind of pointy-eared terrier breed running back and forth in a frantic figure eight pattern at the base of the embankment. As we watched, it suddenly broke away and burst up the slope, disappearing into the high weeds. Thirty seconds later it shot back out of the weeds again, yipping even more shrilly than before.

And then we heard the voice calling after it: "Get out of here ... damn dog, damn dog ... stay away, damn dog!"

"Grandma?" the brown-haired woman said, her tone rising hopefully. She quickened her step, heading in the direction of the voice. I hurried to keep up with her.

At our approach the terrier skittered away and its yips seemed to take on a plaintiff tone, as if protesting our intrusion. The brown-haired woman turned and started up the slope of the embankment at approximately the same point the dog had made its recent ascent and then hasty retreat. I stayed on her heels, shining the beam of my light out ahead of us.

We climbed for maybe a dozen yards through high weeds and bramble brush before the ground leveled off into a little clearing of shorter grass where there was a scattered heap of broken rocks and rubble. On her knees beside the rubble was a white-haired old woman in a house dress and apron. She looked around sharply at our arrival, her expression an equal mix of annoyance and anger.

"You got no business here—go away and keep your pesky little dog away, too!"

The brown-haired woman walked slowly closer to her grandmother, then paused. Leaning slightly forward, she said in a gentle, soothing voice, "That wasn't my little dog, Grandma .... It's me ... Cindy .... We don't have a dog, remember?"

The old woman put a hand up to shade her eyes from the glare of my flashlight. "Cindy?" she said, as if trying hard to place the name but finding it only vaguely familiar.

"Grandma, don't you think you should come home now? You really shouldn't be out here. My goodness, you could have fallen and seriously injured yourself."

The old woman gave a sudden, almost violent shake of her head. "No! No I did *not* fall .... That's what he always made me tell people—that I'd fallen or bumped into something. But it was never true and everybody knew it. The only times I fell was when that bastard knocked me down!"

"When who knocked you down?" I said, edging forward.

The old woman scowled at me for a moment, but then her eyes softened. "Who are you?"

"My name is Joe. I'm here to help you," I told her.

Her gaze shifted to Cindy, eyes softening even more. "Heaven's sake, Sandra, you should have told me you had a new beau stopping by. Don't you imagine I would have appreciated the chance to freshen up ... I've been working in the garden all afternoon, I must look a sight!"

Cindy cast me a sidelong glance and said in a low voice, "Sandra was my mother. We lost her five years ago to cancer ... Grandma gets confused sometimes and thinks I'm her."

The grandmother beamed up at the two of us. "Are you two youngsters going out on a date tonight? A nice dance somewhere? Or just to the movies? Young couples these days don't seem to go to dances like they did in my time." Then the sweet smile went away and her expression turned stern as she said directly to me. "You may as well know right now, young man, that I do *not* approve of the drive-in movies .... *Passion pits*, that's all those blasted things are and I do *not* approve."

"That's all right, ma'am," I told her. "I wasn't planning on taking Cin—er, Sandra to the drive-in. I just wanted to stop by and introduce myself, maybe sit and visit for a spell."

"Well, what a nice idea ... I think that would be very enjoyable."

I stepped forward and held out my hand to her. "Let me help you up from your gardening, then, and we'll just go—"

My words stopped short. Sticking out of the pile of rubble, on the edge of the pool of light thrown by my flashlight, were several partially exposed bones from a human skeleton.

The old woman turned her head and stared down at the bones with me. Neither of us said any-thing. Cindy took a step forward, not yet aware of what we were looking at. "What is it?" she wanted to know.

"Nothing to worry about, Sandra dear. Nothing at all." Now the grandmother's voice was the gentle, soothing one. "Mee-Dah has gone away, that's all. Everything will be okay now. He won't frighten you any more ... and you won't have to watch him hurting mommy ever again ...."

❖

It was late. Full dark. Quiet.

The night air was heavy. Sky overcast, starless. Felt like it could rain.

I was leaning against the fender of my vehicle parked out front of the Lemoyne house shared by Doug and Cindy Collard and Cindy's grandmother, Betty Boardman. All were inside. Cindy had called Doug home early from his job at the truck stop in Big Springs. Sheriff Knaack was in there with them.

I'd been inside with the rest of them … until I'd heard enough. Then I came out here, poured myself a cup of coffee from the thermos I always took on patrol rounds, and tried to let the quiet and the night absorb me. I tried not to think about what was being discussed inside that house, and most of all not to think about the consequences that ultimately had to come of it. Out here it was a pleasant night, even with the hint of rain. In there it was a lousy one … lousy as hell.

I'd just topped off my cup and was waiting for it to get cool enough to take another sip, when the door of the house creaked open and Knaack came out. He walked over to where I was standing.

"You got any more of that?" he said, pointing to my steaming mug.

"Got more coffee in the thermos. But this is my only cup."

He went over to his car, leaned in through the passenger door a minute, then returned carrying one of those wide-bottomed travel mugs into which I poured some of my brew. Neither of us said any-thing more for a few minutes, blowing across the tops of our cups once in awhile, gingerly taking sips.

"Good coffee," Knaack said at length.

I grunted. "If it is, it's the only thing good about this rotten situation."

"Yeah, I know what you mean … can't help but feel for the old gal, can you?"

"Uhmm ... she still out of it? Thinking her granddaughter is her daughter and like that?"

"She drifts back and forth a little bit, but mostly, yeah, that's where she's at in her mind right now. The granddaughter says she's never been this far out for this long before. Chance she may never come back to the full reality of the present."

We drank some more of our coffee ... make that *my* coffee.

"You got to admit," said the sheriff, "that if you were just hearing about it and not caught up in having to *deal* with, it makes a kinda fascinating tale."

Yeah. Fascinating ... and tragic.

Fifty-odd years ago, Betty Boardman got fed up with her abusive husband knocking her around and frightening their baby daughter all the time. One night she finally fought back, coldcocking him with a frying pan and killing the bastard. Only instead of owning up to it and going for a self-defense plea, she panicked and decided to cover it up. Buried the body by the dark of the moon in the back yard of their modest house just within the city limits of the original town of Lemoyne. Told the neighbors that her husband had abandoned her and the daughter, giving no clear idea why or where he was going. Because everybody who knew him knew what a jerk he was, they all figured it was good riddance to bad rubbish and nobody seemed to think much more about it.

And when the lake got formed and the body ended up being buried under not only just the back yard sod but a few million gallons of dammed-up river water, Betty breathed an added sigh of relief and told herself that after that no trace of him could turn up to *ever* give anybody a second thought.

Except until all these years later, when the drought caused the lake to roll back. All of a sudden the burial spot was freshly exposed to the trampling crowds of curious gawkers who came to tromp all over the old town and the yards of the old neighborhoods, poking and picking and nosing through everything. In recent years, after it became more and more difficult for her to get about on her own (necessitating the arrangement for her granddaughter and grandson-in-law to come live with her) Betty had found quiet pleasure from sitting in her room and gazing out upon the lake through the window with a pair of strong binoculars, watching the fishermen and colorful boaters and other activities that always seemed to be taking place on and around the water. Only now the activity she looked upon no longer brought pleasure, but rather dread—the dread of her decades-old crime being revealed after all this time. The state of her confused, near-senile mind only added to the paranoia. And on the afternoon she watched Dusty bring me to peer into the hole under the old foundation steps, she knew with a terrible certainty what it was that must have been uncovered. The fact that the spot we were focused on wasn't anywhere near to where her former back yard had been was lost to her dementia. And so that night, in the middle of the storm, she had gone down there and removed the bones—the damnable *bones* of the bullying bastard who had caused her so much misery and humiliation when he was alive, threatening from the grave to cause her even more. She'd taken the bones to the pile of rubble on the embankment slope and hastily reburied them there. Earlier this evening had been her first chance to get away and return to try and do a better job of concealing the telltale remains.

Some of this was conjecture. The rest was conclusion based on a combination of circumstantial evidence, bits of history that Cindy was able to fill in, and the somewhat disjointed yet convincing ramblings of Betty herself.

"Mee-Dah," I said softly and somewhat abruptly into the still night air.

"What's that?" Knaack asked.

"Something Betty said when we found her at the rubble pile, down where I first spotted the skeleton bones she was trying to do a better job of covering back up," I explained. "Cindy and I were able to figure out what it meant when we got her back up to the house, before you arrived."

"So what *does* it mean?"

"Sandra, Cindy's mother, was just a toddler when her father ... went away. Barely two, still learning to talk, pronouncing certain things in that funny, quirky way like kids sometimes do. 'Mee-Dah' is what Sandra called her father."

"So it was supposed to be, like, 'me dad' or 'my dad'—that's what she was trying to say?"

I looked at him. "That's what you might think, isn't it? But remember she was referring to the guy she mostly heard hollering and bitching practically every minute he was around the house, and who she regularly saw pound bruises on her mother so that the poor woman had to lie to friends and neighbors about falling or bumping into things .... No, Sandra wasn't calling him 'my dad' or 'me dad', Gene. With a little kid's brutal honesty, she was calling the piece of crud what he truly was and what he deserved to be called ... 'Mean Dad'."

Knaack made a sour face. "That's a hell of a thing."

"Apparently Sandra never really knew the truth about what happened to her father. She was left to think, like everybody else, that he simply took off and abandoned her and her mother. And eventually all the term 'Mee-Dah' meant to her was her childish name for a man she barely remembered."

"And good for her that she *didn't* remember any of the rest."

"Only Betty knew the whole story," I said. "And all these years she's had to live with it ... marrying a monster she had to endure hearing her own child call 'Mean Dad', putting up with the pain and humiliation of his beatings for as long as she could, fearing for the day he might start to turn that same wrath on the child. Then finally lashing out and ending it. And after that ... carrying the weight of the guilt she felt over what she'd done, and the grinding fear that one day it might all somehow be brought to light and come crashing down on her."

"And now that day has arrived," Knaack said huskily.

I let his words hang in the air for a minute then said, "Doesn't really *have* to be that way."

He gave me a look. "What are you saying?"

"I'm saying what we're both already damned well thinking ... no way that old woman in there deserves a police hassle or to have any kind of criminal charge brought against her."

"Yet you called me out here to listen to her confession."

"I called you because I owed it to you. I couldn't *not* do at least that much. But it can still end right here."

"She's admitted to killing a man, Joe. Granted, it sounds like a case of self defense. Hell, maybe the creep deserved it. But that ain't for me to say. She did it and then she covered it up. Literally. Buried the body and hid the evidence for all these years. That's too much for me to just turn my back on because I feel sorry for her."

"What would you actually be turning your back on? You don't even have a body. All you've really got is the ramblings of an obviously confused, half-senile old woman. For all we know she could have her memories tangled up with something she saw in a movie or on a TV show."

"That sounds like the pitch of a slick defense lawyer. No, we don't have a body. But now that we've got reason to believe there may be one down there somewhere, we can go after it."

"For the sake of gaining what, exactly? If you managed to dig around and actually find any remains, what are the odds of that old woman ever being declared competent enough to stand trial? So the only thing you'd accomplish would be trashing her good name, embarrassing and humiliating her family, and maybe hurrying her into some kind of care facility where she's almost certain to end up, anyway. Can you show me how justice would be better served by any of that?"

Knaack put his free hand to the back of his neck and slowly rubbed it from side to side. He kept looking at me as he did this, his eyes wary and thoughtful, face pulled long by an expression of hangdog sadness mixed with wavering resolve. After a while he turned his head and gazed out across the empty blackness where the lake should have been.

"Lake'll be back one of these days," he said, sighing. "Drought can't last forever."

"Nothing lasts forever," I allowed.

"Gonna take time, though. Take some heavy snow packs melting out of the Wyoming mountains. And rain ... lots of rain. Feels like there could even be some tonight."

"Uh-huh."

The sheriff cleared his throat. "One of the oldest sayings in the book, I'd guess, is the one about having enough sense to come in out of the rain." He turned his face back and looked at me again. "Maybe that should be our cue to get out of here and go on home before it cuts loose. You think?"

Our eyes held. I said, "Sounds like a good idea to me."

He cleared his throat again. "Suppose I should go tell the granddaughter and her husband that we're leaving, then ... and warn them they'd better keep a little tighter rein on Granny from now on because I've got better things to do than waste my time chasing after some batty old broad's twisted-around notions about what happened fifty years ago."

I couldn't help grinning. "Yeah ... yeah, that's exactly what you should do, Gene."

And then, while I stood there waiting for him to come back out, damned if fat, cold drops of rain didn't start spattering down around me. †

NIGHT TERRORS
Jake Hinkson

When the stranger next to me screamed in her sleep, I tumbled out of bed and smacked my face on her nightstand. Darkness and exploding red suns spun around me as she shrieked like someone was killing her. I struggled to my feet and steadied myself against the wall, trying to let my vision clear. When it did, I saw her thrashing about in blue moonlight and clawing at the sheets like she was possessed. Finally she twitched, curled into a ball, and began gently snoring.

For a moment, I just stood there naked listening to the angry thump of my heart.

Then I realized I was bleeding. I inched my way across our clothes piled on the carpet and searched for her bathroom in the dark. When I found it, I closed the door and turned on the light.

In that sudden glare, I looked like hell. Three bright streams of blood ran down my face from a gash on my forehead. Blood dotted my chest and arms and dripped on her sink and floor. My hands still shook with adrenaline as I tried to wash up, but I finally got the job done. When everything was clean, and I was calmed down, I turned off the light.

As quietly as I could, I dressed in the dark. Normally, I wasn't the type to sneak out in the middle of the night, but I wasn't going to stick around with a screamer. I thought about leaving a note, but I decided against it. What was there to say? *Nice to meet you? Thanks for the sex? Do you know you shriek in your sleep?*

Outside, the temperature dropped fifty degrees, and I considered going back inside where it was warm. Maybe crash on her couch. But, of course, the door was locked now. The Metro had stopped running, so there was nothing to do but hike home through the cold.

I was still thinking about her. What was her name? Lynn? Yes, Lynn, after Loretta Lynn she'd told me. Her dad was a big country music fan even though they weren't from the south. I nodded. That's right. Lynn. I couldn't recall her last name. She had honey-blonde hair and calculating green eyes, eyes that were always thinking. Nice girl. We'd had a few drinks, talked about music and movies, and then we went back to her place, tipsy but not too drunk. A couple of condoms later, we kissed goodnight and fell asleep. I was going to give her the usual fake number in the morning.

Walking home before the sun had even begun to rise, though, I started to feel bad for not at least leaving a note.

I shrugged and braced myself as a truck rumbled past me. I'd be lucky if I didn't get mugged. And I was freezing my ass off. I didn't feel too bad for her.

She played a couple of songs on the jukebox. The first was "Somebody to Love" by Queen. She came back to the bar, three stools down from me. I leaned over. "Good choice," I said. "I haven't heard this song in a while."

That last part was a lie. Every time I came in this bar someone was playing that song.

She smiled and brushed some hair back behind her ear. She was tiny—not more than five two, but she was wearing some heels to give herself another couple of inches.

"Yeah," she said with a thoughtful nod. She leaned toward me and said, "To tell you the truth, I sang this song for American Idol."

"Seriously?"

"Yeah. Didn't work, obviously. I stepped up, sang, and they told me to beat it. I didn't even get on TV." She lifted her glass as if to toast fate. "Just another piece of cattle."

I leaned over to say, "Nice to try, though."

She nodded.

I pointed at her empty glass. "Can I buy you another?"

"Sure."

The bartender was slicing up limes. I motioned to our glasses and eased down the bar.

I told her my name.

We shook. Her hands were small and soft. "I'm Lynn," she said.

Two days later, I was standing at my kitchen counter waiting on the coffee to brew when I read in the *Washington Post* that she'd been murdered. Her name was Lynn Byers, and she was an assistant manager at the Apple store in Arlington. I stared at her name, and my stomach turned to ice. She had been murdered the night I was with her. I tried to sit down, but my knees collapsed beneath me. I landed on the linoleum.

There was a picture of the front door of her apartment with police tape around it. In the corner of the article there was a small picture of her: Lynn sitting on a couch, laughing and pointing to someone or something off camera. It was an older picture and another hairdo, but it was her.

She'd been strangled in her bed by an unknown assailant. The police were investigating leads.

I dropped the paper. *The police were investigating leads.* What did that mean? I looked at my front door. I picked up the paper again. The police were investigating leads.

Oh, Jesus. They wouldn't think …. No, no. Why would they?

I got to my feet. Why would they? I took the paper to the kitchen table and tried to read the article again.

A neighbor knocked on her door after seeing Lynn's shattered back window. When no answer came, the neighbor grew suspicious. When he noticed that Lynn's car was parked out front, he called the police.

Someone had broken in and murdered her after I left. That thought sunk down to the bottom of my stomach.

I touched the crusty gash on my forehead and thought of the towel stained with my blood. I'd probably dripped blood on the bed and floor, too.

I hurried to my front door and cracked it open. Empty street, empty sidewalk. A wind kicked up suddenly, shaking the maples in front of my apartment and sweeping their scarlet leaves down the sidewalk. Across the street, a man was watching his dog piss on a tree trunk. That was it.

Back inside, I didn't know which way to go. I picked up the phone, but I didn't have an idea who I might call.

The cops? They would find me anyway. I was the last one to see her alive—

No, the killer was. That thought made me shudder. Tears sprang to my eyes.

She had been murdered, choked to death. Lynn. Lynn Byers. I hadn't even known her last name. I'd had sex with her, had been inside her body, had felt her breathing quicken and settle. And now she was dead. That thought was too horrible. I could still taste her mouth, could still feel her skin. She had a mole next to her left nipple, and I could tell she was sensitive about it when she took off her clothes. She was embarrassed, but not too embarrassed. She mostly wanted to judge my reaction. Her eyes were always thinking.

But not anymore.

I picked up my phone and punched in 911, but I hung up.

I walked a circuit between the kitchen and the den. I made myself stop and sit down and think. But then I got up again.

I prayed for the first time in fifteen years. *Please God. Please God. Don't let this happen.* I didn't get any farther than that when I realized that I was more scared than upset.

That thought sickened me. She was dead. I didn't really know her and she was dead and I was too scared to feel anything except fear.

I read the paper again looking for something new.

I walked to the den and back again.

I skimmed the paper again. My lungs felt like they were going to pop. I was going to lose it.

I ran and looked out the front door. A light rain was falling now, and wet leaves spread across the sidewalk like open sores.

I slammed the door shut and ran to my bedroom. After I threw on some clothes and a heavy coat, I ran out of the house without locking the front door.

I also didn't look behind me to see who might be there.

After a few minutes of hurrying nowhere in particular, I saw the Metro. I slipped inside and dashed down the escalator to the trains. A green line train pulled up as I got to the platform, and I jumped on board. A moment later, we shot down the tunnel. For the first time that morning, my heart slowed to a steady beat. My stomached settled. There were about twenty people on the train, mostly people in suits on their way to work.

Then it hit me. I was supposed to be at work. I dug in my pocket for my cell phone, but I couldn't find it. I dug through every pocket I had three times before I accepted that I'd left it on the kitchen table. I hadn't left home without it in years.

I asked a woman across the aisle for the time. She pushed back the cuff of her coat and said, "Ten-thirty."

I was supposed to be at work at nine. That realization actually stopped me for a second. I'd never been late to work. Ever. Punctuality is like a religion with me. But now I was on a train, heading the opposite direction. How would that look to the cops? I hadn't even called in to tell work I'd be late. As the train rumbled out of the tunnel, my bowels roiled like a cauldron.

I tried to calm myself. First thing: I had to go to the cops. I had to go to them and tell them what happened. I met her, we had sex, and I left. That's it. When I left, she was alive. The truth, that's all I could tell them.

We found your blood, they would say.

I fell out of bed, I'd say. She had a screaming fit in the middle of the night, and I fell out of bed and bumped my head.

And someone broke in after you left? Just happened to break in and kill Lynn Byers in the same bed? That's what you're trying to tell us?

They wouldn't believe me, but I didn't have anything else to tell them. They would find me. They would go to the bar, talk to the bartender, find out who she was talking to, check the debit card receipts. They could be at my house right now, but they'd see I wasn't there. They'd find out that I failed to show up for work today.

Next stop, I thought. At the next stop, you get off this train and get on one to take you to the cops. Get this thing settled.

I bought her another Stella and had one myself. The bartender went back to his limes.

"I've tried out for all kinds of things," she said. "TV shows, reality shows, plays, talent searches. Never got anywhere." She shrugged. "No talent."

"Well, I don't know anything about that stuff," I said, "but isn't rejection a part of the game?"

"Sure, and that's what I told myself. But you have to face facts sooner or later, right? You tell yourself, everyone who ever hit it big got the door slammed in her face at some point. Then you think, well, so did all the people who never made it."

"I guess that's true."

"Yet everyone is always telling you to follow your dreams."

"I guess."

"Thing is, most dreams never become reality. So okay, Kelly Clarkson had the dream of being a world famous pop star, and now she's a world famous pop star, but the other ten million people who tried out for American Idol *had exactly the same dream, and for them it was all just bullshit."*

I didn't know what to say to that. She was right, but I didn't want to let her wallow in it. If she got drunk and depressed, I'd be going home alone.

"Well," I said "most people can't sing well enough to be famous. No shame in that. You're probably good at other things."

She ignored me. "Think about the night sky. Seems full of stars, but most of the sky is just a big empty nothing. In fact, that's what makes a star shine so bright, all the nothing around it. There's only a few stars. Most of us are the nothing."

I glanced up at the bartender. He didn't look at me, but I could tell he was listening. I bet he heard a lot of sob stories.

I looked back at Lynn, and now she was staring at me.

She laughed.

"The hell with it," she said. "You want to get out of here?"

When the train stopped at Fort Totten, I slid off and sat down on an empty bench. It was good to sit down and breath in some fresh air. Rain tapped against the uncovered portion of the platform, and I sat there watching it, waiting for the next train.

A lot of people had exited the train with me and most of them went directly to the escalators.

It seemed like one guy didn't, though. People milled around on the platform—kids in Catholic school uniforms, men and women in business attire carrying satchels and briefcases, a guy in military fatigues—but something told me that one of the people who got off the train with me hadn't moved very far.

While I glanced around like I was looking at the trees and apartment buildings in the distance, I scanned the people on the platform. In a glance, though, there's nothing special about anyone.

After a minute, a train barreled up, opened its doors and released some passengers, and then all of us who were waiting got on. I glanced around to check out faces.

You're being paranoid, I thought. *No one is following you.*

No one unusual. No one familiar. Just people. An old man took out a hearing aid and messed with it. Two girls—one white, one black—held hands and shared the headphones on an iPod. Some people read the paper. Some people stared out the window. No one looked at me.

No one in our car.

But when I glanced at the back door, I saw that someone was watching me from the next car. He looked away when I saw him, but I'd seen his face for a good second or two.

The bartender.

I smiled. "Sure," I said. "Let's get out of here."

I waved the bartender over. He was short and blocky, with a smooth, bland face and prematurely gray hair.

I motioned at our glasses. "I need to settle up for both of us," I told him.

Lynn laughed. "Aw, you don't have to do that," she said, nudging me playfully.

My dick got hard.

"Easier this way," I said, nudging her back. "You can get the bill next time."

She said, "I'll tell you what: you know the liquor store down the street?"

"Sure."

"Well, I live next door."

"Really? Wait a second! The little green place with the big bathtub out front?"

She laughed. "Yep, the big bathtub full of flowers. Don't ask. It was there when I moved in."

"It's cute," I said. "I always wondered about the bathtub house."

She smiled and put her hand on my forearm, "Wanna see it up close? I can buy us a bottle on the way there."

"Sounds good," I said.

The bartender handed me the bill. He didn't say a word. As I dug out my wallet, he just looked at Lynn.

My thoughts bickered while I tried to figure out what the hell do to.

It couldn't be a coincidence. Couldn't be.

I glanced at the window again, but he'd moved away.

How long had he been following me?

Why?

The train slowed and came to a stop at New York Avenue and people got off. Others got on. I stayed where I was and watched the platform, but I didn't see him.

We pulled away from the station, and I switched seats to get a look at the next car from another vantage point.

He was there all right, wearing a non-descript brown coat and blue shirt. He stood by the door trying to blend in. His face was as smooth as a child's, but his hair was nearly completely gray. When he caught me looking at him, he flinched and moved to another seat. We stared at each other through the cars for a moment, but I was the only one who was frightened.

I opened the doors between cars walked in and sat down next to him. People glanced at us and then glanced away.

I said, "Why are you following me?"

"Here's what's gonna happen," he said under his breath. "Next stop, we're getting off. Just so we can talk."

I took a deep breath and something odd happened. I thought of Lynn. I thought of the way she'd screamed in her sleep. I would never know what her nightmares were about, and I would never want to know how horrible the waking nightmare had been when this man crept into her room and murdered her, but in that moment I felt an anger rising that dissipated the fear.

My hands steadied. They went dry. My entire body seemed to cool. I turned to him.

"Why her?" I asked.

He glanced around at the other people on the car. No one was paying us any attention.

"Why?" I said. "Why Lynn?"

The train began to slow, and he turned to me and jerked his head at the sliding doors. "Get up. Let's go talk about this somewhere."

"There was no reason, was there? You just wanted to hurt somebody. You saw her, and you wanted to hurt somebody, so you decided it would be her."

"I told you to get up."

"What'd you do, follow me home that night and then go back and kill her? If you were smart you'd just let the cops pin this on me, but you didn't think of that, did you? You're too much of a sick fucking psycho. You just wanted to hurt someone."

The train lurched to a stop.

He pulled a gun from under his coat long enough to show it to me then put it in his pocket. "Get up now," he whispered, "or I'll start shooting. I'll kill everybody on this train, starting with you."

I got up and he followed me to the doors. A crowd waited impatiently on the platform, and we had to push our way through them. He kept one hand on my back and one on his gun, but I spun around suddenly and grabbed his wrist and shoved it deeper into his pocket. I rammed my knee into his balls. "Gun!" I yelled. "He's got a gun!"

The place erupted. Everyone seemed to move at once. People around us heaved through the train doors trying to scramble inside as the people inside the train tried to rush out. Then the gun blasted a hole in his pocket and everything barreled into a roar that echoed down the darkened tunnel. As people stampeded us, I kept my hand on his wrist. Some guy grabbed him in a choke hold and then other people—men and women—piled on him. It was chilling to see a horde descend so quickly on one person. The sheer power of the group surged like an undercurrent dragging a hapless swimmer down. Blood pounded through my veins. I could feel the blood pounding in the crowd around me. I thought we might trample him to death.

Soon enough, though, the cops pushed their way through. Hands tightened around my arms and shoulders. Someone pulled me off of him.

Bloodied and nearly crushed, he was taken away on a stretcher once the EMT guys showed up. I was hauled in for questions, but when they found his gun, along with my address scribbled down on the back of my debit card bill, they pieced it all together. After a few hours, they took my statement and let me go home.

That night, I rode home on the Metro in a daze. People bustled around me, but nothing seemed quite solid or connected. When I got off the train, I staggered home like a drunk man.

Even though I was exhausted, it took a while for me to fall asleep. At three the next morning when I finally drifted off, I dreamed that Lynn was lying in bed next to me. I knew she would scream, that whatever had scared her would come back, and I wanted to tell her she'd be okay. I wanted to say that this time I wouldn't run away.

But I couldn't. I had no mouth, just a deep, thick scar where a gash had sealed shut. All I could do was lay next to her in the darkness. Her breathing grew erratic. I couldn't breathe at all. When she screamed, I jerked awake. †

LOST VALLEY OF THE SKOOCOOM
a "Maple Jack" tale

Matthew P. Mayo

This here story is as real as a case of hydrophoby. Happened years ago, back when I was a young man, on a hunt with my friend, Tilquata, a Chinook warrior. It's something so strange and drop-jaw unbelievable that if it were anybody telling it other than me, Maple Jack, you might have cause to doubt. Just the same, if you get to feelin' skeptical, I'll ask you kindly to get out of my cabin. But hand me that jug first.

The notion that something was wrong come to me early on our eighth day out, whilst I was hunched up behind a fire-leaf bush. I ate too much berry paste the day before and it went right through me like a spring freshet through a mountain gorge. Only not so pretty, I can assure you. I'd nearly passed out twice and was fixing to rejoin the land of the coherent when I looked up from finishing my business, and I see a pair of eyes, not ten feet away, watching me.

You know the look I'm talking of. It's the one a mountain lion settles on right before it decides to pounce. Or the wide-open stare a grizz will give a man just as it recalls that it was a man who shot her cubs.

I couldn't maintain that pose for too long, buckskins half-shucked and wavering as I was. So, slow as you please, I slid them trousers back up to where they belonged and did my best to stand. And do you know, that whole time them eyes stayed on me, peeking through the wagging green leaves. Dark like black river rocks, those eyes were, and if they blinked, I didn't see it.

I wanted to shout to Tilquata. He was upwind from me—smart man—back at the campsite, but I didn't dare do anything more than creep backward toward camp, moving like I was riddled with rheumatism. Still, them eyes stayed on me. Like a fool, I was armed with nothing more than my skinning knife. I'd rather have had my revolver. You got to kill a thing before you can skin it, and most often, killing a thing's a whole lot easier with a gun than a knife—and not so close-up.

I'd backed a good six feet when that thing in the bushes shifted, grew taller, and I realized it had been crouching down. Up and up it stood, right out of the saplings and brush. And by the time it stopped, danged if I wasn't looking at a fully haired man, brownish and shaggy, half again as tall as me and wider at the shoulder than a rifle is long. There was something else, too—a godawful stink had dropped on me like a wool blanket dipped in a gut pile. I realized then that it wasn't me, but the creature that smelled so bad.

I spun, reaching out to run, and grabbed me a handful of hair. Slammed straight into a solid, muscled wall of it, in fact. I backed up, frantic, thinking that Old Ephraim was finally on me, and that I was about to end my days as a grizzly mauled carcass.

Pushing away from that mass of hair, the first thing I noticed was the stink, worse than before—a godawful rankness that was equal parts boiled dog and festering canker, with a goodly amount of sour sweat poured over the top of it. A face stared down at me, more confused than angry, looking like nothing I'd ever seen before—more man than grizzly and more grizzly than man is the only way I can describe it. And if it was possible, this hairy man was bigger than the first.

Now I'm not a small man, and I will admit to a gut I have acquired in my dotage. But back then, when I was green, I fancy I was lean and a bit taller than your average trapper. But this big brute was easy near twice my height. It stared at me, all haired up in that full-body beard. It had yellow teeth as long as my small finger, and some of them were pointed, like a wolf's, but that's where that similarity ended. This thing breathed down on me, and a growl like a low, deep moan squeezed out with its rank breath.

I nearly fell to my knees, so weak had this experience made me. Then I heard branches snapping and knew the first one was coming up behind me—I was caught between two of the creatures! The sound behind me was not the alternating crushing gallop of a bull grizzly, but the two-legged run of a man, and drawing closer with each stride.

I turned my head in time to see that creature plow right into me, and my bean hit the ground hard on what must have been a rock. When I came to, I was fuzzy headed and couldn't seem to make my legs or arms do what I told them to. That brute had pinned me, and was closer than most men get to their wives' faces each day. It panted, pushing hot gouts of fetid breath deep into my mouth and nose, its tongue a quivering, slick pink thing cupped just behind those curved yellow teeth. A thick sound worked upward from deep within the beast's gut, and I knew I was about to be its next meal.

But then it just sniffed at me. Now, I've never been accused of smelling like a flower, but this thing seemed mighty interested in what I smelled like—my hair, beard, ears, the works.

The big one stood looking down at me, squinting like it was trying to remember something important. Then its eyes widened and bulged a bit. I saw it stagger and I thought as sure as the day is long that it was going to drop on top of me, too. That's when I saw bare arms close around its neck and I knew Tilquata had come to my rescue.

That big creature turned on my friend, raging full bore, and grabbed at the Indian swinging on his back. As they spun, I saw Tilquata's short axe, half the head driven between the beast's shoulders, red blood steaming in the chill morning air. Tilquata dropped off and scampered a few feet away, taunting and luring the wounded creature. But that creature wasn't done, not by a long shot. It bellowed and ran straight into my warrior friend, knocking him down.

Now I'd known Tilquata for years, and let me tell you, he was as muscled a man as you'll find. Like most of the men of his tribe, he was lean and hard as wood and not accustomed to backing down from a scuffle, nor afraid to start one. But in this instance, I feared Tilquata had met his match.

The beast continued to bellow in a roar equal parts bull-grizz and raw, crazy-man howl. It picked up Tilquata with his two giant hands and whomped him all over that little clearing, flinging him in the air, into trees, against the earth.

Within seconds the brave was a crushed, broken man, with bones poking through one arm's skin like shiny decorations. One of his legs was bent wrong, and dark purple welts covered his arms, neck, and bread basket where the thing had grabbed him. Even his buckskins had been ripped away like paper off a parcel.

As I watched that thing batter Tilquata around the camp, overpowering him in every way, and me nearly useless to help him, addle-pated and lolling as I was like a little girl's dolly, I realized that the stories were true—the Skoocooms lived.

Folks of Tilquata's tribe had mentioned the creature at night, at times when the fire was low and tobacco had been enjoyed. Then they would say that one word—skoocoom. And as I watched that thing lean low over Tilquata's nearly still body, I recalled what little the Chinook had said about skoocooms.

Called 'em angry spirits who were neither man nor beast, said they walked upright on two legs and had toes and fingers instead of claws. At the time I remember thinking that Indians were just like whites—always looking for reasons behind things rather than just taking things as they are. But seeing that thing savage my friend, I knew that at least part of the story had been true—this was neither man nor beast. And it was damn angry.

My friend landed hard on the ground less than ten feet away from me, his head bouncing on a spongy matte of pine needles. High on his shaved forehead, I saw the white glisten of bone beneath where the skin had peeled away when he'd been smacked against the rough bark of the pine, and blood pumped from a raw crater beside his eye. Then I saw Tilquata smile at me. I kid you not, even as the light of life dulled in his eyes, he smiled.

The skoocoom bent low, grunting and chuffing, and grabbed Tilquata by the shoulder. As his near-limp body flipped over, the warrior's long, fine-steel skinning knife flashed upward and found purchase to the hilt in the beast's gut. It howled a ragged cry that shook the very trees around us, and I knew then why Tilquata had smiled. Gouts of hot, steaming blood pulsed outward, dousing my friend, and still he smiled. though by then Tilquata was dead.

And there I was, so useless from that knock cn the bean that I could do nothing for the man, my best friend, but watch as he died. I couldn't even figure out how to raise a limb. Oh, I tried, and I must have raised some sort of noise, for that creature that had been sniffing at me, turned his attention back to me. His dark eyes widened and he commenced to whomp on me like you might on a friend, just to show how strappy you were.

It had all happened so fast that I was confused, and guessed I was near death myself. I watched that murderous haired brute lurch about the clearing, spraying his blood all over our strewn gear, the smoking remains of the campfire, the rabbits we'd intended for supper.

For a moment, as his big, blood-slick hands wrestled with that knife, which must have been wedged hard in bone, that skoocoom's eyes settled on me. His nose worked hard at the cool morning air, blood threading out of his open mouth, and we looked at each other, eye-to-eye, man-to-man. I tell you what, that massive beast looked as scared as any creature that knew it was breathing its last. Despite what he did to me, to my friend, I felt true sadness for that skoocoom.

His eyes bore no anger, no vengeance like you'll often see on a dying man. Just sadness and maybe a little confusion. He dropped to his knees, then I saw the other, smaller skoocoom grab him by the shoulders. They yammered in grunts and barking noises I couldn't make out, then that big one wobbled, and the smaller one eased him down on his side. The last thing I heard was a groaning, sobbing sound. Then I, too, faded. Never suspecting I'd wake up again. But I did.

Something like a fist rapped me hard enough on the head to revive me. I forced an eye open. It was a tree trunk and my head had rapped against it. And then another one. God almighty, didn't that throb. It took me a few minutes before I remembered what had happened to me, to Tilquata. And then a few more until I came around to the possibility that I wasn't dead. And if I wasn't dead, I reasoned, then where was I?

The landscape kept changing, rising and falling. At some point, while my world swirled like water eddying in a mountain stream, I realized I was being carried. There was some sort of stink, and hair, lots of hair. I don't know how long it went on, I was that addled. Then I was dropped. Hard. I moaned, I know because I heard it. And whoever carried me heard it too.

The smell seemed worse than ever and I worked hard to open my eyes. They fluttered and finally cracked. Dabs of dark and light worked through what must have been crusted blood on my eyes. I squeezed them shut and opened them wider. The dark bits took shape, like when you twist a field scope, until I saw what must have been a dozen skoocoom faces staring at me. I closed my eyes again and wished to god I'd died back at the campsite with Tilquata.

Her touch surprised me with its gentleness. I never expected those massive, callused hands could convey such kindness. In truth, she didn't seem to know much doctoring, but she did apply a poultice of sorts to my chest, made of leaves and mosses and something that smelled an awful lot like camphorated dung. The entire matted affair was wetted down, though I hate to say by what, and I was forced to lay there naked under that dripping mess. At some point, those beasts had stripped me of my buckskins.

All of them, too, were naked, but they had the advantage of being covered in hair. I may be a bit of a hairy man, but I ain't no skoocoom. They must have seen I was hairy enough, though, what with my beard and chest and whatnots, and that the buckskins weren't attached to my own hide. I guess that must have shocked them to see that they could peel off my skin and I'd still be alive, all them days and weeks later. I kept trying to gander about the cave, see where it was they kept my clothes and possibles bag and such. But it was no use. They'd probably tossed it away or eaten it, for all I know.

So I was sprawled right out there in the middle of a cave, them skoocooms gawping at me all hours of the day and night. It was a family of them. Girls and boys and fathers and mothers. Old ones, too—I could tell 'cause they were slow and frail looking, and a bit gray around the edges.

The little ones would come over and point at me and poke me. If I could have moved anything more than my mouth, I would have showed 'em where the bear went through the buckwheat. But I was crippled up and still addled in my head. And my voice seemed to have no effect on them. At first they'd stare when I spoke, then they ignored my yammering. That same she-skoocoom wouldn't hardly ever leave my side, and I'd usually wake up with her drizzling water into my mouth from handfuls of wet leaves and pine needles.

For all their stink and grunts and odd noises, they were not much different than any human family you'd find. Seemed like half the time the males and the females argued, waving their arms, hitting at each other, jabbering and pushing. And the young were the same as human children, playing and what sounded like singing and bothering the old ones and getting hit for it. They cried, too, and sounded just like people.

I tell you what, you want to learn all about something, you just lay back and look and listen and keep your yap shut, and you'll do some learning, by god. I know what I'm saying. I lay there for what must have been a couple of weeks. Early on, the cave, a damp, cool place of rock and earth, would start to move and get fuzzy on me and I'd pass out for a spell. As time wore on, though, such episodes grew less frequent.

After a few weeks, she started feeding me wriggling grubs and the soft bits of pine cones and roots that tasted as awful as a handful of sand. Then one day, I felt a throbbing in my hands. Pretty soon, I felt like I fell onto a giant mound crawling with them angry red ants, like I was on fire and being chewed alive at the same time.

I kept from whimpering for as long as I could, but soon there wasn't nothing for it and I howled and screamed like a birthing woman. As I did, I saw my own hands come slapping up at me and claw at my face, my chest. I whipped off them rank poultices and soon I was up on my knees and wobbling in circles, barking and drooling and screaming to get the fire off of me. The entire time this was happening, that skoocoom family made its own noises, pointing and covering their mouths and generally keeping clear of me.

For all that bother, the feeling only lasted a day or so, then I come out of it all right, I reckon.

Well, sir, I saw seasons come and go, and I reckon what few friends I had must have long since given Tilquata and me up for dead. I had pretty much given up on ever seeing a human again. But do you know, if you live with something long enough, after a while you sort of get used to it. That's the way it was with me and the skoocooms. I guess I even sort of got used to the smell, though in truth I did breathe a lot through my mouth.

My time with them gave me plenty of opportunity to think about things. Like, for instance, why that young male skoocoom dragged me home I'll never know. Nor will I know if he was the son of the big one who got ambushed by Tilquata. I am convinced that they were just curious and wanted to sniff us, inspect us a bit. But I reckon Tilquata figured they were fixing to eat me, so he had attacked. And that was a most valiant thing for him to do. One of the kindest things anyone ever did for me, in fact.

But that young skoocoom, I saw him now and again. He was one of the males who always seemed to keep an eye on me when I was well enough to wander on my own outside. They never tried to get me to help gather food—they ate everything but meat, which I found odd. I had reckoned that those creatures would need piles of meat to keep their bodies that big. They did eat with gusto, but it was all day long, and lots of everything, from moss and bark to grass and leaves, nuts, roots. And in berry season of late summer, they looked to be in heaven. All big-bellied and smeared with paste. Yessir, I survived in decent order.

What I did miss, though, was my clothes and a warm fire. And as the seasons grew colder, it was that lack of fire that changed my life forever. One night in late fall, it was colder than a gravedigger's backside. Them skoocooms, being covered in thick hair, were sprawled out all over the cave, flopped and snoring like full dogs. But that chill air was making me tremble as if gripped with the ague.

I huddled up as best I could, but I had nothing to cover myself with. Every time I'd tried to gather up strips of bark or pine boughs for just such a purpose, they'd up and eat them on me. I reckon they figured it was like I was hoarding a feast, when all I was looking for was a bit of warmth.

This one night, the she-skoocoom saw me shivering up a storm. She eased over to me and gathered me up in them big long arms and hugged me close like she was happy to see me, as if I'd been gone away a long time. Well sir, she warmed me up. That's all I'm saying on the matter. But there were an awful lot of cold nights that came and went, and I doubt I would have survived had she not taken pity on this poorly haired fellow.

❖

One day in early spring, I wasn't watched that closely by the young male who'd saved me in the first place. More to the point, I reckon, now that I've had years to think back on it, he might have been sweet on the she-skoocoom who'd been keeping me warm all winter. Whatever the reason, I found myself unguarded and in solid health. It was early in the day and the melt was on, so I kept wandering, heading east, looking back over my shoulder every so often to see if I was being trailed.

I'd been kept a near-recluse for the better part of a year in or near that cave, and yet when I was away from it, I admit I missed it a bit. But I kept walking. I walked for days with little rest, just long enough for a smidge of shut eye, and then I was up and at it again. Come to find out, I'd been in a little valley, hidden and protected by happenstance, so as to look like nothing more than an impossible tangle of trees and rock.

Once I had climbed up and out of it, which took me most of a morning, I looked back and couldn't tell just where it was, so thick were the trees and so oddly angled were the boulders. I gave a grunt and a wave and turned my back on that little valley forever.

❖

I knew I'd never see that big, hairy girl again. But I like to think that somewheres out there, running around in that strange little lost valley, is a creature I'm proud to call my own. I hope it's a boy, gone on to raise sons of his own, but mostly I hope it's happy. Happier than I've been since then. For what I thought I was looking for, what I left the valley for, is something I never found in all these years.

Don't look so shocked. There's love and there's other types of love and there's affection and there's survival and there's instinct. I reckon what I had with that she-skoocoom was a knotted up tangle of all them things. Just don't you judge me, lest you want me to judge you, too. I know what people get up to. I know. And no, I ain't trying to change the topic, neither.

If I thought I could make the journey, I'd lay in a request right now and have someone help me get back there. But even if I was up to it, I don't know where that valley is or how to get there. I tried, oh how I tried. I spent what amounts to years of my life going back to where I thought it was. But I never could find it. Not to say that it was some magical place or something I only imagined, because it wasn't.

Why, even today I'll be off in the woods alone and I'll get a whiff of something rank. I'll sit there for a longish spell, until my horse decides he's had enough. I'll have been thinking back on the sweetness of memory. Something that I doubt you're believing, even though, I'm here to tell you, Maple Jack ain't never told a lie in his life.

Now fetch me my jug before I have cause to jump up from this bed and take a round or two out of you for being an insolent pup. †

SHADOW OF THE CROW
Larry D. Sweazy

June 11, 1933

The glass exploded out of the back window of the Chevrolet sedan like somebody had thrown a brick from the inside out. Once he saw the muzzle flash, it only took Lyle "Sonny" Wolfe half a second to realize that someone had taken a shot at him.

There was no question who was doing the shooting. It was the Barrow Gang, Bonnie and Clyde themselves, just out of the Ritz Theater in Wellington, Texas, for a night of entertainment. It was hard telling what was next with these two. Less than a year before, back in August, Clyde had killed a deputy in Stringtown, Oklahoma, launching a killing spree that had captured the nation's attention, and made the pair as famous as the dead actor, Rudolph Valentino.

Sonny was alone, coming off duty in the small panhandle town that had been his home for nearly as long as he could remember. He was surprised at his luck, recognizing the two of them, walking arm-in-arm to their car, like they didn't have a care in the world, like nobody would know, or care, who they were. Their picture was plastered across the front of the newspaper every other day. Or maybe they just didn't give a rat's ass, maybe they were laying in wait for another shoot-out, another opportunity to have their names slipping off the tongues of every man, woman, and child in Texas, and beyond.

It didn't take Bonnie and Clyde long to figure out that they were being followed by a Texas Ranger—the cinco badge emblem and announcement that it was a Ranger's car, was plastered across the side of the black 1932 Ford in hard-to-miss six-inch white letters.

Thankfully, they had made their way out of town before the discovery occurred to them, off on a nearly deserted dirt road, when the shooting started.

With no way to communicate with anyone back at the company headquarters about his lucky find, Sonny was on his own to bring the pair of lawless gangsters in for justice—if that was possible.

The shot from Bonnie's weapon had pierced the windshield, shattering the glass in the pattern of a bull's-eye just before it exploded inward in a million little pieces.

It was a near miss. The bullet whizzed by Sonny's right ear just a couple of inches away from its intended target—his forehead. Luckily, he had tilted his head in the right direction. The wrong way would have put him directly in line with the shot, and it would have been lights out. Another notch on Bonnie and Clyde's belt. A Texas Ranger added to their growing collection of law enforcement kills.

It was a sobering thought, dying this close to the end of his career, the days ticking off until he no longer wore the badge. The word for retirement didn't exist for him, it was just time to quit—he was getting too old, and the world was changing too fast. Sonny wasn't sure what the future held for him, but up until a few minutes prior, he wasn't too concerned about living to a satisfactory old age. He just wanted to finish what he had started; being a proud Texas Ranger, and alive, to boot.

The shattering windshield sounded like a bomb had gone off directly next to Sonny's ears.

He was pelted with stinging shards of the broken glass, and it felt like he'd fallen face first into a hornet's nest. But that didn't stop him. His fingers tingled as he gripped the steering wheel. The skin above his chest felt like it was going to rip open; his heart was racing a mile a minute. He could feel blood trickling down from his brow, but his eyes were safe, not hit, not blinding him—he could still see the Chevrolet swerving in front of him, trying to get away, or to get a better shot at him, one or the other, he wasn't sure.

Nothing short of death would stop Sonny now. He could see no better way to wrap up his last days as a Ranger than bringing in Bonnie and Clyde, effectively cutting the head off the snake of the Barrow Gang. That would be a fine capper. If he could have smiled at that thought, he would have.

The older model Chevrolet that Clyde Barrow was driving was no match for Sonny's newer Ford. The '32 Model B had a flathead V-8 engine, and was fast off the start with 65 horsepower under the hood, an amazing thought, considering Sonny had been born long before the advent of automobiles. Back then, all of the Texas Rangers, including his own father, had ridden horses across the state of Texas, pursuing the worst of the worst outlaws, like King Fisher and John Wesley Hardin. As a boy, Sonny would've been incapable of imagining so much power in one vehicle. Times had changed—all too quickly, as far as Sonny was concerned.

He pushed the accelerator to the floor and rolled down the window. His gun was loaded, and in hand almost magically, like a magnet had drawn it to his fingers. He aimed the Colt .45 Government Model Automatic Pistol with confidence, and lack of fear, at the busted out window of the Chevrolet, and returned fire.

Barrow swerved the car again, fish-tailing it on the gravel road, spraying the hood of Sonny's car with hundreds of pebbles; little pings and thuds that sounded like gunshots finding their target, but posed no real threat.

Bonnie Parker poked the rifle out of the rear window and fired again. Her blonde hair flowed behind her, and her angelic face was twisted with demonic focus as she struggled to find her aim. Sonny had seen her face plenty of times on wanted posters and in the newspaper, but seeing her live and in person, with the intent to kill him, was an experience he never thought he would have.

A hot, orange flash exploded from the end of the barrel of Bonnie's gun, and did not stop at one. Bonnie wasn't shooting a riot gun or a deer rifle. She meant business this time around. She was shooting a Browning Automatic Rifle, a fierce weapon that could empty a twenty-shot magazine in three seconds.

The noise was excruciating, metal piercing metal, ripping into the fenders, then shattering what remained of the windshield. Sonny could hardly take a breath or gather his wits about him. He wasn't ready to die.

The radiator exploded, sending a geyser of steam spraying upward to the heavens, clouding Sonny's vision. Bullets whizzed by his ears, as he pulled the trigger of his .45, not stopping until every bullet had been fired.

He thought for certain he heard a tire explode, thought he saw a sign to his left warning that the road ahead was closed, under construction, that the bridge was out, but thoughts no longer mattered. He had been hit.

A bullet ripped into his shoulder, sending white hot pain screaming though his body; blood popped out of the wound like a dam had been breached, an artery severed. Bonnie had hit her target.

Another bullet hit him, not far from the other, and Lyle "Sonny" Wolfe screamed with pain, frustration, and fear. Reality left him, and his fingers slipped from the wheel, sending the '32 Ford careening into a ditch. He felt like he had been hit twice by the largest, heaviest, hardest sledge hammer anyone could ever imagine.

The last image Sonny saw before the car rolled and he blacked out was Bonnie Parker laughing like a maniacal child who had just watched the funniest movie she had ever seen at the Ritz Theater.

❖

Bonnie Parker climbed into the front seat, grabbed Clyde Barrow around the neck, and kissed him hard on the cheek. She was unscathed. Blood raced through her veins, and she felt invincible, more than human. The bullets had passed by her like she was protected by some imaginary shield.

Barrow, a thin, dark-haired man who looked much more handsome in the newspapers than in person, laughed, then pushed Bonnie off of him. "Did you get him?" The Ranger's bullets had missed Clyde, too, but he was sweating and his face was pale, the joy of the encounter lost on him, unlike Bonnie. Gunfire turned her on. She'd be purring, wanting, demanding ... when all Clyde was interested in, at the moment, was escaping, making it back to Oklahoma unscathed and alive.

Bonnie shrugged, feigned a pout at Clyde's rejection, and ran her hands through her hair as she settled into the passenger seat. "I did. I think I really did, Clyde." She laughed, but suddenly grew serious, the joy and high of the shoot-out vanishing quickly from her face. "Clyde!" she screamed, pointing straight ahead.

There was no bridge over the river. It had washed out, and was being rebuilt. Clyde was driving as fast as he could to get as far away from the Texas Ranger as possible. He jerked the steering wheel and slammed on the brakes.

The Chevrolet slid sideways. Clyde had his foot pressed down on the brake as hard as he could, as far as the pedal would go, but he lost control of the car anyway. The rear-end clipped a spindly locust tree just big enough to bounce the car across the road, sending it careening down a deep ravine.

They hit an oak as big around as a beer barrel, head-on. The impact stopped the car dead in its tracks, but not hard enough to seriously injure either one of them as they bounced forward and back. Clipping the locust had slowed them down just enough from slamming too hard into the tree.

But the impact *was* hard enough to send the battery flying upward, busting opening the hood, spiraling through the air, through the windshield, and landing directly on Bonnie Parker's thigh.

The pain was too much to bear as the boulder-like battery toppled over, spilling acid on Bonnie Parker's leg, gobbling at her flesh like a hungry bear after a paw full of honey.

Bonnie's screams echoed across the river and into the air, but no one heard her. No one but Clyde, and he didn't know how to help her.

❖

June 14, 1933

The volume of the radio was turned down low, the voices distant but decipherable. "The Nazi Party was made Germany's only legal political party today. Any political opposition is punishable by law ...." the announcer said in a droning voice.

Sonny reached over with his left arm, and was about to turn the radio off when he heard the announcer go on to say, "And in local news, the manhunt for Clyde Barrow and Bonnie Parker continues after their car was found wrecked and abandoned just outside of Wellington. They are to be considered armed and dangerous. If you see the duo, or know anything of their whereabouts, contact your local police or the Texas Rangers. Bonnie Parker is reported to be injured."

Sonny took a deep breath as he struggled to turn the radio off. His right arm was bound and unmovable, and he had always been right-handed. Any coordination and strength that he had in his left hand was lacking, to say the least. He really wasn't supposed to move, but he didn't want to hear any more news, even though he was reasonably interested in hearing about Bonnie and Clyde, and what had happened to them after he had been shot. It was the first time he'd heard they'd wrecked. The idea that he had something to do with that settled easy on his shoulders, but it didn't make the pain, or lack of use of his arm, go away. All he really wanted was silence, at the moment, and nothing more.

He eased down onto the hospital bed, and stared out of the third-floor window.

Summer had set in with a vengeance.

The windows were cracked, but there didn't look to be a breeze outside. Every tree he could see was still as a statue, their leaves droopy. The sky was perfect and clear, the color of a roan mare he used to know, and the sun was a red hot plate, beating down relentlessly on the earth, scorching everything in sight; the grass had already given up all of its green, and browned out. The landscape out the window was desolate, hopeless, but familiar. Hot, uncomfortable summers were just part of the deal when you lived in Texas.

The door to the hospital room was cracked open, and a murmur of low voices found its way to Sonny's ears. He couldn't make out the words. It was like a small group was consulting three or four doors down, all whispering in soft, professional tones.

He closed his eyes, and hoped for sleep to come and take him away from the reality he'd woken up to, but that wasn't to be.

The door pushed open slowly, along with Sonny's eyes at the noise. A very old Mexican man, hair as white as cotton balls, skin as brown and leathery as a hundred-year-old holster, pushed a mop and bucket into the room, trying to be as quiet as possible. He was unsuccessful in the attempt. The wheels on the mop bucket squeaked like fingers slowly scraping down a chalkboard.

The man wore a blue short-sleeved work shirt with a pack of Chesterfields poking out of the pocket. He had the largest collection of keys dangling from his belt that Sonny had ever seen.

It was tempting for Sonny to close his eyes again, and let the man do his job, but he couldn't keep himself from acknowledging the janitor's presence. "*Hola,*" he said, his voice weak, but steady, as he stared directly at the man. The patch on the Mexican's work shirt said his name was Frank, but Sonny doubted that was really the case.

Sonny had startled the old man. His shoulders jumped, then he looked up, glancing over at Sonny sheepishly, then back to the floor, as he pulled the mop out of the water. "*Hola,*" he answered. "*Hablas Español?*"

Sonny nodded, and tried to pull himself up. "Yes, I learned to speak Spanish a long time ago," he said, speaking fully in the Mexican's language.

The janitor smiled, relaxed a bit, then pulled up the mop, and let it drain through the ringer. "You speak very well."

"I was raised by a Mexican woman."

"Really?"

"Yes. She was with me every day until I grew up, and left home."

"What happened to your momma?"

"She died when I was born," Sonny said, looking away from the man, out the window. "What's your name?" he finally asked, pushing away his childhood the best he could.

Sonny was sixty-two years old, and should have been long past the sadness of losing his mother and nanny, if the woman who raised him could be called that, but Sonny thought about Ofelia Martinez every day. She taught him everything he knew about being a decent, Anglo man living in Texas.

"My name is Franco," the Mexican said.

Sonny smiled. He knew it wasn't Frank.

"And what is your name, *señor*?"

"Lyle. Lyle Wolfe. But everybody calls me Sonny. They have ever since I was four or five."

Franco returned the smile. "You are that Ranger that was shot by Bonnie and Clyde, aren't you? You are lucky you are not dead, *señor*."

"Yes, I know."

"Your arm, will it get better?"

Sonny shook his head no. "I'll be lucky to feel anything, or be able to use my hand ever again."

"Then you are done working. It is all over for you?"

"Seems that way. Times are tough all over. Another man can take my job. I've had my life, and it's been pretty good up until now."

"Yes, yes, times are very bad. This Depression seems like it will go on forever. I, too, am happy to have a job. I have hungry mouths at home who depend on me, even at my age. What about you, do you have children?"

Sonny nodded yes. "A son. He's a Ranger, too, down in Brownsville. He's married with a couple of little ones of his own." A smile crossed Sonny's face, then quickly flittered away. He hardly ever saw his grandchildren. The distance between them was too far to encourage a closeness, and that seemed just fine with his son, Jess. They never seemed to see eye to eye on anything. It had always been that way, and Sonny didn't expect it to change now.

"You are lucky then. You will have someone to help you when you go home."

Lyle didn't answer, he looked away, and stared up at the ceiling. There was no use telling Franco that he'd be all alone when he left the hospital. The house was empty, a collection of dusty furniture, and a clock that ticked to no one. Martha, his wife, had been dead for ten years, struck down in a single, unforeseen blow, by a massive heart attack. The emptiness was his sadness to bear, and no one else's.

Franco didn't broach the silence. He let it hang in the air knowingly.

Like his father, Sonny had always been tall and rangy, and he could only imagine how he must look to the Mexican; skeletal, gaunt, each breath a rattle on death's short chain. He closed his eyes then, the strength not in him to push away the memories of the past. Ofelia, Martha, Jess, the good times, and the bad.

When he opened his eyes again, it was dark in the room, and chilly. It was like he had been abandoned in a tomb, and Franco was gone, as if he had never existed at all.

August 12, 1933

Bonnie and Clyde's Chevrolet was sitting inside a barn. Three bullet holes had pierced the rear fender, and both of the tires on the driver's side were flat. Straw and dust covered the roof of the car, and a red tabby cat lay sleeping in the back seat, the coils poking up through the brown velvet material that was slowly being carted away, one mouthful at a time, by a herd of opportunistic mice ... when the cat was away, of course.

Sonny stood back staring at the car, afternoon light filtering in through the barn walls, and the August heat stifling and humid made him sweat just at the thought of walking the rest of the way inside.

"Been chargin' a nickel a peek," Carl Halstaad said, a dairy farmer the size of a bull himself, as he chawed a big wad of Red Man tobacco in his right cheek. "But I 'spect I won't charge you a penny since you're the man who put them bullet holes there."

"I appreciate that, Mr. Halstaad."

"Carl. You can call me, Carl, Ranger Wolfe." He spit a long stream of brown liquid from his mouth, splashing a good two feet from Sonny's boots.

Sonny nodded. "My Ranger days are behind me now."

"Ah, heck. I can see you got a bad limb, there, but once a Ranger, always a Ranger, right?"

"Well, yes, I suppose so." The doctors had wanted to amputate the arm. They feared gangrene would set in, but so far it hadn't. It just hung there useless and numb, an annoying reminder of the times when he felt whole, and young. Most days he kept busy, didn't allow himself to feel sorry for the loss, or grow too angry. He just regretted not being a better shot. Killing Bonnie before she pulled the Browning on him.

He walked up slowly to the driver's door, and peered inside the window. The windshield was shattered, and the battery lay on the floor in front of the passenger's seat.

"People say Bonnie's got a limp now," Halstaad said. "The acid burned her bad, but maybe not bad enough."

"Maybe not," Sonny said.

"Some folks up in Dexter, Iowa, seen them at an amusement park a couple weeks back. Bonnie was bandaged up pretty good. They was surrounded, but somehow they managed to get away again. Must be magicians, or blessed with dark skills. The one they called Buck died after surgery for a gunshot wound. And they just left him, ran from him like thieves in the night. There are no true friends to those two."

"What are you going to do with it?" Sonny asked, pulling himself from the window, ignoring the news about the Barrow gang's whereabouts. The inside of the car smelled like cat urine, pungent and sour, mixed acid and dried blood. His stomach lurched.

"The car?" Halstaad asked.

Sonny nodded.

"I suppose I'll just hang onto it, keep gettin' my nickels from it for as long as I can. Why? You want to buy it?"

"No, I've seen all I need to." Sonny turned and pushed past Halstaad. He knew about the Dexter, Iowa, incident. He followed Bonnie and Clyde's every move on the radio and in the newspapers. He'd been practicing shooting left-handed, just in case another chance at them ever came his way.

❖

May 23, 1934

Clyde Barrow had given up on Chevrolets, and now preferred Fords, particularly '32s with V-8 engines. A quick getaway meant the difference between life and death. There would be no prison for him. The Feds wanted him dead. Wanted retribution. Revenge. Bargaining was out of the question now. Now that he'd pulled the trigger and killed nine lawmen. Every breath could be his last. Nobody knew that better than Clyde.

Dawn was just beginning to break over the horizon, and the world was silent, still asleep. The first robin had yet to chirp, and the stars pulsed like little drops of mercury clinging to the solid black sky.

Clyde pulled back from peering out the window, took a long, last draw off a cigarette, and stubbed it out as quietly as he could.

Bonnie lay on the bed, nothing on but a pure white satin slip, and a lace Kestos bra. She looked blissful, like an angel sleeping on a cloud, instead of a wanted killer holed up in a dingy motel room with a bum leg.

Clyde bristled at the thought of Bonnie as a killer. Truth was, she could hardly hurt a fly. The picture of her with a machine gun and a cigar had been for laughs, but the world, and newspapers, took it seriously, made a legend of her meanness when none existed. As far as he could remember, Bonnie had only fired a gun three times, and that had been to save their ass every time.

He hated to wake her. The road had been long, and she was getting jumpy, tense. Bonnie knew their bargaining days were over, too. They'd talked about it, come to terms with it, but both of them were only twenty-three. The doomed road ahead was certain.

They joked about getting old together, about having kids that would turn out to be better outlaws than them, but they both knew that it was all a joke, a dream, a sad longing that was never to be for either of them. Fate had conspired long before they ever met as to how things would end. That's just the way it was for the likes of them.

Clyde slid into the bed, and hugged Bonnie, pulled her close, breathed in her sweet smell. He had his pants on, an undershirt, and no shoes. He'd already shaved. He was ready to go, but he couldn't restrain himself at the sight of her. He nibbled at her neck.

"Hey, baby, wake up. We need to get across the state line before daylight." One of Clyde's survival techniques had been to ride the state line wherever he went, crossing over at will, dashing out of jurisdiction at the last second, leaving his pursuers with no law to hang onto.

Bonnie stirred, stretched her arms, then flittered open her eyes, and smiled. "I was havin' a real nice dream, Clyde."

"That's good, baby." He propped himself up on his elbow. "Was I in it?"

"Always." She reached up and kissed him softly, then pulled away. "What's wrong?"

"Nothing."

"You're lyin'."

"Just got a bad feeling, that's all."

"You've had those before." There was concern in Bonnie's voice, like she didn't believe what she was saying.

"You're right."

Clyde kissed Bonnie again, deeply, more passionately, the thought of restraining himself, and getting across the state line before daylight, vanishing quickly in a wash of desire and need that he couldn't, and didn't, want to control. Their hands became a tangle of knowledgeable moves, each one to the delight of the other, and they made love with the same force and enthusiasm as the day they had met.

The Ford was loaded down with two sawed-off shotguns, two machine guns, ten automatic pistols, and fifteen-hundred rounds of ammunition. The sun was slowly rising into the perfect blue sky, and the fragrant smell of spring was in the air as Bonnie and Clyde crossed over into Louisiana. They were ready for anything that came their way.

It was a quiet road, little traffic. It was a little after nine o'clock in the morning, and Clyde was in a hurry, trying to outrun the bad feeling he'd had hours before. Bonnie sat next to him, and he rubbed her bad leg nervously.

"Once we get to Methvin's house, we need to lay low," Clyde said. "Take some time off the road. Have a real life for a month or two, give the newspapers something else to yak about. We'll sleep till noon and eat fried chicken for breakfast if we want. That sound good, baby?"

"Sounds dreamy to me," Bonnie whispered, snuggling up to Clyde as close as she could.

The road lay out flat in front of them, plain and open, trees and shrubs thick on both sides.

At first Bonnie thought she heard a thunder clap, but the sky was clear. It only took a breath, a second, to realize that it had been a gunshot she'd heard.

The driver's side window shattered, and the bullet smacked Clyde's head so hard it nearly tore it clean off. He didn't even have time to scream, to yell out in pain. The shot killed him instantly. Blood splattered everywhere, raining down on Bonnie as the Ford rocketed toward a ditch.

Bonnie did have time to scream, time to try to reach for a gun, but that's all the time she had.

They had been ambushed, and a storm of steel-piercing bullets exploded into the Ford relentlessly. Before it was all said and done, Bonnie and Clyde's bodies were so riddled with holes that the mortician couldn't even fill them with embalming fluid.

❖

May 29, 1934

Sonny watched a car come up the road, leaving a trail of dust behind it a mile long. It was a fine spring day, and he had been sitting on the front porch, relaxing, drinking a cup of coffee, and reading the newspaper.

He stood up when he recognized the car, surprised, since he wasn't expecting a visit.

The car, a year old Plymouth, was covered with dust, and belonged to Sonny's only son, Jess. He came to a quick stop a few feet from the house.

"What're you doing up this way?" Sonny said, ambling down the steps, steadying himself the best he could. His balance was never going to be the same since they'd cut off his arm. Gangrene *had* set in, like the doctors feared. He was glad to be without the pain—except sometimes in the night, the pain was still there, like his arm was attached and nothing had ever happened to it. He woke up screaming then, but there was no one there to hear him.

"Come to see how you're gettin' along, that's all, Pa," Jess said. He was alone, dressed for work, wearing a white Stetson and the Texas Ranger cinco badge.

"You expect me to believe that?"

Jess stuck out his right hand for a shake, and Sonny stared at it, then offered his left hand, and shook it weakly.

"You heard about Bonnie and Clyde," Jess said, heading to an empty chair, next to the one Sonny had been sitting in.

Jess favored his mother, was a little shorter and rounder than most Wolfes, but there was no mistaking his heritage, his facial profile was the spitting image of Sonny's, and Sonny's father, Josiah.

Sonny nodded. "I heard."

"Frank Hamer told me to send you his regards."

"Were you there?" Sonny sat down, steadying himself as he did.

"No, I wish I would've been."

"It was some shoot out."

"There were six of them that ambushed 'em," Jess said. "Each one of them had a shotgun, automatic rifle, and pistols. Hamer put his manhunter skills to use, and since Clyde was such a creature of habit, always skirtin' the state line, it was an easy task in the end. They caught them unawares."

"They'll just be more."

"What?"

"Somebody else'll take their place."

"What makes you say that?"

"Just the way it is."

Jess stared at Sonny, started to say something, then restrained himself. Instead, he dug into his pants pocket, and offered something to Sonny.

Sonny held out his hand, and Jess dropped a shell casing into it. "A souvenir."

"From the shooting?"

"Hamer thought you'd like to have it. He knows you would've like to have been there, taken a shot. He did it for you as much as the rest of the fellas they killed."

Sonny handed the casing back to Jess. "You take it. I've got enough to remember. This is just the end of my life. It's not my whole life. Those two didn't take that from me. The bad ones never can, no matter how hard they try."

"You sure?"

"Sure as it's daytime. You want a glass of lemonade, or do you have to get back to work?"

"No, I can sit here with you for a while."

"Good."

Sonny stood up and walked into the house, a smile on his face, glad to have a moment with his son, glad that time could stop for an hour or two, glad that the past was gone, and the future didn't exist. †

A World You Don't Know

James Reasoner

I swung down off the bus in a medium-sized burg where I'd never been, and the first thing I saw was some guy beating on a kid.

Four leather-jacketed punks had him surrounded in the mouth of an alley next to the bus station. Light from the station window spilled over them. One of the punks had hold of the kid's shirt. His open hand cracked, back and forth, across the kid's face. Music throbbed from some juke joint down the street, and although the blows didn't really fall in time with the notes, it seemed that way to me for a second.

The boy was twelve, maybe fourteen if he was small for his age. He wasn't fighting back or trying to get away. He just sort of hung there as if he'd given up, letting the punk slap him.

I slung the duffel on my back and walked over to the alley.

"Hey, Brando. Let the kid go."

All four of them looked around, obviously surprised that anybody would interfere with their fun. They were eighteen or nineteen and husky. Might've played some ball before they decided they were too smart to do what the coach told them and got kicked off the team. The redheaded one slapping the kid was the oldest, twenty or maybe twenty-one. I was willing to bet he'd been left back a few times before he finally got old enough to drop out of school.

"Go away, mister," he told me. "This is none of your business, and if you stick your nose in, you'll get hurt."

"What's playing at the Bijou this week? That where you got that line?"

He stared at me. I'd confused him, the poor baby.

To make it clear, I pointed at the kid and said, "Let him go."

"Run this loser off," Red told his buddies.

The three of them were so confident they didn't even pull the switchblades they must've had in their hip pockets. They thought they could bust me up with their fists and those motorcycle boots they wore on their feet. I stepped aside from the first punch, threw my heavy duffel in the faces of two of them, and broke the third one's nose with a short left that traveled about six inches.

The other two caught their balance and rushed me. I tripped one of them, sunk a left in the other one's gut, brought the right up in a punch that landed cleanly on his jaw and put him down and out. The one I'd tripped was trying to get up when I kicked him in the ribs and sent him rolling across the dirty sidewalk.

The show wasn't lost on Red. When I turned around he had let go of the kid and was coming at me with a knife in his hand, held low like he knew what he was doing. When he slashed upward, aiming to slice open my belly, I twisted away from the blade, caught his wrist, and squeezed. Bones ground together. He opened his mouth to scream, but I closed it with my other fist. He went down.

The bus was still sitting there half a block away, engine chugging. Some of the windows had the pale blur of faces in them, looking out. A few people had come out of the station and gathered in front of the swinging door. They gawked at me and the limp shapes scattered around me. I didn't care. I never like drawing attention to myself, but somebody had to help the kid and I had a hunch nobody else around here would've stepped in to do it.

He still stood there, but he didn't look overwhelmed by defeat anymore. He was gawking, too. When he found his voice, he said, "Mister, how ... how did you ..."

"Military training," I said, which wasn't really a lie. I didn't say whose military.

"I never saw anybody fight like that. Not John Wayne, not anybody."

I reached down and picked up my duffel. "What's your name, kid?"

"Davey. I mean, David. Or Dave."

Or anything but Davey, which was what his mama called him, I figured. But he was too grown up for that now.

"Where do you live?"

Eyes narrowed, instantly suspicious like somebody who spent a lot of time on the streets. "Why do you want to know?"

"Because you're out pretty late, and you've already gotten in trouble once tonight," I said, sounding reasonable as I inclined my head toward the four punks, who were starting to stir around and make little pained noises. "I thought I'd walk you back to your house and see that you don't get into any more."

He didn't fully trust me despite what I'd done for him, which is actually pretty smart. A lot of people will tell you they want to help you when that's not what they have in mind at all. I'd learned to look out for people who wanted to do things for my own good.

But he didn't want to walk home by himself in the dark, either, so he said, "I'll show you."

I shouldered the duffel. "Let's go."

Behind us as we walked off, somebody from the bus station called, "Hey, you'd better wait for the cops!"

"No, you shouldn't," Dave said. "You don't want to wait for the cops."

I looked down at him. "Why not?"

"Because the chief of police is Carl's dad. Carl's the redheaded guy who came at you with the knife."

"The one who was hitting you."

"Yeah."

"I can see why it would be better not to wait."

I couldn't afford to let myself get locked up in some jerkwater town. Not with the mission I had to complete.

At this time of night, all the businesses along the main drag were closed except the bus station and an all-night drugstore in the next block. We passed a barber shop, a hardware store, a butcher shop, a little market, a beauty parlor ... the sort of places you find in all the little towns in this country. It was a lot different than where I came from. I didn't see a single soldier.

"I told you my name," Dave said as we walked past a park where all the swings and slides were empty at this time of night. "What's yours?"

"John," I said.

Dave gave me a skeptical grunt. "John Smith, I bet."

"No, as a matter of fact it's John Reeves."

"Oh. Sorry, I didn't mean to sound like a smart-aleck."

"Don't worry about it."

"My last name is Conley."

"Pleased to meet you, Dave Conley. What are you doing out so late?"

"I went to the movies. *The Thing From Another World.* My mom didn't want me to see it, so I, uh, sort of snuck out."

It was all I could do not to laugh. I knew what he was talking about, all right.

"So you're going to be in trouble when you get home."

"Maybe not. Not if I can sneak back in without Mom knowing about it. You won't tell her what I did, will you, Mr. Reeves?"

"I don't think I'll have to. You, on the other hand ...."

I let my voice trail off as the woman I had spotted coming toward us on the sidewalk suddenly broke into a run and called, "Davey! Davey, oh, my God, is that you?"

"Oh, shoot," Dave said under his breath.

We had reached a residential neighborhood, nice old houses behind lawns and under big trees. Houses with porch swings and windows that glowed with warm yellow light. Yeah, a lot different than where I'm from.

The woman slowed as she came up to us. Even though I couldn't see her face very well in the shadows, I could tell by the tense stance of her body that she was scared. Some of it was leftover scared because she'd discovered that her kid was out there somewhere in the night, and some of it was fresh because she found him walking along with a big, ugly stranger.

"Um, hello," she said to me as we all came to a stop on the sidewalk.

I smiled and nodded. "Good evening, ma'am."

Probably hoping that I wasn't an immediate threat, she turned to the kid and took him by the shoulders. "Davey, where in the world have you been? I looked all over the neighborhood for you, and I was about to come downtown—"

"I'm sorry, Mom," he said, and he sounded like he really meant it. "I snuck out and went to see that movie."

"Oh, my goodness. You ... I can't believe you would ...." She stood up straighter and her voice didn't have any give to it as she said, "I'm glad you're all right, of course, but we're going to have a long talk about this when we get home, young man."

"Yeah," he muttered. "I know."

"You go ahead now while I speak to this gentleman."

"Mom, there's something I have to tell you—"

"I don't want to hear any excuses. I made it quite clear that I didn't want you to see that silly movie."

"It wasn't silly—" Dave stopped himself this time. "Mom, listen to me. I got in some trouble."

Her hand went to her mouth. "What did you *do*?"

"*I* didn't do anything. Carl Wilcox and some of his buddies jumped me after I came out of the movie. Carl started whaling on me for no reason." Dave paused and added, "Well, no reason except that he's a jackass."

"Davey!" She took hold of his shoulders again and turned him one way and then the other, studying him in the dim glow from the streetlamp a block away. "You're bruised! Are you all right?"

"Yeah. I might have a black eye in the morning." He sounded like that wouldn't be the worst thing in the world. "It would've been a lot worse if Mr. Reeves hadn't stopped 'em."

She kept her hands on his shoulders but looked at me. "Mister ... Reeves, was it?"

"Yes, ma'am," I told her. "John Reeves."

"I'm Evelyn Conley."

"My pleasure, ma'am."

"You rescued my son from those hoodlums?"

"You should've seen him, Mom! He tore 'em up! John Wayne or Randolph Scott couldn't have done better!"

"You're lucky," she told me. "Carl Wilcox and his friends have bad reputations. They're rumored to have hurt some people pretty badly."

I shrugged. "I've dealt with worse."

"Yes, I imagine you have." She looked at me a little longer. "You were in the war, weren't you?"

"Yes, ma'am."

Again, I didn't say which war ... or which side.

"Well, thank you for helping my son. You may wish you hadn't, though, when Ed Wilcox gets through with you."

"That's the Wilcox boy's father? The chief of police?"

"I guess Davey told you. Ed's a stubborn man. He refuses to see just how bad Carl is. If you fought with Carl and his friends, Ed will probably arrest you."

"They attacked me," I said. "I was just defending myself. There were witnesses who can testify to that."

"Maybe they could ... but they won't. Not in this town."

So it was like that. I'd been in other places where the local bigshot ran things with the proverbial iron fist. But I wasn't scared of Chief Ed Wilcox. He couldn't do anything to me that was any worse than a lot of things I'd run into in the past.

"I don't have much money," Evelyn Conley was saying, "but I know a lawyer who might be willing to help you ...."

"Don't worry about it. I'm sure I'll be fine."

"Well ... why don't you come back to the house with Davey and me? I can offer you a cup of coffee, anyway. Somebody ought to welcome you to town."

"How'd you know I'm new here?"

"You're carrying a duffel bag, and I don't remember ever seeing you around town before. Also, you just look like somebody who's not from around here."

I smiled. She could have said that again.

❖

Evelyn Conley was a nice-looking woman in her early thirties, with brown eyes and dark blonde, curly hair that she kept cut short. Dave hadn't said anything about his dad, only his mom, so I figured she was either widowed or divorced. When I saw the photograph of the smiling guy in uniform on the wall of their living room, I decided on widowed.

"Your husband?" I asked with a nod toward the photo when Evelyn brought cups and saucers from the kitchen. She'd already sent Dave upstairs and told him they'd have their talk in the morning.

She placed the saucers on the coffee table in front of the divan where I was sitting. "That's right." She moved an armchair a little closer to the table rather than sharing the divan with me. "He was a Marine. He didn't make it off Okinawa."

"I'm sorry."

"It was a long time ago," she said, although it really wasn't, not in the big scheme of things and not in the lives of the family left behind, either. But if it helped her to look at it that way, it was none of my business.

To change the subject, she went on, "What brings you to our town, Mr. Reeves?"

"Just passing through."

"You're a veteran, too. You didn't come home and settle back into the life you had before the war?"

I smiled. "Things had changed." I picked up the coffee and took a sip. "And I guess maybe I was just too restless to settle down right away. I decided I wanted to see as much as I could of the country. You know, take it all in."

She shook her head. "I've never traveled much. I've always been happy to stay right here at home." She couldn't stop the sigh that slipped out. "Even though it's not … as nice a place as it used to be."

"Trouble?" I made a guess. "Ed Wilcox, maybe?"

"Ed's wife passed away a few years ago. He's gotten it into his head somehow that he and I …. Of course, I've never encouraged him. I couldn't do that to Davey. Ed's boy, Carl, he's made life miserable for Davey for years now. You know how it is with some people, it's like all they have to do is lay eyes on somebody and they hate them and want to torture them for no reason, and—"

She stopped short and swallowed. Summoned up a smile.

"My, I didn't mean to start going on like that. This isn't your problem, Mr. Reeves."

I smiled back at her. "Or at least it wouldn't have been if I hadn't beaten up Carl Wilcox and his friends."

She looked at the watch on her slender wrist. "There'll be a late bus through at eleven-thirty. You'd better take it."

"What if it's not going the direction I want to go?"

"Any direction away from here is what you need, Mr. Reeves."

I spotted flashing red and blue lights through her living room window. "It's too late for that."

"What do you—"

The doorbell rang before she could finish the question.

She gasped. "You should go out the back!"

I shook my head. "I don't run from trouble. Besides, if Wilcox is a halfway competent cop, he's got somebody back there." I set my cup on its saucer and stood up. "I'll talk to him outside. There's no need for you to be mixed up in this."

She stood up, too, and shook her head. "You were helping my son. I won't let you face this alone."

Before I could argue with her, she went to the front door and opened it.

The man who stood on the porch had a brown Stetson in his hand that matched his uniform trousers. His short-sleeved khaki shirt had a badge pinned to it. The sidearm on his hip was a Colt Model 1911A. A lot of gun for a small-town police chief.

Ed Wilcox was about forty. Not big, but well put together, with brawny forearms and thick wrists. His head didn't have much hair on it, and what was there was pale and wispy around his ears.

He nodded and said, "Sorry to bother you this late, Evelyn, but I was told that a man who started a fight downtown might be here." He was talking to her, but his pale blue eyes had already looked past her and fastened on me. "Don't want him causing any trouble for you and the boy."

"Mr. Reeves isn't causing any trouble, and he didn't start that fight. Your son did."

Wilcox frowned and half-turned. He gestured with the hat. "Come up here."

Carl came up the steps and shuffled into the light. The belligerence that had filled him earlier was gone. His head hung forward and his eyes were downcast. He had taken off the leather jacket and now looked like a scared young man in a T-shirt.

"Carl told me that an older man, a stranger, jumped him down by the bus station and beat him up, and I believe him, Evelyn. My boy wouldn't lie to me. Not only that, but I talked to the ticket clerk and some of the other folks who hang around down there, and they back up Carl's story."

Of course they would. They all knew Carl would settle up with them later if they didn't.

Evelyn hadn't budged. Wilcox looked past her again at me and said, "Mister, you'd better come along peaceful-like."

"Mr. Reeves is my guest, and he's not going anywhere with you."

"Now, Evelyn, he assaulted—"

"He did no such thing. He was defending Davey—and me— from those hoodlums your son runs around with."

That surprised me, the way she included herself, and it knocked Wilcox for a loop, too. He recovered quickly, though. "Now wait a minute. You're saying you were there?"

"That's right. Davey and ... and Mr. Reeves and I went to the movie tonight, and we were walking home when those boys started saying terrible things to me and pushing Davey around. Of course Mr. Reeves stepped in to put a stop to it. What gentleman wouldn't?"

I managed to keep from grinning, but it wasn't easy. She was good.

"Wait a minute," Wilcox said again. "This fella was with you and Davey?"

"That's right." She turned and came over to stand beside me. "Mr. Reeves is visiting in town. He was friends with Ken in the service. They were on Okinawa together."

All right, I thought. All right.

"Nobody at the bus station said anything about you being there tonight, Evelyn."

I could tell what he was thinking. If he asked the ticket seller and the ushers at the movie theater whether Mrs. Conley and I had gone to the show with Dave, they would tell him we hadn't. But if he did that, it would be the same thing as calling a woman he was interested in a liar. He didn't want that. He was stuck.

"Pop ...." Carl said with a whiney edge in his voice. He was waiting for his old man to do something, but his old man wasn't sure what to do anymore.

Wilcox rubbed his chin. "I think maybe this whole thing was just an unfortunate misunderstanding. Somebody said something that was taken the wrong way, and there was a scuffle, and an accident ...." He was trying to convince himself, at least enough to accept it.

Carl didn't help matters by saying, "That's not the way it was, damn it."

Wilcox turned on him, a short, sharp turn that was violent even though no blow was struck. "You watch your mouth," he said. "Go back to the car."

"But Pop—"

"I said go back to the car."

Carl went, but he glared at Evelyn and me first.

"I'm sorry about all this," Wilcox said as he turned back to us. "Look, Reeves, do you have any identification?"

"Sure." I reached for my wallet and took out the California driver's license my superiors had given me when I was sent here. It was a good one. Nothing else would do.

Wilcox studied it for a minute and then gave it back to me. "All right. You have your visit, but then you're moving on, understand?"

"Ed, you don't have any reason to run him out of town."

"It's all right," I said. "I'm just passing through."

He gave me a curt nod. "You see to it." He looked at Evelyn again, and I wasn't there anymore. "I'm sorry about all this. I'd like to make it up to you. There's a pancake supper at the Methodist church next week—"

"I'm sorry, Ed. I don't think that would be a good idea."

"Fine." He took a deep breath and made it sound more civil when he said again, "Fine. Good night, then."

She didn't close the door until he'd gotten into the police car and pulled away from the curb. Then she shut it and looked over at me.

"You're staying here tonight."

"That's not smart. People will talk."

"Let them. He'll have somebody watching the house. If you leave …."

She didn't have to finish. Wilcox wouldn't hurt me as long as I was under her roof, but if I left, the cops would jump me, haul me down to the basement of the police station … and anything could happen down there.

"All right. But in the morning I'll have to go."

"We'll deal with the morning when it gets here."

❖

She brought sheets and a pillow and blanket and made up the sofa for me. Watching her bustle around reminded me of how long it had been since I was in such intimate circumstances with a woman. Not that I thought anything was going to happen between us. I knew it wouldn't. She wouldn't allow it, and it was against my orders anyway. I had already gotten closer to her and her son than I was supposed to. You can't get too fond of people you're going to invade and conquer.

She told me good night and went upstairs. I didn't stretch out on the divan just yet. Earlier when I'd told her that I was restless by nature, it wasn't really a lie. That was why I hadn't minded when they told me they were sending me here as an advance scout.

I eased the front door open and stepped out onto the front porch instead. Wilcox probably had a man keeping an eye on the place, but he wouldn't do anything as long as I stayed close. I sat down on the steps and lit a cigarette and listened to the night. A warm breeze moved in the trees. Somewhere off in the distance a truck's engine ground through the gears. A dog barked a couple of blocks over.

Somebody stepped onto the end of the porch.

I was up in an instant, turning, ready. The small shape drew back and said, "Wait a minute, Mr. Reeves. It's just me. Dave."

I took a deep breath. "What are you doing out here, Dave?"

"I was watching from the top of the stairs. I saw you come out, and I wanted to talk to you." I heard the grin in his voice as he went on, "So I climbed out my window and shinnied down the oak tree again."

I had to smile, too. "Why didn't you just come down the stairs?"

"Because they creak and Mom would've heard it and known what I was up to. This way she doesn't know I'm not in bed asleep. You won't tell her, will you, Mr. Reeves?" he asked for the second time that night. "I'm already gonna be grounded for a week, maybe two."

I sat down on the step and motioned for him to join me. "No, I won't tell her. I know how sometimes a guy just can't sleep."

"Boy, that's the truth!" He settled on the step beside me. "Sometimes I feel like I'm full of so many thoughts and so many feelings that I'm just gonna bust! Does that go away when you get older?"

I took a drag on the cigarette. "I hate to say it, but yeah, it does. But sometimes you get it back for a little while, if you're lucky."

"Say, could I have one of those butts?"

I squinted over at him. "What kind of question is that from somebody who's wearing ... who is that, anyway, on your pajamas? Hopalong Cassidy?"

Dave sighed. "Yeah."

"You can smoke when you get older."

No, he can't, a voice said in the back of my head. *He won't be alive that long.*

I was trying to shove that thought away when Dave asked, "Where are you from, Mr. Reeves?"

How was I supposed to answer that? What could I say that he would understand?

I blew out some smoke and said, "I'm from a long way off."

"Like New York or Florida?"

"Farther than that." All my training tried to kick in and shut my mouth, but the words kept coming anyway. "There are worlds beyond worlds, Dave. Worlds that you've never heard of, worlds that you don't know anything about. I'm from a world you don't know."

He didn't say anything. Right about now he was probably thinking that I was a little crazy. Maybe a lot crazy.

When he did say something, he sounded like he didn't know whether to laugh or be scared. "You mean, like ... from outer space? Like ... in the movie I just saw?"

I wanted to tell him not to be scared, that it would all be over quick. That when the fleet showed up, there wouldn't be time for anybody to hurt. The ones who'd been sent ahead, like me, would have it all planned out so things would go fast.

But before I could say anything, three cars roared down the street and screeched to a stop in front of the Conley house.

Carl Wilcox came out the back door of the first one, followed by more of his friends. They poured out of all three cars, some carrying baseball bats, some armed with knives, some with chains. Carl must have called in every favor he had out there. Maybe they were all just bored on this warm summer night. I didn't know and didn't care.

"Get in the house, Dave," I said.

"Crap!" Definitely scared now. "There must be fifteen or twenty of 'em!"

"Get inside," I told him as I came to my feet. I caught hold of his arm with my right hand and hauled him to his feet, pushed him toward the front door.

With my left I reached inside my pocket for the weapon that I kept secret when I could. Tonight I didn't have any choice but to use it. If Wilcox did have a man watching the place, he wouldn't dare interfere with Carl's vengeance. In fact, it wouldn't surprise me if the cop was already beating feet away from here. He wouldn't want any part of what was about to happen.

"Dave," I said again.

This time I heard him scramble through the door behind me. Carl laughed as he walked toward me. A short length of chain dangled from his left hand.

"Let the kid run," he said. "It won't do any good. When we get through with you, we'll go in there and get him, too. He needs a lesson. So does his mama. When we're finished with her, maybe my stupid old man won't want her anymore."

After he said that, I didn't feel bad about what was going to happen. Not even a little.

"The rest of you boys should leave. This is between Carl and me. I don't want to hurt you."

Carl laughed again. "Nobody's goin' anywhere except right over you." He slashed the chain in front of him. "Get him!"

The others started toward me. They had made their choice. I brought up the cylinder in my left hand and thumbed the firing button. The rays shot out like a beam of light and played over them, freezing them in place. I could have burned them to the ground, but it was more fun just to disable them.

That way I could take them apart with my bare hands.

They struggled against the paralyzing effects and tried to get away from me, but I was too fast for them. The weapon was heavy and sturdy enough to be an effective club. I waded into them and hammered down several of them. My elbow broke the jaw of another. A couple of kicks that were too swift to be avoided shattered kneecaps. I stuck the weapon back in my pocket, grabbed two of them, banged their heads together. All the close combat tricks I had been taught in hour after grueling hour of training came into play as I plowed into that gang of young hoodlums and put them down, one after another.

They never had a chance.

That left me with Carl.

But he was gone. There were too many of the others, and I had taken too long with them. Carl had shaken off the effects of the ray. Where was he?

A scream from inside the house gave me the answer.

I turned and made it back to the porch in one bound. From the corner of my eye I saw flashing lights coming down the street. I didn't know what was going to happen, but it didn't matter. Dave and his mother were in danger, and I had to help them.

The door was open. I burst in and saw Carl struggling with Evelyn and Dave on the stairs. A sharp reek struck my nostrils. Gasoline. Carl must have gotten a can from one of the cars while I was busy with the others.

"I'll burn the place down around you, you bitch!" Carl screamed. Something was wrong in his head. He wasn't just a punk. He was insane.

Brakes screeched outside.

Carl slashed at Evelyn and Dave with the chain and made them fall back to get away from him. Then he dropped the chain and pulled a cigarette lighter out of his pocket.

"Burn it down!" he screamed as footsteps pounded on the porch. "Kill you all!"

I hit him with the ray.

That froze him in place as Ed Wilcox shouted from behind me, "Carl, no! Drop that lighter!"

Slowly, so slowly because of the ray's effects, Carl turned his head toward us. The ray lit up his face, twisted in lines of insane hatred. His thumb moved toward the lighter's wheel.

Wilcox fired, the blast of the shot from the heavy gun filling the foyer.

The bullet struck Carl in the left shoulder and knocked him back. The lighter slipped from his fingers and bounced harmlessly down the stairs. Carl half-fell, half-sat on the stairs and made a mewling sound as he pawed at his bloody shoulder with his other hand.

"Get him out of here!" Wilcox shouted at the pair of uniformed cops with him. "Take him to the hospital and hold him there!"

They rushed up the stairs and dragged Carl out. He whimpered all the way.

Evelyn and Dave were farther up the stairs, clutching each other. Wilcox holstered his gun and went to them. Evelyn started to pull away from him, but he was saying, "I'm sorry, I'm sorry, I didn't want to believe he was really that bad, I'm so sorry ...."

She let him lift her and pull her into his arms. Dave hung on to both of them.

I smiled. An unexpected outcome, but let them enjoy it while they could. Time for me to go.

When I turned, four big men were waiting for me. "Hello, John," one of them said. "You led us on quite a chase this time. When we stopped at the police station, Chief Wilcox told us where you were."

I lifted a hand. "Get away from me," I said. "You can't interfere with my mission."

They started closing in on me. "You've got us all wrong, Johnny. We just want to help you."

"Get back. I won't be responsible for what happens if you don't!"

"All right, grab him and get him in the ambulance."

I jerked out the weapon and fired. The ray washed over them, but even though they flinched from the brilliance, they didn't stop. Exposure to the ray must have weakened its effects on them. This wasn't the first time they had taken me prisoner.

"Damn it, John." A hand slapped the weapon out of my hand. "I've told you before not to shine that flashlight in our eyes. It's annoying as hell."

They grabbed hold of me and started to drag me out. The punks I had roughed up earlier were still sprawled in the yard, some unconscious, some starting to come to, moving around and moaning.

"You gotta quit doin' this, John," the leader said to me as they forced me toward their craft, which was disguised as an ambulance. "Your old man's gonna get tired of paying people off one of these days."

I managed to twist my head around. Evelyn and Dave had come onto the porch with Wilcox. They were all staring at me.

"Don't believe them, Dave!" I called to him. "Whatever they tell you about me, it's not true! You know who I am!"

They started dragging me inside.

"Worlds beyond worlds, Dave! Worlds beyond worlds!"

The rear doors of the ambulance slammed shut. A needle stabbed my arm. I started to slip away.

It didn't matter. The fleet would be here soon, and Dave would know the truth. They all would. †

STATE ROAD 53

Alec Cizak

"Bud?"

"Yeah?"

"Tell Lynn I want to see her."

Bud sighed.

Ron felt bad for him. The entire town knew what was happening while Bud worked the night shift at Liberty Steel. He sounded glummer than usual. Ron figured it was on the count of the strike. Bud Gorski couldn't satisfy his wife and now his bosses refused to pay him what he was worth. Ron thought he was a good guy. He made it possible for Lynn to raise their boys without her having to get a job. Most important, he understood he just didn't have the gump to give her what she needed in bed.

Ron didn't consider himself an especially skilled lover. He figured the demon energy he brought back from three tours in the jungle provided animal attributes Lynn mistook for prowess. Whatever the reasons, he tried to keep things cordial with Bud. He didn't want to see the twins grow up without their father. Nothing had ever been officially spoken. Bud worked the graveyard shift in the mill Monday through Friday. Two or three nights during the week, Deputy Sheriff Ronald Quinn went to work on Bud's wife.

Bud said he'd pass the message. "You going to wait until I'm gone?"

"Sure thing." Ron hung up. He went back to his cruiser and started for the north side of town. He radioed the station. Nobody answered. He figured Beth, the night dispatch, had fallen asleep. No big deal. Haggard hadn't seen any serious crime since the 1930s, before Ron had been born. Occasionally, a carload of teenagers from Gary drifted too far south on State Road 53 and he or Sherriff Dudek would pull them over and remind them, in a manner most friendly, that they couldn't possibly have any business in a nice town like Haggard.

He parked across the street from Bud Gorski's one-story house on Old Ridge Road. It was protected by a thin sheet of painted aluminum and had a small, covered stoop with three steps leading to the front door. Just like every other house on the block. Ron smoked an unfiltered Pall Mall while he waited.

Bud stepped out and crossed his snow-covered lawn with a picket sign and lunch pail under his arm. He unlocked the back door to his Chevelle and tossed them in. Then he opened the front and glanced over. From across the street, Ron could see any remaining enthusiasm Bud had for life drop right out of his eyes. Bud got in his car and drove away.

Lynn Gorski answered the door in a pink nightie. She had her dusty-blonde hair up in a beehive. Ron thought of the covers of fashion magazines he had seen at Union Station in Chicago. Women in big cities had already abandoned that style. It didn't matter. He'd have her hair down and wrapped around his fist soon enough. "Twins asleep?"

"Of course." Her voice quaked. "I'm glad you called." She grabbed his ear with her teeth and slid her tongue around the rim. "Don't ever make me wait a whole week again." Her fingers marched down his chest and unfastened his gun belt. She almost let it drop. Ron caught it and pushed her away.

"Take it easy, baby," he said. His gun clanked on the round table in the kitchen as he set the belt on it. Crusted spaghetti sauce stained three of four flower-patterned placemats laid out.

Lynn stood back. She brushed her hand along her forehead. "I'm cool."

"The hell you are." Ron laughed. "Can I get a beer?"

She nodded toward the fridge.

Ron found a can of Schlitz. He peeled the lid off and tossed the tab into a trash can by the sink.

Lynn walked toward the bedroom. "I changed the sheets before Bud left."

"Probably should've waited." He took a noisy swig.

"Nothing we can do about it now." Lynn stood in the doorway, resting against the frame. Her fingers crawled up and down her thigh, pushing her gown higher and higher.

Ron finished his beer and strode toward her, unbuttoning his shirt along the way.

"How was work?" she asked.

"Boring."

"Same old, same old?"

❖

Ron and Lynn lay in bed. They shared a cigarette. She said something about going to Chicago together. He sighed. "You know that ain't going to happen."

Lynn wrapped her legs around him. Running her fingers in the cross-pattern on his chest, then down to the left, where a small chunk had been taken from him when a VC shot him in the side, she said, "You won't let nobody in."

"Lost enough people to know better." He dragged on the cigarette and passed it. "Besides, you don't ever tire of telling me how much you love Bud."

"I do love Bud. I also love you."

"That ain't even possible."

Gunshots exploded down the street. Ron grabbed Lynn and rolled her off the side of the bed. He crawled out to the hallway and into the twins' room. He woke Sam and Andrew Gorski long enough to help them from their bunk beds to the floor. "Stay low," he told them.

When he returned to the master bedroom, he stopped. Lynn stood by the window, holding a Marlin across her naked body. "It's just the intimidators," she said. "From Liberty."

Ron pointed at the rifle. "That a recent addition to the family?"

She smiled. "Bud bought it after that preacher was shot in Memphis. While you were gone, you know." She looked down. "He was worried the riots might spill over."

Ron took the gun away from her. It was loaded. "Careful, baby."

She rolled her eyes. "I grew up in Kentucky, Ronald."

He realized he missed what she said when he first returned and saw her holding the gun. "Liberty Steel?"

"They send a truck full of goons every night. Since the union ok'd the strike."

"Why ain't I heard of this?"

Lynn shrugged. "Not really police business." She got back on the bed. She lay on her side, tracing the curve of her hips with her fingertips. "Why don't you put that away?" She nodded to the shotgun.

Ron asked her where she kept it. She told him Bud's closet, on the top shelf. "Next to the box of shells."

Lynn smacked the 'Off' button on her alarm clock at 7:10. Ron got dressed while she stayed in bed, smoking. He saw two holes in the wall, just to the right of the window. Leaning in to get a better look, he stuck his pinky in one of them.

Lynn rested on her elbows. "They blasted at this side of the street three nights ago."

"Why ain't you talking to me?"

"It's Liberty Steel, honey. They built every town in Lake County."

"You could get hurt."

"Bud says this'll pass when the union gets its way."

"I don't like it." Ron stuffed his shirt into his pants.

Lynn stretched her leg out and caressed him with her toes. "I appreciate your worries. Bud's got it all took care of."

Ron kissed her goodbye. He grabbed his gun belt on the way to the front door. He stepped outside just as Bud's burgundy, rusted Chevy pulled into the driveway. The two men exchanged curt nods. Ron laid tracks in fresh snow, across the lawn and street to his Ford. He got in and started the engine.

Bud moped along, arched over, like a hunchback, staring at his feet. He seemed more miserable and pathetic than ever. Ron felt like saying something. He couldn't think of anything that would help.

Ron parked his cruiser behind a ground-level billboard with a strawberry lollipop on it advertising Haddaker's Drug Store. Toward the front of his mind was the notion that he was looking out for the people of Haggard. On the other side was a suspicion that he was just bored. He had been in a stupor since coming home. The only physical excitement he got was from Lynn Gorski. Now he had something resembling a *mission*. What was damn clear was that nobody else in town cared about the Liberty Steel gun thugs. It didn't make sense to him. He hadn't slept since leaving the Gorski house that morning.

He caught the sheriff just before lunch, asked him if he was aware of the truck full of rifles spitting bullets on Old Ridge. "Nope," said Sheriff Dudek. The old man twisted the toothpick in his mouth round and round and lowered his eyes.

Ron had done enough interrogation work in the war to know when a human being was lying to him. "Gorski's house has got holes in it."

Sheriff Dudek laughed. "I thought you was plugging them holes!" He looked back at Gretchen, the daytime dispatch. She obliged with a giggle.

Ron said, "I don't think this is something we can shrug."

The sheriff stepped closer. He inflated his chest and nodded up to face the young deputy. "Things happen, as you're well aware, that the law don't have any say regarding." Then he turned to walk away. "Get on them roads. Write some tickets and make us some money so we can have us a nice Christmas party."

The sheriff stepped into his office and slammed the door. As Ron made his way out of the station, Gretchen stopped him. "You're fortunate to come back in one piece, Ronald," she said. "Don't be stupid. Not now."

He thanked her and left. While he ate a hot dog and soft-serve cone for lunch, watching icicles melt off the gutters of the Dairy Queen in downtown Haggard, he decided he would chase the truck by himself and arrest the whole lot. "I like to see them suits cross 53 and explain themselves." He thought of *Rio Bravo*, his favorite movie when he was a kid. He thought about how John Wayne might have handled the situation.

He almost fell asleep, waiting there in the dark for the truck. The sound of a larger vehicle, struggling in the cold, cut through the country silence. He sat up to crank the ignition on his Ford. A blood-colored Dodge Power Wagon rumbled past him. Ron turned the key but the engine wouldn't fire.

"Dammit!"

Guns went off down the road. Glass broke, women screamed, and doors opened and slammed. Ron got the cruiser started and tore out from behind the billboard. His wheels spun on packed snow. He straightened the car and flipped his sirens on.

The Ford roared up behind the truck. There were four men in the back wearing potato sacks over their heads with half-dollar-sized holes cut for their eyes. Two of them aimed their shotguns at Ron. The thug closest to the cab beat on the rear window and motioned for the driver to step on it. The muffler coughed black smoke as the Dodge mustered speed. It continued on Old Ridge and nearly tipped as it veered right, onto State Road 53.

Ron put his foot on the gas and the Ford threatened to fly past the truck when he whipped the steering-wheel. The pickup fish-tailed its way over the ice-coated bridge connecting Haggard and Gary. There were no rails and the men in the back braced themselves for the possibility of going over the side and plunging into Lake Arthur. Ron slowed down. The truck was able to gain a mile on him by the time he was across.

He chased them up 53, passing white fields outside of Industry Row, where nine companies employed most of the labor in Lake County. Smokestacks belched smog into the sky twenty-four hours a day. The entire town smelled like rotten eggs.

A Gary Municipal flashed its sirens and zoomed in front of Ron. The driver tapped the brakes, forcing him to pull over. The officers stepped out of the cruiser and approached him as though he were possibly on the wrong side of the law, dancing their flashlights across his windshield. He opened his door and nudged his way out with his hands raised.

Ron recognized the officer who had been driving. They did basic together at Fort Harrison, down in Indianapolis, in '67. They spent the Summer of Love crawling through mud while their drill sergeant called them maggots and other encouraging insults. "What's going on, Calvin?"

"At ease, soldier. We ain't going to do you like you do our folks any time they wander into Haggard."

Ron lowered his hands. "Just don't do me like you did that Italian girl at the funhouse in Kokomo."

Calvin laughed. "I'm unaware of any such activity, nor would I say shit about it if I was." He kept his flashlight aimed at Ron's eyes. "What you doing this far north?"

"I was hoping to apprehend the men in that pickup that passed here a few minutes ago."

The Gary officers looked at each other. They offered their best impressions of confusion and ignorance.

"We didn't see any pickup."

Ron sighed. He was sick of people thinking he was too stupid to figure out when they were lying to him. "You didn't see that red Dodge? There was four men in the back with shotguns, wearing masks. They looked like ghosts."

Calvin shrugged. "No idea."

Ron stepped back toward his cruiser. "Mind if I drive in to town and have a look?"

Calvin shook his head. "Best thing for you is to head back to Haggard."

Ron stopped.

Calvin's partner rested his free hand on his pistol.

Calvin said, "No need to go begging the Man to dig us early graves. Not after the shit we've been through."

"Lake County Sheriff's Department's got jurisdiction."

"That so?" Calvin reached down and unfastened the button keeping his gun in his holster.

Ron considered his odds. "All right," he said.

Calvin smiled. "Good seeing you, soldier."

Ron got in his car, turned around and drove slowly toward Lake Arthur. He kept an eye on the rearview mirror, hoping Calvin and his partner would move on. They didn't.

As he approached Old Ridge Road, he saw an ambulance from St. Mary's near the Gorski house. Sheriff Dudek's car was parked across the street. Families gathered on the lawn.

Ron pulled up behind Sheriff Dudek's cruiser. Bud Gorski's neighbors let him know what happened. He got to the mailbox posted at the end of the driveway and stopped. The front door opened and two paramedics carried a body, covered with a white sheet, to the ambulance. The sheriff followed behind the medics. When he saw Ron, he pushed past a crowd of huddled wives.

"Where you been, Deputy?"

Ron told him.

The sheriff studied him the way his father did when he was younger, just before he got drafted and all he ever did was drink and fight and get thrown into the drunk tank. "I wonder if you had done like you was told and kept to Haggard, if Bud Gorski might be alive right now."

Ron wanted to get inside, to talk to Lynn. He tried moving around the sheriff.

"Where you headed?"

He nodded toward the house.

"Whatever for?"

Ron looked at him.

"If you was so concerned about happenings in Haggard you sure as hell wouldn't have taken a joy ride up to Gary."

"I told you …"

The sheriff got close enough for Ron to smell Wild Turkey on his breath. "Not a thing in there needing your attention." He waited for Ron to stand down. Then he strolled over to his cruiser, telling regular folks there was nothing more to gawk at.

A third paramedic helped Lynn outside. Ron strained to make eye contact with her. There were too many people between them. She seemed dazed, stumbling and twisting her head side to side, as though she were expecting another attack. She reminded him of older women in Vietnam. The ones who helped stack or bury their dead.

"Who's watching the boys?" he wondered, out loud.

Sheila Hyatt, who lived two doors from the Gorski's, informed him, "Beth's got them over at her place. Scooped them up before anybody goofed and let them know what happened."

The paramedics closed the doors on the ambulance. Lynn and her husband were taken to St. Mary's where a doctor could file the necessary papers, making Bud's death official.

The morning after Bud Gorski was murdered, a knock fell on Ron's door while he was eating a bowl of Quaker Oats. He lived in a one bedroom apartment on the second floor of the building Haddager's was located in. There wasn't much furniture. Just a table and a single chair to go with it and a cot he picked up from a surplus store in Chicago. He was still in his boxers. He scratched his front and back on his way to the door. As he opened it, he got the idea it was Lynn, that she had come to tell him she wanted to get married. He decided he would say yes. He wouldn't even make her sweat it.

Three men in jeans, flannel shirts and potato sacks over their heads shoved Ron into his room. One of them said, "Mind yourself. He's a vet." They kicked him and punched him until he collapsed. Two of the thugs stepped on his right arm, one at the wrist, the other at his shoulder. The third man produced a tire iron.

"This here's a suggestion." He knelt down and splintered Ron's arm. When he stopped, he wiped blood off of the iron and said, "Poke your snout in the wrong place one more time. I dare you."

The men left the apartment without closing the door.

Ron caught his breath and rolled on to his left arm. He pushed himself off the ground. He would have to go down to the drug store to use their phone. Most likely, he figured, someone would catch sight of the bone poking through his skin and call an ambulance for him. When he got to the stairs, he passed out.

Ron Quinn didn't have nightmares about Vietnam. He had bad dreams about the future, about what he was going to do with his life back in the States. His parents split before he ever got to know his mom. While he was fighting the war, his dad got lung cancer, probably from working in the cement factory on the east side of Haggard. Most of the folks who earned a living there ended their days in hospital beds with tubes in their throats.

When Ron returned from the jungle, the women his age were already married. The men who had stayed behind, who had weaseled out with money or left the country, looked at him funny. They probably felt guilty. He dated Lynn in high school and when he ran into her a few days after coming home, he realized he had what she needed. He believed she could do the same for him. But her kids would never be his kids. She was hooked on something Bud provided. Maybe Bud was smarter than him. Maybe Lynn was smarter, too. Ron Quinn tossed and turned while he slept because he knew he was, and always would be, alone.

He woke up at St. Mary's. A nurse was changing bags of fluids pouring into an I.V. plugged into the back of his left hand. They must have been giving him morphine. He couldn't feel a thing. Lynn stood by the only window. He thought of the last night they had made love.

"Hey, baby," he said. His throat felt like it was filled with rocks.

Lynn drifted over and ran her fingers along his right arm, which was covered in a cast. "We're putting Bud in the ground tomorrow. Catholic funeral."

Ron tried to meet her hand with his left. The I.V. prevented him from crossing his body. "I'll be there."

"Doubt they'll let you loose from here that soon."

Ron asked her what had happened. She explained that they were asleep when the shooting started. She said Bud's blood sprayed her face and the bullet angled off into their headboard. Then she asked, "Who did this to you?"

"Pretty sure it was the same people."

"Figured so."

He told her how he chased the gun thugs to Gary.

"State Road 53?"

"What you thinking about, Lynn?"

"Nothing." She turned away from him.

Another goddamn liar, thought Ron.

Lynn stayed with him until the nurses kicked her out. They sneered when they spoke to her. Ron told them to back off. When she was gone, the head nurse whispered, "You two are going *straight* to hell."

Ron was released from the hospital two days later. He missed Bud Gorski's funeral. Sheriff Dudek told him to take it easy. The last thing Ronald Quinn wanted, though, was more time to himself. He went back to work the next day with a bottle of Darvocet hidden in his glove box. The sheriff called him to his office.

"You clear, now?" He nodded toward a wooden chair on the other side of his desk.

Ron declined the offer to sit. "What do you mean?"

"Your job is to write tickets and chase the coloreds back up to Gary. You ain't Mickey Spillane. You ain't Sam Spade and you sure as hell ain't no hero. Confine yourself to Haggard, or find another way to pay your bills."

Neither man spoke for a moment. Then the sheriff repeated his first question.

Ron thought he was stupid for even asking. The strike would be over, regardless of how it turned out for Liberty or the workers, long before his arm mended. He assured the sheriff he wasn't going to do anything but burn fuel driving round and round Haggard city limits.

Ron parked in the lot of the Dairy Queen that night to take a nap. The air outside was freezing. He rolled the windows up and turned the heater on. The speaker on his police radio crackled and the night dispatch told him to get to the bridge on State Road 53.

He turned his lights on and raced over ice-coated roads. He passed Old Ridge and got a feeling things were never going to be the same. When he drove up to Lake Arthur and the iron bridge, there were a dozen squad cars from three different police agencies gathered, sirens turning. Police walked off the side and down a slope toward the water. Ron's eyes followed them. There was more activity by the shore. He parked and got out. The ground was slick from a sheer layer of ice.

Sheriff Dudek stood among a group of Gary Municipal officers. Ron approached him. "What's going on?"

The sheriff directed his attention to the frozen lake, just beyond the edge of the bridge. A crane was hoisting a red pickup truck from a crater in the ice. "Where you been tonight?"

"Minding my own."

The sheriff said he believed him.

The officers examining the truck made their way to the top of the bridge. One of them explained, "Front tires was shot out."

Sheriff Dudek took him aside. "Bud Gorski have any guns in his house?"

Ron stuttered. "Doesn't everybody?"

The sheriff raised his chin and smiled. "Go get the Gorski broad. Bring her to the station."

Ron moped back to his cruiser. He remembered watching Bud walk the very same way. He got in the Ford, fired it up, turned around and drove toward Old Ridge Road.

Most of the cars on the street were frosted over. The ice on Bud's Chevelle had been cleared. Pieces of it were still breaking off and sliding down the windows. Ron parked in the driveway, to the side of Bud's car. He approached the front door with his .38 already drawn, wondering if Lynn Gorski had it in her to shoot him. He knocked and waited.

She let him in. She was wearing her coat and the twins were seated on the dull yellow couch in the living room, dressed in matching parkas. Ron looked at his watch. It was after midnight. "You fixing on taking the boys out for a milk shake?"

Lynn opened her mouth to speak, but said nothing. Ron crossed the room and noticed she was trying to hide three suitcases standing in the narrow hallway between the bedrooms. He pretended he wasn't aware of them.

"I just wanted to see the damage from the ...." He glanced back at the boys. "Well, you know what I'm getting at."

Lynn remained still. Ron slid past her and into the bedroom. He knelt down and studied the hole in the wall caused by the shot that killed Bud. He stood up and approached Bud's open closet. The rifle rested on the shelf where it was supposed to be. The box of shells was turned on its side. Empty.

Lynn stood in the doorway, staring at him.

He reached up and took the Marlin down. "Baby," he said. He closed his eyes. When he opened them again, she was gone.

The front door slammed shut.

Ron Quinn took a deep breath. He put his finger in the hole in the wall across from the bed. Then he counted, "One Mississippi, Two Mississippi ..." At three Mississippi, he heard the engine on the Chevy rev. Ice cracked like thunder as the wheels rolled over it. He put the shotgun down and moseyed out of the house.

He got in his cruiser and casually turned the sirens on. He took his time backing up and taking off after Lynn Gorski and her sons. He kept a good distance between them so that she wouldn't panic and crash. She was smart and took 35th Avenue to I-65. Ron followed her onto the highway and made sure she crossed the Illinois state line. He slowed down and watched the Chevy's taillights thin to darkness, hoping the she'd have the sense to go all the way to Canada. Then he made a U-turn and drove back to Haggard. He grimaced, like he had bitten into something awful, and rehearsed the lie he would tell to guarantee he never saw Lynn Gorski again. †

THE HAND THAT FEEDS HIM
Patricia Abbott

A cardboard coaster depicting a bucolic Irish pub sat beneath my watery glass of Scotch. Long past sodden, the green mat told me in a rather pushy way that I'd drunk more than my share over the past three, okay, five hours. Looking for a replacement, I wondered whether the invention of a decent coaster was an impossible task. The fuckers clattered to the floor, stuck to the glass, got saturated—none did the job. The only ones I'd seen do the trick were the cotton booties my parents slipped on their endless rye-and-sodas back in the fifties. Couldn't remember the last time I saw one.

Half-emptying the glass, I sent the disk flying and slammed the glass down on the bare wood as punctuation. Served Tudge's right if it made another of the thousand half-moons enameling the sticky surface. What I hadn't counted on was breaking it, which I did, and cutting my hand, which I did too.

Kenny came hurrying over, flashed me a now-familiar look of annoyance, and cleaned the mess up. Didn't offer to make good on my lost booze though. Just dropped a ziplock bag stuffed with gauze and adhesive on the bar in front of me. Standard procedure, I guessed, from the efficiency with which it came.

"Wash it off and bandage it up, Frye," Kenny said, nodding toward the toilet, a grimy cubicle to be avoided if at all possible.

Of course, Tudge's being a bar, and us being men, dodging it for long wasn't an option.

"Stopped bleeding already, Ken." I held up my hand. "And look there's enough alcohol on this bar top to disinfect it ten times over." I licked my finger to prove it and then waggled it in his fat face. God knows, his mug was plump. Sacks of loose flesh swayed rhythmically from his chin as he shook his head. Even his ear lobes were fleshy purses. Below his shoulders, he was a stick though. How does a thing like that happen, I ask you?

Looking over at the rest of his customers obliquely, Kenny said, "You guys heard me warn Frye, right? No lawsuit if he comes in here with a nasty infection."

Complete indifference on their part. No sense getting between the source of booze (Kenny) and the guy who could and would whip 'em (me). Lately, I'd been looking for an ass to kick.

For instance, I'd listened—for the last forty minutes, mind you—to Butcher. He was sitting his usual four stools down, telling stories about his minor-league days in the Phillies' farm system. Tonight's audience was too far gone to interrupt him. All of 'em sat shit-faced and spellbound by his nonsense, like they'd never heard this story before. Jesus. If Butcher once spent a day in Philly, it was in the Eastern State Pen.

I was halfway to believing that every last embellishment came straight from my mouth. We'd known each other long enough. If he'd ever been more than an hour or two outside of Detroit, I'd be gobsmacked. Butcher was borrowing my God-forsaken life. What a crappy past he must've had to pinch my sad story. What would he do without me?

He was still going on with it despite the groans and head shaking I shot his way, recounting a double play he'd made against the Dodgers' Triple A team. There never was a guy in Tudge's who hadn't played sports of some kind—no riders of the pine in this dive. But only Butcher was nervy enough to claim major league experience. Most guys were content to give accounts of high school hijinks—state tournaments, you know. Only had to look at Butcher to doubt his story. The guy barely cleared five-foot eight, and his upper arms weren't made to drive a ball past the infield. A shortstop, he insisted, but I'd seen him run more than once; he was slow and clumsy. He stunk the stink that clings to a guy even years after being the last one picked for every team.

I grabbed the towel Kenny had left lying on the bar and tossed it in Butcher's direction. "Think fast," I hissed, as the cloth sailed past his jabbering mouth.

Five men watched silently as the cloth slapped the floor. Butcher was the last to spot it, having no idea he'd been expected to grab it mid-air. *Thinking fast* had been lost on Butcher three drinks ago. *Acting fast* had probably never been his strong suit. Any professional would've grabbed it instinctively. Goddamn bullshitter.

"Last call," Kenny said, scooping up the cloth from the floor and throwing it into the bar sink. Most of the men, myself included, ordered a final round. The others finished quickly and left one by one. Me and Butcher exited together through the back door, same as always.

"Haven't you two got a home," Kenny said, flapping his bar apron at us when we moved too slow.

We felt the breeze of the door slamming behind us, heard the lock snap. Nearly caught my heel on the loose metal on the door threshold thanks to Kenny's bum's rush. It was insulting considering Tudge's would close in a month without our business.

"Guess our host's off to a late night assignation," I said, checking my shoe for damages. We'd been coming here for years, but I had no idea whether Kenny had a wife.

Butcher had other things on his mind. "You sure drank a hell of a lot of booze for a guy who can't cough up rent money." He turned and looked at me. "And do you have to use three-syllable words every time you get the chance? Assignation, my ass. No wonder nobody can stand you. All that faggy talk gives 'em a headache."

"Four syllables," I corrected him. We hadn't gone half a block and were already at it. "And I don't give a good fuckin' fig whether any of those idiots like me."

"Temple's just like Wayne State, right? City school. Easy to get in."

I nodded. He was talking about my college years again, always a sore point with a high-school drop-out.

"And you put in what … two years? Or was it less?" He chuckled when I didn't respond. Our footsteps were the only sound after that interchange on the desolate street.

Home, a ten-minute walk from the bar, was a cinderblock box of tiny, nearly windowless apartments, mostly rented by divorced and hard-drinking men. Had its share of ex-cons and druggies too. We'd shared the place for the last week or so. But Butcher and I'd been roomies several times over the years. Between wives, hospitals stays, jail time, evictions, whatever, we drifted back to this arrangement. This place was the worst of our bad housing history. Twenty-four apartments and not a woman to be found except for the stray Saturday night score, an irate wife or a female dealer. Few were the sort of girl you'd brag about.

"You'll have your dough by the weekend."

That was a barefaced lie. I'd no way to come up with any money. I was tapped out. Paying some fines and overdue bills the week before finished me off, and I hadn't had the energy or inclination to look for work. Jeez, I was coming up on sixty. How many men my age were on the job market in Detroit? Washing dishes in a diner seemed harsh. Waiting to be robbed behind a convenience-store counter for minimum wage was even worse. Men a few years older than me usually wore a name tag and pointed people toward the right elevator at the hospital or to Aisle 11 at Walmart.

"Don't know why I ever took you in, Moocher convict."

"Don't know why I ever asked you to, Bullshitting slumlord."

We paused, sizing each other up for the hundredth time. I had every advantage over Butcher except I was a lot drunker. Some days it seemed like yesterday's buzz hadn't worn off before I started in again. Today had been one of those days.

We started walking again.

"I'm no convict. Just took a swipe at my wife and got caught. She's a slut, a liar, and a thief. Believe what she says then you're a fool." Priscilla could drive any man to splash some egg on her face.

Butcher snorted. "I was the one picked her up at St. John's, and it was more than a swipe. Beating up on a woman who weighs ninety-five pounds. You couldn't last a week without me to take care of you. To put you up, feed your face." He shook his head. We were almost home now, and I held my tongue while I followed him inside.

The apartment was little more than a studio: rented furniture, Salvation Army linens and dishes; a sheet instead of curtains at the one window; trash bags lined a wall. The smell took some getting used to. Over the years we'd known each other and lived together, it was always like this. We never could work out a routine for keeping a place clean, human even. If I'd been depressed before, the sight of this shit-hole filled me with rage and despair. Two men in their fifties without a prayer of things turning around. Is a decent home too much to ask for? I'd considered voting for Obama for such a thing: If he gave help to the blacks, would he leave an old whitey behind? 'Course I wasn't registered, had never been.

"Wipe your filthy feet," Butcher ordered me, gesturing to a ripped piece of gold shag carpeting he called a welcome mat. My pent-up anger exploded, and I threw an arm around Butcher's neck, forcing him down on the pulled-out bed. If I had to say why I tackled him just then, I couldn't tell you. It seemed inevitable: the walk home, the insults, the sparring in Tudge's—all leading to this moment. And Butcher gave the odds of us having a fight a boost with his filthy feet remark.

"Always thought you were a fag," Butcher said.

His face, squashed into a pillow, muffled his voice. He was almost laughing, which made me madder still, and I wondered if Butcher's old revolver still lay in the top dresser drawer. I calculated I could probably hold Butcher down with my knee and reach over for it. The feel of the cold metallic butt on his neck would stop that laughter pretty damned quick. Still laughing, God help him, Butcher bucked upward as if I intended ....

Everything went red-black: swirls of smoke, a funny smell, a bitter taste in my mouth that trickled down to my stomach, a weak-kneed feeling, general numbness. Jeez, it was awful. When my head cleared, and I wasn't sure how much time had passed, Butcher was lying on the bed with a shoelace wrapped tight around his neck. It looked to be tied with some sort of fancy sailor's knot. Nothing I knew about. He wasn't on his stomach anymore either. I sat up and looked down at my feet. Loafers, no laces. What the hell.

I shook Butcher. Rattled him good. His spine seemed to have turned pulpy, his face was swollen and dark. Several bruises were beginning to bloom, and the whites of his eyes were sprinkled with little red dots. Maybe he'd been sensitive to the pillow stuffing. But there was that shoelace to explain. That swollen neck. Holy Mother of God. He looked about as dead as anyone I'd ever seen. Not that I'd seen many dead men.

Truthfully, I didn't think I'd done it. What would have driven me to such an extreme act? I couldn't picture myself stopping to unlace a shoe when I could just as easily have strangled Butcher with my bare hands. Or used the gun in the drawer, or what the hell, a kitchen knife. I looked around, half-expecting to see signs of another person. Had to be that someone sneaked in while we were tussling on the bed. One of the guys who hung around this hell hole looking for trouble. Maybe Ernie down the hall. The super had a key. Someone other than me anyway. Maybe he—they—left thinking we'd both bought it, 'cause I didn't feel any too good myself. How had I fared in this scuffle?

I got off the bed, nearly tripping over a shoe. Butcher's? The unlaced one. The left one was still on his foot. Shit. I had a vague memory of him waving his foot in my face earlier, egging me on. And that shoe was as dirty as the ones he demanded I wipe. I remembered pointing that out to him, Butcher agreeing in a shaky voice. "Sure, whatever you say, Frye."

I limped off. In the bathroom mirror, my face didn't look much better than Butcher's. Clearly we'd gone at it pretty good. A bite mark near my nose looked to be a contender for infection. Apparently I hadn't killed him before we'd pummeled each other. Had I strangled him then? In all the years I'd tangled with various things, various people, nothing half as terrible as this had happened. Why last night?

Funny thing was—the weird thing—I wanted to talk to Butcher. Ask what happened? What should I do next? Where should I go? Pathetic, right? Butcher was my only friend, come down to it. Those guys in the bar, I barely knew their names. The men in the apartments, I'd only been here a week. Even thought of calling my ex, Priscilla, trying to get her to take my side, help me figure out what to do. No kids to call on—no one.

Every once in a while, this notion that I was alone in the world swept over me and I began to cry like a five-year-old. Before tonight, I could always name Butcher as a friend. I sat for a long time, until my head cleared. Till I had some sort of idea to work with. And my idea was this: I needed some dope; stuff that would make the sick feeling in the pit of my stomach go away. I needed a place to stay.

"No money, no honey" was the password at my neighborhood pharmacy. Most of all, I couldn't stay here a minute longer. Perhaps all our scuffling hadn't gone unnoticed even if hours had passed.

I looked around, wondering what I could hock. And then it came to me: Butcher wasn't going to raise a fuss if I borrowed a few bucks. Or took all his money for that matter. Grimacing, I flipped him over and reached into his back pockets. Empty. I looked through the sheets, under the bed, in his coat pocket, and then I spotted his wallet on the bureau. Somehow he'd had time to clear out his pockets before I jumped him. Inside was about two hundred dollars plus a Visa and an ATM card. Sounds cold, but I was still pretty lit and couldn't think of a single reason not to take all of it. He wasn't gonna be needing it, I'm ashamed to say.

I had neither a car nor a license, so I ordered a Shamrock Cab. Not so unusual in Detroit, friends. I'd thought about my next move in the half-hour I waited, and I decided that one: I had to get some food if I wanted to think rationally; and two: I didn't want to take a direct route to my eventual destination. I owed my dealer a little money, but now I had some. Plus access to more.

I glanced over at Butcher one last time and decided a little set decoration was called for. I went into his drawer (guess what, no gun after all) and amidst things like shoe horns, paper clips and dirty combs found some snapshots and put a picture of his kid next to his head. Maybe this odd gesture would obscure what had happened. Maybe it showed feeling on my part should it come to my needing to display some. I don't really know what I was thinking.

Marlene, his kid, was making her first communion in the snapshot I picked—must have been twenty-odd years old. I removed the shoelace from his swollen neck and put it back on the shoe. At no point, did I really believe I would get away with it, but it was the best I could do. Thinking beyond the next hour was impossible.

The cab picked me up outside a deserted movie theater about two blocks from the apartment. No sense associating myself too closely with the murder scene. The driver, an eastern-European twenty-something, let me off at Anita's, one of the million Greek cafes in Detroit, and where I'd occasionally eaten breakfast over the years. It was a five-minute drive, and I sank into the upholstery as much as I could, thinking the less chance Omar could identify me, the better. Just another old man to him.

In the restaurant, I chatted up the waitress. She knew me—or my face—at least, but had never seen me at this hour before. Six A.M. I still hadn't filled in the dots as to how long I'd been out cold on that bed with Butcher. Hours with a corpse turning cold and stiff, and I was too drunk to catch on.

I struggled to remember her name.

"Suzie," I finally spit out. "Give me two eggs over easy, ham, rye toast." I slapped grape jelly on the bread as soon as it arrived.

Suzie was already pouring a second cup of coffee with a big smile on her face. "Joe, isn't it?" she asked.

"John. John Frye."

"Right."

I took a second cab from another company. No cell to order one, of course, but Anita's was the sort of dive that still had a public phone on the back wall. My drug dealer was on the west side of Detroit, but the cabbie let me off at an ATM a few blocks away. I withdrew the allotted $200, figuring Butcher used the same code he had for the last twenty years. I teared up for a second, punching in his mother's name.

My dealer lived on Ashley. Only three intact houses remained on his street. What sort of people still managed to mow their lawn or shovel their walks on a block like this one? I slunk down the street, fitting in like the slime bag I'd become.

My destination, 1703, was not one of the three undamaged houses; it was missing any number of architectural details. Like legitimate lighting and heat. Nobody actually lived there, my dealer reasoned once, so he jerry-rigged an electrical system. Tarp covered a large section of the roof. There were several missing windows now boarded-up and making the place as dark as hell. The ceiling leaked plaster in any number of places. Unless you counted the jugs of water on the floor and the rusted sink resting on its side, there was no plumbing. A place to buy drugs—and maybe, occasionally, to sleep drugs off.

The place was run by a guy called Kylie, who quickly cleared my debt on his shiny new Apple laptop and provided me with a new supply of dope. The quick transaction put him in a good mood. I wanted something simple and not too dodgy. Kylie, far from the stereotypical hip-hop trader, was dressed in a neatly pressed blue oxford shirt and creased chinos. A well-trimmed goatee underscored an otherwise well-shaved face. Corporate weekend attire.

"Where'd you get the money, Frye?"

It was conversational more than informational. He didn't care whether I'd knocked off a liquor store or landed a job. Just so long as no cops had followed me.

"Guy owed me some dough. Gave me his bank card to get it."

Kylie rolled his eyes. "Whatever you say, Chief."

"Mind if I hang around a while?"

Kylie raised his eyebrows, rubbed his lips, and looked around the house. "Now why would you want to do that when there's a Comfort Inn half-a-mile away? You apparently have some money."

I didn't respond.

"What does 'a while' mean? An hour?"

"Couple hours, maybe a little longer. I need some sleep."

I flung off my jacket and looked for a seat, trying to appear relaxed. A sofa that was more frame than stuffing was the only place to sit so I flopped there. Dust rose, but it wasn't too bad. There was also a table and two chairs, an old TV, a boombox, a mattress. Home.

"Gonna get me into trouble, Frye? Don't like trouble."

I shook my head. "Just for the night. More or less."

He rubbed his lips again. "How much dough you got on that bank card?"

I shrugged.

"Give it here," he said. "What's the guy's name? Dude who *gave* it to you?" He squinted at me in the near dark. I told him and he pulled out his cell and called the bank, me feeding him the information the bank requested.

"$6400," he said, hanging up. " 'Course you can only take out $200 a day. Still I can fix you up for that."

"So theoretically, I could take out money for thirty days?"

He looked at me more closely, nodding. "Looks like someone tried to bite off your nose. Frye. Ain't this dude gonna report the card missing?"

"He's out of town."

Kylie shook his head, but didn't question it.

Who would think to go into that rat-hole apartment on the east side of Detroit and find Butcher before the rent was due— fourteen days from now? With all those bags of garbage lined up along the wall, no other smell would be noticed.

I settled back on the sofa, and when he tried to give me back the card, I waved it away. "Month's rent in advance," I told him.

"Rent? A month? You gotta be kidding." He looked at me hard. "Much as I appreciate your company and the dough, I don't know if that's a good idea." Kylie rubbed his lips again. "I thought we were talkin' about buyin' pharmaceuticals here."

Truly, I don't know how he had any lips left with all that rubbing. "Free sentry at night?" I flexed my muscle, but inside I was begging him. "Home minder."

He snorted. "Can't even take a dump here, Frye."

"Dunking Donuts right down the block."

"Look, you paying me for rent or drugs?" he asked.

"Some combination."

Finally, he shrugged. "It'll only keep you out of harm's way for so long."

I'd stayed in worse places and "so long" was about all the time I had.

"Got any more cards in your pocket?"

I handed the Visa over. †

A SPECIAL KIND OF HELL
Hilary Davidson

"You understand this isn't about sex, don't you, honey?"

Paige hated it when her husband called her *honey*. It sounded so insincere as it rolled off his tongue. She bit the soft tissue inside her cheek to tamp down her anger. "Yes," she muttered.

"You're sure you're okay with this?"

"I've told you a hundred times. What more do you want from me, Derek?"

Her husband sighed and glanced around the bistro. It was late Tuesday afternoon and the place was empty except for the staff. Paige wondered what they thought of the fortyish couple refusing to relinquish their corner table. She caught their loaded looks as they set tables for the dinner crowd, murmuring subversively in Spanish.

"Dr. Shapiro says it's a bad idea for me to go through with it if you're not okay with it," Derek said.

She gulped her third glass of Chardonnay. It was an amazing trick Derek had pulled on her, really. He was forcing her to give him permission to indulge in a twisted fantasy. If she didn't do it, she was a bad wife. *A fetish needs an outlet,* Dr. Shapiro had told them when they'd gone for counseling. *You can't think them away. They need a channel so that you can have a satisfying life as a couple.*

Bullshit, Paige had thought at the time. She hadn't changed her mind about that. "I don't understand why you want a dominatrix to torture you." Her face flushed as the words gushed out.

"Dr. Shapiro explained it to you, didn't he, Paige?" He took a sip of club soda, then steepled his fingers, taking on the serious, steady demeanor he assumed in front of juries when speaking on behalf of his shady clients. "Every day, literally hundreds of people look to me to take care of them. My employees, my clients. Charities I support ...."

"I'm the one who helps charities," Paige said.

"With my money." Derek's voice was even. "Our money, of course. But I'm the one who has to go out and earn it. I have so many people depending on me. Think of what the kids' schools cost."

That jolted Paige. Everything had seemed fine between her and Derek when the kids were at home. But then Derek had insisted on shipping them off to Swiss academies. Once it was just the two of them at home, minus the sunshine and cover the kids provided, Derek's darker desires had flourished like poisonous plants. "But you're the one who insisted ...."

"I'm in control twenty-four/seven, and it's exhausting. I'm not complaining about how I live my life, but I need a release," Derek went on. "You understand the dominatrix and I aren't going to have sex, right? That's why the dungeons are legal, by the way. No sex. You can legally hire someone to beat you with a whip, so long as there's no sexual contact."

Paige hated the way he slithered behind lawyerly arguments when discussing something personal. Did he really think that highlighting the technicalities of a morals law was going to make her comfortable with the fact her husband was going to go into a dark room with some leather-clad woman with a whip? Paige couldn't put her finger on the part that bothered her the most. Her personal trainer liked to talk about trigger points in the body, and Paige felt that a bunch of hers were being hammered at the same time.

"I just don't understand ...." Paige started to say, but Derek had already opened his wallet and dropped several bills on the table.

"This doesn't have to be a big deal, Paige, unless you make it one. This is about satisfying my needs."

"But what about my needs?"

He stood without answering that. "Look, my appointment's at three. I want to be on time."

He meant his session at the dungeon, of course. It didn't matter how she felt; he was going no matter what she said.

"Let me put you in the car." Derek took her elbow. That made her feel older suddenly, like someone's maiden auntie. "You've had a lot to drink."

"I can get to the car." She pushed him away.

Derek called his driver. Finally, the black town car turned the corner and double-parked in front of the bistro. Derek stepped off the curb and opened the door for her.

Paige started to get in. "Why did you tell me, Derek? Why didn't you just do it quietly? I probably never would've known."

Derek gave her that flat, broad smile that worked on juries. "I couldn't keep secrets from you, honey." He nudged her into the car and shut the door. When she turned to look at him, he was already on the sidewalk, his shoulders squared and his step swift, as if he couldn't wait to get where he was headed.

"Home, ma'am?" the driver asked.

"Yes, please." Paige sat back and rubbed her eyes. Had it really come to this? Seventeen years of marriage to a man who secretly craved dungeon paddlings? Whips and chains? A ball gag? Paige wasn't even completely certain of the nature of his cravings. A couple of sessions at Dr. Shapiro's townhouse hadn't enlightened her about that. The doctor talked mostly about how trust is the most important thing in a relationship and how you have a responsibility to satisfy your partner, even if their desires don't match up with yours.

I've been doing that for years, Paige had said.

I'm sure you think you have, the shrink told her.

She wanted to tell him about the occasional threesomes Derek wanted. She'd gone along with that, even though she hated them. She didn't care about kissing another woman. Paige had friends who liked to think they were sexually liberated and open, and they'd sometimes say over cocktails how wonderful it would be to have a threesome. Only, it wasn't wonderful when you were the one who was shoved aside in bed. There was nothing more humiliating than sitting there, sweaty and wet, while your husband and a rented siren went at it beside you. Paige had never known what to do then. Play with herself and pretend she was enjoying the show? Derek wasn't looking at her anyway.

As the car went up Madison, she caught sight of a mannequin in a plate-glass window. It sported a corset rimmed with black lace, and slender ribbons of garters that secured sheer black stockings. It was like looking at a retro pin-up, one holding something red in her hand. The light changed and the car surged ahead.

"Stop!" Paige shouted. "Stop here!"

"What is it, ma'am?" the driver asked, pulling over.

"I need to see ... something ... wait here."

Paige's legs were wobbly on the sidewalk. In front of the window, she realized the mannequin was holding a red paddle. It looked like suede, and Paige reached out to touch it, swaying slightly as her nails tapped the glass. The paddle had a red heart cut out of it near the top; that missing piece dangled from a red cord attached to the handle.

Would the dominatrix Derek was seeing hit him with something like that? Maybe the woman even shopped at this store. That thought made Paige recoil, as if she were standing on enemy territory. She gulped for air before she opened the door, expecting scorn. But the saleswoman who greeted her smiled, apparently not unaccustomed to the sight of confused, middle-aged ladies on the Upper East Side.

"I want that paddle in the window," Paige blurted out.

"Of course. Would you prefer red, pink, or black?"

"It comes in different colors?" Paige's words came out quietly, as if she'd used up all the air in her lungs on that first outburst.

"Yes. We also have one with a crystal handle. Well, that's more like a riding crop, but—"

"I'll take them all."

"Would you like them gift-wrapped?"

Paige shook her head. The woman leaned closer. "If you want, I can bring them into the dressing room for you to inspect. And if there's anything you'd like to try on …."

"Yes! The whole outfit." Paige turned to study the mannequin again. If that was what Derek wanted, she'd give it to him.

The saleswoman led her to a pink-walled room with a giant three-way mirror and rosy lighting. She sized her up and returned with a series of lacy corsets and garters, then came back with gloves, boots, and paddles.

"I look ridiculous," Paige said.

"Don't be silly. You've got a great figure. Your arms are better than Michelle Obama's."

Paige smiled at the compliment.

"Do you have any idea how many women come in here for *exactly* the same thing? The kitten-with-a-whip fantasy is *huge* in these parts."

"My husband would laugh if he saw me dressed like this."

"I promise you, he won't. You'll do just fine." The saleswoman handed her the black paddle. "When you get the boots on, you'll look like Catwoman."

It felt like a flyswatter in Paige's hand. "How hard can you hit someone with it?"

"Don't worry. These are all very safe."

"It isn't even close to Halloween," Paige tried to joke.

"Listen, putting on a costume might feel weird, but what's the alternative? Sending him to a dominatrix?" The saleswoman chuckled and patted Paige's shoulder, mistaking her look of panic for nerves.

❖

Paige worked through her anxiety by playing with the toys at home, mock-swiping at the leather armchair Derek liked to read in. When she finally wound up and hit it with a pink paddle, it let out a dull thud. As the wine wore off, she felt foolish, and hid the toys in their bedroom closet. Then she took a pill and waited for the panic to subside. It receded a little, like the tide, but waves lapped at her, some brushing her skin and making her shiver.

When Derek came home that night, he had a bouquet of red roses with him.

"How did everything go?" Paige asked. Her question was oblique, even though it was only the two of them in the cavernous apartment.

"Great." Derek smiled. "It was great."

"That's good." Paige wished she could bite off her tongue as soon as she said the words. "Do you want to talk about it?"

"Not particularly. You know when you've fantasized about something for so long, and then you get to experience it, and it's even better than you hoped? It's hard to really describe that to another person."

Derek's voice was warm and smooth, but each word hit her like the smack of a paddle. *Great. Better. Than. You. Hoped.* She bit the inside of her cheek to keep from crying out.

"So, what did you do with your afternoon?" Derek asked.

"I went shopping."

"There's a surprise."

"I bought something you'll like."

"Really?"

"Wait here."

She went to the closet. She thought about putting on the corset and stockings and boots, but she'd need more wine to manage that. Instead, she took out the paddles, examining each before settling on the red. In her mind, the dominatrix wore all black; she didn't want to mimic that. She held the paddle behind her back and went to the living room. Derek had already poured himself a Scotch and was checking email.

"Did you want to see?" Paige asked.

"See what?" He didn't look up.

"What I bought this afternoon."

She held out the paddle. He took it from her, and a slow, sly grin crept across his face. "Oh, Paige. I never would've thought you had it in you. Where did you find that?"

She'd been terrified he'd burst out laughing, and she suddenly felt relieved. "I thought you might want to try it." Her voice was shy, almost girlish.

"Sure, I would. Put out your hand."

She reached to take the paddle from him, but he pulled it back. "Don't you …?" *Don't you want me to take it?* Before she could choke the words out he turned her hand over and whacked her palm.

"How'd you like that?" he asked.

She was ready to burst into tears. Not because of the pain—really, it was about as harmful as the snap of an elastic band—but because she was so baffled. Wasn't this what he wanted? What was wrong with her?

"Well?" he prodded. "Did you like it?"

"Yes?"

"Good. What's for dinner?"

Afterward, when Derek took a work call and left her cleaning up the remnants of the meal, she went to the closet, pulled out the toys and the corset and the accessories, and put them down the garbage chute.

❖

Derek made another appointment with the dominatrix, then another, and another. Each time, he made sure Paige knew what he was up to. "No secrets. That's the most important thing to me," he said one evening, after a politician's fundraising dinner that he'd dragged her to. They were in the backseat of the town car. "Don't you agree, Paige?"

"Yes."

"You know what's special about us, Paige? We can tell each other everything. I don't have to hide who I am from you and you don't have to hide things from me."

She'd been drinking, which always made her a little bolder. "How long do you think you're going to see this dominatrix?"

He raised his eyebrows. "Why?"

"I just want to know."

"Does it bother you? I've been completely upfront with you, Paige. I'd think you could return the courtesy."

"The courtesy?"

"Of trusting me. You know what's going on. What more do you want?"

"I thought you'd get this … *thing* out of your system. I didn't think it would just go on and on and on."

"Paige, you need to deal with your own issues."

"My issues?" Her voice was so loud the driver glanced at them in the rearview mirror.

"Shh! This is about your own insecurity, Paige. Maybe this is about you aging, and feeling unattractive because of that."

"Feeling unattractive?" He'd struck a nerve that vibrated through her whole body. It wasn't about age though; these issues had run through their marriage, with Paige feeling less substantial with each passing year. Living with Derek had hollowed her out to the point that the exterior had become brittle and tough to maintain. It was like a fine building that was ruined inside; sooner or later, the façade would come crashing down.

That night, she couldn't sleep. Even though Derek lay beside her, she felt a bridge between them that she couldn't cross. She wanted to be close to him, to bring him over to her side, but she had no idea how to do that. It wasn't until the next morning that she realized there was one person who could help her.

She hesitated when she stepped out of the cab in front of Dr. Shapiro's Gramercy Park brownstone. She'd called ahead, so he was expecting her. A middle-aged redhead she took for his wife answered the door and ushered her into an anteroom filled with towering bookcases. When Dr. Shapiro finally appeared, she'd picked up an art book and was leafing through it.

"Waterhouse. Interesting choice." He was a round man with a bald head and owlish glasses. His skin was pale, as if the sun never touched his face, and as smooth as a baby's.

"Is that some kind of test, having these books here? What does choosing the Waterhouse say about me?"

"This isn't a Rorschach test, Paige. It's a book. But, if you want something to consider, show me the paintings that intrigued you."

Feeling faintly ridiculous, Paige turned to an image of a flame-haired woman in a long, gauzy dress; her face was turned away from the viewer and she peered into a gold box that she'd started to crack open.

"*Psyche Opening the Golden Box.* Interesting. Any others?"

It was like being asked to pick a tarot card by a fortune teller, Paige realized. She'd gone through a phase, a couple of years back, when she'd seen plenty of those, until she'd gotten wise to their tricks: the vague statements that were really questions, the hushed, anguished expressions when they pulled certain cards, their way of reshaping statements that didn't fit. Paige flipped through the book and showed Dr. Shapiro a dark-haired woman in a bold red dress, sitting at a loom and staring out a window.

" '*I Am Half-Sick of Shadows,' Said the Lady of Shalott,* " Dr. Shapiro read. "Fascinating."

"Oh, and this one." Paige opened the book to a bare-breasted, alabaster-skinned woman lying dead on the ground, with a Roman centurion and wailing people in the background. "*St. Eulalia,*" she added, before he could read the name next to it.

Dr. Shapiro gave her a sour look, as if she'd spoiled his fun. "Highly symbolic. Let's go into my office." He led her to the room at the back of the townhouse. There was a walnut desk and a big chair behind it, and a couple of plush chairs that she and Derek had sat in when they visited.

He closed the door. "You said on the phone you needed to talk. I should explain that, while I don't have an ethical problem treating both you and your husband, I cannot tell you anything from his sessions or vice versa. Is that understood?"

She felt like slapping the smugness off his face. Given what he was charging for a fifty-minute appointment, she was sure he'd have taken a sewer rat on as a patient if it paid in cash. "Yes."

"Well then," he settled into his seat. "What would you like to talk about?"

Paige cleared her throat. "I'm still struggling with my husband's ... *fascination* with seeing a dominatrix."

"That's understandable. Is there a particular aspect of it that bothers you?"

"Aspect?"

"Do you think about the woman, or fear your husband gains more pleasure with her than with you, or ..."

He went on suggesting scenarios. What Paige wanted to ask was why her husband didn't want her to dominate him. Did he think she was unattractive? Did he think her a prude? That was at the heart of what tortured her, but she couldn't give it voice. Instead, she burst into tears.

Dr. Shapiro set a box of tissues on the chair next to her, but he didn't interrupt. She was glad, though she realized what a mistake she'd made by coming to his office. He couldn't help. No one could.

"I should go."

"Paige, I understand this is difficult to talk about. May I make a suggestion? Go home, and think about your reaction when your husband told you he wanted to role play."

"Think about what? Derek never told me he wanted to role play."

"But when he first spoke to you at home about his desire to be dominated, how did you respond?"

"He never brought the subject up. The first time I heard about it was in your office."

Dr. Shapiro frowned. "You mean to say that your husband never broached this subject with you first? You had no indication from him of his desires?"

"No." Hot shame flooded her face as she answered. The humiliation, being married to a man for seventeen years and not understanding the seamier sides of his mind, not even knowing it was there. "One day he said we needed to go to couples counseling here, with you. That's when he dropped that bomb."

"But he told me the story of what happened when he tried to talk to you about it."

"That never happened."

She started to leave.

"Interesting," Dr. Shapiro said. "The games couples play with each other."

"This isn't a game. Not to me."

"Well, it may be to your husband."

When Paige went home that afternoon, she ran a hot bath and took a bottle of wine with her into the tub. Maybe she would drown, like the Lady of Shalott. Wait, was that how the lady had died? It was in the Arthurian legend, something about a boat, but she didn't really remember it, and the painting in the book had just shown the lady staring out the window, daydreaming about Lancelot.

My husband hates me, she thought. *He's playing some sick game with me, and I don't even know it.* Derek needled her all the time, in small ways that were hard to point out to other people. It was a special kind of hell she found herself alone in. It was almost as if he derived pleasure from torturing her. *Sadist,* she thought.

She sat bolt upright, splashing water out of the tub. Was that what his game was about? Watch how she reacted when he caused her pain, and see how deep the wound went?

Paige clambered out of the bath and wrapped a towel around her. In her bedroom, she cursed herself for throwing away the corset. It had actually been pretty. Instead, she pulled on a black bra and panties and zipped up a pair of black boots with kitten heels. Over that outfit went a beige raincoat she belted closed.

She took a taxi to midtown. Five o'clock. Derek would still be at his office for a while. The receptionist smiled and greeted her, but Paige ignored the woman. She had something to ask Derek, and she was chewing the inside of her mouth, to work up the nerve.

His door was open and she walked in, shutting it behind her. Derek's desk was an uncluttered glass showpiece. His framed diplomas were on the wall, along with photos of Derek with politicians and his more infamous clients. His civic awards and golf trophies dotted the office. It was a temple to self-congratulation.

Derek looked up from his laptop. "Well, this is a surprise."

"Why did you never ask me?" Paige demanded.

"Ask you what?"

"Ask me to act like a dominatrix, if that's what you wanted. You've never been shy telling me what you want!" She opened her coat, letting it drop to the floor. She moved so that she was right in front of his desk.

He closed the computer. "Oh, Paige, I was just sparing you from making a fool of yourself."

"How?"

"This isn't about costumes or accessories. If I asked you to dominate me, I'd have to stage-manage you through the whole process."

"Is that what you think of me?" Paige demanded. "That I'm weak?"

"You're a hopeless pushover."

"That's not true."

"It doesn't matter what I do, you don't say no."

"That's not true!"

"You're weak, Paige. You always have been."

Without thinking, she grabbed one of the trophies and swung it at him. The wooden base connected with the side of his head, and a seam of blood opened and dripped down his cheek. Derek stared at her, stunned into silence. She swung again but he ducked and reached for the phone. Paige grabbed its base and swung, connecting with his face. Derek made an awful yelping cry, dropping the phone and putting his hands to his face. "Stop it!" Blood oozed over his lips when he spoke.

"No."

Paige struck him again, bringing the phone down on top of his head, and he crashed into the desk, cracking the glass. She grabbed a wooden plaque and smashed it against the back of his neck. There was blood and glass everywhere, and Derek was on the floor, curled up like a baby, sobbing. She pounded him again and again, all the while thinking, *I hope you're enjoying this.* †

A GOOD KILL IS WORTH REPEATING
C. Courtney Joyner

The bullet ricocheted by Richard Conte's shoulder as he pressed against a dungeon wall of the Tower of London, huge rubber chains dangling by his head.

He half-smiled, "Mr. Hyde's not going to miss all night, kid," then brushed the Fuller's Earth from his cashmere jacket. "This isn't exactly what I signed on for."

"Me either, sir," Jimmy said, with his back against a tower parapet, holding his flashlight like a club and wishing it was a .45. He and Richard were separated by a few feet of plywood disguised as stone; a medieval walkway along the top of the Tower wall, where twenty years before, royal guards had stood with cardboard shields and fired flaming arrows on a crowd of angry peasants in the open courtyard below.

The shrapnel that had been sleeping in Jimmy's hip bit hard into muscle, spitting pain down the side of his left leg. Jimmy felt the blood pooling around the joint, swelling it, but he didn't dare make a move or take a loud breath. He swallowed the fire, thinking he heard the bolt on a rifle being thrown; a distant, metallic click.

Richard barely shifted from the shadowed protection of the archway where he was standing when a bullet blew a melon-size hole in the plaster wall by his knee, just kissing the razor crease of his gray flannels. "It's those damn kliegs. Can you make him out at all?"

On the opposite side of The Tower, Mr. Hyde was just a shape, moving in front of the sun-hot glare of the gigantic klieg lights that had been set up on the adjoining Western street to light a night shoot-out.

Shielding his eyes, Jimmy could make out the monstrous silhouette, in opera hat and cape, racing along the top of the turreted wall. Hyde carried a high-power rifle with a sniper's scope and dove behind an archer's pulpit. It was all a squinted blur, curtained by the flaring white of the movie lights.

Jimmy closed his eyes, greenish dots squirming behind his lids. "He's on the far wall."

Hyde's rifle flamed from behind a pulpit, the slug tearing the meat in Jimmy's shoulder, burning flesh and fabric together. He cried out, as deep red soaked through his security tan. Another five shots reported, but they came from the Western street, echoed, and died phony against the San Fernando mountains.

Richard leaned out of the shadows with, "Hang on, Navy. Where's the Winchester '73?"

Jimmy tasted blood and spit it out. Richard's voice was lost in a sea of sound and pounding memory: men screaming, the roar of a Mig, and Lou Costello barking, "Hey, when are we gonna shoot this crap?"

❖

Charles Lamont checked his watch, and then low-whistled through his light gray moustache as Lou kept it up, "You're supposed to be the director of this thing, Charlie. Why the hell isn't the gag ready? I'm ready, and you're not! Know what that means? Quittin' time!"

Lou threw off his policeman's bobby and blue jacket in a single motion, handing them to the bent wardrobe woman who was instantly at his side. Lamont got up from his director's chair, thumbing his well-worn script for *The Boys Meet Dr. Jekyll and Mr. Hyde*. An assistant director reminded the Victorian dress extras through a bullhorn to, "Stay in your positions, ladies and gentlemen. The company is not dismissed."

Lou raised a hand before Lamont could say a word, "They're not, but I am."

"Lou, the effects guys are on break. As soon as they're back, we'll get the trap door working."

"Then you'll be all set for tomorrow. Check your watch again, Charlie. That's the one I gave you for Christmas, ain't it?"

Lou made his point with a little soft shoe and a twirl that brought chuckles and bits of applause from the Hyde Park crowd, as he started for the large caravan that was parked at the end of the cobblestone street, and served as his and Bud's dressing room. Lamont felt a pat on his shoulder as Bud Abbott, also dressed as a London copper, leaned in with just a hint of Maker's Mark, "Sorry, but if the little fella goes, I go. Don't worry, pal. We'll get it first thing."

Jimmy Pearl took another bite of his tuna sandwich, folding back the wax paper so it wouldn't scatter on his uniform, and watched Bud give the extras a wave before falling in with a couple of sun-burns in shark-skin suits, who were chattering over a racing form.

Bud passed with a wink, "Don't do anything I wouldn't do, pal."

Jimmy responded with a quick, "Yes sir," and a Navy salute; it was an automatic reaction, having just been separated from the USS *Iowa*. Jimmy's hip gave him a twinge, and he stretched his leg in front of him, leaning against the giant doors of Notre Dame Cathedral. He looked up at the gargoyles, met their cement stare, and smiled at the "James Pearl" etched by their feet.

Jimmy's dad had just started as a set builder when he fashioned the gargoyles where Lon Chaney's Quasimodo perched. Old Man Pearl never left Universal, and his production tales were Jimmy's bedtime stories. He was on the job, building a saloon, when his heart stopped. The hammer slipped from his hand, and he was dead before it hit the ground, on the very day his son had been promoted to Petty Officer, Second. The congratulation and condolence telegrams arrived for Jimmy stapled together, and they were in his pocket when a North

Korean fighter strafed the deck of the *Iowa* and he caught one in the hip.

When Jimmy called his Mom at the Universal commissary, where she still works as a waitress, she burst into tears and put Lana Turner on the phone to beg him to come home. Now that's exactly where he was. Jimmy checked his security guard's uniform for any stray tuna, brushing the front of his shirt.

"You look like you're going on parade."

"Doing honor to the post, sir."

Charles Lamont laughed in his easy way, slipping an arm around Jimmy's shoulder, "I'm sorry I couldn't make the homecoming, kid. We'd just started shooting. But we're all real proud of you. How long you been on the job?"

"This is my third week."

"I spent three weeks here twenty years ago, and haven't left yet. Same sets. *Inside Information*, a doozie with Dick Foran. Jesus, that was '39 and your Dad brought your Mom around—she was big as a house, carrying you."

Lamont half-stepped away, "Jim, could you pass by tonight and make sure the effects guys are on the trap door?"

"Part of my rounds."

Jimmy almost saluted again, but instead tossed the last of his sandwich. Grips shut down the lights, the burning arcs whining as they cooled. Traffic cones were placed at all four corners of Hyde Park while a yellow rope was strung around the bandstand, with caricatures of Bud and Lou warning, "Hot Set! Staaaay Awaaaay!"

A mush-faced grip planted a flag by the faulty trap door. It was just a few feet from the side of the bandstand, and the artificial grass had been pulled back to reveal it. Mush-Face gave the door a stomp with his size twelve's, but it didn't give. He made a gesture with his stubbed fingers and sauntered off, while Jimmy moved to his security box to check in.

That's when he saw the cat's pawprint in blood.

It was a jagged smear of red on the edge of a cobblestone, still wet to the touch. Jimmy knew the almost-black look of blood on the ground too well, and dabbed it with his fingertip. For a heartbeat, he heard his own screams on the deck of the *Iowa*. The feeling passed.

The next smear was a foot away, toward the park, and more distinctly the outline of a shoe. Jimmy moved to the next print by the edge of the lawn, with the cat's paw marking the center in drying brown.

Jimmy ignored Bud and Lou, and shone his flashlight under the bandstand. Perhaps an animal had been injured and crawled away, but all he found was a litter of coffee cups and call sheets. Jimmy straightened, his hip throbbing, when he looked down at the trap door and saw the thickening blood oozing around the rude edges.

A diamond-clean Chrysler New Yorker convertible pulled up and Richard Conte smiled, "Hey, Navy, can you do me a favor and let me out the back gate?"

A sniper shot tore the Tower of London, shredding a bogus granite pillar. Richard said again, "Navy, listen to me, where's the Winchester '73?"

Richard let the sound of the shot fade, then asked one more time. There was no hint of crisis in his smooth voice, and he kept repeating the question to bring Jimmy back from his pain, "The Winchester, kid, the Winchester."

Jimmy coughed and angled his head toward a small set of iron stairs for camera crews to haul up equipment. The Winchester '73 rifle was lying just below the second step.

Richard backed into a corner hidden by the archway, grabbed a Guard's pike cobwebbed to the floor, and moved as close as he could to the border of the dark of the set and bright light of the kliegs.

Jimmy rolled his shoulders to ease the burn, but stayed huddled against his stone protection. Richard reached out with the pike, arms stretching, trying to hook the Winchester's finger lever. A shadow moved passed the kliegs, and Richard lifted the rifle, caught the gun in mid-air, pumped a shell into the chamber, and fired blindly toward the hot white.

A slug blasted the plywood-stone at Richard's feet as he stepped from the shadows, firing at the phantom on the opposite wall. Richard was in constant motion, bringing down the lever action, hefting Jimmy from behind the parapet, and pulling the trigger. It was all sound and flame as Conte emptied the Winchester and they dove for the iron stairs.

Jimmy's legs numbed beneath him as Richard threw an arm under his shoulder for support, hauling him down through the Tower's hollow walls. They felt the heat as a bullet screamed against the iron supports around them, then spun off into a wheelbarrow full of sand with a dead thud.

They reached the bottom, and Richard handed Jimmy a monogrammed handkerchief, "Around here this kind of stuff is supposed to be make-believe. We've both had our fill of the real thing."

Jimmy pressed the handkerchief against the bullet wound, "Yeah, but an old Winchester rifle filled with blanks just saved our bacon. Real is getting kind of mixed-up, isn't it? There's a secret entrance right there."

Richard pushed aside a pair of faded Zulu warrior shields and a spokeless wagon wheel to get to the cut in the canvas that was the back of the Tower set. He twisted the wire ties that held the opening as Jimmy steadied himself, using the pike and Winchester for crutches.

"Careful. I cut myself a million times on those when I was a kid."

Richard deep-sliced his finger on the last tie before pulling the molding canvas open, "Thanks for the warning, now let's get the police."

Jimmy's answer caught in his throat and Richard froze, as they saw Hyde, a few yards away, standing next to an English buggy. Richard let the canvas drape back as Jimmy whispered, "Can we get around him?"

"Too close to the car," Richard took the Winchester, "He can hit us any second. Think you can swing that thing?"

"Yes, sir."

Richard gripped the edge of the canvas and yanked it back in a quick motion. Jimmy half-leapt through the opening, smashing the pike between Hyde's shoulders as Richard swung the rifle hard into the back of Hyde's skull with a loud crack.

It was a solid base hit; Mr. Hyde's head spun cleanly away, eyes unblinking and crepe hair flying, before bouncing off the trunk of Richard's Skylark and landing in a pile of artificial shrubbery. Blood didn't geyser, and Hyde's body was only bent at the waist where a steel spine held it together, his apelike arms swinging free.

Jimmy held up the head. The thick lips over exposed fangs, flared nose, and hanging, wrinkled brow were a perfect recreation of Boris Karloff's monster that was terrorizing Bud and Lou on Stage Four.

Richard lit a Newport with his gold Dunhill, "Westmore does great work, but we sure didn't need this tonight. Somebody's having us, Navy. This is the big put-on."

"The dead man wasn't a put-on; I don't know about the rest …."

Richard ran his hands across the dented trunk, bullet holes, and shattered glass of his once-pristine convertible, "Don't take this wrong, kid, but I really wish I'd gone out the front gate tonight."

Richard Conte looked at his watch, as if he could retrieve the last two hours, and remake his evening sweet and easy, like he had planned it. That is, before he saw Jimmy standing in Hyde Park, asking him for a favor.

Jimmy stepped away from the trap door, and examined his heels for blood, as Richard climbed from his convertible with, "Are you all right, Navy?"

"Mr. Conte, can I borrow your tire iron?"

Richard laughed, "I guess so. What's going on?"

He looked down at the wet red spread across the trick doors by the bandstand and then Jimmy said, "Lou Costello was supposed to fall through these doors this afternoon, but they jammed."

"It's a gag that didn't come off. Happens all the time."

Jimmy slipped the tire iron between the small doors and pried. The hinges moaned as the wood split, but refused to give until Richard stood on one of the doors, holding it down, as the other broke open.

Jimmy and Richard Conte took a step back.

The man's body had been corkscrewed into the hole with such force one of the shoulders was dislocated and pressing against his cheek. The left eye was obliterated by a high caliber round that exited just below the ear. The side of the face that wasn't corrupted was young, with leading-man features, and his black hair was meticulously combed. His cut-away jacket and striped trousers were soaked in a soup of bloody, brackish water, and a bowler hat was clutched in his hands.

"Jesus, Navy, who is he?"

Jimmy reached into the young man's jacket, and pulled out a folded time card. Richard leaned over Jimmy's shoulder, "C'mon, kid, you can call the cops from my dressing room."

The wine tasted warm as it went down, and Richard refilled Jimmy's glass. "I never knew a studio cop who didn't have a bottle someplace. Nur, made from Pomegranates. A gift from Akim Tamiroff. Take a minute."

Richard put the bottle of wine on a script-heavy coffee table. Jimmy sank into the couch, studying the red in his glass. "I thought I'd seen my last dead man."

Richard handed Jimmy a telephone, "They're going to fire a lot of questions at us, Navy, so you better call the cops now. Then I'll call my wife, my lawyer, and my agent."

"How long have you known my family?"

"Fifteen, sixteen years, when I first came out. Your folks were very good to me."

"That's who they are. When I was in Tokyo, fighting this hip, all I could think of was coming home. Here. Universal's home for my family, and I don't want the stink of this to hurt them."

"That's great, kid, but this is a job. You've got to bring in the police."

"Of course, but a murder investigation could touch anybody whoever walked through that front gate."

Richard put down his glass, "I was calling my agent and my lawyer, just because I was standing next to you. Funny how fast you can switch into 'Hollywood' mode."

"It's still my shift and right now we know more than the police. A little investigating on the QT could help wrap this thing up really fast."

Richard lit a fresh Newport. "We take care of our own, huh? My old man was a barber, you grew up in this business. The hard fact is there never was a scandal in Hollywood that didn't end up as a publicity heyday."

"For all the wrong reasons. These people are family to me, and I want—have—to protect my family."

"Sounds like dialog from one of my old pictures. Rumor is you took it in the hip pulling two buddies to safety."

Jimmy shrugged, "That's what I was supposed to do."

"I'm probably going to regret this." Richard Conte moved to his make-up mirror, snapped on the framing lights and studied himself, "I still don't know how a singing waiter ended up here; nobody gets anywhere alone, Navy. Your buddies owe you, and I owe your old man. So we'll see what we can find out, and then we bring in the cops. Deal?"

"Deal."

"The only ID is a time card?"

The boy's handwriting was a mixture of crude printing and a try at cursive, with some letters inverted. Richard smiled, "It reminds me of my son's first attempt at a father's day card. Was this kid ... okay?"

Jimmy called production, and they read everything they had about the dead man: "Name's Owen Franks; he reported at nine

A.M. as a dress extra for Abbott and Costello production 3456, and he got a salary bump for riding a bicycle through a shot."

Richard drew smoke deep in his lungs, "So he was one of ten thousand kids who get off the bus every year. That was vicious, what was done to him. You have to hate pretty good to do that kind of violence. How could a kid make that kind of enemy?"

Jimmy turned over the call sheet and on the back was scrawled, "S.L. at 8."

"The initials of someone he was supposed to meet?"

"I need to find someone who knew him. Other than Abbott and Costello, the only other picture he worked on was a Western, and it's still shooting."

Richard Conte angled the Skylark along the edge of Universal Lake, where painters were adding another fresh coat of white to the Mississippi Riverboat.

Jimmy said, "I called special effects and told them not to bother with the trap door. I didn't want them finding the body before I completed my ... mission."

"Navy, for somebody who's only been on the job for three weeks, you've got your neck stuck out a hundred miles."

Jimmy agreed in silence as Richard parked his car next to a prop van stacked with antique rifles and pistols. Lee, a gangly bit player in denims and six guns, sprawled on the tailgate rolling a cigarette, "Well, well, look here, the man in uniform. Whatever it is, I didn't do it."

Lee extended one of his enormous paws to Jimmy, "How are ya, Navy? Gonna stay and see me bite the dust?"

"I might, Lee. Got much in this one?"

"One week and ten lines. That's enough. And it's an honor to work with Audie. Semper Fi, kid."

Lee grinned, waiting for Navy to take the challenge, but Jimmy just shook his hand, "Semper Fi."

Audie Murphy sat in a swayback chair, a binder resting on his knees, studying his lines, when he looked up and saw Richard Conte walk onto the Western street dressed for dinner at Chasen's, and not a showdown. Audie tipped his black hat with a shy smile, but remained focused on the multi-colored script in front of him.

Richard returned the nod as his eyes fixed on Audie's co-star, Susie Lane. The petite, raven-haired beauty was standing on the porch of the saloon, trying to lasso a piece-of-leather stuntman. Beyond her, the camera crew was rolling klieg lights off a flatbed truck for the night scenes.

The lasso tangled with Susie laugh; her eyes and smile danced as she tried one more time, the rope settling cleanly over the stuntman's chaw-stain beard to his shoulders.

"Good throw, honey."

Susie bowed with a giggle, "Thank you, Gil. I didn't feel right playing all these cowgirls and not being able to throw a rope!"

"Next we'll work on your quick-draw."

"Believe it or not, that I can do!"

Susie's smile froze when she saw Richard standing by her chair. She brushed the dust from her blue jeans, walked over, kissed Richard on the cheek, and said quickly, "Good to see you, Richard, and I think I know why you're here. Owen, yes?"

"This really is the smallest city in the world."

"I see security talking to the assistant director, and he's with you. Simple arithmetic. Is Owen causing problems on your set, because I don't want to get him into trouble."

Richard lit a Newport, handed it to Susie, "Why would you ask that?"

"Because he caused me problems, but I didn't report it, until—"

"What?"

"He's been with us on *Silver Creek* all week and kept asking me out. I said no about a hundred times but he wouldn't hear it. I have a dressing room filled with flowers and candy from a total stranger! That's when I left a message at security. Isn't that why Jimmy's here?"

"It's about Owen, yes."

"I just wanted him to leave me alone. He even got it in his mind I was going to meet him tonight, even though I'm working."

"That's not a problem now, honey."

Susie Lane looked directly at Richard with, "You're being gentle and not telling me directly."

"Maybe you should sit down."

"You just said it all." Susie eased into her chair. "You're the third person in two days to ask me about him."

"They're going to be more, Susie. And probably before morning."

"The police?"

Richard Conte nodded, and Susie squeezed his hand, eyes fixed straight ahead, "I stay to myself, Richard. Owen was kind of sweet, but he frightened me. My life is my private business, but I never would want anything bad to happen to anyone."

"I know. The cops are going to want to know about the other guy, the one who was asking questions."

"He never spoke to me, he just talked to the A.D. like Jimmy is now. Don Siegel got pretty annoyed, because he was trying to get a shot. You did the right thing, telling me."

Richard nodded toward Jimmy, "The kid's trying to defuse the situation, keep it here on the lot."

Susie Lane wiped her eyes and smeared make-up with a quiet, "That would be nice."

At the prop truck, Lee was checking his Colt's as Jimmy and Richard returned to the Skylark. Lee whipped one of the pistols from its holster, spun it on his finger, then dropped it back in its leather. "You know what's missing from your new picture, Dick? Me."

Richard slapped Lee on the back, "You just might have a point."

Richard slid in behind the wheel when the shot blew apart the driver's mirror, an explosion of silvered glass and metal, then spider-webbed the tinted windshield.

Lee bellowed, "Whoa, what the Christ was that?"

Richard snapped on his headlights to show up the railroad water tower, as a cloaked shadow leapt from a slap-board ladder to the ground, and ran like hell. "Right there!"

Jimmy said, "Lee, security will be here in five minutes, but we don't want a panic!"

Lee shrugged, "I'm not panicked," then pulled a Winchester '73 repeater from the prop truck, and tossed it to Jimmy, "Don't let the bastard think all you've got is a flashlight!"

Richard Conte dropped the Skylark into gear and punched the gas, spit gravel, and was gone. He gunned the 'Lark, roaring past the old steam locomotive, across a rickety trestle, before turning hard onto New York Street.

They fishtailed wild, then slowed as Richard and Jimmy kept their eyes on the phony rooftops, the rumble of the V8 backing them up. Richard said, "He had to come this way. If he turned back, he would have ended up at the lake."

"No, they're prepping it for some kind of a monster movie, he'd be running right into a crowd. Hold up—"

Richard braked as Jimmy nodded toward the fluttering curtains in the upper window of a rubber-and-plaster brownstone. Something was moving. Richard's words were measured, "No more chances, Navy. Let's get to the nearest phone."

"The Tower of London."

Mr. Hyde suddenly leapt across the hood, rolled, and came up shouldering the K98 Sniper's. Gunfire from the *Iowa* echoed in Jimmy's ears as he pulled the Winchester. Richard floored it, whipping the front end of the car at the monster, tires burning. Jimmy cracked off two shots. Hyde fired wild, shattering a street lamp, as the 'Lark jumped the sidewalk, the bumper hot-sparking the curb.

Hyde dove out of the way, recovered, and took out a taillight as the Skylark exploded through a balsa-wood fruit stand. Richard checked over his shoulder to see Hyde running hard in the opposite direction before skidding to a stop beside the Tower's arched walls. Jimmy leapt from the car for the security phone and grabbed the receiver just as a slug blew it in half. He hit the deck.

Bullets from nowhere hard-punched the car as Richard kept low, rolled out of the passenger side, and yelled, "Navy! You all right?"

Jimmy grabbed the Winchester, "We'll take cover in the Tower!"

❖

An hour later, and Richard Conte was trying to make sense of Hyde, Jimmy, Susie Lane, and his near-dead Skylark. He wanted his wife, a Scotch, and sleep, but knew that none were coming soon. He picked up Mr. Hyde's head with, "Friend, you've caused me a hell of a lot of trouble. I won't forget it," and tossed it into the backseat.

Around the Tower, sheriff's deputies roamed the sets, shouting to each other, flashlights barely slicing the valley fog rolling in over the hills. Richard blanched as one deputy shone a light in his eyes, "Wow, Mr. Conte? Richard Conte? This is really something to find you here!"

Richard smiled, angling the flashlight away from his face, and regarded the man with the shaved head and ill-fitting uniform. "Well, this is a movie studio."

"I just saw *The Raiders*. Really liked that one."

"Thanks, I don't get the chance to do Westerns very often."

"So what happened here, anyway?"

Richard soft-punched his words, "It was like a night in an asylum, but I think we're supposed to give a formal statement to your chief in the morning."

The deputy smiled, "Understood, I'll just continue with my assignment. Oh, I should take that."

He reached for the rubber monstrosity and Richard stopped him with a look, saying, "I think we're supposed to wait for the detectives. I made a mistake and touched it, and you're not wearing gloves."

"I am part of the investigating team, Mr. Conte."

"Just doing what I was told. You cut your fingers?"

"Yeah, making dinner."

Richard rubbed the deep cut on his finger, "I did too, on some wire. Not making dinner."

The deputy swallowed a laugh, "I've wasted enough time and we're still looking for your so-called monster. I'd like to clear a few things up, so I'll be right up this road when you're ready to talk."

After adjusting his cap to shadow his eyes, the deputy strode up the curving lane that led to Frankenstein Village. Richard watched, as Jimmy limped over to the car, sporting a clean shirt, bandaged shoulder, and two A&Ws.

"My mom's in tears again; these are from her," Jimmy handed Richard one of the root beers. "Susie's giving a statement about Owen. They don't have a thing except Bud Westmore reported a Hyde mask stolen."

"Have them check wardrobe for a missing deputy's uniform. That's the bastard right there, Navy."

Jimmy turned to see the deputy stride the pathway with slow, deliberate steps. He tasted the fog in the back of his throat as the deputy moved deeper into the mist. Richard's voice was low, "Bastard's playing us."

"No, he's trapping himself."

Jimmy grabbed the top edge of the false, plaster-rock wall and jostled it loose, revealing a tunneled entrance next to the Tower's drawbridge. He said, "This was my clubhouse. It connects with the Frankenstein Village so the crews can haul special effects rigs. There's nowhere he can go I can't get first."

"And waiting with that rifle."

Jimmy opened his shirt to reveal the Navy automatic tucked in his belt, "This is the last place I ever thought I'd be needing it—for real."

"What about the sheriff?"

"Ready. A warning shot and they'll swarm."

"So you're doing this by yourself?"

"I have to. My watch, my screw-up."

"I told you, I owe your old man, so I can't stand by while you put yourself in jeopardy. You got lucky once. Barely."

"This is all on me, Mr. Conte."

"Something's driving you, kid. I don't like being played for a sucker, or to be anybody's target practice." Richard tossed away his Newport. "Okay, I'll walk point, give you a chance to sneak attack. With that hip and shoulder, you need all the help you can get."

"You don't have to do this."

"Don't remind me."

The fog curtained heavy around Richard as he walked across the Tower's drawbridge. He lit a cigarette, pausing for his face to be seen in the flame. By his feet, Jimmy peered up through a grating, and threw the star a salute.

Richard said, "Okay, Navy, let's go," then started toward a small, wooded spot. The trees were twisted, knotted shapes glistening with moisture, and standing beyond them was the village of Frankenstein.

Below the road to the village, Jimmy's footsteps echoed the length of the underground tunnel as he followed his flashlight to the doors that lined the walls. They were worn, guarded by spiders, and painted with barely readable numbers that indicated which set they led to. Jimmy swung his flash on the grating just above his head, and saw Richard walking passed the Burgomaster's office to the village square. Richard's voice echoed in the tunnel, "Deputy, I think you and I should talk."

Richard Conte stood by the town square fountain, where the four streets of the village convened. The deputy hung back in a doorway where the Wolfman once sprung, the sniper's rifle resting against his hip. The fog embraced both men, and the dark windows of the faux buildings around them were the eyeless sockets of so many skulls in a row.

"I've made a lot of pictures, but being here gives me the creeps."

The deputy smirked, "My Mr. Hyde terrified you."

Richard smiled, "You had the rifle, we had nothing, and gave you a pretty rough time."

"And you still have nothing?"

Richard put his hands up, "Just like that kid you shot. How many cops do you figure are in the studio right now?"

"They're spread out everywhere. They won't hear us. Move."

Jimmy's hip and shoulder seared as he made his way to the last door in the tunnel, and threw his weight against it, forcing it open.

The large surgical table with restraining straps and electrodes for the monster's head dominated the center of Stage Six. Two large steel orbs suspended between neon tubes hung above it, while heavy cables and liquid-filled spirals connected the table to a series of life-giving devices from which electricity jumped.

The deputy kept the rifle at Richard's stomach as he motioned him into Frankenstein's lab. Richard stepped around a table with a glass container marked "Human Brain," and asked, "Is this yours, deputy?"

"Typical American arrogance that you'd make a joke now."

"Where are you from?"

"I was never born."

"Does that mean you can't die?"

Hot-blue lightning burst from the orbs over the table, blinding the deputy for a heartbeat as the bullet punched through his phony badge. A jet of red sprayed, the deputy dropped, hands wrapped around the rifle.

Jimmy stepped from behind a cone-shaped laser cannon mounted on a trolley, the gun in his hand still smoking. Jimmy threw another switch, and the other machines jump-sparked to life, "My dad showed me how."

Richard grabbed for the rifle, but Deputy held it fast, "It doesn't happen like that—this isn't the movies."

Jimmy put the .45 against the deputy's ear, "Who was that kid to you?"

"Nobody. A target, with poor choice in women."

Richard asked, "Susie Lane? She knew about this?"

"She is blissfully ignorant. There is a man who loves her, who insists that anyone who causes her distress be dealt with, and she goes innocently on. In your parlance, she would be a femme fatale who isn't even aware of it."

Jimmy pressed the gun into the deputy's cheek, "Who's the man?"

"Someone you don't want as an enemy, and now you have him. Very powerful, very jealous, and with a thousand like me. You're wasting your strength, sailor boy."

Gunfire and screams pounded in Jimmy's ears, as he smashed the deputy's nose with the pistol, screaming, "Tell me who the enemy is!"

Blood smeared the deputy's teeth when he smiled. Jimmy's eyes dropped to see he'd slipped his thumb around the rifle's trigger. He whispered, "You'll find out," jerked the barrel under his chin, and fired.

Jimmy and Richard didn't see the slug hit the electrode box, only the fireball that exploded from it. The lab burst into plumes of orange flame, sparks danced wild, and chemical fire erupted. Acrid smoke strangled the air. Jimmy and Richard made it to the stage door, the deputy's body buried under a mountain of old, burning props.

Jimmy Pearl sat in the wooden booth facing Lankershim Boulevard, the *Variety* headline in front of him screaming, "Frankenstein Fire Destroys Stage!" and a column below it, "Susie Lane to Br'dwy Debut." The cars streamed in, and Jimmy checked ID's, but his thoughts were someplace else. He opened the gate for Martha Hyer, all blonde and sunglasses, and then returned to reading about how "The Great White Way is just wild about Susie," his Navy .45 beside him in his lunchbox.

Richard Conte pulled up, playfully beeping the horn of his new Skylark, "How have you been, Navy?"

"They wanted me to take a couple of weeks off, but it's better to keep on watch. This is home, after all." Jimmy pulled a card from his pocket and handed it to Richard. It said "Jimmy Pearl, Private Investigations."

Jimmy said, "What do you think?"

Richard Conte put the card on his sun visor, with "I got some friends who just might need you."

Jimmy pressed a button, and the wooden gate lifted with an electric hum. He watched the movie star angle his convertible past a group of Indians heading into the studio commissary, before throwing Jimmy a quick salute. †

DRIFTER FROM WENATCHEE
John D. Nesbitt

I was sitting on the steps outside my room when a stranger pulled into the auto court in a yellow-and-white Chrysler. He parked in front of number 23, which had been vacant, and went inside with a brown bag of groceries. A little while later, Roxanne came out and sat in a metal chair in front of room 21. She did that just about every night while her father and mother and brother sat inside drinking beer and watching a black-and-white television. I went over to talk to her, hoping as usual that I would get next to her one of these nights.

Roxanne was a dishwater blonde with a pale complexion for someone who worked in the fields. This evening she was wearing a sleeveless white blouse and sand-colored shorts, so her pale legs were noticeable.

"Hi," I said. "How'd it go today?"

"About the same. And you?"

I shrugged. "About normal." She and her family were picking peaches just as I was, but for a different outfit, and it was rare that anything new happened either in the orchard or in the camp.

"It got hot today."

"Oh, yeah," I said. "I drank a lot of water."

She lit a cigarette, and her mouth held the shape of an "O" as she blew the smoke away. Then her eyes looked past me.

I turned to see a guy with dark hair slicked back on the sides and over on top. He was wearing a gold-colored shirt with the collar turned up and the short sleeves cuffed. As he strolled toward Roxanne, I noticed the name "Carol" above his left bicep.

He was an older guy in his mid-thirties, and he had a cocksure air about him. He ignored me as he lifted his head and tossed a glance at Roxanne. "Hey, there," he said. "My name's Vince. I just moved in next door." He pointed with his thumb at number 23.

She said, "Uh-huh," but she didn't look at him.

His head swayed. "Just thought I'd say hello."

She looked up at him with her mouth twisted and her eyebrows drawn, but she didn't say anything.

His voice had a down-home accent when he said, "You look kinda cute when you give me that go-to-hell look."

I didn't care for his kind of hustle, so I said, "I bet you get a lot of 'em."

His face went hard, and he gave me a cold stare. "I don't get any from the likes of you, buddy."

I shut up. I knew he could kick my ass, and he seemed ready to prove it.

He moved his head back toward her. "What's your name?"

"Roxanne."

"Roxie," he said. "Roxie-Doxie."

She took a puff on her cigarette.

"Well, it's nice to meet you," he said. "I'll come back when you can talk more. Maybe we'll go for a spin. Have a milkshake or somethin'. Don't you think?"

"I don't know."

He strolled away, doing a kind of hoodlum walk I'd seen in the movies.

When he went inside, I said to Roxanne, "That guy thinks he's pretty smart."

"He's just tryin' to be friendly."

"Yeah, I noticed."

❖

The couple on the other side of me in 29 worked in the same orchard I did. The man's name was Jimmy. He was about fifty, a typical guy in field work except that he had a young Mexican wife. He told me he met her through an ad in a magazine. She was somewhere near thirty-five, I'd guess, and her name was Celestina. He called her Sally.

When we took a break at mid-morning, Celestina went to the can. Jimmy sat on the second rung of his ladder, lit a cigarette, and spoke in his squeaky Texan voice. "You know that feller that moved in last night? Well, he's no stranger, and I'll tell ya, I don't think he's up to any good."

"Do you know him from somewhere else?"

"Wenatchee. He was pickin' cheeries where we were. Had his eye on Sally, I could tell. 'Course, he never got anywhere, but that don't stop his kind."

I didn't wonder why he took the trouble to tell me that the guy didn't get anywhere. I hadn't been all that impressed with Celestina's love for her husband. She was gloomy most of the time and spoke to him in a cross voice. If I was older I might have seen more in her, because she had a nice figure. But she didn't seem to care for me, and I didn't worry about her at all. As for Jimmy, he reminded me of the saying that there was no fool like an old fool. I had the basic feeling that she would leave him some day, and it didn't make me feel sorry.

"Do you think he followed you down here?" I asked.

"Could be. I bleeve he knew where we were goin' next."

I didn't doubt that. A lot of people like Jimmy followed a pattern—pick cherries in Stockton, go up to Washington and pick some more, come back down here to work in the peaches or pears, and so on. The government called them migrants, but the common term was fruit tramps.

Jimmy took another drag. He had small, narrow eyes, kind of a washed-out blue, and he squinted as he nodded his head. "I don't think he'll git anywhere, though, not with Sally. If she pisses up the rope on me, she won't get her papers."

❖

That evening I told Roxanne she might want to be careful with this guy Vince. I didn't give her particulars, but I told her Jimmy knew him from before and thought he could be trouble.

"Don't talk too loud," she said. "He's in there drinkin' beer with my dad."

I felt a sinking in my stomach, but I tried not to show it. "He moves pretty fast, huh?"

"He works on the same crew as we do, so he met my dad that way."

"Well, just a word to the wise."

"No need to worry about me."

I hung around for a few minutes more until Vince came out doing his hoodlum walk. He flinched when he saw me, but he raised his head and ignored me as he tapped Roxanne on the arm.

"Hey, babe, your dad says you can go for a spin with me. What do you think?"

"I don't know."

"We won't be gone long. Just get a six-pack." He wagged his eyebrows. "Come on."

"Oh, okay."

❖

I was sulking in my room a little later on when I heard a knock on the door. When I opened it, Vince was standing on the step.

"Come outside for a minute."

"What for?"

"I've got something to say to you." He stood with his arms bent, like he was ready for action.

"You can say it from where you are."

His hand came from nowhere, and he grabbed me by the front of the shirt. He dragged me out through the doorway, switched hands, and punched me on the left side of my face. I stumbled and fell down.

"That's for sayin' shit about me," he said.

Jimmy's voice came up from behind. "That's enough! Leave that kid alone. Come in here startin' trouble."

Vince turned halfway and sneered at him. "Aw, shut up."

Jimmy had most of his teeth, but his lips pushed together like an old gummer's. His voice was high-pitched and loud. "Shut up your own self. Better yet, git out. No one wants you here."

Vince used both hands to grab Jimmy by the shirt, swing him halfway around, and slam him up against the building. "Don't make me hit you, you old fuck." He let go of Jimmy and walked away.

Jimmy's voice rose again. "You stay away from me, and my wife, too. No one needs you."

Vince stopped and turned. His chest was heaving up and down, and I could see it took an effort for him not to do any more. He gave Jimmy a scowl and went into his room.

Jimmy took a couple of steps toward me as he brushed at his shirt. "Just a drifter. That's what he is. And a trouble-maker."

❖

Roxanne was snippy with me when I tried to talk to her the next evening. "You and Jimmy, one of you's as bad as the other. Stirrin' things up."

The Chrysler was gone, so I said what I thought. "Us? Casanova here, he's the one that caused all the trouble. That's what I get for warnin' you. If you ask me, I think you're a fool to have anything to do with him."

She rolled her eyes. "Well, I'll do what I want, and I don't have to ask you."

I took a close look at her. I felt as if I just then knew something about her. "You're probably fool enough to run off with him."

She wagged her head as she blew out a breath of smoke. "Even if I did, it shouldn't be anything to you."

❖

I didn't talk to her for about three days, and I tried not to pay any attention to what she did. But I saw her coming and going with Vince a couple of times, and I hoped like hell she didn't throw herself away on someone like him.

❖

I was sitting on the steps in front of my room when I heard loud voices in Jimmy's cabin and saw Celestina come out with a pair of suitcases. They were the old pasteboard type, light tan with leather corners. She set them down in front of the doorway and went back inside.

I had seen Vince leave on foot about ten minutes earlier, so I didn't know what to make of Celestina packing her bags. For all I knew, it was something she did when she and Jimmy got into an argument. And from the way I'd heard his voice go up and stay on a whiny pitch, I thought he might have been drinking.

The next time Celestina came out, she had two grocery sacks crammed full. She set them next to the suitcases and stood there.

Jimmy came to the doorway and said, "Put that stuff back inside. You're not goin' anywhere."

"I do what I want," she said.

"Well, so do I." He walked the few steps to his car, unlocked the door, and got in. It was a 1954 Ford, brown and white. He kept it backed into its parking place like some people did, in case the battery went dead and he had to push-start it. So he was on the other side of the car from where I was sitting, and I couldn't see him very well.

A few minutes later, Vince came walking along. He was carrying a paper bag with a carton of cigarettes sticking out. He seemed to change his pace as he turned into the auto court, and he was gazing in the direction of room 21 where Roxanne and her family lived.

Jimmy started up his car, and I didn't think much of it even when I heard him slip it into gear. He rolled out of the parking place, and when he was in the middle of the lot he goosed it. He headed straight at Vince.

I was impressed by how quick Vince was. He didn't turn and stare. He took two quick strides toward the cabins, and when he saw the car still bearing down on him, he jumped into the air. The nose of the Ford hit him on the legs, and he flopped onto the hood. The carton of cigarettes went sailing.

Jimmy slammed on the brakes, and the motor died.

Vince scrambled off the hood, went around to the driver's side, and yanked the door open. Jimmy leaned away and batted at Vince with his hand, but Vince got a hold of him and dragged him out of the car.

Celestina was shouting, "Yeemee, you crazy, you stupid!"

People came out of almost every room in the auto court. Someone hollered, "Call the cops," and someone else said, "Let 'em fight."

Vince hit Jimmy three or four times until the old man fell down. Then Vince piled on him and started hitting him with both fists.

Now Celestina was yelling, "Don't hit him. You going to hurt him."

Vince didn't let up, though, and it was sickening the way everyone just stood and watched. I knew I was in for a few punches myself, but I jumped in to try to get Vince off of Jimmy.

It worked better than I thought. As soon as I tackled Vince, he left Jimmy alone and went to work on me. He pushed me off, got to his feet, and came at me swinging. He hit me solid on each side of the face, and I went down.

When I got back on my feet, Jimmy was leaning into his car and reaching under the driver's seat. He came out with a lug wrench.

His voice was high-pitched and shaky as he said, "Now, you son of a bitch, we'll see how tough you are. See what you say to this."

Vince stood there with his eyes narrowed.

"Come on," Jimmy said. "Step up."

"Maybe I will." Vince walked to the passenger's side of his Chrysler, unlocked the door, and opened the glove box. He had a full audience when he turned around and pointed a dark-barreled pistol at Jimmy.

It sure stopped me, and the whole auto court went quiet. I caught a glimpse of Celestina, and she had the kind of expression on her face that you would expect a woman to have when the cops told her they arrested her husband for having a girl buried in the cellar. If she had had even half an idea of taking off with Vince before, it was gone now.

Jimmy's voice came out, squeaky but not as shaky as before. "You're real brave with that thing in your hand."

"Shut up."

"Real brave."

"Don't think I don't know how to use it." Vince looked around at me and Celestina and came back to Jimmy. "It's just not worth it with any of you. But don't push me." He lowered the gun, turned back toward his car, and pushed the door shut. Then he went into his room.

Roxanne's father walked out to the parking lot, picked up the carton of Lucky Strikes, and set it on the hood of the Chrysler. Jimmy started his Ford and backed it into its place while Celestina carried her bags and suitcases inside. Others around the court went into their rooms, and so did I.

I left my door open, though, and about half an hour later I heard Vince come out of his room. From where I sat I could see him as he opened the doors on the driver's side of his car. Within a few minutes he had his stuff packed up and was gone.

❖

Things seemed to get back to normal. Roxanne sat outside the next day, so I went over and talked to her. She said Vince was gone from the picking crew and she guessed he'd moved on.

We chatted for a few minutes more, and when she mentioned that she was out of cigarettes, I offered to drive her to the store. She said that was fine, so I started up my '50 Chevy as she went inside to get some money.

I liked having a girl in my car, and she didn't seem to be in any hurry. I drove the length of town and back, then pulled into the Chinaman's market, where she got out and bought two packs of Marlboros.

When she was back in the car, I asked her if she wanted to drive around some more.

"Might as well," she said. "Nothin' else to do."

I drove out south of town until I came to a turnout. It was shaded by a grove of eucalyptus trees, and it looked like a good spot. I turned in and came to a stop.

We had both windows rolled down. She lit a cigarette and tossed out the match.

"Do you ever think about just goin' someplace?" she said.

"Oh, sure. But it takes money. Where would you go?"

"Up to Reno."

"I don't know what kind of work there is up there."

"Jesus," she said. "I'd want to go somewhere where you don't have to work."

"Someone would have to work at some point."

"Oh, I guess."

"I went on a vacation once," I said. "Me and another guy. We worked for a month straight, no days off, and we saved our money. Then we went to the coast. Fort Bragg."

"What was that like?"

"Cool weather. Almost cold, after being here in the valley."

"That's the way Reno and Tahoe are."

To get to Reno and Tahoe, you had to go east up into the Sierras. To get to Fort Bragg, you went west over the Coast Range. I liked the idea of Fort Bragg better. Reno and Tahoe sounded like a lot of money.

"Over on the coast," I said, "you don't have to do anything. Some people fish, or go for abalone. We just loafed around. Watched the waves come in. Built a little fire on the beach."

"That sounds all right. 'Course there's more to do in Reno."

"You could go one place one time, another place the next time."

She nodded and didn't say any more until she finished her cigarette. "Well, I guess I'd better get back, so they don't think I'm doin' anything."

❖

Two nights later in the same spot I got her into the back seat, and things went the way I hoped. She had better movement than some girls I had been with, and I wondered where she learned it. I wasn't sure I wanted to know, though, so I kept my questions to myself and enjoyed what I could.

When we were in the front seat headed back to town, I said, "You ought to think about goin' to the coast. Nothin' to do except lay around the motel room and walk along the beach. Eat some seafood."

"It would be all right."

She didn't sound very eager, and I guess I was jealous for a minute. I said, "Maybe someone else has you talked into going to Reno."

She leaned forward out of the draft to light a cigarette. When she blew away the smoke she said, "I wouldn't go anywhere with someone that had a gun."

I didn't find her very convincing. First, she could have run off with the guy before she knew he had a gun, and second, I thought she was capable of going off with him anyway. He was the type to put stars in her eyes. But I didn't say anything. I thought about that nice magical moment when I got her shorts off, and I hoped I would get to do it again.

❖

I didn't get a chance the next couple of evenings, but everything seemed normal until I came home from work the third day. Her family was standing outside and talking to the neighbors. As soon as I got out of my car, her father called me over.

He was a light-haired man with a pot belly. His name was Hershel, and he smoked Pall Malls. He had one bobbing in his lips when I walked up to him.

"Have you seen Roxanne?" he asked.

"No, I haven't. Why?"

"She disappeared last night. I didn't know if she went somewhere with you."

I shook my head. "No, not at all. Last time I saw her was yesterday evening. She said she didn't want to go anywhere."

"Well, she must've went somewhere. She wasn't here this morning, and neither was you."

"I went to work. I was gone by about five-thirty."

Hershel looked at his wife and back at me.

I said, "You can ask Jimmy and his wife. They were on the next row."

"We looked for her all day," he said.

"I hope she didn't take off with that drifter."

"Who? Halterman?"

"Vince. I don't know his last name."

"That's him. But I think he's gone."

"I don't know. He could have come back." I thought the action with Roxanne was good enough to make him want to, but I kept that to myself.

I went to my room, got cleaned up, and reheated some spaghetti for dinner. All that time I was thinking about Roxanne and how I hoped she had more sense than to go somewhere with that guy.

❖

I woke up in the middle of the night. Something was strange. The swamp cooler was rumbling like always, but a cool, hard object was pressed against my face between my cheekbone and my nose. Someone else was in the room, next to my bed.

A small flashlight came on. I saw that the object was a gun, and the person holding it was Vince.

"What do you want?" I asked.

"Get up."

"What for?"

"Because I said so." He stood back and kept the gun leveled at me.

I sat up and swung my legs around.

"Get dressed."

My head was clearing. I wondered how he got into my room, and I figured a guy like him could pick the lock on any door in the court. "What's goin' on?" I asked.

"I said get dressed."

"Why?"

"I already told you why."

I put on the clothes I had laid out before I went to sleep. When I finished tying my shoes, he spoke again.

"Get your car keys. And don't do anything stupid, or you'll get this thing in the guts." He motioned with the gun.

When we stepped outside, he said, "You're drivin'. Open my door first, then go around and open yours. You get in, and then I will."

I did as he said. My interior light didn't work, but I found the ignition next to the steering column, poked the key in, and turned it on. I stepped on the clutch and hit the starter button, and the engine fired right up.

"Don't turn on the lights till you're about to pull out onto the road."

I backed the car around, drove to the edge of the lot, and switched on the lights.

"Turn right."

I eased onto the highway. The night was warm and the inside of the car was musty, so I rolled down my window. The town was asleep. I drove south, past the turnout spot, and still didn't see any headlights.

After about three miles he told me to turn left. I drove through farm country, where there were orchards and hayfields. He had me turn right and left down dirt roads and then right onto a canal road. Out in the middle of nowhere, I saw the reflection of my lights on the bumper and tail lights of a car.

Closer, I saw that it was his Chrysler.

"Pull right up behind it," he said. "Leave the lights on, but shut off the motor and give me the key."

I left the car in gear when I shut if off. When I handed him the key, he told me to stay put. He got out, walked around in front of my car through the headlights, and came to my window.

He pointed the gun at me and said, "Get out." When I did, he herded me through the narrow space between the two cars. "Stop there." He shifted the gun to his left hand and stuck a key into the trunk latch of the Chrysler. He clicked the lock, and the lid lifted.

In the glow of the headlights I saw a body bent and turned away. Without seeing her face, I recognized the light-colored hair and clothes of Roxanne. My stomach was in a knot, and my heart was pounding.

"Lift her out of there."

"What?"

"Look here, you punk. I'm not fucking around with you. Either you lift her out, or I put a bullet through you."

I reached over and pushed her shoulder, and she was stiff. I braced my legs against the back of the Chrysler as I pulled and shifted and got the dead weight up into my arms.

"Carry her around back of your car."

He followed me, then got ahead and unlocked my trunk.

I lowered her in, and he pushed the lid closed.

"Now get back in the car like before."

As I did that, he walked forward, slammed his trunk closed, and opened his driver's door. He took out a brown paper bag and a red plastic cup that must have come off of a thermos bottle.

He crossed in front of the headlights again and got into my car on the right side. "Shut off the lights," he said.

The night went dark. I heard him crack the seal on the bottle and pour liquid into the cup.

"Drink this."

I took a sip. It was whiskey.

"Drink it. Down the hatch."

I almost choked, but I got it down. I sat for a couple of minutes in the strange silence and breathed with my mouth open.

"Give me the cup." He poured more whiskey into it and handed it to me. "Drink it."

"I can't. I just drank a cupful."

"I don't care. Drink some more."

It burned my throat on the way down, and my stomach churned so bad I thought I was going to puke, but I held it down.

"Give it here."

I gave him the cup.

After another long moment, he spoke. "She said you fucked her."

"I don't see where that makes any difference."

"You will." He unscrewed the cap on the bottle. "She said you told her I was no good."

"I don't remember exactly what I said."

"You shit." He poured more whiskey.

I was getting drunk fast, and I tried to think straight. I wondered what his plan was, whether he was trying to make me drink myself to death or whether he wanted to get me falling-down drunk and then shoot me. Either way, I was sure he planned to leave me there dead, with Roxanne in my trunk.

"Here."

"I can't drink any more."

"You just think you can't. I said drink it, or I'll splatter your brains all over the inside of this car."

I took the cup, and the smell almost gagged me. I forced the whiskey down, but it came right back up. I got the door open just as I heaved. I coughed and sputtered and vomited some more. My eyes were watery, and I saw little circles in the dark.

"Pick up the cup."

I realized it had hit the ledge of the door and fallen on the ground. I had my right hand on the steering wheel, and my head was leaning out through the open door. "I don't think I can reach it," I said.

"Lean down and pick it up. Don't piss me off."

As I reached with my left hand, I lost my grip on the steering wheel. I fell out on the ground.

Vince opened the door on his side, and the next moment he was kicking at me. "Get up, you worthless puke."

"I can't."

He poked the barrel of the pistol under my left cheekbone. It pulled me together. Somewhere in the center of my drunk self I found a clear spot. I got up onto my feet, grabbed the steering wheel, and pulled myself into the car.

"Get your feet in."

When I did, he slammed the door and went back around the front.

From the clear spot inside me, two things came up that I knew about my car. I could start it in gear with no clutch if the ignition was on, and since I had pulled the key out in the straight-up position, I could turn the switch without the key. As Vince walked between the two cars and set his pistol hand on the hood of my Chevy, I turned on the ignition with my right hand and pushed the starter button with my left.

The car lurched, jammed him into the Chrysler, and lurched again. The gun clunked across the hood and rolled off the right fender.

Vince's scream filled the night. He banged his fist on the hood, then hollered, "Get me out of this."

I realized I had him pinned. The clear spot in my mind told me I needed to make myself move. I opened the door and got out, and I almost fell over.

He yelled again. "Get me out of here, you fucker, or I'll kill you."

I leaned over, took a full breath of air, and heaved out another gush of whiskey. When Vince pounded on the hood again, I got moving.

I walked for what I thought was a long time, and I still heard him banging. When I got to where the canal road met the dirt road, I didn't hear him any more.

I followed the dirt roads as well as I could remember, and I came to a paved road where the faintest light was showing in the east. I started walking in the other direction, toward town.

In a little while, a pair of headlights came into view. A car was coming my way. When I waved it down, I saw it was an old pickup. The driver had his window rolled down, and the lights from his dashboard cast a glow on him and the dog in his lap. The music from his radio echoed in the metal cab.

"What do you need?"

"A ride to town if I can get it."

"Are you in trouble?"

"Not as much as some people. But I need to talk to some cops."

"Well, get in. I guess those cows can wait a little while." †

GIVING DAD THE FINGER
Keith Rawson

Me and Jeb had just put in an eighteen hour shift and were laying out in the back of my truck drinking piss warm Coors Light trying to come down from the bumps of speed our super had pumped into us during the last two hours of our shift—the crank was good shit that had burned all the hairs out of my nostrils and had made Jeb's bleed a little bit, so chances were we weren't coming down any time soon no matter how many beers we poured down our throats.

We were covered head-to-toe in dried red mud from running the hose out at the mine. Eighteen straight hours of dredging copper was shit, but when the owners were paying triple time, that kind of money was hard to pass up. Not like I had much use for the extra cash, but it felt kind of nice come payday to feel that wad in the hip pocket, knowing that any time I wanted out of town I could just pack up my room and head out. Not that I had any desire to pull up stakes, but you never know.

Jeb was in a different boat entirely then me. He worked long shitty hours because he spent his high school years sticking his dick into any girl he could get drunk enough to spread her legs for his ugly ass, and he'd managed to get three or four of them girls knocked up. So most of his cash went to buying diapers and school supplies and keeping roofs over the heads of their deadbeat mamas, most of who seemed to have the habit of spreading their legs for any jackass who sprang for an eighteen pack, popping out one bastard after another, and collecting child support and government aid.

Jeb had been the first person I'd met when I moved to Strawberry for the mining job two years ago, and he was still the only one I knew other than a couple of Mormon missionary boys from Idaho who'd taken it upon themselves to save me from my sinful life and a few slutty girls who were trying to do the same with what was between their legs—none of them were having much luck converting me.

I was finishing up my third beer and thinking about taking a piss out in the sagebrush. I stood up and stretched, my bones popping, my worn-out muscles begging me to sit back down for a couple of minutes longer.

"I've been thinking some," Jeb said.

"Shit, that ain't normal for you." Which was pretty close to the truth and whatever thinking he did do was usually with his cock. I mean, how else do you explain a 22-year-old man with six kids?

He shook his head, spit and tossed his beer bottle out into the dark.

"I'm being serious, dude. I've been thinking a lot about getting out of town, maybe starting new somewhere."

Jeb was a native going back three generations and all of them worked the mines. The town was mixed into his blood thicker than the mud dried to our coveralls. I cracked another beer and decided to just take a piss where I was standing.

"Where you thinking about heading?"

"I don't know. Phoenix, maybe."

All these small town Arizona guys were the same when they got to talking about where they'd go if they left. Me, I'd had a belly full of Phoenix. I'd spent most of my life there getting bounced back and forth between my grandma's trailer and whatever group homes the state would stick me in whenever she felt like she couldn't handle me anymore. I liked Strawberry, it was quiet, it was clean, and sure, the people were dumber than a bag of hammers, but that was everywhere as far as I was concerned.

"Oh yeah," I tucked myself back in and zipped up. "I guess it's just as good a place as any. How you planning on leaving? It ain't like you got any money or nothing."

"Well, I've been thinking about that one, too. Me and Susie have been talking, trying to figure a few things out."

Susie was Jeb's on-again-off-again cooze and one of the few girls Jeb hadn't managed to knock up. She wasn't all that bad looking either, which made me think she must've been pretty hard up to be hanging out with Jeb, that or she got a little ego boost from feeling superior to him, not that that was a big stretch.

"So what's she got to say? It's not like she's got any money either." I was starting to think Jeb was working himself up to ask me for a loan. Not that any money I gave him would be a loan.

"Naw, she don't. But her daddy's got a whole bunch of it."

"Her Daddy? Who's her daddy?"

I was drawing a blank, I didn't know of nobody in town who had any kind of real money, not that I didn't know Susie's life story or nothing like that. I'd only been around her a few times and those times had been when I was out drinking with Jeb and we'd somehow made it over to her double wide so Jeb could get his dick wet.

"Bill Tillets … you know …?"

"Who?"

"You know, the guy Stevens got the pick-me-up from."

Tillets.

Yeah, I knew him, everybody in the county knew who Tillets was. Not that anybody saw hide or hair of him. He was one of those small town characters that was more like a rumor than an actual person. He was a drunk-talk story people got yammering about when they got sick of bitching about work. And, of course, if you wanted something a little stronger than beer—as I was apt to want—Tillets' name was a sign of quality in what you were buying.

"Shit, I didn't know Susie was Tillets' kid? Why ain't she got the same last name?'

"She's got her ma's name. Her folks never got married and Susie's ma ended up leaving him when she was three. But she's Tillets' only kid."

"So you gonna ask him for a loan or some shit?"

"Naw, he don't like me all that much 'cause of all my kids and whatnot."

"Ya gonna go and work for him then?"

"No ... no ... me and Susie were thinking about something else ...." He started talking, his ears glowing red in the dark as he tried to tell me what him and Susie had planned and how they wanted me to help them.

In the hour he talked, I somehow managed to piss myself.

❖

Me and Jeb had the next day off, and we decided to meet at Susie's place so she could do a more thorough job about the details of what they had planned.

I hadn't gone to sleep yet from the effects of the crank grinding through my blood and getting worked up over Jeb's little plan. Overnight I'd gone from kind of liking him to resenting him for thinking I'd want anything to do with the line of bullshit he'd spit out.

Maybe I should have been listening to the Mormon boys and given up my wicked ways and ditched Jeb for Sunday sermons and Thursday night Bible study. I know it would be a hell of a lot better for my health than what Jeb and Susie had planned.

"It ain't rocket science, you know. We fake me getting kidnapped, we send a ransom note to daddy, he hands over the cash and we get the fuck out of this dump." I never noticed before how hard Susie was. Maybe it was the beer goggles I always seemed to have on when I'd been over to her place before, but I'd never noticed the sleeve of tattoos on her left arm or the tweeker welts dotting her forehead. I'd thought of her as this delicate flower type that you might want to take home to mama instead of screwing her in the bed of your pickup. But looking at her now, she was definitely just another trailer park girl with a decent back side.

"You keep saying 'we' like I already said yes to this fucker. I've gotten kind of fond of this 'dump' and ain't got no plans for leaving or getting buried by your hillbilly daddy."

"Who the fuck you calling a hillbilly?" She asked as she reached between her legs and gave her clamshell a couple of stiff scratches. "And why wouldn't you want in on something like this? I mean it ain't like you gonna have to actually kidnap me or nothing. Ain't like you got to wrestle me to the ground and tie me up. All you got to do is make some phone calls and then go pick up the money when daddy hands it over."

"Are you even listening to me? I said I like living here. I said I like being alive. The minute I go picking up any cash, your daddy and his boys are gonna jump on me and put a bullet in my head if I'm lucky. Besides, why don't you just get Jeb to be your mule?"

"Come on, he ain't going to kill you. The asshole loves me and wouldn't want no harm done to me even if it costs him fifty thousand bucks. And if Jeb tried doing any of this shit, daddy would know it was a scam in a dead second, that is if Jeb didn't fuck it all up first."

Jeb just kind of sat there looking hang dog, his bottom lip poofed out, a sheen of tears clouding his eyes, trying to choke back reacting to Susie's little jab. Jeb was a stupid motherfucker, but he was still smart enough to know he was being treated like human buttwipe.

"Daddy don't know you, never talked with you and probably never seen you neither. And the way we're gonna work it, he ain't ever gonna see your face. We'll work out drop off points for the cash and we'll hand some line of bullshit about how I'll be killed if you don't show back up an hour after the drop off or something. Like I said, it's easy and you'll be ten grand richer for maybe two hours of your time."

I rubbed my hand across my face and fished around in my pockets for a smoke.

"Fuck ten grand, I want half."

"No goddamn way you're getting half!"

"I'm gonna be the one taking all the risks."

"Fifteen!"

"Twenty or you can kiss my ass goodbye right here and now."

She shut up for a couple of minutes, worrying her bottom lip between her teeth. She finally looked up at me and said, "Alright, I guess twenty's fine, but if you try fucking us over with the money, you ain't gonna have to trouble yourself about daddy putting a bullet in you because I'll do it myself."

I was pretty sure she was going to try killing me no matter what, but I'd deal with it when we crossed that bridge.

"We got a deal," I said. "Let me ask you something, though. If your daddy loves you so much, why don't you just ask for the money instead of going through all this?"

"Shit, he don't love me that goddamn much."

We went to work on Susie and Jeb's plan a couple of days after I'd negotiated my cut. The "kidnapping" base of operation was an old hunting cabin that used to belong to Jeb's grandpa until the Feds decided the land it was on needed to be protected against the ravages of mining and logging. It was a dilapidated clapboard and tarpaper heap with dirt floors and no electricity or indoor plumbing. Hell, Jeb had rushed into everything so headlong that the only heat or lighting in the place were a few rusted oil lamps, and with the plan being for Susie to stay up there tucked away in the woods while we mailed out our ransom notes, the girl would have been straight-up fucked seven different ways and freezing her titties off. Luckily it had been a warm September, so Susie's high beams were safe.

Me and Jeb went about our normal routines, going to work and picking up extra shifts when they were available. I kept myself even-steven, nose to the grindstone and out of other people's shit like usual, but Jeb was going in about a million directions at once. Couldn't keep himself focused on anything and started fucking up at work, coming close to hurting a few people with the hose, myself included.

"Dude, you gotta chill out!" This was after the shit had nearly knocked my head off with the brass nozzle he was supposed to be handling.

"Fuck this job, man! I don't need this shit no more!" I wanted to smack the teeth out of his mouth. The kid had no sense at all and for some reason he'd failed to grasp the dynamics of a small town: small town people are bored, so small town people talk when something's even a bit out of the ordinary. And that talk tends to get around to folks who you don't want hearing it.

I stopped myself from slugging him because chances were all it would do is cause a bigger stink. I kept to myself, worked, racked up the overtime and waited for Susie's daddy to come up with the cash to save his only daughter from having her brains blown out.

❖

Two weeks went by and no word from Tillets. We figured the note we'd sent him must've gotten lost in the mail (which wasn't too far of a stretch considering Strawberry's single mail carrier was a mean, sloppy drunk). So we put together another note, this time using letters clipped out of magazines just like in some shitty Lifetime movie and I dropped it into the mail with a stack of bills.

Two more weeks, nothing.

Susie was going bugshit and Jeb was getting whinier by the hour, always whispering and asking me what we should do? I'd give him a blank stare and shrug my shoulders, wanting to say: "It's your show, Einstein, figure it out."

After week three rolled by, Susie finally had enough and made Jeb go and buy a throwaway phone from the Circle K so we could call daddy and let him know we meant business.

❖

I was the one who got talked into dialing Tillets. Both Jeb and Susie said he'd recognize their voices and since I was a stranger to him and all ... well, shit.

I wasn't taking any chances of him recognizing my voice though. I cut out the bottom of a Pepsi can and talked through the tab end in a deep, gravelly voice and kept it on speaker phone.

The dude took forever to pick up, twelve rings total.

"Yup ...." Finally.

"Tillets?"

"You're the one calling, so it must be me. Who the hell is this?"

"The person who has your daughter."

"Hmmmm, I was wondering why you were talking funny. Thought it was a bad connection or something, but I guess you're just trying to disguise your voice, huh? So how's my little honeybunch doing? My bet's by now she's managed to make you want to pay *me* fifty grand to take her back?"

"So you've received our notes?"

"Yep. Tossed out the first one, wiped my ass with the second one. Managed to give myself a paper cut."

"Now why would you do that, Mr. Tillets? Don't you know we'll hurt your daughter?"

"Well, shit, son, I figure you either will or you won't? Don't matter one way or the other."

I kept an eye on Susie. She was turning fireball red. I kept expecting her to explode at any second. But maybe Tillets knew all of this was bullshit? Maybe he knew his little girl was sitting on the other end of the line waiting for her to lose it?

"Excuse me?" I asked.

"Son, let me tell you something, I don't like being threatened and this ain't the first time someone's tried getting a little money off me by trying to hurt my blood. So I'll tell you the same thing that I told the last motherfucker who tried pulling this shit. I don't negotiate with no fucking terrorists."

And he hung up.

We let Susie throw her fit.

Jeb and I sat back, sipped a couple of beers as she threw around some tables and chairs, broke a few of the chipped plates that came with the cabin, and let lose the longest string of cuss words I'd ever heard a woman speak.

Even longer than the time I busted up my grandma's car, and trust me, that woman knew how to cuss.

After an hour, she managed to settle herself down and she turned and spat at Jeb, "It's time we showed this fucker we mean business! Go and get the axe like we talked about!"

❖

Jeb was gone a looooong time.

By the time he came back, we'd lit the oil lanterns and he stunk like he'd thrown back a case of beer and tossed it right back up. But he seemed as sober as monk and kept the hatchet pressed against his leg.

Susie explained their little contingency plan while he was gone.

She knew her daddy was stubborn old man. The type of stubborn old man who'd only get the point if they sent something bloody home to him. Nothing big and nothing Susie would miss all that much when it was gone.

Susie's pinky finger, the one on her left hand.

Sure, it would hurt like hell when Jeb did it, but she was convince her daddy would hand over the money once he saw it.

Me, I wasn't too sure about that and I figured neither of 'em would have the balls to go through with it.

Right up until Susie pressed her left hand out flat on the tabletop and Jeb held it down at the wrist, that is.

Neither of them said a word, just nodded.

I wanted to run the hell out of there, maybe go puke my guts out and forget any of this shit ever happened. But, goddamn, how often do you get to see somebody get a piece of their body chopped off? Hell, that's got to be a once in a lifetime kind of thing?

Jeb tensed himself up, raised up the hatchet over his head and brought it down fast.

And flinched, turning his head at the last second.

Let me tell you something, you don't ever forget the sound of somebody's hand being cut off. I can't even describe it, don't even want to try.

Or the sound of Susie's screams.

Or the way she kicked at Jeb like a mule, sending him crashing into one of the oil lamps and setting his head on fire.

That I don't mind describing so much: He looked like a match head right when you strike it with a thumbnail.

Of course, after I saw him fall on top of Susie, I hauled ass out of there to my truck and watched the cabin burn up in my rearview.

After a few miles, I patted down my pockets, making sure my last two paychecks were there and thinking there was probably a town in New Mexico just as nice as Strawberry. †

GHOST OF A CHANCE
Howard Hopkins

Angel de la Ruse had the most stunning cherry-wood eyes, even in death. But the way she sightlessly stared up at me as I knelt by her side would haunt me until the day I joined her in the grave.

And a ghost is not easily haunted.

My name is George Chance and I am a magician by leisure, detective by choice. But I'll fill in the details later. Right now all that mattered was the dead woman lying before me and my failure to prevent her untimely demise.

People were gathering around us in the Sapphire Lagoon, forming a circle of horrified faces and widened eyes. One woman let out a shriek that rattled my spine, then promptly fainted, only to be caught by a fellow wearing a Marley Brooks suit. To tell you the truth, I was relieved she'd fainted, because another scream like that and I would have become a lot more unnerved than I was already ….

❖

Twenty-eight hours ago ….

I probably should have expected trouble when I heard the rap on the door of my brownstone. Trouble has a way of finding me, especially since retiring from my life as a revue magician to "dabble" in mystery and detection. I run the New York School of Magic in my spare time, having made a fortune in prestidigitation, but when the opportunity arises I lead a double life, one where I aide New York's finest as a figure the underworld fears and reviles, a being called the Ghost.

The knock sounded again, a trifle more insistent, so I extricated myself from the divan and headed to the door.

I was right: Trouble perched on my doorstep, the kind of trouble that made men's legs go weak and their minds surrender any semblance of common sense.

"Well, are you going to invite me in, or just leave me standing out here catching my death?" asked the raven-haired beauty poised on my stoop.

I should have left her standing out there, but chivalry got the better of me.

She brushed past me, walking to the divan and with a sweep of her chinchilla coat nearly knocked over the vase holding a red rose that sat on a small table. No, that wasn't quite accurate. Angel de la Ruse didn't walk, she sashayed. The woman carried herself with a confidence that made men turn handsprings and women glare green-eyed murder. But, if I recalled correctly, that confidence was a veneer she painted on when she needed it.

I left the door open a crack because it suddenly felt a hell of a lot warmer in the room than it had a moment before. When I turned to her she swept back the folds of her fur coat to reveal a form-fitting emerald dress that made my mouth hang open.

"Well, what do you think?" She winked. My legs almost buckled. "Still the same old Angel?"

I tried a smile and struggled to walk straight as I came over to her. "You've filled out ...." I am not sure why I said it, but couldn't think of anything else.

She laughed that airy little laugh of hers I remembered from our time together six year ago. She'd briefly worked in my act, but had quickly outgrown it—and me. I'd kept up with her career, even owned her phonograph record.

"It's been a long time, George," she said. I could suddenly see something in her cherry-wood eyes, eyes that used to turn my legs to syrup and my heart to jelly, something that belied the self-assured air she affected.

Indeed, trouble *had* come to my door.

I gave her a small laugh I hoped sounded nonchalant. "I never expected to see you on my doorstep again, Angel."

She smiled a honey smile. "I'm singing at the Sapphire Lagoon tomorrow. I was hoping you'd be able to come. I'll sing 'Ghost of a Chance' ... just for old time's sake."

I studied her face, which wasn't easy considering the tightness of her dress and the diamonds that dripped from the necklace caressing her olive throat. Something was wrong. She was here for more than simply inviting an old friend to a torch performance.

"What is it, Angel? What's wrong?"

She chuckled but the sound came without any humor. "You always could read me, George, couldn't you?"

"I thought so, up until the night you left without a word." Was that bitterness in my tone? I believe it might have been.

"Oh, that." She gave a dismissive wave of her hand. I remembered that gesture only too well. I still despised it. Everything had always revolved around Angel and the feelings of others came secondary to whatever she desired at the moment.

"I got over you."

Her laugh was more sincere this time. "Did you really?"

"I'm engaged." Now my tone was a trifle defensive and I didn't like that. Merry White, my fiancé, wouldn't have liked it, either.

"How nice for you." She paused, her cherry-wood gaze sweeping the room, then landing back on me. It was smoldering. It always was when she wanted something. "You're right, George. I did come for another reason. Lately ... well, lately *things* have been happening. I need your help."

"Things?" I was a bit puzzled. Angel wasn't the type to ask for help from anyone. She was too used to extracting it through other means, mostly her womanly charms.

"I think something's after me, George, trying to frighten me to death."

"You'll have to explain, Angel. I'm feeling a little confused this evening."

She smiled and let her long finger nails drift over her diamond necklace to a spot just below it between her breasts. "I imagine you are." The smile went away and fear replaced it. Not much about Angel was genuine, but that fear was.

"I have been hearing voices, in my dressing room, sometimes in my hotel rooms."

"Voices?" Angel had a great many things lurking beneath her surface; insanity wasn't one of them.

"They tell me to do things, George. To kill myself, mostly, but they say other things, too. Sometimes they simply try to frighten me. I think I am being haunted."

"Sounds like a doctor might better serve you than I," I said, before I could stop myself. I didn't mean it, but Angel always had a way of making me say things I didn't mean. That had not changed in six years.

"I'm not crazy!" An edge formed on her voice capable of slicing a man in two. "I *do* hear them, George. I hear them after every performance. Someone is trying to hurt me, destroy my career. When I arrived here in town I remembered the way you used to expose those fake mediums in your shows sometimes. I thought—"

"That you could simply step back into my life and make me do tricks, the way you did six years ago."

The look that crossed her cherry-wood eyes was not one you'd want to see twice, but it softened an instant later. "It's not like that, now, George. I was young, then; I wanted to experience the world."

"Did you?"

"It experienced me ...." Sadness crept into her voice and I might have actually believed then she was sincere. It was hard to tell with Angel and the years might have only made her a better actress. "Please say you'll come, George. I really want you to. I need you to hear those voices and stop them."

I did something silly, then. I suppose I couldn't help myself, but it was something I used to do when I knew her. I reached up to the side of her raven hair and produced a rose from thin air, then handed it to her. I hoped she hadn't seen me palm it from the vase on the table next to me, since a stem's not the easiest thing to hide.

She smiled and accepted the rose, sniffed it, gazed at me with those eyes again, and before I knew it I promised her I would be there.

"Seven o'clock," she said and started to step past me with her rose, but stumbled. I caught her and the feeling of her body in my arms ... well, it was right up there with expensive Fleming Brandy.

Women think men don't catch on when they pull the tripping trick, knowing that they'll catch them. But men do know. They simply don't care, because playing hero and holding the prize is all that counts.

She kissed me, then, her lips as soft and sweet as velvet wine. I almost lost the rest of my senses but pushed her back and set her on her feet before that could happen.

"Well, don't we all just have a nice case of the cozies ...." a perturbed voice came from behind me. I cranked my head to see Merry White standing in the doorway, her expression matching her tone.

I grinned what could only be called sheepishly and from the corner of my eye I caught the look of challenge on Angel's face. Angel stepped by me, then brushed past Merry, who'd taken two steps into the room. Angel raked Merry with a dismissing gaze, then glanced back to me.

"We had something once, George. I'm sure we could again ...." With that, she left, but her ghost might as well have stayed in the room.

Merry locked her arms together and started tapping her foot. I had the feeling the rest of the evening was going to be a long one.

❖

One hour ago ....

After my senses cleared I quickly figured out Angel de la Ruse hadn't come just because some voices were terrorizing her. She had come because she had blown into town and remembered what we used to have and decided she wanted it again. At least for the moment. And what Angel wanted she usually got. Merry White figured that out a hell of a lot faster than I did and I am the one who is supposed to be the detective. But women can read other woman instantly and Angel and Merry had judged each other as competition, both promising to mark their territory.

I would have to let Angel down easy, but I was afraid she wouldn't see it that way. She had a degree in tantrums, if I remembered correctly.

Before heading out to The Sapphire Lagoon, I went down to a secret room just off the workshop in my basement. The hidden chamber, brilliantly lighted, contained the equipment I used in my outings as a detective. Because George Chance wasn't attending Angel's performance tonight—the Ghost was.

I stood in front of the three-paneled mirror and inserted small wire ovals into my nose, which elongated my nostrils and tilted the tip. I then darkened each nostril with brown pigment and used brown eye shadow to smudge the pits of my eyes. I gave my features a ghostly pallor courtesy of a powder box, then highlighted my naturally high cheekbones. Over my teeth I placed celluloid shells of old ivory. By the time I added a specially made suit and yanked a crusher hat over my blond hair I no longer looked like George Chance. I was just any other man, not especially attractive, yet nothing frightening, either. At least not until I decided to pull my lips back to bear my teeth and cast a vacuous expression to bring out the Ghost.

Although I am a poor shot, I made sure my flat automatic was in place beneath the suit, which held myriad pockets stuffed with magic apparatuses. Sheathed in my right sleeve I carried a double-edged throwing knife. That I *was* good with.

I was ready for a haunt and by the time I got to The Sapphire Lagoon ten minutes later, the place was starting to fill up. I slipped into the joint and took the three steps to the floor, selecting a table a half-dozen feet from the grand piano, atop which sat a sparkling glass of champagne. The Lagoon itself was a masterpiece in elegant blue, with royal curtains and glistening cobalt fountains spouting sapphire streams. Cigarette smoke infused with blue lighting gave the impression of floating smoky blue opals and glasses never stopped clinking.

At a glance I saw Merry White and Merry White saw me. She had wrangled herself a job last evening after I told her of my plans to help Angel. How she had done it I didn't really care to know, but when it came to flirting her way into things Merry was a virtuoso. I am pretty certain the flaring white satin skirt rising eight inches above her knees and painted-on, red satin blouse that accentuated her bosom had a lot to do with it. That ten-thousand-watt personality of hers shined with each graceful step she took toward my table.

She carried a tray of cigarettes and cigars and as she reached my table she said, "Cigarettes?"

I nodded, and pulled out a billfold. "What's the lay?" I kept my voice low, and Merry glanced about, ducked her chin slightly toward the piano.

"See the girl?"

I did. She was boyish, dressed in a flapper style popular more than ten years ago, with flattened breasts under a loose blouse, a beaded headband and bobbed hair, short skirt and generously applied makeup.

"Who is she?"

"She's Angel's piano player. Spent some time as a nurse for the Stockbridge Circus, catering to trapeze artists who had ungraceful nights before landing a gig as Angel's protégé. Angel lets her chirp a number or two near the end of her first set. She's like a sister to Angel, comforts her after her frequent tantrums."

Merry took all too much pleasure in telling me that; I could see the twinkle in her sparkling green eyes. "Next." I didn't want to give her too much time to gloat on it. With a flip of her dark hair Merry indicated a heavyset fellow wearing a rumpled suit and matching expression standing to the right of the piano.

"He's Joe Pasquorelli, Angel's bodyguard. Bad one, spent some time in prison. Rumor has it he ran some dope for Capone years back, and one of his girlfriends met with a mysterious death. He's got a thing for Angel."

"You discovered all this how?" I asked, amazed at what she'd been able to ferret in such a short period.

She winked. "Bartender has an eye for gams and honey-coated smiles."

"Oh," I said, not sure I liked that answer. "Anyway?"

Merry's eyes cut to another figure, who was leaning against the bar. The man had unkempt graying hair sorely in need of a clipping. It was wispy and hung nearly to his shoulders and he must have been looking at the underside of sixty. His suit was cut perfectly for his spidery frame and probably cost more than most men earned in a year. His gaze, narrowed, was stalking about the room like a jungle cat scouting for an antelope.

"Miguel Epiñada, a regular Svengali, from what I hear. He's Angel's manager and apparently, *lover.*" Merry took quite a bit of joy in the emphasis she placed on that last word. It gave my stomach a twinge, but I wasn't sure why.

"Nobody with a reason for scaring our little songbird," I said, not wanting to give her the satisfaction of seeing me react.

She shrugged, handed me change, and danced off.

My eyes focused on the bodyguard, whose arms were crossed like two iron beams and whose eyes promised doom to anyone stupid enough to get in his way. I would have liked to pin him for Angel's problems, but had nothing to go on other than that feeling I got around criminal types.

The tinkling notes of the piano distracted me and I saw flapper girl smiling a glowing smile as her hands glided over the keys and her eyes flowed warmly for the woman stepping from behind the blue velvet curtain.

I stifled a gasp and noticed Merry staring at me, her green eyes suddenly three shades greener because of the expression that must have been on my face at Angel's entrance. Angel flowed like silk onto the top of the piano, swung her legs right and her shapely hips left. Her cherry-wood eyes swept over the room. I'd like to think she was looking for me.

Her blue-sequined dress caressed her body the way men would have killed to do and its plunging neckline revealed glimpses of her ample charms. A sapphire necklace glittered liquid blue under the lights. Wisps of smoke danced around her, opal angels. Her voice was as velvet as the curtains and the haunting lyrics of "Little Girl Blue" could have melted a glacier. She looked right at me when she sang it, though I doubt she recognized me. She did not know me as the Ghost; only six others did and of them only Merry White was at the Lagoon tonight.

I watched, mesmerized, feeling the same pangs of the yearning I had six years ago, but with age and wisdom knowing better than to let myself get too lost. I was here for a reason, to discover who was trying to frighten her and why. That meant I needed to get back stage, and with King Kong standing near the piano, that might take some magic. Angel finished her song, then took a long drink of her champagne while flapper girl tinkled the keys and Mr. Svengali eyed Angel like he was looking at a gold-plated Stutz Bearcat. Angel made a peculiar face, glanced at her glass, then at flapper girl, who shrugged. Angel set the glass down and slid off the piano, wavering a second, then gaining control of herself.

She began to sing, the beginning lyrics to "Ghost of a Chance" unearthing something silky inside me. No one sang that song the way she did. But her voice seemed ….

It was hard to put into words, but something had changed from her previous song; something in her dulcet tones had cooled. A few moments later, at the end of the song, they became downright shaky.

An instant later she doubled over, clutching her stomach. I was out of my chair before I knew it, but even then it was too late. Angel hit the floor with a sound only the dead can make.

Men started murmuring and women started gasping. Merry White shucked her cigarette tray and headed toward us. Miguel Epiñada, face suddenly purple, shoved his way toward the body.

I turned Angel over onto her back and saw her death stare, knew her fears had been all too real. Someone had tired of trying to persuade her to kill herself and done it for her, right in front of the Ghost.

Foam bubbled out of her mouth and her lips contorted. A sinking feeling came to my gut, as if I had just lost something I never really had.

I looked up at the gathering, seeing Miguel Epiñada peering down with a look that said his meal ticket had just taken the train. I didn't see much feeling for Angel in his eyes. Tears streamed down flapper girl's face, dripping onto her blouse and mingling with small pink stains on the material. She appeared on the verge of fainting. Joe Bodyguard had a scowl on his fat lips and was yelling something about nobody moving and killing whoever had done this to his Angel.

I avoided any contact with the foam dribbling out of Angel's mouth, since there was a slightly acrid odor I recognized. She had been poisoned, that much was obvious.

I gently placed her head on the floor and let my hand drift over her swelling eyes, to close the lids.

After I got to my feet, I went to the piano and examined the champagne glass. I waved a hand over it, wafting its scent into my nostrils. The same acrid odor.

I returned to the gathering, seeing the bartender on the phone, most likely to the police.

"I demand an answer to this!" Miguel Epiñada shouted, fury on his face, now that some of the shock had worn off. "I demand to know who murdered my Angel." He said "my Angel" in the same way someone says my house or my car. Something he owned, not loved.

"I can tell you who did it," I said, looking over flapper girl, the bodyguard and Miguel Epiñada in turn. I put on the ghost, then, and a gasp came from flapper girl, a growl from the bodyguard and not much of anything but annoyance from Epiñada.

"And who are *you*, sir? What connection have you to *my* Angel?" Epiñada folded his arms, expecting an answer like he owned the world.

"I'm someone who used to care about *your* Angel," I answered, not because he had asked but because I needed to say something to get my own nerves under control. "Someone who perhaps still does."

"You say you … you know who did it?" asked flapper girl, tears still streaming, hands now quaking.

I nodded. "Carbolic acid—phenol—in her champagne and a lot of it."

"She was poisoned?" The bodyguard's eyes narrowed. "Why?"

"She was poisoned," I said. "But the why … flapper girl can answer that better than I can."

A startled look jumped onto flapper girl's face and the tears stopped as if a spigot had been closed. "Me? How would I—"

I stepped over to her. "Phenol sometimes appears red or pinkish if it's not pure." I pointed to the pink dots on her blouse. I reached out, pulled the blouse down slightly to reveal whitish marks on her skin. "You were a trifle clumsy when you put it in her champagne. Phenol is absorbed through the skin, incidentally, and causes gangrene after a while."

Horror replaced the grief on her face like a shade had been drawn. "I … I have no idea—"

"Carbolic has been sometimes used medically. You were a nurse. Your circus background might give you access to fake mediums, so I imagine you picked up some tricks. Angel told me she was hearing voices in her dressing room. The only question is why?"

Flapper girl looked ready to deny it, but a sudden flood of tears gushed and she bowed her head. Sobs wracked her body. "I … used microphones, wax recordings. I thought if I frightened her and was there to comfort her afterward … she … she would run into my arms. I ... I loved her ...." I told her so last night and she ... she laughed ... said I was a silly little girl. Said I should dismiss such foolish notions and find myself a man to change my ways."

"Well, that's just mighty peculiar ...." came Merry's voice beside me.

"She said she had gone to see the man she was going to marry and that after this engagement she was going to find herself a new piano player." Flapper girl's head came up; makeup streaked down her cheeks. "I couldn't live without her, don't you understand?"

Six years ago I would have understood. Now ... now it just brought a sick feeling to my stomach.

Flapper girl screamed, "I never wanted to kill her, but I couldn't let anyone else have her!" She tried to make a break for it, but Joe Bodyguard grabbed her arm and held her fast. With the look on his face I hoped there'd be something left for the police when they arrived. Miguel Epiñada seemed stunned into silence for probably the first time in his life. Outside, sirens wailed, coming closer, and I said goodbye to Angel ....

❖

Three hours later ....

I sat on the divan in my brownstone, Merry's head nestled against my chest. A scratchy recording revolved on the phonograph, filling the dimly lit room with Angel's voice. I felt little of the satisfaction I usually did after wrapping up a case. When Angel died she took something of me with her, a part of my past, perhaps.

Merry sighed. "What that girl said, about Angel saying she had seen the man she was going to marry ... that was you, George, wasn't it?"

"Angel always wanted something, Merry—usually only until she tired of playing with it, which never took very long."

"But if she hadn't ... died ... would you ...?"

I knew the question on her mind: Would I have thrown her over for a beautiful torch singer with whom I obviously had a history?

I chuckled, reached up to her hair, and produced a rose from midair. "Not a ghost of chance ...." ⚜

THE QUICK ... AND THE DEAD
Bill Crider

She keeps it in a cedar box on the nightstand by her bed.

Her father made the box. She remembers his hard hands as he worked, the smell of the cedar shavings.

His hard hands, the smell. The sawdust in the creases of his hands.

Sometimes she hears it during the night when it flops against the sides of the box, a dull, dead sound.

When she wakes, she looks out the window and sees leaves falling from a tall pecan tree. A bird sits on the window sill and looks in at her, its eyes like black beads.

She hasn't seen a bird in a long time, and she goes to the window to get a closer look. But by the time she gets there, the bird is gone.

She sits at the dresser and combs her lank black hair, then twists it into a knot at the base of her skull. Her face in the mirror is white and drawn, the eyes deep and dark. The mirror is streaked with dust.

She looks over at the cedar box.

The box is still, its surface smooth and polished. It has always been smooth, but over the years her hands have continued to polish it as she rubs its lid, its sides.

The lid of the box fits snugly into the sides. It is beautifully made. One can hardly see a space where the lid joins the box.

She does not look into the box before she leaves the room.

❖

Her father.

She remembers the hands. The way they gripped the wood as he shaped the box, the way they gripped her arms when he—.

She pushes the thought out of her mind and tries to find something to eat in the kitchen. She cannot remember when she last ate real food. She has been existing for weeks (months?) now on whatever she can scavenge from other houses, from stores. There is never much. Others who are still alive have always been there before her, and she has to be wary of them. The others are more dangerous to her than the dead.

It is the dead she seeks.

She finds a box of Wheat Thins in the kitchen, more than half empty. The crackers are old and they no longer crack when she bites them, but she hardly notices. She swallows them almost without chewing and fills a glass with water at the sink. It takes a long time for the glass to fill. She wonders what she will do when there is no more water.

Maybe by then she will have found him.

She knows that he is coming back. She knows that he will be looking for her.

She looks at her arms. The marks that she expects to see are not there, the red marks left by his fingers.

❖

She is sitting on his lap. She is five years old, wearing a white organdy dress.

"Serena," he says. His hands grip her arms. "You know you're my special darling." One hand releases her and he fumbles with his pants.

"No," she says. "No."

"Yes," he says. He pulls her closer with one hand and she twists away. His hard hand holds her and draws her to him.

"Look," he says.

She does not want to look, but she does. Then she turns her head away.

"My angel," he says. "My special one."

"No," she says, but he is pulling her hand now and she is going to have to touch him.

He sighs and pulls her even closer, moving his hand under her organdy dress.

"No," she says. "It hurts, Daddy. It hurts!"

"No," he says. "Let me show you. It doesn't hurt."

But it does. It hurts and hurts and she screams, shaking her head from side to side, her face furiously red.

"No," he says. "Be quiet, my darling. It doesn't hurt. It doesn't hurt."

But it does, and she screams and she screams and then—

She looks at the box of Wheat Thins, but she is no longer hungry. She opens the drawer of the cabinet and takes out the steak knife. It is eight inches long and has a serrated edge.

She sticks it through the knot of her hair.

In the living room there is a shotgun lying on the couch. It is a Mossberg pump, the eight-shot Persuader model with the pistol grip. There is a box of twelve-gauge shells beside it.

She opens the box of shells and fills the red hip purse that is strapped to her waist. She had earlier been lucky enough to find a sporting goods store that had not been looted, and she has an entire case of shells that she has not yet used.

She slides her fingers along the ridged red shell casings as she loads the pump.

She closes the door quietly when she leaves.

❖

—and then she is no longer screaming but crying, the tears like hot round lead on her cheeks, running into her mouth and off her chin. She can feel them soaking into her organdy dress, and she can feel—

❖

There are not so many of the dead now as there had been. They decay rapidly, disintegrating even as they stumble along the streets looking for new victims, for tender flesh to rend.

The zombies they beget with their toxic bites live on after their creators have crumbled, and crumble in their turn, but in the meanwhile they are there for the taking.

It is easy to avoid them if you know how, easy to pump a shell into the chamber of the Persuader and brace it against your shoulder while holding tight to the pistol grip. Easy to pull the trigger and blow off an arm or a leg, blow a huge hole in stomach or chest.

The dead do not always die again from such a wound. Their bodies fall and writhe in spastic dances, but they do not lie still.

Some of them can be stopped completely by blasting the head to bits, destroying absolutely and forever the brain, but not all of them can be stopped by even that means.

The virus, the radiation, whatever it is that animates them continues to enliven the body parts.

The solitary foot hops across the road, the hand pulls itself along by the fingers, even the eyeballs roll along, gathering dirt on their slimy surfaces.

But these are not the things that interest her.

❖

—feel it pushing, pushing, hurting. And the tears continue and the screaming begins again and her daddy is saying "Yesyesyesyes," but she is screaming "Nononono" and then—

❖

She sees two of them, both men, emerging from an alley. They are recent changeovers as she can tell by the fact that they are moving quickly and with an apparent determination. She can see the tears in their clothing where the dried blood still clings to them.

The shirt of one is open and there is a hole in his stomach. The shiny guts are spilling out, half eaten. The small intestine flops as he walks.

They were young when they changed. Neither is the one she is seeking.

She does not hesitate. She pumps the shotgun and fires. Pumps. Fires.

The heads explode and a red and grayish haze fills the air around them. The bodies stumble forward and then fall. The fresh ones are the easiest to kill. They always fall and remain still.

She hardly notices them as she steps across them, reaching into the purse for two more shells, her fingers caressing them as she shoves them into the pump.

He eyes move up the street, looking for more prey.

❖

—and then something wet and warm and he is hugging her and he is crying too.

"You can never tell your mother," he says, sobbing. "It will be our secret. Our secret, my darling."

She does not answer. Her tears have grown cold.

"Our secret," he says. "Ours. It must never happen again. And you must never tell."

His hands release her. There are marks, red marks on her arms.

She gets off his lap. The pain is between her legs and in her head. She hates him.

And she loves him.

And she knows—

❖

She sees him coming out of the bank. She does not even wonder why he has been inside it. Why do any of them do anything, other than eat?

She does not know. She does not care.

He is the one. His hair, what there is of it, is touched with gray. His hands are large and hard. He is the one.

He is not a fresh one. Strips of skin hang down from his face where something appears to have scratched him. One foot is entirely gone, but he can still walk, a strange unbalanced walk.

He still has his hands. His hard hands.

He is the one.

She blows a hole through his chest. Something that might be blood but that is more like green slime explodes out his back, along with still-white backbone, and he flies into the brick wall of the bank.

He slides slowly down the wall, feeling for purchase with his hands. He is definitely not a fresh one. All parts of him are alive, though *alive* is almost certainly not the right word.

She fires again and his head becomes nothing more than a smear on the wall.

❖

—and she knows, somehow she knows, that it *will* happen again and that she will scream and cry and that he will cry too and promise her that "this is the last time, the last," but that it will never be the last, never, until she is old enough to escape, and she knows, too, that no matter how far she goes, no matter how old she becomes, she will never escape.

Never.

❖

It is not dead.

Even without the head it somehow moves.

The hands twitch, the foot jiggles, the legs jerk, the arms quiver.

The twelve-gauge pellets pulverize the hands. She smiles. She has killed the hard hands.

She walks up to the still-pulsing body and reaches behind her head for the knife. She slits the belt and pulls down the pants and frees the throbbing penis.

She takes it in her left hand, gently. Then she squeezes it once, twice, three times.

Still smiling she cuts through the root with the serrated edge of the steak knife. She cuts slowly, taking her time.

When she is finished, she holds it up.

It continues to twitch and throb. Pubic hair still clings to it.

She unzips the purse and puts it inside.

As she walks back to the house she can feel it bumping her hip. Her smile stretches her lips and makes them tight.

She opens the cedar box. She can smell the shavings, see the dust in the wrinkles of his hands.

The one inside is quite still now, shriveled. Nothing lasts forever. The virus, the radiation, whatever it is, has left it, seeking another host, or died.

She neither knows nor cares which.

She opens the window and tosses it out. She wonders briefly about the bird, then closes the window.

She takes the penis from her purse, holds it throbbing in her hand. A pubic hair drops to the floor, but she does not notice.

She puts it into the box. It flops to the side and knocks against it. She watches it for a moment, then puts on the lid. It fits smoothly. She can hardly see the spaces between it and the sides.

She smiles.

That night she opens the box.

It spasms to the side as if to avoid her reach, but she catches it easily and takes it out.

She brings it to her face, where it throbs for a moment, then moves it down.

It touches her there and there and there and there.

She cries, but she cries silently. There is no one to hear her cry.

After a time she returns it to the box and replaces the lid. It does not move.

She lies in the bed, but sleep does not come until much later, after she hears the movement in the box, hears the soft knock against the cedar sides.

"Goodnight," she says. "Goodnight, Daddy."

And then she sleeps. †

RIFT
Nik Korpon

Glass crushes under my sneakers. I kneel down and grab a handful of Slim Jims, stuff them in my Dickies. They're snack sticks, not the jerky Anna likes, but it'll have to do. Old Sang stands behind the masonite counter, tilted toward the shelf by his knee, eyeballs bobbing back to me like he's watching a tennis match.

"Don't say I didn't warn you, friend."

He straightens himself. I snatch some Chili Fritos from the wire rack and tear open the bag, and I'm pretty sure that echo is corn chip hitting the bottom of my stomach. Should've forced down that sandwich rather than letting anger get the best of my gut.

"Just so we're on the same page, this isn't something I wanted to do. I know I don't need to tell you that, but I think it's important to know."

"Then go home." He points at the front door, spiderwebs sprawling from a muzzle-shaped hole in the glass. "Go home to your wife and TV dinners."

"Like I told you, Sang, there's the problem."

"My name's Rudy."

"I can't go because I've got nothing to go home with. Look here." I pull back my canvas jacket and he flinches, covers his face. "Come on, Sang, I'm not going to hurt you. Look here a sec."

He peeks around his hand. "What?"

"That's my soul. It's too light and airy. I need something to weigh me down so I don't float off into the clouds on my way home." Zipping up the jacket, listening to the growl in my stomach, I'm glad I at least remembered to rip the threads from my name tag. Hopefully he can't ID grease-stained knuckles in a lineup. It'd be my luck, but. "Don't you think my wife would be upset if I just floated off into the clouds on my way home?"

Fluorescent overhead lights flicker and buzz. I adjust Anna's stocking on my head, moving the black-line design away from the middle of my eyes. What the hell's wrong with just a normal stocking? Why do they have to have so many lines on them today? He nods like his head is a melon carefully balanced on a gutter nail.

"I think so, too. So, I need something to weigh me down. You can help me here, Sang—"

"Rudy."

"Sang, you can help me here by putting the rest of the money into that bag so I can go home to my wife. Got me?" On the TV chained up in the corner, the mayor waves his hands like a flightless bird in a windstorm, though I assume it's not in response to his slashing municipal pensions. Must be election season again for him to be so up in arms. That, or some little girl got raped and gutted again.

"Sir, I told you, there is no more money."

I topple the wire rack beside me. A couple bags of chips pop but it's not as dramatic as I hoped. "Nah, I still don't cotton to that. That's lawyers' tricks. *Store carries no more than thirty dollars. You have to be this tall to ride.* I know those tricks, Sang. City lawyers shoved my ass so full of them I should be reciting them to you."

"Sir, really—"

I sweep my Mossberg across his condiment shelf and get the shattering I was hoping for. Fragments of ketchup bottles and relish jars skitter across the cracked tile floor. Sang rears back behind the counter. Wedging my sneaker against the middle shelf, I kick hard as can and feel a sense of accomplishment when the shelf actually topples backward, until it knocks over the next two and the poor man's going to have a hell of a clean up.

Behind me, a click. I look up to two barrels of Sang.

"Put that down before someone gets hurt, now."

"I told you there was no more. I told you to get out of my store." The barrels tremble in his soft hands.

Pressing air beneath my palm, keeping identifiable tattoos inside my jacket, I tell him again to put it down while sidestepping broken condiments, finding cover behind a shelf. My finger stays on the .22's trigger. His barrels stay on me.

"Rudy, this doesn't need to get ugly. Just take a breath, calm down—"

There's a pop.

I swing my arm and pull the trigger.

I'd barely closed the mustard jar when the doorbell rang. The Felix clock hanging over the range said it was 2:30. Earlier than I'd expected. I dropped my cigarette in a cup, swished the coffee over the old butts, then checked my dentures in the mirror and went to the door.

"My sweet potato pie." Arms extended, I invited her in.

"Hi, Daddy." She gave me a peck and said she's not a little girl anymore.

"You'll always be my little girl."

She touched a palm lightly on my cheek, and she went right to the fridge. I followed behind her.

"Do you have any turkey? I forgot to eat before my shift."

I handed her my plate, said I'd make another.

"Jesus, Daddy, it's mustard." She set the plate down, crossed her arms and cocked her hip out like her mother used to.

"You don't like mustard anymore?"

"There's got to be something to make it a sandwich, is my point. Cheese, meat. Lettuce?"

I took a bite and then set to rummaging around the fridge for something to do. The root beer was flat and about tasteless, but cold. She cleared her throat three times before drawing me out.

"What happened to your food?"

"Been hungry."

"What happened to your check? When's the last time you went shopping?"

I pushed more sandwich in my mouth, offered her the rest again. She just stared. I smoothed my sideburns as I chewed, noticed a dried glob of ketchup stuck on the wall. At least, it looked like ketchup.

"I've been spending a lot of time in the garage, is all. Just slipped my mind."

The chair scraped across the floor, hopped when it caught in the hole of missing linoleum. She lowered herself with a sigh. "Did you get it running yet?"

"Nah. Not sure if she'll even run anymore, old girl is so nearly seized. Keeps me in shape. Just in case, you know?" I sat beside her, pushed my plate to the middle of the table. "Like I always told you, you need to be ready for opportunity because it doesn't knock twice nor take messages."

"Yeah, I remember." She picked a strip of crust off my sandwich. Her shoulder mic squawked about a robbery up on Edmonson. She turned an ear to it, then quieted the box. A couple more pins on her chest that I hadn't noticed before. Wonder if she got a promotion. "You ever hear anything from those names I gave you?"

A cough echoed down the hallway. The bedroom door whined open, floor squeaking to the bathroom. She chewed on her bottom lip.

"They didn't have much use for diesel. Guess busses and cars are more clocks and watches than just gears like I'd figured. So many damn computers in the engines these days."

"Well, keep looking, I suppose." She spoke to me but didn't look at me. The bedroom door closed again.

I reached over and took her hand. "Look, sweet potato, I need to ask a favor."

❖

The popped bag of Utz Crab Chips crushes under my sneaker. Stupid son of a bitch. Jumpy bastard. Can't tag a damn rat with some aim but you can shoot a chinaman's eye on a fucking humbug? What the fuck, Louis!

I slink behind the counter like old Sang's liable to spring up on me, swing his barrels around and say, *you have to be this tall to fuck off*. Sang, though, he can't do much more than lie there and make the floor red, staring at me with one eye.

This is not good. Not good at all. This is not how it was supposed to happen.

I creep around his body, staying below the row of windows. The last register I operated was at Hutzler's in high school, and this one is a far cry from that, so I grab a screwdriver and start prying. It gives with a surprising lack of torque. Cheap little Mexican-made machines.

Sang appears to have been lying, but he's not far from the truth, either. Eighty-seven in paper, probably four-fifty or so in coin. Plus the forty-six he gave me to get the rat gun out of his face. So, one dead chinaman equates to roughly twelve minutes of treatment for Anna. A fucking joke.

And up in the corner, the mayor's red in the face, saying he's bringing a new day to Baltimore.

The TV doesn't spark as much as I'd expected when I shoot it, though it's one of those movie things I've always wanted to do.

I step behind the counter and shove half a dozen packs of USAs into my pockets, another dozen in my jacket and a loosey between my lips. Avoiding blood on my knees, I kneel down and thumb Rudy's eyelid closed, say the only prayer I can remember, one Janey taught me:

"Saint Michael the Archangel, defend us in battle. Be our protection against the wickedness and snares of the devil. May God rebuke him, we humbly pray."

I say amen because the rest escapes me, then trace a small cross on his forehead. Sorry if you're Buddhist, Rudy. Don't mean for you to go to Hell, or wherever.

Strike a match, pull the stocking from my face, and unlock the door.

The air is like biting into a fresh apple. A touch of smoke lingering, probably leaves burning in an alley trashcan. Skeletal fingers of pink evening loom above, the night drawing close. Check my legs again to make sure there's no blood, nothing to attract wandering eyes. I take a long drag off my smoke, look up, and clock two cruisers, double-barreling down Ostend, straight at me.

❖

"I'm not giving her shit."

"It's not her, sweet pota—"

"Dad, please, stop fucking calling me that."

"Janey, I can't afford it anymore. Your stepmother—"

"That cunt is not my mother."

"Your stepmother—"

"You remember when I was a freshman and I asked you what running a train was? Yeah, that was her." She slammed back in her chair, leaving an indentation in the drywall. "Christ, she fucked an Aerosmith roadie just for a T-shirt."

I kneaded my fingers on my forehead. "We've all done our trespasses, Janey."

"Aerosmith, Dad? You don't even like Aerosmith."

I opened my mouth, closed it, like a dog eating hornets. The floorboards in the bedroom creaked.

"Your stepmother is sick, Janey."

"It's called liver failure, Dad. It's what happens when you've got a street's worth of tar in you." Janey jumped up, chair cracking against the floor. Her finger in my face, though whether trembling or shaking it, it was a toss-up. "Wake the fuck up, Dad. She's a dope fiend. She's in withdrawal and she's going to die sooner or later." She flung my sandwich into the trashcan, dropped the dish on the pile in the sink and I was shocked nothing broke. A dull *thump-thump-thump* I took for the 2:45 freight chugging through the yard. Her foot on the floor, fingers gripping the edge of the sink, head swinging from her neck like a pendulum. She was so angry I could hear her breathe.

I clicked open my lighter, touched flame to my smoke, folded it shut. "You remember when we took you to Wild World, back when you were, I don't know, five? Six?"

She grunted.

"You were so angry 'cause your mom wouldn't let you in the wavepool after she saw the bandages floating on the surface."

Nothing to that, just a measured exhale that sounded like descending numbers. More and more like her mother, like when we used to argue. I'd told her she could become an accountant with all the time she spent counting.

"I miss her, too, Janey. It's hard being in this house." The cherry crackled as I inhaled. Ashes fluttered to the floor. "It's hard being alone. It sucks."

Her shoulder squawked again, another robbery. This time on Scott and West Cross. She spun on her heels, walked past me with her hand in pocket, then paused by the door, breathing, breathing. She pulled her fist from her pocket, uncurled it. Two bills fell on the coffee table.

"Sometimes life sucks, Daddy." Halfway turned, so I could only see her profile. "You told me that the same afternoon."

The door clicked shut.

No creaking bedrooms. No chattering daughters. Just the echo-memory of a dead wife's moaning, the ghost of a static blast. I lit another cigarette, held it till I could feel the smoke fill in my eyelids.

Robbery at Scott and West Cross. No one'd go back that way twice.

❖

Bars of red and blue light strobe through the store, twisting and swirling like they're caught in the wake of angels' wings. Back pressed against the fallen shelf, I peek around the corner, clock three silhouettes of Baltimore's finest kneeling behind their cars' hoods, guns trained on the store. Bugs flock to their headlights. Big Man bullhorns me again, says I won't be hurt if I come out now.

"That's all right. Think I'm fine here." I chew a filter into dust. Burnt tobacco falls on the back of my hand.

"I give you my word that—"

"Fuck your word, Captain." I bite off a mouthful of Slim Jim, which tastes like a dead dog's asshole, and swallow. Light another cigarette to give my hands something to do besides shake. "I've had enough words from all you people. They don't mean shit when it comes down to it."

"Sir, I repeat, I promise that if you put down—"

"I put down the gun and come out, then everything's fine. No one's going to open my ass up as soon as I step out that door?" I inhale until it hurts, until my chest tingles with burning. "Fuck you. I know how you all do."

"Look motherfucker, you got till ten, then I'm coming in and I'm going to shoot you in the fucking face."

Maybe it's meant for the TV, for the mayor and his vote-collecting budget slashes, the ones that leave working men without insurance. Maybe it's for Big Man, for all big men, the ones who let cutthroats like the mayor cut our throats. Or maybe it's just because I'm scared to go home to Anna anymore. I don't know why my hand does it, but I watch it lift the gun, point behind me and fire three times.

A volley of shots shatters the front door completely. Someone hoarse-whispers, "By the door, bottom right." Tiny bits of tile pop and scatter as bullets slip wide. One hits the ceiling, plaster dust sifting down. I have a flash of snowflakes landing on Janey's toddler eyelashes, looking up and seeing her mother with the same. In the aisle, a ketchup bottle explodes, two glass shards stabbing into my leg. I stop to roll in pain then grab the floor, push myself the opposite way. It takes a good four seconds to pull the shards out, at least an inch of blood-covered glass. I see Janey and her mother eating shave ice from Pascal's on Wicomico, their lips garish red. My thigh is warm and wet. I swing the gun up, pull three more times. A metal ting, and I think I hit the inside wall of the shop.

Seven shots till, *click. Louis, what were you ever thinking?*

The bullhorn feeds back. Scuttling outside. I peek around, catch two police sneaking up the flank. One shot, into the ceiling, just for effect. Just to see my girls' eyelashes.

The bullhorn shrieks. A woman's voice rings out.

"Sir, please. We can work this out so no one gets hurt. My name is Sergeant Tanzen. I won't let you get hurt, and you can trust me. Sir, what's your name?"

I light a cigarette. "Sonny Wortzik."

"Mr. Wortzik, we can work together and everyone will be safe."

I take a long drag, exhale through my nose, watching the smoke spiral away from itself, watching oblivion on a micro, natural level. I shouldn't be surprised. I should've foreseen this the day I met Anna. She's just got that air about her.

"Mr. Wortzik, I need you to put the gun down."

Tipping my head back, I blow two smoke rings into the air and watch them overlap, dissapate, then call out, "After you, sweet potato. After you." †

BIG DARLENE THE SEX MACHINE
Matthew J. McBride

I'd been out of prison just three days when I broke a man's chin with a crowbar.

I was changing a tire outside of Bland, Missouri, when a cop who didn't like tattoos harassed us. We'd had a blow out in Darlene's Bonneville going sixty-eight in a thirty-five and I drove a few miles on the rim.

I'd met Darlene at the end of my third year at Algoa. I was doing a five-year stretch for armed robbery. My partner got sixteen years, but he deserved it. He shot a kid in the head during the hold up. The kid lived, but now he breathes through a tube. My lawyer said his parents keep him in their basement hooked up to a machine.

I felt bad about the kid, but I didn't shoot him. I was in the back of the store—sucking the life from a can of pressurized whip cream. Duke's the one who got tough with the boy. He hit him in the face with a pistol, told him to cough up the money.

What happened next is a mystery because I was high from the whippets, but I heard two gunshots that sounded like firecrackers then the kid hit the floor. Duke said he'd gone for a weapon, but the cops never found one. Duke was a liar. He just liked to shoot people.

❖

Life in prison was as bad as it could be. There were fights, stabbings, and rapes.

I did the first year and a half without trouble. I kept to myself and I walked with my head down. My lawyer told me I had five years to serve but stay off the radar and be out in three. So I stayed off the radar. Until that first day of summer when I hit a prisoner named Jerome Delmont in the throat.

Jerome Delmont had it coming. He must have had something to prove to his boys, because he gave me a hard shoulder in the mess hall and grabbed a biscuit off my tray. He and his boys laughed.

I laughed too, but my smile was ripe with hate.

The next day came and I waited at the back of the line. I watched the other prisoners in front of me give hard looks to each other, but that didn't bother me.

Hard looks never killed anybody.

I watched a cook named Jerry Dean work the noodles loose from a deep pan of spaghetti and slap them on my tray. There was no meat, only sauce.

Another inmate shoveled a load of mashed potatoes with an ice cream scoop and plopped them on the noodles.

I nodded, grabbed a box of juice, and walked toward Jerome.

Jerome Delmont was a lifer. He looked up when I approached and showed me a mouth full of gold fronts. "Oh, here come this cat from yesterday. Let's see what this mu'fucker gotta say."

"How you spooks doin' today?" I asked.

That stopped them cold—so I tossed my orange juice to Jerome. When he looked down to catch it, I turned the tray upside down and let that slop fall to the floor.

Quickly, I rotated my body in a complete circle, and using the momentum, I spun and hit that black bastard in the Adam's apple as hard as I could with the edge of my plastic tray.

The tray snapped in half and part of it flew across the room.

Jerome fell off the bench and landed on his back and I stomped his throat. One of his boys yelled, "Damn!"

I walked to the other end of the mess hall and set my broken tray on the trashcan with the other empties. I walked out into the scorching sun and found a place against the chain link fence in a small patch of shade.

❖

It didn't take long before word got out that I'd put a hurt on Jerome. A guard named Ray Hall asked me if it was true. Was I the one who smashed his throat?

"What if I did?"

Hall laughed. "Don't matter to me none, bud. Far as I'm concerned, you done good."

I liked Hall after that. I'd hated him before, but that kind of reassurance in a man was enough to spark a friendship.

Ray Hall was a country boy. A big man with a barrel chest, wide shoulders and a sharp smile that carved into his fat cheeks every time his lips parted. He told me I wasn't so bad. He said he had a sister if I was interested. "Was I?"

I said of course I was interested.

He never told me she was a big girl. I guess he didn't want to ruin the surprise.

❖

I spent a few weeks in the hole. That's what they called it, *the hole*. But it wasn't a hole; it was an ancient room with concrete walls that were stained with piss and a concrete floor stained with shit. I'd seen closets that were bigger than the hole, but I didn't complain. I ate one meal a day, and three days a week they'd set a bucket of water on the floor so I could bathe. It wasn't so bad.

I did my time like a man and kept my mouth shut. I pissed on the wall and shit on the floor just like everybody else. Days passed. Then weeks passed. Finally I was out, and my first day back I hit Jerome in the throat with a five-finger death punch that sent him to the shower floor choking on blood. His friend backed up, told me he was cool, but I went after him anyway and bit a piece of meat out of his back.

I went back to the hole for a long time after that. But this time they put me in a new hole. A real hole. They brought me down two short flights of concrete steps that were long and wide, then lead me to a basement under the mess hall that I didn't know was there.

There was a long fluorescent light above my head they never turned off. There were no windows. They left me in a pair of prison boxers stained with ten thousand skid marks and they didn't come back for days.

❖

In the hole, time became my enemy. Days went by and weeks became months. They only fed me when they remembered I existed—and they didn't bring a bucket of water, they brought a fire hose. Once a week they'd kick the door open without warning and blast me with enough force to rip my skin open.

Then one day I was out. The guards returned me to gen pop and asked if I'd be good.

I swallowed hard and spit on the floor. I told the guards I liked the hole. Told them leave the light on for me, I was pretty sure I'd be coming back.

Ray Hall handed me a stack of envelopes before he locked me in my cage. "These here letters are from my sister."

He said her name was Darlene.

I spent the next few days lost in Darlene's world. She said she had a lot of love to give. She was alone, and she was looking for a guy like me. She said all she'd ever wanted was a man to hold her hand and love her. And spank her when she was bad.

Her words were magic and they heeled my wounds like medicine. I'd be out in a week. I'd walk through that gate and she'd be waiting there—in her golden chariot, with a bottle of champagne and a wet mouth that promised to suck away all my problems.

Ray Hall came to get me the following Monday—and the night before I was restless. I didn't sleep. I couldn't eat. I did sit-ups and push-ups and pull-ups instead.

I wanted to look good for Darlene. I was one hundred eighty-two pounds of lean hard muscle and my body looked like someone carved me out of granite with a switchblade.

Ray told me I was looking good. "Just don't hurt her," he said.

I told him not to worry. But still, even then, Ray never told me she was a big girl.

❖

I left Algoa in faded Levi's with a hole in the knee, a pair of steel-toed boots, and a T-shirt that advertised Snag's Pool Hall and read *Liquor in the front, poker in the rear*. It was my favorite shirt when I went in, but now it was a size too big.

When I passed the main gate, a black guard with a face that looked like it had been used to put out a grease fire warned me not to come back. Then I stepped into that harsh golden sunlight and what I saw stopped me in mid stride like a brick wall.

Darlene had parked her '77 Bonneville up front in a handicapped spot, and she was perched on top of the hood like an ornament. There was a GPC fused to her lip with at least three inches of ash. She blew me a kiss with bloated lips the color of red paint then dropped her GPC on the parking lot.

When she stood the whole car moved and I saw a mess of hair that had been many colors at many different times, none of which ever seemed to wash out. Darlene had a solid frame with shoulders as wide as her brothers and a face just as fat. Her hands were the size of catcher's mitts, each tit the size of a medicine ball.

I climbed into her Pontiac and there was a case of warm beer between the seats. A set of pink fuzzy dice hung from the rear-view mirror that looked like they'd been drug behind a garbage truck.

Darlene had me by a good eighty pounds. She told me her and Ray were twins. Then she hugged me, kissed me, and jacked me off in the parking lot while a song I'd never heard played on the radio.

We spent the next two days at a dump called Bud's Place where the best room in the house was forty-five bucks and it smelled like the final resting place for animals when they came to die. The air conditioning worked when it wanted and the carpet smelled like hobo piss, but the bed was soft, and I spent the first night doing things to that woman that only three years in prison could make a man do.

The first time we fucked I rolled off of her and puked in an ashtray. I told her it was the seventeen hot Stags I drank on the way to Bud's Place. The next few pokes went a little smoother, though she was a bit rough with me at times. I forgave her for being rough, but I couldn't forgive her for looking like her brother. Ray was probably laughing right now.

We ate prescription diet pills like candy and drank cheap rum. The room reeked like sex and cigarette smoke. I thought about a girl I used to know and then I turned Darlene around so it didn't feel like I was pounding Ray from behind.

❖

I went through parked cars at night so when we left Bud's Place, we had an extra forty dollars and a hot new pistol. I found the gun in a station wagon with a bumper sticker that read *Ted Kennedy's car has killed more people than my gun!*

I looked in the mirror at the cut above my eye where Darlene hit me with the ashtray once I said I'd had enough.

Big Darlene was a sex machine with an appetite that knew no boundaries—but a man could only take so much.

I rubbed my finger along the cut and took a big gulp of rum. Darlene squeezed my leg and crammed a handful of diet pills down my throat. We'd been eating them for days and that was the primary reason for all that fornicating back at Bud's Place. I'd given her the pounding of a lifetime but I hadn't come close to wearing her out.

I raced the Pontiac at a high rate of speed as we blew down the back roads of Gasconade County. I hadn't driven in years but the wheel felt natural in my hands.

This seemed to excite Darlene. She yelled for me to go faster, so I punched the gas pedal and we listened to the Pontiac choke. The carburetor gagged, and the car pumped an oil cloud of thick black smoke as the motor screamed, and pleaded, and tried not to blow up.

Everything was fine until we took a corner outside Bland in the wrong lane and the right front tire blew off the rim.

Darlene screeched as the wheel dropped onto the asphalt and began grinding down. Sparks flew up into the window and peppered her big, freckled arm.

"Goddammit," I yelled, and I yanked that lead sled to the shoulder.

"My Bonnie," Darlene cried, as she gnawed a stick of beef jerky.

I pulled over once I'd found good shoulder and hoisted the bottle upright. I poured the rest of the rum down my throat and asked Darlene if she had a spare.

She grabbed me and hugged me, but I pushed her away and told her she smelled like sweat. "Spare?" I asked. "Do you have one?"

Darlene shrugged, so I walked to the back and slid my key in the hole but she never got out. She fired up a GPC instead and blew a mouthful of smoke out the window.

In the trunk I found bags of dirty clothes, and trash, and a box filled with sex toys. I didn't see a spare.

"Oh, it's there," she assured me.

I set the box on the roof, dug a little deeper, and found a semi bald tire under a pile of dirty whites that no amount of laundering could ever sanitize. I rolled the tire to the front of the car and then went back for the jack.

❖

I was on my knees when the officer pulled up and gave me a hard look with his eyes.

The cop walked to the front of the Bonneville and my heart beat in my ears. My mind was on fire from three days of sex and beer and Benzedrine.

"Y'all's goin' a little fast back there, huh, speedy?"

I shook my head and told the pig I was sorry.

He stood over me just as tall as he could like a good old boy and grinned.

"I bet you's sorry. You's doin' sixty-eight in a thirty-five."

I tightened the last lug nut when the cop grabbed the box of vibrators off the roof.

"And just what in the hell is this crap?"

I looked up at Darlene and smiled.

"Those belong to her."

The cop tossed the box on the hood. "What kind of sick shit is this?"

He looked me over. He didn't like tattoos.

"You just get out of the pen, boy?"

I told him I had. We had a flat to change, but now we'd be on our way.

The cop stood a little straighter and stuck his chest up. "You wait just a second. I need to see some ID, right now. Hers too." He pointed to Darlene but she didn't move.

"Come on, sweetheart, you too." But she rolled the window up and shook another GPC loose from the pack.

The cop turned his head sideways and looked at Darlene. Then he looked at me. "Listen, you tell her to get her big ass out of the car right now."

He had his hand on his mace and he meant to use it.

I looked at Darlene and remembered the gun I'd found at Bud's Place.

The cop beat on the hood with his fist and told me I'd better get that fat bitch outta the car "toot sweet" or we'd both end up in jail.

When he popped the top on his mace, I jerked that tire tool up that was dangling by my side and gave him an uppercut to the chin with the steel handle that blew his jaw apart.

The cop stumbled back into the road as a grain truck roared by and it slammed him to the pavement. The truck screeched and bounced and it swerved into the ditch with its brakes locked up. The cop's body was scattered in pieces along Highway A.

Darlene screamed and danced, and the whole car rocked—the worn out springs heaved and bounced.

I jumped behind the wheel and hit the key. The Bonneville cranked and coughed, but she finally started. I shoved the shifter into gear and stomped the pedal.

Darlene was wet with desire as I pulled onto the road. She grabbed me and told me she loved me in a way she could never love anyone else. She'd do anything to please me and she put her head down under the steering wheel to love me the best way that she knew how.

The gun was between our seats and the cops were behind us—ready to blow out our tires then blow holes in our heads.

Darlene took me in her mouth as the Pontiac screamed across the pavement defiantly while black smoke pumped from the tail pipe in a powerful cloud.

I thought about Algoa, and Duke. About Jerome Delmont and Ray Hall.

When the engine threw a rod through the oil pan. I knew the Pontiac was done.

I picked up the gun as Darlene's Bonneville died and rolled to a stop, and cops surrounded the car, guns drawn, telling me to put that fucking gun down.

I pushed the barrel into my neck and said I was never going back to the hole.

Darlene stopped long enough to tell me that she loved me, and the Pontiac backfired, and the cops unloaded hot rounds into the doors. I never said I loved her back. †

MAYBE SOMEDAY
Sean Chercover

Above all else, it was the taste of her he could not forget. Every day, the memory returned. A sense memory, rising spontaneous and unbidden, the taste *right there* on his tongue, as intense and intoxicating as the hot summer night she'd spread her long legs and invited him in.

Every day. And with it came a flood of other memories. Freckled face, beautiful and creased by middle age; proud nose, nostrils like elongated teardrops; hooded eyes, intelligent, perceptive, but also wounded and needy. Slender fingers stroking his cheek, then clutching the hair on the back of his head as he went down.

And every day, he picked up his cell phone, brought her number up on the screen, determined to either call or delete the number from its memory. But he couldn't call, and he couldn't erase her number from his phone, and above all else, he couldn't erase the taste of her from his mind.

He didn't believe in love at first sight. Love at first sight was the stuff of fairy tales and romance novels.

Might as well believe in unicorns.

But something happened in his chest the very first time their eyes met, and from the way she darted her eyes away he could tell it had happened to her also. They were at opposite ends of a long table, in a large group, hadn't said a word to each other, hadn't even been introduced. When she looked away she reached for her drink, adjusted her wedding ring with her thumb, bringing the diamond setting upright on her slender finger. An unconscious gesture, like the tell of a poker player. The message was clear: *I'm married.* But was it a signal meant for him, or a reminder to herself? He couldn't say.

That was their first meeting, in a large group of friends out for drinks after work. One of those things where two circles of friends overlap and then become one. Among the members of the group, the after-work drinking sessions were called "going for herbal tea." Each Friday around lunchtime, someone would send a mass email to the group: *Who's going for herbal after work?* If enough people jumped in, they'd meet at Sheffield's patio, where they'd drink expensive craft beer or single malt scotch while sharing funny stories about their nightmare bosses, commiserating over the ongoing futility of the Cubs, deconstructing the latest novels they'd loved or hated.

Minutes after their eyes first met, someone in the group introduced them and the thing happened in his chest again as he shook her hand and he had no idea what he said or what she said in reply, and the rest of that first night was a blur.

He didn't want to get involved with a married woman. And he didn't believe in love at first sight. But the next week, when the email went around and he saw her name on the list of recipients, he felt queasy. And when she responded to the group, saying she'd join them for herbal, goddamn if that thing didn't happen in his chest again.

It was just a case of sexual chemistry, he told himself. Just pheromones at work, a genetically programmed response to a good breeding partner, and pheromones don't care who's married and who's not. That's all it was, nothing more. Hell, he didn't even know the woman. They might not even like each other.

But he joined the group for drinks after work. And they did like each other. She was smart and funny and beautiful, and clearly as disturbed as he by what they both were feeling. She talked a great deal about her husband and her three children, and she kept propping up that damned diamond with her thumb. Even so, she talked mostly to him that night, and he to her. The rest of the group just seemed to melt into the background.

For the next five Fridays, they both attended every herbal, and they sat across from each other and talked like old friends, or new lovers. But he never made even the suggestion of a pass, and she never missed an opportunity to mention her family.

On the sixth Friday she seemed nervous as she told—someone else at the table, not him—that her husband had taken the kids camping for the weekend. She avoided his eyes for a good five minutes after that, which told him more than if she hadn't.

The group stayed late that night. When it was over, he offered to walk her to Belmont and she said yes, and he silently prayed that none of the others were taking the train.

They weren't.

Outside the station, he told her his apartment was just a few blocks away on Melrose and he had a bottle of Talisker and a rooftop deck with a fabulous view of the city.

"I'm sorry," she said.

"Just a drink," he lied, "and some conversation. Nothing more." He held his breath. Waited.

"I don't know. I should ..." she looked at the entrance to the station, then back at him. "All right."

They sat on his rooftop deck and drank Talisker and watched thin white mist-clouds drifting across the John Hancock building, and they talked about their lives, and he found himself telling her things he'd never told anyone else. He talked freely of the profound sense of isolation that had been his constant companion, even in childhood, even with his parents, who loved him but never really knew him.

And telling her this, he felt completely exposed, and completely comfortable with it. Not isolated at all.

He realized then, it was far more than sexual chemistry, and had been from the very beginning. It was as if this moment of intimacy had somehow been contained in that very first look. It was the feeling that, when their eyes first met, they had seen right into each other, behind the masks, seen each other fully and truly, and liked what they'd seen. And more, they'd seen themselves being seen by the other, and neither covered up. Yes, they'd looked away, but each time they looked back, they were right there again, willing to see and be seen, unwilling to shut the other out.

She felt it too, right from the very first look, and that night on his rooftop deck, they talked about it. And then she went with him to the bedroom.

But in the morning he woke up alone.

She called the next afternoon and apologized, both for leaving and for leading him on, and he apologized for inviting her to his apartment, for putting her in that situation to begin with. She insisted that she loved her husband, and he believed her. She vowed that she would never allow her children's lives to be shattered by divorce, and he believed that too. He said he didn't want to break up her family, and he meant it.

Then she told him the connection they'd shared was real, was maybe even love, but could never happen again. After she hung up, he cried a little. Then he saved her number in his cell phone. He couldn't help himself.

She stopped coming out for herbals, and after a few weeks he stopped as well. He couldn't do it anymore, couldn't sit on the patio at Sheffield's making small talk with the group, staring at the door, hoping for what he knew wasn't coming.

He got on with his life. Eventually he had other women, other relationships. But he never felt that level of connection with any of them, that sense of truly seeing and being seen, completely exposed and comfortable, not like he'd felt with her, and he just couldn't see the point without it, and the relationships never worked out.

He told himself that maybe someday she would call again. Maybe someday they could be together. Maybe after her kids were grown and out of the house. Or maybe her husband would get cancer and die—and he hated himself for wishing it, but he *did* wish it just the same. And each time he upgraded to a new cell phone, he transferred her number over, for when the time came.

But *maybe someday* never came. She never called.

He never called.

You don't break up a family, just because of love.

❖

He sat and stared at the phone, beside the newspaper that lay open on the kitchen table. There was no use calling now, she wouldn't answer. It occurred to him that he'd been sitting there for hours, unmoving, as the day had darkened to night. He reached for the phone, picked it up. Just like all the previous days since they'd been together, he put the phone back down on the table, hating himself for his lack of will. How hard could it be to simply wipe her number from the phone and never have to look at it again?

The sense memory returned, the taste of her on his tongue.

Every damn day ... even now.

He stood and opened the fridge and pushed his face into the cool white light and held it there, feeling his sweat turn cold, breathing through his mouth. He grabbed the last bottle of Old Style from the shelf and returned to the table, not looking at the cell phone or the newspaper, and drank the beer down in one go.

To wash the taste away.

It didn't.

He lit a cigarette. Picked up the newspaper and read her obituary again.

Maybe someday.

He didn't believe in an afterlife, any more than he believed in love at first sight—the stuff of fairy tales and romance novels.

Might as well believe in unicorns.

He pulled the half-full bottle of Talisker from the cupboard. He'd put it away after their night together, promised himself he'd only bring it out when she came back to him. Hadn't touched it since.

He took the bottle up to his rooftop deck. It was a hot summer night, like the night they'd been together, years ago. But tonight, there was no mist. Tonight everything was clear.

He sat and drank the scotch and remembered. It didn't wash the taste of her away, but he no longer wanted to wash it away.

After the bottle was empty, he walked slowly to the edge of the rooftop.

He didn't believe in an afterlife.

Love at first sight.

Fairy tales … romance novels.

Unicorns.

He stepped over the edge, into the empty space beyond.

Someday. †

THE OLD WAYS
Ed Gorman

For Norman Partridge

There had been a gunfight earlier in the evening, but then, in a place like this one, there usually were gunfights earlier. And later, for that matter.

The name of the place was Madame Duprée's and it was one of the big casino-drinking establishments that were filling the most disreputable part of San Francisco in this year of 1903. The Barbary Coast was the name for the entire district and, yes, it was every bit as dangerous as you've heard. Cops, even the young strong ones, would only come down here in fours and sixes, and even then an awful lot of them got killed.

The way I got this job was to get myself good and beaten up and tossed in an alley behind the Madame's. One of her men found me and brought me to her and she asked me if I wanted a job and since I hadn't eaten in three days I said yes and so she put me to work as a floater in her casino. What I did was walk around with a few hundred dollars of Madame Duprée's money in my pockets and pretend to be drunk. Inevitably, rubes would spot me as an easy mark and invite me into one of their poker games. Thanks to a few accoutrements such as a holdout vest and a sleeve holdout, I could pretty much deal myself any cards I wanted to. Eighty-five percent of my winnings went back to Madame Duprée. The rest I kept. Not bad pay for somebody who'd been raised on an Oklahoma reservation and seen three of his brothers and sisters die of tuberculosis before they reached eight years of age. I'd gotten my memory back and wished I hadn't.

What Madame Duprée didn't say—didn't need to say, really—was that an Indian was a perfect mark because he was held to be the lowest form of life in these United States, even below that of Negro and Chinaman. What rube could possibly resist taking money from a drunken Indian? Or, for that matter, what Indian could resist? You saw a lot of red men along the Barbary Coast, men who'd worked or stolen their way into some money and now wanted to spend it the way white men did. The Barbary was about the only place in the land where no distinction was made among the races—if you had the money, you could have anything any other man could have. This included all the white girls, some of whom were as young as thirteen, though this particular summer a wave of various venereal diseases was sweeping the Barbary. More than six hundred people had died so far. A Methodist minister had suggested in one of the local newspapers that the Barbary be set afire with all its "human filth" still in it. I wasn't sure that Jesus would have approved of such a proposal, but then you never could tell.

Tonight's gunfight pretty much started the way they all do in a place like this.

On the ground floor, Madame Duprée's consisted of three large rooms, the walls of which were covered by giant murals of easy women in even easier poses. As you wandered among the sailors, the city councilmen, the crooked cops, the whores, the pickpockets, the professional gamblers, the farmers, the clerks, the disguised ministers and priests and even the occasional rabbi, the slumming socialites, and the sad-eyed fathers looking for their runaway daughters, you found gambling devices of every kind: faro, baffling board, roulette, keno, goose-and-balls, and— well, you get the idea.

Tonight a drunken rube suspected he'd been cheated out of his money. And no doubt he suspected correctly. He got loud, and then he got violent, and then, as he was being escorted out one of the side doors by a giant Negro bouncer with a ruffled white shirt already bloody this early in the evening, he made the worst mistake of all. He pulled his gun and tried to shoot the bouncer in the side. And the bouncer responded by drawing his own gun and shooting the man's gun away. And then the bouncer threw the man through the side door and went out into the dark alley.

Everybody who worked here knew what was going to happen next. Every bouncer at every major casino in the Barbary had a specialty. Some were especially good with knives and guns, for instance. This man's specialty was his strength. He liked to grab the top of somebody's head with his giant hand and give the head a violent wrench to the left, thereby breaking the neck. I'd seen him do it once and I couldn't get the sight out of my mind for a couple of weeks afterward. The funny thing was he was called Mr. Stevenson because late at night, at a steakhouse down the street, he read Robert Louis Stevenson stories out loud to anybody who'd listen. Mr. Stevenson told me once, "I was a plantation nigger and my master thought it'd be funny to have a big buck like me know how to read. So he had me educated from the time I was six and a couple of times a week he'd have me come up to the house and read to all his friends and they just couldn't believe I could read the way I did." That gave us something in common. An Oklahoma white man who ran the town next to my reservation put me through two years of college. I probably would have finished except the man dropped straight down dead of a heart attack and his son wasn't anywhere near as generous.

That was how Mr. Stevenson and I were the same, the education. How we were different was his physical strength.

After Mr. Stevenson finished with the rube, I got myself a good cigar and wandered around in my good clothes, weaving a little the way I did to let people know that I was a drunken Indian, and I got pulled into three different games in as many hours. I won a little over four hundred dollars. Madame Duprée would be happy—at least she would be if she'd gotten over her terrible cold, which some of us had come to suspect was maybe something more than a cold. Be funny if one of the owners died of venereal disease the way their girls and their customers did.

Around ten, I saw Mr. Stevenson working his way over to me. He wore his usual attire, a bowler perched at a rakish angle on his big head, his fancy shirt with the celluloid collar, and a sparkling diamond stickpin through his red cravat.

"You catch a drink with me?" he said as he leaned over the table where I was playing.

"Something wrong?"

He nodded. He had solemn brown eyes that hinted at both his intelligence and his anger.

"Five minutes."

"You know that coon?" one of the rubes said after Mr. Stevenson had left.

"Met him a little earlier. Why?"

The rube shook his head. "Scares the piss out of me, he does. I heard about how he snaps them necks." He shuddered. "Back in Nebraska, you just don't see things like that."

I finished the hand and then joined Mr. Stevenson at the bar. As always, he drank tea. He took his job very seriously and he didn't want whiskey to make him careless.

I didn't much worry about things like that. I had a shot of rye with a beer back.

"What's up, Mr. Stevenson?"

"Moira."

"Oh."

There was a group of reservation Indians who had collected in the Barbary over the past two years or so. Maybe a dozen of us, all employed in various capacities by the casinos. One was a very beautiful Indian girl who'd been called "Moira" by the Indian agent where she'd grown up. Mr. Stevenson was sweet on her, and in a terrible way. He'd go through periods where he couldn't sleep; you'd see him standing in front of her cheap hotel, staring up at her window, doing some kind of sad sentry duty. Or you'd see him following her. Or you'd see him sitting alone in a coffeehouse all teary-eyed and glum and you knew who he was thinking about. Or I did, anyway. I'd gone through the same thing with Moira myself. I'd been in bitter love with her for nearly a year but then I'd passed through it. Like a fever.

Not that you could blame Moira. She was as captivated by another reservation Indian named Two Eagle as we were captivated by her. Did all the same things we did with her. Followed him around. Bought him gifts he didn't want. Wrote him pleading little notes.

Then they got a place and moved in together, Moira and Two Eagle, but word was things weren't going well. He was one of those Indians too fond of the bottle and too bitter toward the white man to function well. Kept a drum up in his room and sometimes in the middle of the night you'd hear it, a tom-tom here in the center of the Barbary, and him yowling ancient Indian war cries and chants. He was fierce, Two Eagle, and he seemed to hate me especially, seemed to think that I had no pride in my red skin or my ancestors. I returned the favor, thinking he was pretty much a melodramatic asshole. I was just as much an Indian as he was. I just kept it to myself was all.

Only time I ever liked him was one night when I ran into him and Moira in a Barbary restaurant, real late it was, and Two Eagle gentle drunk on wine, and him telling her in great excited rushes about the old religions of ours, and how only the red man—of all the earth's peoples—understood that sky and sun and the winds were all part of the Great God spirit—and how a man or woman who knew how to truly speak to God could then address all living creatures on the earth, be they elk or horse or great mountain eagle, for all things and all creatures are God's, and thus all things in the world, seen and unseen alike, are indivisible, and of God. And he spoke with such passion and sweep and majesty that I could see tears in his eyes—and I felt tears in my own eyes … and I saw that there was a good side to his belligerent clinging to the old ways. But his bad side ….

Moira liked white-man things. Back when she'd let me take her to supper a few times, we'd gone for a long carriage ride by the bay and she'd enjoyed it. Then we went up where the fancy shops were. She made a lot of little-girl sounds, pleased and cute and dreamy.

This was the part of her Two Eagle hated. By now he'd got her to dress in deerskin instead of cloth dresses, her shining black hair in pigtails instead of tumbling tresses, her face innocent of the "whore paint," as he pontifically called it. He worked as a bouncer in a place so tough it might have given Mr. Stevenson pause, and she worked behind the bar in the same place. Pity the man who got drunk and started sweet-talking Moira. Two Eagle would drag him outside and make the man plead for a quick death.

Now that I was over Moira, I didn't especially like hearing about either of them. But you couldn't say the same for Mr. Stevenson. He was as aggrieved as ever, all pain and dashed hope.

"She went out on him."

"Oh, bullshit."

"True," he said. "Few nights ago. They got into a bad fight and he kicked her in the stomach. He didn't know she was just startin' to carry a baby. Killed the baby and nearly killed Moira, too."

"The sonofabitch. Somebody should kill that bastard."

"You haven't heard the rest of it."

"I'm not sure I want to."

"He wants to cut her."

"Cut her?"

"The old ways, he says. What the Indians used to do back when I was on the plantation. When a woman went out on a man like that. You know—her nose."

"That's crazy. Nobody does that shit anymore."

"He does. Or at least he says he does. You know how he is. All that warrior bullshit he gets into."

"Where's Moira?"

"That's the worst part. She thinks she's got it coming. She's just waitin' in her room for him to come up and cut her. Says she believes in the old ways, too."

I shook my head. "That sounds like Moira." I took my pocket watch from my breeches. "I've got some time off coming. I can tell Madame Duprée I'm going for the rest of the night."

"You're tough, man, but you aren't that tough. Two Eagle'll kill you." He showed me his hands. How big they were. And strong. And black. "Fucker tries to cut her, I'll take care of him." He nodded to the front door, his bowler perched at a precarious angle. Sometimes I wondered if he had it glued to his head. "Let's go."

We went.

Making our way along the board sidewalks this time of night meant stepping over corpses, drunks, and reeking puddles of vomit and blood from various fights. Every important casino had a band of its own, which meant that the noise was as bad as the odors.

It was raining and so the boards were slick. But we walked fast, anyway. Two Eagle had a couple of rooms on the second floor of a livery stable. Moira lived there, too. She'd waited a long time for him to marry her. I figured she'd wait a lot longer.

A drunken rube made a crack about Mr. Stevenson, but if the black man heard, he didn't let on. Just kept walking. Real quiet and real intense. Like he had only one thought in the entire world and everything else just got in the way. Moira can make you like that.

The Barbary looked pretty much as usual, a jumble of cheap clothing stores for drunken sailors, dance halls where the girls were practically naked, and signs that advertised every kind of whore anybody could ever want. There was a new one this month, a mulatto who went over four hundred pounds, and a lot of Barbary regulars were giving her a try just to see what it'd be like, a lady so fat.

Half a block away you could smell the sweet hay and the sour horseshit in the rain and the night. Closer, you could hear the horses roll against their stalls, making small nervous sounds as they dreamed.

We went up a long stretch of outside stairs. The two-by-fours were new and smelled of sawn wood, tangy as autumn apples on a back porch.

Stevenson didn't knock. He just kicked the door in and stepped over the threshold. The walls inside were stained and the floors so scuffed the wood was slivery. She'd put up new red curtains that were supposed to make the shabby room a home but all the curtains did was make everything else look even older and uglier.

Moira, sad beautiful Indian child that she was, sat in a corner with her head on her knees. When she looked up, her black eyes glistened in the lantern light. She wore a deerskin dress and moccasins. The walls were covered with the lances and shields and knives and arrows of Two Eagle's tribe. He liked to smoke opium up here and tell dream-stories about ancient days when the medicine men said that the bravest warriors had horses that could fly. But the toys on the wall looked dulled and dusty and drab. Every couple of weeks he had his little group of Barbary-area Indians up here, Moira had told me once. The last stand, I'd remarked sarcastically. But she hadn't found it funny at all.

"This is crazy shit, Moira," I said. "We're gonna get you out of here before he comes back."

She had wrists and ankles so delicate they could make you cry. She stood up in her red skin, no more than ninety pounds and five feet she was, and walked over to Mr. Stevenson and said, "You don't have no goddamn right to come here, Mr. Stevenson. Or you either," she said to me. "What happens between Two Eagle and me is our business."

"You ever seen a woman who's been cut?" I said. I had. The man always took the nose, the same thing the ancient Egyptians had taken, just sawed it right off the face, so that only a dark and bloody hole was left. No brave ever wanted a woman who'd been cut, so many of the women went into the forest to live. A few even drank poison wine to end it quickly.

She looked at Mr. Stevenson. "We don't have no whiskey left."

"So the nigger goes and fetches you some, huh?" he said in his deep and bitter voice.

"I need to talk to Jimmy here, Mr. Stevenson, that's all. Just ten minutes or so."

He brought up his big murderous hands and looked at them as if he wasn't quite sure what they were.

"Rye?" he said.

She smiled and was even more beautiful. "Thanks for remembering. I'll get some money from Two Eagle and pay you back."

"I don't want any of his money," Mr. Stevenson said, and fixed her with his melancholy gaze. "I just want you."

"Oh, Mr. Stevenson," she said, and gently touched her small hand to his wide, hard chin. Sisterly, I guess you'd say. She was like that with every man but Two Eagle.

"You don't let him lay a hand on her," Mr. Stevenson said to me as he crossed the room to the door.

I brought up my Colt. "Don't worry, Mr. Stevenson."

He glanced at her one more time, sad and loving and scared and obviously baffled by his own tumultuous feelings, and then he left.

"Poor Mr. Stevenson."

"He's a decent man," I said.

"Kinda scary, though."

"Not any more so than Two Eagle."

"I just wish he understood how I felt about Two Eagle."

"Maybe he finds it kind of hard to understand a man who kicks a woman so hard she loses the baby she's carrying—and then wants to cut her nose off."

"He didn't mean to kick me that hard. He was real sorry. He cried when he saw—the baby."

I went over to the window and looked out on the Barbary Coast. One of the local editorial writers had estimated that a man was robbed every five minutes in the Barbary. At least when it rained, it didn't smell so bad.

I turned back to her. "I want to put you on a train tonight. For Denver. There's one that leaves in an hour and a half."

"I don't want to go."

"You know what he's gonna do to you."

Her eyes suddenly filled. She padded back to her corner and sat down and put her head on her knees and wept quietly.

I went over and sat down next to her and stroked her head as she cried.

After a time she looked up, her cheeks streaky with warm tears that I wiped away with my knuckles.

"He caught me."

"It's not something I want to hear about."

"I was so mad at him—with the baby and everything—that I just went out and got drunk. Didn't even know who I was with or where I was."

"Moira, I really don't want to hear."

"So he came looking for me. Took him all night. And you know where he found me?"

I sighed. She was going to tell me anyway.

"Up in some white sailors' room. There were two of them. One of them was inside me when he came through the door and found me."

I didn't say anything. Neither did she. Not for a long time.

"You know what was funny, Jimmy?"

"What?"

"He didn't hurt either one of them. Didn't lay a hand on them. Just stood there staring at me. And the guy, well, he pulled out and picked up his clothes and got out of there real fast with his friend. It was their own room, too. That's what was real funny. By then, I was sober. I tried to cover myself up but I couldn't find my clothes, so I went over and held Two Eagle just like he was my little boy, and then he started crying. I'd never heard him cry before. It was like he didn't know how. And then I got him over to the bed and I tried to make love to him but he couldn't. And he hasn't been able to since it happened, almost a week now. He's not a man anymore. That's what he said to me. He said that he can't be a man ever again after what he saw. And it's my fault, Jimmy. It's all my fault."

I wanted to hate him, or her, or myself, I wanted to hate some goddamned body, but I couldn't. It was just sad human shit and at the moment it overwhelmed me, left me ice cold and confused. People are so goddamned confusing sometimes.

She laughed. "You and Mr. Stevenson must have some conversations about us, Jimmy."

I stood up, reached back down, and took her wrist. "C'mon now, I'm taking you to the train."

"You ain't takin' her nowhere."

A harsh, quick voice from behind me in the doorway. When I turned I was looking into Two Eagle's insane dark eyes. I'd never seen him when he didn't look angry, when he didn't look ready for blood. He wore a piece of leather tied around his head, his rough black hair touching his shoulders, his gaunt cheeks crosshatched with myriad knife slashes. His buckskin outfit gave him the kind of Indian ferocity he wanted.

He came into the room.

"Why can't you be true to our ancestors for once, Jimmy?" he said, pointing his Colt right at my head. "Cutting her is the only thing I can do. Even Moira agrees. So why should you try to stop it? It's our blood, Jimmy, our tribal way."

"I don't want you to cut her."

His hard face smiled. "You gonna stop me, Jimmy?"

He expected me to be afraid of him and I was. But that didn't mean I wouldn't shoot him if I had to.

And then Mr. Stevenson was in the doorway.

Moira made a female sound in her throat. Two Eagle followed my gaze over his shoulder to the huge black man in the doorframe.

"You're smart to have him around, Jimmy. You'll need him."

Mr. Stevenson came into the room carrying a bottle of rotgut rye in one hand and a single rose in the other. He carried the flower to Moira and gave it to her. Then, without any warning, he turned around and backhanded Two Eagle so hard the Indian's feet left the floor and he flew backward into the wall. The entire room shook.

Mr. Stevenson wasn't going to bother with any preliminaries.

He went right for Two Eagle, who was trying to right his vision and his breathing and his ability to stand up straight. He'd struck his head hard when he'd collided with the wall and he looked disoriented. Bright red blood ran from his nostrils.

Mr. Stevenson grabbed him and it was easy to see what he was going to do. Maybe he thought that this would ultimately give him his first real chance with Moira, killing Two Eagle by snapping his neck.

"No!" I shouted.

And dove on Mr. Stevenson's back, trying to pull him off Two Eagle.

But it was no use. I clung to Mr. Stevenson like a child. I could not even budge him.

By now he had his hands in place, one on top of Two Eagle's head, the other on the bottom of his neck—ready for the single wrench that would kill Two Eagle.

Two Eagle used fists, feet, even his teeth to get free, but Mr. Stevenson paid no attention. He was setting himself to perform his most magnificent act ....

Moira shot him once in the side and then raised the gun and shot him once on top of the head. His hair flew off, a bloody black coil of curls affixed to the wall by pieces of sticky flesh and bone.

The funny thing was, he kept right on going, as if he refused to acknowledge what Moira had done to him.

Getting ready to snap Two Eagle's neck—

And then she ran closer, shrieking, and shot him again, and this time not even Mr. Stevenson could refuse to acknowledge what had happened. Blood poured from his ears.

An enraged Two Eagle was now able to bring his hands up and seize Mr. Stevenson's throat, holding tight, choking him, as the big black fell over backward, Two Eagle riding him down to the floor and then grabbing the gun from Moira's hand.

Two Eagle put the barrel of the .45 to Mr. Stevenson's forehead and fired three times. Didn't seem to matter to him that Mr. Stevenson had died a little while ago.

With each shot, Mr. Stevenson's head jerked upward from the coarse board floor and then slapped back down.

Two Eagle was calling him nigger and a lot of other things in our native tongue.

Then he was done, Two Eagle, pitching forward and lying facedown on the floor, very still for a long time.

I got up and straightened my clothes and picked up my gun from the floor where it had fallen when I'd jumped on Mr. Stevenson.

Moira said, "You two shouldn't have come up here."

"I guess not." I nodded to Mr. Stevenson. "He was trying to help you was all."

"It wasn't none of his business and it ain't none of yours, either."

"I guess he didn't see it that way. Seeing's he loved you and all."

"A nigger," Two Eagle said, getting up from the floor suddenly. "A nigger, lovin' Moira. Maybe you think that's all right, Jimmy, but then you gave up bein' a true man a long time back."

And then he went for me. Couldn't help himself. He still had all this fury and it had to light somewhere.

So he came at me, but he was stupid because he didn't look at my hand.

I felt his powerful arm wrap around my neck. I smelled his sweat and whiskey and tobacco.

He pushed me back against the wall.

And that was when I raised my Colt and put it directly to his ribs and fired three times.

He was dead before he hit the floor.

She was screaming, Moira was. That was about all I can tell you about my last few minutes in the room. She was screaming and Two Eagle had fallen close by Mr. Stevenson and then I was running. That's about all I can remember.

Then there was the night and the rain and I was running and running and running and tripping and falling and hurting myself bad but no matter how far or how fast I ran, I could still hear Moira screaming.

❖

Week later it was.

I was back doing my nightly turn at Madame Duprée's, winning upward of five hundred dollars this particular night, when I saw Lone Deer come in the side door by the faro layout.

She looked frantic. I figured it was me she wanted.

Being as we were waiting for some liquid refreshments at our table, I got up and went over to her.

When I reached her, she said, "She's goin', Jimmy. Leavin' us. Twenty-five minutes, her train leaves. I didn't find out till half an hour ago myself. Thought I'd better tell you."

"I appreciate it."

I suppose, like Mr. Stevenson, I'd had the idle dream that Moira and I would be lovers now that Two Eagle was gone. I didn't have to worry about any recriminations from the law getting in my way. A dead nigger and a dead Injun on the Barbary Coast don't exactly turn out a lot of curious cops. They're just two more slabs down at the morgue.

I'd figured I'd give it a few weeks and then go see her, tell her how what I did was the only thing I known to do—kill him to save my own life. And then I'd gentle-like invite her out for some dinner and ….

But that wasn't to be. Not now.

Moira was leaving.

"You'd better hurry," Lone Deer said. And then took my arm and drew me closer. "There's something else I need to tell you."

❖

Less than two minutes later I was running toward the depot. It was crowded and the conductor walked up and down all pompous as he consulted his railroad watch and shouted out that there were only a few minutes left before this particular train pulled out.

I found her in the very back of the last coach. The car was barely half full and she looked small and isolated there with the seats so much taller than she was. Moira. She'd always be a child.

I dropped into the seat next to her and said, "Lone Deer told me what you did."

"I wish she wouldn't have. I didn't want nobody to see me off."

"I love you, Moira."

"I don't want to hear that. Not with Two Eagle barely a week dead. Didn't I betray him enough?"

I'd seen the soldiers drag my grandfather from the reservation one day when I was very young. They were taking him to a federal penitentiary where he would die less than two months later at the hands of some angry white prisoners. I could still feel my panic that day—panic and terror and a sense that my own life was ending, too.

That's how I felt now, with Moira.

"But I won't betray him no more," Moira said. "You can bet on that."

"Is that why you did it?"

"Why I did it is none of your business."

I looked at her there in her black mourning dress and black mourning hat and black mourning veil, a veil so heavy you couldn't make out anything on the other side.

"No man'll ever want to bother me again. I made sure of that."

I was tempted to lift the veil quickly and see what she looked like. Lone Deer had said that Moira had used a butcher knife on her nose and that nothing remained but a bloody hole.

But then I decided that I didn't want to remember her that way. That I always wanted her to be young and beautiful Moira in my mind. Every man needs something to believe in, even if he knows it's not true.

"You got a ticket, buck?" the conductor asked me. Ordinarily, I'd take exception to his calling me "buck," but at the moment it just didn't seem very important.

I leaned over and kissed Moira, pressing her veil to her cheek. I still couldn't see anything.

"Hurry up, buck. You get your ass off of here or you show me a ticket."

I squeezed her hand. "I love you, Moira. And I always will."

And then I was gone, and the train was pulling out, all steam and power and majesty in the western night.

Then I walked slowly back to Madame Duprée's where I got just as drunk as Indians are supposed to get. †

PULP ART: AN APPRECIATION
Cullen Gallagher

The phrase brings to mind a whirlwind of brazen, brightly colored covers of damsels in distress and various states of undress, of bigger-than-life villains and even bigger heroes, of an entire culture's fantasies and nightmares splashed upon the page in the most violent hues imaginable. It invites the most ludicrous adjectives and far-fetched explanations, and promises thrills that most ordinary stories could never deliver. But one look at a pulp cover and you know that you're not dealing with ordinary stories, or with ordinary artwork. Magical, frightening, sexy, thrilling: pulp literature, and pulp art, is something truly special.

Historian and critic Robert Lesser summed it up perfectly in his book *Pulp Art*, among the finest books on the subject ever published. He called it "nightmare art" and compared it to "hard whiskey," but he really nailed it on the head when he described it as "storytelling art in motion."[1] It is that sense of movement, even in completely still pictures, that distinguishes the style. Not even still frames from a movie have the same dramatic propulsion that pulls the characters from one moment and hurls them into the next. We might not be able to see the "before" and "after" like we can in a movie, but we can see a fully charged "now" infused with anxiety, tension, and anticipation.

Charles Ardai, celebrated novelist and publisher of Hard Case Crime, has illuminated not only the emotional thrill of pulp art,

---

[1] Robert Lesser. *Pulp Art: Original Cover Paintings for the Great American Pulp Magazines.* 10, 17.

but also the meticulous and studied craft: "The vigor and velocity; the sex appeal; the larger-than-life quality. The technical skill as well—the best of the paintings had an outstanding grasp of composition and anatomy and chiaroscuro. I like to think that if Caravaggio had lived a few hundred years later he'd have been a pulp artist. The best of them were of his caliber."[2]

The heritage of pulp art grew out of the front covers of pulp magazines in the first half of the 20th century. After the pulp industry collapsed in the late 1940s, the artists moved over to the booming paperback industry in the 1950s and 1960s. These covers manifested visually all of the visceral emotions contained within the pages. It wasn't all bombast, bullets, beefcake and bosoms, however. Amidst the seething lust and irrepressible violence, a unique and, at times, beautiful style developed. The best covers display a great deal of subtlety, nuance and craftsmanship. And even when they don't, there are always the screaming babes and the blazing gats—and there's nothing wrong with that!

The artwork is as complex and diverse as the literature it illustrated. Just as there are differences between writers like Carroll John Daly and Dashiell Hammett, or between Max Brand and D.L. Champion, there are distinctions between the great pulp artists like Rafael De Soto and Hugh J. Ward, Rudolph Belarski and Norman Saunders, Walter M. Baumhofer and .... The list does, and will, go on, but first let's take a trip back to the first pulp magazines to see where it all came from.

Humble Beginnings

The first pulp magazine was the effort of a Mainer named Frank J. Munsey. He left his Down East home for New York City and started a publication called *The Golden Argosy*. The original format wasn't uncommon for its day, what was then called a

---

[2] Charles Ardai. Personal Interview.

"storypaper," sort of a newspaper but filled entirely with short stories. In 1888 the name was shortened to *The Argosy*, and in 1894 the format was changed to a side-stapled publication that opened like a magazine and printed on the cheapest "pulpwood" paper available. Thus, the basic shape of the pulp magazine was established.

The cover art, however, still had a long way to go. Phil Stephensen-Payne's *Galactic Central* website features a terrific archive of covers that literally illustrates the evolution.[3] Originally, the front of *The Argosy* featured black-and-white realist illustrations of portraits or domestic scenes and occasionally something exciting like a horse chase or someone hanging from a cliff. In 1896, however, due to low sales, Munsey cut out cover artwork all together. For the next 10 years, readers were enticed by copy, such as: "192 pages crowded from cover to cover with rattling good stories," "Don't fail to read it," and, "All for ten cents." Somehow, it worked, and Munsey kept his business alive. Even though this hardly resembles the libidinal illustrations of *Spicy Detective* and its Depression-era newsstand compatriots, they do share one thing in common: shoestring economics. Cheap paper, cheap printing, and cheap prices. Anything to keep the business afloat.

In 1905, *The Argosy* brought pictures back to the forefront, this time in color. Early covers show Native Americans, sea captains, knights in shining armor, runaway horses. While any of these subjects could have appeared in the earlier incarnations of the magazine, three things stand out. First, they aren't lost amidst a sea of text on an oversized newspaper-style layout; instead, a single image occupies the entirety of the cover with only sparse copy text to announce the date and to briefly advertise the contents. Second, the use of bright color, like red and blue, are much more attractive to the eye than the earlier black-and-white designs. And third, the pictures themselves are more action-packed. You won't see any cleavage or blood puddles, but you

---

[3] Phil Stephensen-Payne. *Galactic Central*.

can see the genesis of that movement-oriented visual storytelling that Robert Lesser alluded to. Horses crash into one edge of the cover and break through the other; a car careens around a mountain cliff, racing down the narrow road toward the reader; seafarers maneuver a ship through a battering storm. These are narrative images that imply a story.

For the images to get saucier, so too would the stories.

Coming of Age

The pulps were an industry. Like with any business enterprise, competition breeds improvement and innovation. In 1903, Street & Smith launched *The Popular Magazine*, with even more colorful front covers. In 1905, Munsey hit back with another magazine, *All-Story*. Still, these aren't the images that scream bloody pulp with every brush stroke. The covers of *The Popular Magazine*, *All-Story*, and other early pulps remind of Norman Rockwell and Winslow Homer. They're classic Americana, with an emphasis on harmony and balance between nature and man, the sort of stuff you might see in your grandparents' living room. Even though the October 1912 edition of *All-Story* features a Clinton Pettee cover of Tarzan strangling a lion and lifting a dagger poised for the kill—an exciting image for its time—the golden hues make the image seem somehow calm, as though the battle is already won and all is right with the world.[4]

But all was certainly not right with the world when the first issue of *Black Mask*, the most famous of all pulp magazines, first hit the newsstands in April 1920. William Grotz's cover painting is morbid and bleak, and it set the tone for a whole new breed of writing that was about to take over the world: hardboiled crime fiction. In the foreground, a man in a top hat is in the midst of dying as blood drips down his neck, and his dropped cane is about to hit the pavement. In the mid-ground, a man in a fedora

---

[4] Lesser 76.

strangles another man in the back of a truck. In the background, there is the city, dark and sinister, filled with unknown terrors. This is not the world of Rockwell and Homer; this is the world of pulp fiction.

Black Mask's stories provided morally ambiguous heroes who sometimes more closely resembled the bad guys than the good guys. This same ambiguity can be found in the magazine's covers. The May 1924 issue is a strong example. A man with a black fedora pulled low over the eyes, a shifty gaze, a cigarette dangling from the corner of the mouth, and a revolver cocked and ready to fire. From the looks of things, he's a dead ringer for an iconic villain. Look more closely, however, and you'll realize that he's wearing a tin star. So, he's one of the good guys? Maybe, but maybe not. I haven't read the story. The point is that there is the potential for him to be on either side, and that in this morally uncertain universe, the only character for us to relate to is someone with equally uncertain morals.

The Golden Years

Nothing says "pulp" more than the pages of *Spicy Detective Stories*. While inside the magazine Robert Leslie Bellem was making roscoes belch "chow chow," on the outside artists like Hugh J. Ward were making readers salivate over some of the most lurid paintings yet to be displayed in public. Again, Robert Lesser's *Pulp Art* provides two great examples. On the cover of the August 1936 issue, a fiery redhead's green dress and white bra have been torn to shreds; meanwhile, she clutches a snub-nose revolver in one hand and tears at her male attacker's lip with the other.[5] Sex plus violence—it's a winning formula.

It was Ward's April 1942 cover, however, that might have gone too far. The picture is of a woman hanging from a meat hook next to a dead cow. A fat, sweaty man with a knife stands in front of her, but he is looking over his shoulder. A silhouette of a

---

[5] Lesser 102.

gun is cast on the fat man's body. Whomever is holding the gun is not pictured, but still their menace—and their gun's shadow—looms large. We can assume that the fat man is frightened by this mysterious shooter, but why is the woman still frightened? Isn't she about to be rescued? Or is it possible that the man with the gun will do even worse things to her? Is he our hero, the one with whom we are to identify? This proved too much for New York City's Mayor La Guardia who, according to Lesser, exclaimed, "No more damn *Spicy* pulps in this city!"[6]

Hugh J. Ward wasn't the only one pushing the boundaries of violence. Rafael De Soto is among the most distinctive pulp artists. His sharp use of vivid, contrasting colors, unrestrained violence, and expressive physical gestures graced the covers of many pulp magazines. While his most famous works were his covers for *The Spider*, some of his best paintings were done for *New Detective Magazine* and *Black Mask*. The July 1946 *New Detective* shows a woman at an emergency Police Call Box being accosted by a man behind her. He emerges from the darkness, and all we can see is his right hand covering her mouth; his left hand jamming a .45 automatic into her neck; and his grimacing, scarred face. A variation appeared earlier on the front of the September 1944 *Black Mask*: a blonde woman in a red dress tries to scream, but a man behind her is choking her with the phone cord. De Soto's use of pitch-black backgrounds is striking. His villains emerge from a great void to do harm, and then disappear anonymously into nothingness. The existential terror of his paintings is matched only by the very real pain felt by his subjects.

One can't discuss pulp art without mentioning these other artists, too. Walter M. Baumhofer virtually defined masculine heroism with his *Doc Savage* covers in the 1930s: wispy locks of blond hair, bronze toned muscles, and always a babe in his arms and a villain close by. Who can forget George Rozen's iconic paintings of *The Shadow*, with his beak nose, flowing red scarf,

---

[6] Lesser 100–102.

alert blue eyes, and sleek black body as graceful as a bird? Then there are Margaret Brundage's eerily erotic female nudes for *Weird Tales* that display an almost classical Greek body structure, but with a decidedly pulpy perversity. James Van Hise, author of *Pulp Masters*, praises Brundage's paintings for their "startling vividness of color and technique."[7] And, of course, there are Rudolph Belarski's singular covers for *The Phantom Detective*, with the masked gentleman looking out knowingly in the background. Belarski also had a way with skulls, and managed to fit them into most genres of pulps: one rides a cockpit in *Air War*, another smokes a cigarette in *G-Men Detective*, and one even covers his face in shame in *Popular Detective* because, as the cover reads, "Death Has No Love-Life." John P. Gunnison's *Belarski: Pulp Art Masters* is rife with the Pennsylvania-native's era-defining imagination.[8]

Scaling Down: From Pulps to Paperbacks

The pulps survived the Great Depression and the paper rations of World War II only to close their doors in the late 1940s. Movies, comics and radio all contributed to their downfall, but it was the birth of the paperbacks that spelled the permanent death-knell for the pulps. Just as many pulp publishers jumped on the new bandwagon, so too did many artists. Belarski became one of Popular Library's best artists. His palette of exaggerated pastel tones was as unmistakable as his screaming blondes (like on the cover of Steve Fisher's *I Wake Up Screaming* [Popular Library, 1947]) and his skulls (which he managed to work onto the front of David Dodge's *Death and Taxes* [Popular Library, 1949]).

Piet Schreuders' marvelous book, *Paperbacks. U.S.A.: A Graphic History, 1939-1959*, gives a much fuller history of the industry, but here's the short version of what happened. The

---

[7] James Van Hise. "The Art That Dared to Be Wild." 104–106.
[8] John P. Gunnison. *Belarski: Pulp Art Masters*.

paperback novel got its first big break as a mass-market commodity in America in 1939 when Pocket Books issued its first 10 titles. At that time, the pulps were still in full swing, and the primary way to get fiction was in hardcover. Pocket Books sought to carve out a new niche audience by reprinting hardcover titles and selling them at low prices. The gamble paid off and Pocket Books became the leader in a brand new field.[9]

Early Pocket Books editions, however, did not resemble the pulps at all, and borrowed more from various modern art styles. Donald A. Wollheim's *The Pocket Book of Science-Fiction* (1943) sports a multi-colored Modernist cityscape; Leo Manso's cover to Jonathan Latimer's *The Lady in the Morgue* (1943) is a haunting, Surrealist spectre of a disembodied head screaming; and H. Lawrence Hoffman's neon cityscape on the cover to Raymond Chandler's *Farewell, My Lovely* (1943) is a blending of Expressionism and Art Deco. The most pulp cover is perhaps James M. Cain's *The Postman Always Rings Twice* (1947), which displays a blonde woman leaning her side and showing little (very little) cleavage. Over the next decade, more and more paperbacks would follow in this direction, only with less clothing and larger bosoms.

Other paperback publishers also tried various approaches to cover art. Penguin's 1946 edition of Carson McCullers' *The Heart is a Lonely Hunter* sports a famous cover by Robert Jonas: a symbolic collage of a bird, a heart, a fist, and a chain, which suggest the book's themes rather than illustrate a scene. Dell had their famous "mapbacks" (maps of the novel's locations on the back cover), mostly drawn by Helen Meyer. One of Bantam's leading artists was Norman Saunders, one of the greatest and most prolific pulp artists, and who had worked for nearly all the big magazines. He provided Bantam with some of the most boldly colorful Western covers in their lineup before moving on to Ace.[10] Signet had Social Realist-inspired covers by James

---

[9] Piet Schreuders. *Paperbacks. U.S.A.: A Graphic History, 1939–1959.* 18–31.

Avati, Stanley Meltzoff, and others who, like the "Ashcan School" of painters in the early 20th century, were interested in the grittier aspects of life instead of the glossy parts.

The most iconic paperback art—and the most inspired by the pulps—was not in the hardcover reprints, but in the paperback originals (PBOs). Fawcett started the bandwagon rolling in 1949 with Gold Medal, the first and arguably the best PBO imprint. They not only had writers like David Goodis, Vin Packer, Harry Whittington, and Clifton Adams (to name only a few of my favorites), but they also had cover artists like Barye Phillips, among the most distinctive PBO cover artists. He painted people very realistically, but his backgrounds were much more impressionistic. Both Day Keene's *To Kiss, or Kill* (1951) and Vin Packer's *Spring Fire* (1952) display another of his characteristic touches: a deft, unrealistic use of black lines to accentuate shapes and textures.

Dell's biggest gun was Robert McGinnis. No one paints women like McGinnis. His covers for Brett Halliday's Mike Shayne series (and for Signet's Carter Brown lineup) supply some of the longest, leanest, most shapely gams in the history of art. His use of soft, pale hues for backdrops also gives the women an uncanny glow. Another famous Robert is Robert Maguire, whose cover to David Goodis' *The Blonde on the Street Corner* (Lion, 1954) is one of the cornerstones of noir imagery.

Lion Books was another strong publisher, and often their covers for Jim Thompson's were both unusual and exceptional. No artists name graces *The Criminal* (1953) or *The Golden Gizmo* (1954), but both show the same bold, unconventional stylizations. In *The Criminal*, a boy sits backward in a chair while the furnishings in the room appear only as traced outlines. The same technique is used in the background for *The Golden Gizmo*, while the characters in the foreground show more of an influence of Social Realism. These covers don't scream "sex" and

---

[10] David Saunders. *Norman Saunders*.

"violence" like so many other paperbacks, but engage the reader through atmosphere and sophistication.

For a while, the pulps may have worked their way into some of the paperback covers, but it was by no means the only strategy, nor would it be permanent.

Death and Rebirth

The lurid age of paperbacks didn't last forever. By the 1970s, the paperback market had proven that it had lasting power. Its markets were expanding and changing—and the books had to change with it. Cover art became less salacious and more respectable. Charles Ardai explained to me in an interview that the reasons for the evolution were manifold. It had as much to do with aesthetics and marketing as it did with the economic reality of publishing.

Part of it is just that tastes and styles change as times change, and most publishers want to look modern and cutting edge rather than producing work that looks like it's of an earlier decade. But it's also more expensive and time consuming to commission original illustrations—especially paintings—than it is to make a cover out of type and abstract design elements. Instead of working with only one artist per book, the author, you have to work with two. It increases your risk, your labor, your cost. Publishers aren't in the business of taking bigger risks for more money, especially not when the result will make them look old-fashioned.[11]

Stephen J. Gertz, in his book *Dope Menace: The Sensational World of Drug Paperbacks, 1900-1975*, suggests that another reason for the change: bookstores, instead of the old newsstands, were selling paperbacks. "The last place you'd go to find a paperback book now began stocking them …. They required covers to appeal to a different class of buyer. And, significantly,

---

[11] Ardai. Personal Interview.

sales to schools had become a growing part of the paperback business. The sensational covers had to go."[12]

So, where did they go? The sensational covers naturally went the way of the sensational books: Evening Reader, Midwood, Beacon, and other sleaze and softcore publishers. But, something wasn't the same. They're sleazy and cheap in a way that McGinnis, Maguire, DeSoto or Ward never were. The uncredited cover to Curt Colman's (Harry Whittington) *Flesh Mother* (Evening Reader, 1965) shows a nude woman bending over a bed, while behind her a shirtless man waves a lamp in one hand and holds a curtain over his crotch with the other. Now, don't get me wrong, I totally love the cover—but it is ludicrous, crude, and poorly executed. It lacks the polish, finesse, creativity, and craftsmanship of the pulps and early paperbacks.

Paperback artists like Robert Maguire just adapted to industry changes and stayed where the money was; he wound up doing poster art for James Bond movies and *Barbarella*.[13] Norman Saunders moved into creating trading cards, buttons, and other toys.[14] They were artists, but artists needed to eat. The whole history of pulp art is tied into the economy of publishing, all the way back to Frank A. Munsey. So, it is only natural that as the industry changed, so too did the artwork.

Unfortunately, much of the current state of mass-market paperback artwork doesn't show the influence of James Avati, Barye Phillips and their contemporaries. Today, we're all too familiar with the stock atmospheric photo—or worse, computer generated image—with the author's name in huge letters. Regardless of publisher, most of mass-market covers look the same, something you could never say about the old pulps or paperbacks. Each painting had its own distinctive elements, and each bore the traces of a human hand, a human artist.

---

[12] Gertz, Stephen J. *Dope Menace: The Sensational World of Drug Paperbacks, 1900–1975*. 18.

[13] *R.A. Maguire Cover Art.*

[14] Saunders. *Norman Saunders.*

But, all is not lost! There are a number of terrific artists (and publishers) working hard today that believe in providing distinctive cover art in the pulp tradition. Charles Ardai's Hard Case Crime has revived not only lost, forgotten, and unpublished crime classics, but it also boasts a stellar lineup of artists including none other than original PBO legends Robert McGinnis and Ron Lesser. Hard Case Crime also brought a new generation of pulp painters to the forefront, including Glen Orbik, Richard B. Farrell, Gregory Manchess, and many others whose work would have fit right in amongst the old Gold Medal and Lion paperbacks. Jeff Wong also brings a unique and informed style to his covers, such as Ross Macdonald's *The Archer Files* (Crippen & Landru, 2007). Wong's approach was an historiographic reinterpretation of Mitchell Hooks' original cover to Macdonald's *The Name is Archer* (Bantam, 1955) that replaces Lew Archer's face with Macdonald's own. Richie Fahey's covers to Megan Abbott's *Die a Little* (Simon & Schuster, 2005), *The Song is You* (Simon & Schuster, 2007), *Queenpin* (Simon & Schuster, 2007), and *Bury Me Deep* (Simon & Schuster, 2009) are steeped in noir nostalgia that captures the essence of the time without descending to kitsch or parody. Celebrated graphic artist James O'Barr, who has done excellent art for both *BEAT to a PULP* anthologies, merges comic book sensationalism with pulp attitude.

Among the most innovative of new artists is photographer Thomas Allen, who creatively reuses the actual paperback covers themselves by cutting out the figures, popping them up, and turning the books into 3-D scenes, and then photographing the creations. In Allen's "Timber" (2005), a cowboy is literally knocked through a wooden railing and off of the cover of Max Brand's *Timber Gulch Trail* (Popular Library, 1952, cover art by George Rozen), and in "Recoil" (2006), the cowboy on the cover of Ernest Haycox's *Trail Smoke* (Popular Library, 1952) shoots a deep hole through Bliss Lomax's *Rusty Guns* (Hillman Books, 1949, cover art by Charles Wood).[15]

Forgive me for stopping short and for not naming all of the classic or contemporary cover artists whom I admire, but this could go on all night otherwise. The point is this: the pulps turned their last pages over fifty years ago, but pulp art is far from over. Pulp art, pulp literature, and pulp culture continues to thrive. Online. In print. In readers hands. New generations continue to discover and appreciate the pulps and paperbacks, and I predict that those art forms of yesteryear have a long, prosperous afterlife ahead of them.

Bibliography
Allen, Thomas. *Uncovered: Photographs by Thomas Allen*. New York: Aperture, 2007.

Ardai, Charles. Personal Interview. 6 Aug 2011.

American Art Archives. 1 Aug 2011.
<http://www.americanartarchives.com>.

The George Kelly Paperback and Pulp Fiction Collection - University of Buffalo Libraries. 1 Aug 2011.
<http://libweb.lib.buffalo.edu/kelley/index.php>.

Gertz, Stephen J. *Dope Menace: The Sensational World of Drug Paperbacks, 1900–1975*. Port Townsend: Feral House, 2008.

Gunnison, John P. *Belarski: Pulp Art Masters*. Silver Spring: Adventure House, 2003.

Lesser, Robert. *Pulp Art: Original Cover Paintings for the Great American Pulp Magazines*. New York: Gramercy Books, 1997.

R.A. Maguire Cover Art. 1 Aug 2011.
<http://www.ramaguirecoverart.com>.

---

[15] Thomas Allen. *Uncovered: Photographs by Thomas Allen.*

Saunders, David. *Field Guide to Pulp Artists*. 1 Aug 2011.
<http://www.pulpartists.com>.

---. *Norman Saunders*. 1 Aug 2011.
<http://www.normansaunders.com>.

Schreuders, Piet. *Paperbacks. U.S.A.: A Graphic History, 1939–1959*. Trans. Josh Pachter. San Diego: Blue Dolphin Enterprises, Inc., 1981.

Server, Lee. *Danger is My Business: An Illustrated History of the Fabulous Pulp Magazines*. San Francisco: Chronicle Books, 1993.

---. *Over My Dead Body: The Sensational Age of the American Paperback: 1945–1955*. San Francisco: Chronicle Books, 1994.

Stephensen-Payne, Phil. *Galactic Central*. 1 Aug 2011.
<http://www.philsp.com>.

Van Hise, James. "The Art That Dared to Be Wild." Published in *Pulp Art: Original Cover Paintings for the Great American Pulp Magazines*. Ed. Robert Lesser. New York: Gramercy Books, 1997. 104–106.

ABOUT THE AUTHORS

Patricia Abbott is the author of the collection, *Monkey Justice* (Snubnose Press) and the co-editor of the anthology, *Discount Noir* (Untreed Reads). More than 80 of her stories have appeared in anthologies, print, and online publications. She won a Derringer Award in 2009 for "My Hero." She lives in Detroit.

Charles Ardai is an Edgar and Shamus Award-winning writer and the creator and editor of the Hard Case Crime series of mystery novels. His is also a writer and producer on the television series "Haven" and was the creator of the Internet service Juno. In addition to *BEAT to a PULP: Round One*, his short stories have appeared in collections such as *The Year's Best Horror Stories* and *Best Mystery Stories of the Year*.

Sean Chercover is the author of the novels *Big City Bad Blood*, *Trigger City*, and *The Trinity Game* (July 2012), as well as a handful of short stories. His fiction has received the Shamus, CWA Dagger, Anthony, Dilys, Crimespree, Gumshoe, and Lovey awards, and has been shortlisted for the Edgar, Barry, Macavity, ITW Thriller, and Arthur Ellis. After living in Columbia, South Carolina; Chicago; and New Orleans, Sean returned to his native Toronto where he lives with his wife and son and their bionic dog. You can find him at www.chercover.com. He also spews nonsense on Twitter: @seanchercover.

Alec Cizak is a writer from Indianapolis. His work has appeared in numerous journals and anthologies. He is also the editor of the print journal, *Pulp Modern*.

Bill Crider is the author of more than fifty published novels and numerous short stories. He won the Anthony Award for best first mystery novel in 1987 for *Too Late to Die*. He and his wife, Judy, won the best short story Anthony in 2002 for their story

"Chocolate Moose." His story "Cranked" from *Damn Near Dead* was nominated for the Edgar award. His latest novel is *Murder of a Beauty Shop Queen* (St. Martin's). Check out his homepage at www.billcrider.com, or take a look at his peculiar blog at http://billcrider.blogspot.com.

Hilary Davidson won the 2011 Anthony Award for Best First Novel for *The Damage Done*. The book also earned a Crimespree Award and was a finalist for the Arthur Ellis and Macavity Awards. The sequel, *The Next One to Fall,* a mystery set in Peru, was published by Forge in February, 2012. Hilary's widely acclaimed short stories have been featured in publications from *Ellery Queen's Mystery Magazine* to *Thuglit*, and in many anthologies. A Toronto-born travel journalist and the author of 18 nonfiction books, she has lived in New York City since October, 2001. Visit her online at www.hilarydavidson.com.

Wayne D. Dundee is the author of eleven novels, five novellas, and more than two dozen short stories. Much of his work has featured his PI protagonist, Joe Hannibal (appearing most recently in *Goshen Hole*, 2011). He also writes in other genres, most notably Westerns. His 2010 Western short story, "This Old Star," won a Peacemaker Award from the Western Fictioneers writers' organization; and his first novel-length Westerns, *Dismal River* and *Hard Trail to Socorro*, appeared in 2011. *Manhunter's Mountain*, the first novel-length adventure in the popular Cash Laramie/Gideon Miles series came out in January of 2012.

Titles in the Hannibal series have been translated into several languages and nominated for an Edgar, an Anthony, and six Shamus awards. Dundee is also the founder and original editor of *Hardboiled Magazine*.

Garnett Elliott lives in Tucson, Arizona. He reads and writes pulp, when he's not spending time with family or working with trauma survivors at the VA. Recent stories have appeared or are slated to appear in *Alfred Hitchcock's Mystery Magazine, BEAT* *to a PULP: Hardboiled*, *Needle: A Magazine of Noir*, *A Rip Through Time*, *Pulp Modern*, and *Battling Boxing Stories*. He's just finished a novella called "The Shunned Highway," which will appear in Alec Cizak's anthology *Drive-In Fiction*, and is currently working on another novella featuring David Cranmer's double-amputee hero, Vin. You can follow him on Twitter at @TonyAmtrak.

Cullen Gallagher lives in Brooklyn, NY. He blogs at Pulp Serenade, writes the crime fiction column "The Criminal Kind" for the Los Angeles Review of Books, and records music as Modern Silence Cinema. Currently, he works as a switchboard operator.

Ed Gorman is an award winning American author best known for his crime and mystery fiction. He wrote *The Poker Club* which was made into a film of the same name directed by Tim McCann.

He has written under many pseudonyms including "E. J. Gorman" and "Daniel Ransom." He won a Spur Award for Best Short Fiction for his short story "The Face" in 1992. His fiction collection Cages was nominated for the 1995 Bram Stoker Award for Best Fiction Collection. His collection *The Dark Fantastic* was nominated for the same award in 2001.

He has contributed to many magazines and other publications including *Xero*, *Black Lizard*, *Cemetery Dance*, the anthology *Tales of Zorro*, and many more.

Visit his blog at newimprovedgorman.blogspot.com.

Glenn Gray is a physician specializing in radiology. His stories have appeared in numerous online magazines and in print including: *Needle: A Magazine of Noir*; *Pulp Modern*; *Blood, Guts, & Whiskey* (Kensington 2010); and *BEAT to a PULP: Round One*. He lives in New York.

Vicki Hendricks is the author of erotic crime novels *Miami Purity*, *Iguana Love*, *Voluntary Madness*, *Sky Blues*, and *Cruel Poetry*, the latter a finalist for an Edgar Award in 2008. Her short stories appear in publications ranging from *The Mississippi Review* to Susie Bright's *Best American Erotica 2000* to Otto Penzler's *Murder for Revenge*. A complete collection of her short fiction, *Florida Gothic Stories*, was published in 2010. Hendricks lives in Hollywood, Florida, and teaches writing at Broward College. Her plots and settings reflect participation in adventure sports, such as skydiving and scuba, and knowledge of the Florida environment.

Jake Hinkson is the author of the noir novel *Hell On Church Street* (New Pulp Press, 2012). He is a frequent contributor to the film journal *Noir City* and writes regularly for Macmillan's website *CriminalElement.com*. He blogs at thenighteditor.blogspot.com.

Chris F. Holm was born in Syracuse, New York, the grandson of a cop who passed along his passion for crime fiction. His work has appeared in such publications as *Ellery Queen's Mystery Magazine*, *Alfred Hitchcock's Mystery Magazine*, and *The Best American Mystery Stories* 2011. He's been an Anthony Award nominee, a Derringer Award finalist, and a Spinetingler Award winner. His first novel, *Dead Harvest* (Angry Robot Books, February 2012), is a supernatural thriller that recasts the battle between heaven and hell as Golden Era crime pulp.

Howard Hopkins wrote Westerns under the name Lance Howard and horror novels under his own name, including the popular "The Chloe Files" series for adults and "The Nightmare Club" series for kids. He also edited and contributed to numerous anthologies and comics, most notably with tales of classic pulp and adventure characters such as The Green Hornet, The Avenger, The Spider, Sherlock Holmes, and The Lone Ranger. Howard passed away unexpectedly in early 2012, but his vast body of work lives on. His latest novel is *The Lone Ranger: Vendetta* (Moonstone Books). His work can be found at: www.howardhopkins.com.

C. Courtney Joyner has written the screenplays for more than 25 movies, including the cult films *The Offspring* starring Vincent Price, *Prison, Class of 1999*, and the new *Return of Captain Nemo* starring Hugh Bonneville. He has written extensively about the history of American movies (*The Westerners*) and his latest film book is *Warner Brothers Fantastic*. His Western fiction has been anthologized in *A Fistful of Legends*, *Law of the Gun*, and *The Traditional West*, while his love of horror is on display in *Hell Comes to Hollywood*. Courtney lives in Los Angeles with his fiancée and a ton of movie posters.

Nik Korpon is the author of *Stay God, Old Ghosts, By the Nails of the Warpriest* and will be in the forthcoming collection, *Bar Scars* (Snubnose Press). His stories have bloodied the pages of *Needle: A Magazine of Noir*, *Crime Factory*, *Shotgun Honey*, *Out of the Gutter*, *Powder Burn Flash*, *Punchnel's*, *Speedloader*, and a bunch more. He also reviews books for *Spinetingler*, *NoirJournal*, and *The Nervous Breakdown*. He lives in Baltimore with his wife and son. Give him some danger, little stranger, at nikkorpon.com.

Evan Lewis received the 2011 Robert L. Fish Memorial Award from the Mystery Writers of America for "Skyler Hobbs and the Rabbit Man," which appeared in *Ellery Queen's Mystery Magazine*. More Hobbs stories appeared in the Untreed Reads anthologies *Discount Noir* and *Grimm Tales*, and another is slated for a future *EQMM*. Non-Hobbs stories have appeared in *BEAT to a PULP*, *BEAT to a PULP: Round One*, *A Fistful of Legends*, and *Alfred Hitchcock's Mystery Magazine*. Visit his blog, "Davy Crockett's Almanack of Mystery, Adventure and the Wild West," at evanlewis.com.

Sophie Littlefield writes the award-winning post-apocalyptic "Aftertime" series and the "Stella Hardesty" mystery series. She also writes paranormal fiction for young adults. Her first novel, *A Bad Day for Sorry*, won an Anthony Award for Best First Novel and an RT Book Award for Best First Mystery. Sophie grew up in rural Missouri and makes her home in northern California.

Jodi MacArthur makes up stuff. She reads stuff. She fights psychological warfare with her very naughty rabbit, Foof. And she is never, ever afraid of the dark, except when pale bodies dangle from the ceiling. www.jodimacarthur.blogspot.com.

Matthew P. Mayo is a Spur Award- and Peacemaker Award-nominated writer whose novels include *Winters' War*; *Wrong Town*; *Hot Lead, Cold Heart*; and *Dead Man's Ranch*. His short stories have appeared in a variety of anthologies, including DAW Books' *Timeshares* and *Steampunk'd*. His critically acclaimed non-fiction works include his best-selling "Grittiest Moments" series, plus *Haunted Old West*, and many others. He recently collaborated, with his wife, photographer Jennifer Smith-Mayo, on a series of hardcover books: *Maine Icons*, *Vermont Icons*, and *New Hampshire Icons*. Drop in at www.matthewmayo.com for a chinwag and a cuppa mud.

Matthew J. McBride is the author of *Frank Sinatra in a Blender* (New Pulp Press, Fall 2012). He lives on a farm outside Mount Sterling, Missouri, with his wife Melissa. He has two sons, Nick and Dylan.

John D. Nesbitt writes traditional Western novels and short stories, contemporary fiction, mystery fiction, and retro/noir fiction. He has won many awards for his work, including two Wyoming Arts Council literary fellowships (one for fiction, one for nonfiction), a Western Writers of America Spur finalist award for mass-market paperback original novel for *Raven Springs*, and the Spur Award itself for his noir short story "At the End of the Orchard" and for his Western novels *Trouble at the Redstone* and *Stranger in Thunder Basin*. See his website at www.johndnesbitt.com.

The original 1950s cover of *Spring Fire*—**Vin Packer**'s first book to come out in print and the first lesbian pulp novel ever published—blared, "A story once told in whispers now frankly, honestly written." It sold 1.5 million copies through at least three printings.

Packer recounts: "In the fifties, postal inspectors were not above shipping back to the publisher any books they deemed immoral. A gay book could not have a happy ending, and paperbacks were targets because they went through the mail. If your book fit that label, all the books published with yours went back, too. My editor convinced me it was important to have gay stories, even when they ended unhappily. He was not a big sympathizer, though he was gay-friendly, but he was someone who knew the market. I was amazed at the boxes of mail *Spring Fire* inspired. I was not someone who felt any entitlement as gays feel today. My family was horrified. My friends were sending others out to buy the book at the local drugstore. It was another time and we were grateful for any crumbs thrown our way. The only lesbian book with a happy ending in those days was Patricia Highsmith's *The Price of Salt*. It was a hardcover, so the postal censors couldn't touch it. I never dreamed *Spring Fire* would have a life. I was one of the few females writing pulps in the early '50s. I switched to crime because I got a review in *The New York Times* by Anthony Boucher for a book called *Come Destroy Me*. He made my pulp career at a time when paperback writers on any subject were largely ignored. He was the reason I turned to a life of crime."

Cleis Press re-released *Spring Fire* in 2004.

Bill Pronzini has published more than ten million words of fiction and nonfiction over the past 46 years, including 37 novels in his well-regarded "Nameless Detective" series. His proudest achievement is being named Grand Master by the Mystery Writers of America in 2008, an award he hopes was not predicated on wordage output and longevity alone.

Keith Rawson is a little-known pulp writer whose short fiction, poetry, essays, reviews, and interviews have been widely published both online and in print. He is the author of the short story collections *The Chaos We Know* and *Laughing at Dead Men* (Snubnose Press) and co-editor of the anthology *Crime Factory: The First Shift* (New Pulp Press). He is also a staff writer for *LitReactor* and *Spinetingler Magazine* and the former publisher of *Crime Factory Magazine*. He lives in southern Arizona with his wife and daughter.

James Reasoner, lifelong Texan, has been a professional writer for more than thirty-five years. He is the author of two cult classic mystery novels, *Texas Wind* and *Dust Devils*, as well as the co-creator and co-author of the bestselling Western series "Rancho Diablo." Writing under his own name and various pseudonyms, his books have garnered praise from *Publishers Weekly*, *Booklist*, and the *Los Angeles Times*, as well as appearing on the *New York Times* and *USA Today* bestseller lists. He lives in a small town in Texas with his wife, award-winning fellow author Livia J. Washburn.

Anthony Neil Smith is the fat and grizzled author of *All the Young Warriors*, *Yellow Medicine*, and four other novels. He's the publisher of *Plots with Guns* and the Director of Creative Writing at Southwest Minnesota State University. Visit him at http://anthonyneilsmith.typepad.com or follow him on Twitter at @docnoir.

Larry D. Sweazy (www.larrydsweazy.com) won the WWA Spur Award for Best Short Fiction in 2005, the 2011 Will Rogers Medallion Award for Western Fiction, and the 2011 Best Books of Indiana in the fiction category—the first Western to ever win the award. He has published more than 50 nonfiction articles and short stories, which have appeared in many anthologies and Best-of-the-Year collections. He is also the author of the "Josiah Wolfe, Texas Ranger" series (Berkley), and a stand-alone thriller, *The Devil's Bones* (Five Star). Larry lives in Indiana with his wife, Rose, two dogs, and a cat.

Steve Weddle holds an MFA in creative writing from Louisiana State University and currently works for a newspaper group. He lives with his family in Virginia. In 2009, Weddle and six crime fiction writers created DoSomeDamage, where he blogs weekly. In 2010, Weddle and John Hornor Jacobs created *Needle: A Magazine of Noir*, one of the top journals for contemporary crime fiction. His short fiction has appeared at *BEAT to a PULP*, *Crime Factory*, and *A Twist of Noir* and in *The First Shift*, *Off the Record*, and *D*cked* anthologies.

Dave Zeltserman is the Shamus Award-winning author of "Julius Katz" and the groundbreaking "man out of prison" crime thriller series: *Small Crimes, Pariah,* and *Killer*. Born in Boston, Massachusetts, Dave attended the University of Colorado in Boulder, and currently lives in the Boston area with his wife, Judy. After spending 20 years developing network management software for several of the world's leading technology companies, he now splits his time between writing crime fiction and studying martial arts, where he holds a black belt in Kung Fu. His crime novels *Outsourced* and *A Killer's Essence* have both been optioned for film and are currently in development.

Other titles from BEAT to a PULP available as Kindle eBooks.

www.ingramcontent.com/pod-product-compliance
Lightning Source LLC
Chambersburg PA
CBHW031059030726
47496CB00002BA/287